# NASHVILLE COWBOY

## MEN OF STONE RIDGE

### HEATHERLY BELL

*For my Family*

# PROLOGUE

There's apparently a small matter that I need to address. The very nature of our little town has some young women taking temporary leave of their senses. Yes, you may have heard the rumors, and they're true. We hold the dubious distinction of being the town with the greatest number of runaway brides in…ahem…history.

And though we're never *completely* shocked when this happens, it's still a sad situation. Jilted grooms are not what we'd like our town to be known for. The problem is, because our women have often dated more than one man, and they have such fine choices before them, they hesitate to settle down with one.

Why do they get all the way to the altar before they figure this out, you may ask?

I wish I knew!

You may have guessed, but this is also true: there's a wedding in the works and our very own "Nashville" cowboy, Jackson Carver, will be coming home to be his older brother Lincoln's best man. As luck, or fate, would have it, the maid of honor, Eve Iglesias, happens to be the same woman who left poor Jackson at the altar.

While we don't exactly expect a brawl to break out between these two, anything could happen. And we sure don't want anything to interfere with the Stephens/Carver wedding, a long time coming, believe you me.

To say we're all a *little* sensitive about these upcoming nuptials is perhaps an understatement. We're worried sick!


~ BEULAH HAYES, acting president of the Society of Reasonable, Respectable Orderly Women (SORROW), and author of *The Men of Stone Ridge*, tenth edition ~

# CHAPTER 1

*L*incoln Carver woke to a beautiful naked woman splayed all over him, her long sweet-smelling hair fanned across his chest. Her arm was slung across his waist, one curvy leg between his two legs. Good thing it was his fiancée. Sadie Stephens, also known as the love of his life.

Lincoln Carver was one lucky cowboy and he knew it. He scrubbed a hand down his face. But Jesus. Lucky or not, he was *not* looking forward to today. His brother would be arriving.

"Baby, wake up."

"Hmm?"

"Do you know what I have to do today?"

"Make me coffee?"

"Pick Jackson up at the airport."

"Mm," she mumbled, and then as if just now hearing him, "Oh."

"Yup." She shifted and he tugged her into his arms. "Not going to be a fun time."

She sat up straight, her hair adorably mussed. "Today! He's coming back today."

Uh-oh. He did not like the look on her face, filled with hope and anticipation that had nothing to do with him, or how lucky *he* might get this morning.

"Sadie," he said in a warning tone. "We talked about this."

"I know we did, and I'm not doin' anything but standing by watching, helpless, as Jackson and Eve are reunited once more." She smiled and smoothed down her hair. "You can't stand in the path of true love. All I'm doin' is providing the perfect opportunity. They're going to stand up for us at Trinity Church and when they glance at each other across the altar…"

"He'll reach over and wring her neck?" he provided helpfully.

"No, baby." She settled back down into his arms, resting her head on his shoulder. "They're supposed to realize that could have been them at the altar. And that maybe it's not too late."

"There's a little thing you're forgetting. She ran out on him on the day of their wedding and my brother is not the forgivin' type."

"What if he still loves her?" She propped her chin on his chest.

"There you go getting carried away again."

"I just want them to be as happy as we are. Remember, you didn't want to fall in love and get married, either? And now look at you."

"Yeah, now look at me." He splayed his hands behind his neck. "Mornin' sex. Afternoon sex. Nighttime sex. I'm really sufferin' here."

She thumped his pec. "One-track mind."

Sadie knew he was kidding. Not that he didn't enjoy the constant sex, because he sure did, but he loved this woman. He'd do anything for Sadie. But Jackson would be put through enough having to be the best man while Eve was maid of honor. She was Sadie's best friend. No matter what Jackson said, there was a reason he was still so bitter. He'd gone on to quite a bit of success in Nashville, married a beautiful country singer, even if they divorced after three months. He'd moved on, in other words.

No fool, Lincoln saw quite clearly that both Sadie and his grandmother, Mima, were up to no good. Eve was already living at the Carver house, taking over Mima's duties since she broke her arm. No one wanted to tell Jackson. Lincoln would, but he figured he'd soften the blow and tell him in person.

"I love you," Sadie said. "Did I tell you today?"

Yeah, he'd never get tired of hearing that.

"And I love you back."

And when his fiancée straddled him with a wicked smile, he forgot all about what he would be doing later today, because at least his day was starting off right.

* * *

"THANK YOU FOR COOKING, sugar. Jackson will be expectin' my banana cream pie for dessert," Lillian "Mima" Carver said. "Now make sure you beat those egg whites till they're stiff and beautiful peaks."

Eve Iglesias did as she was told while Mima issued orders from her seat at the kitchen table and simultaneously read her latest book. Secretly, Eve thought Mima was enjoying her time off from the kitchen maybe a little too much. And she was enjoying her new role as Kitchen Overlord in a rather extravagant and obvious way.

"You sure y'all told Jackson about me?" Eve asked, angling the whisk to beat the heck out of those egg whites. Good therapy.

"Of course, darlin'. I'm sure Lincoln and Sadie told him all about you being in the weddin'."

"I don't mean *that*."

Eve prayed for a big dose of saintly patience. It was one thing to be paired with her ex-fiancé at the church. Quite another to be staying at the family home in his old bedroom. "Does he know that I'm living here and taking care of you?"

She glanced heavenward. "Lord have mercy, *why* did I have to break my right arm? Couldn't it have been my left arm? I've got no use at all for my left arm. It could just hang there all day and I wouldn't know the difference. Sugar, I really hope those pork chops are like my Jackson likes them. Juicy and tender on the inside, golden crispy and crunchy on the outside."

For crying out loud, the woman should write a cookbook. "Ode to the Beauty of Food" or something. Eve was already hungry enough. She was dying to bite into a chop. She'd had a long enough day with the Harrisons' colicky mare and the Garcias' pregnant goat. She'd driven an hour in each direction and with nearly the entire day gone, finally come home to the Double C Ranch in time to cook supper. She didn't know if she was exhausted or terrified. Possibly both. Either way, the old pebble in her throat took up its former residency. She could barely swallow, much less eat.

A small part of her was certain that Jackson would have long ago forgiven her for ditching him at the altar even if they hadn't spoken a word since that day. After all, he'd bounced back while the same couldn't be said about her. She'd managed. Survived. Not one to feel sorry for herself, Eve didn't want anyone's pity.

"I followed your directions," Eve said, opening the lid to peek. "They look good enough to eat."

"Smell good, too. You're an angel, that's what you are. An angel sent from up above."

"Aw," Eve said, as she did every time Mima loved on her.

When Eve returned home after graduating from Texas A&M, it was to the surprising forgiveness and open arms of Mima Carver. After her little stunt at Trinity Church, other than her own family, and Sadie, the residents of Stone Ridge turned on her. Some refused to speak to her. The mothers didn't want Eve dating their sons, because even with the shortage of women, no one should take another chance on a runaway bride. Not that she was interested in dating anyone.

But Sadie understood. Sadie knew what it was like to love a Carver cowboy. In Sadie's case, she'd pined away for Lincoln for years, until he'd finally noticed her. Now they were getting married and every last desperate man in town could quit hoping there would be a last-minute change in plans. This wedding was happening because Sadie and Lincoln were made for each other.

"You didn't answer the question," Eve pressed. "Does Jackson know I'm *livin'* here?"

"Well, now, sugar, when would I have time to tell him? I've been busy getting my poor arm broken in three places. Havin' surgery. I think you know all this. Been directing you to cook just the way my cowboys like. Been helping Sadie and her mother plan the wedding. I've got no time at all to spare." She waved her hand in the air dismissively.

Just as Eve suspected. Mortification pulsed through her, followed closely by terror. Jackson would either be cold and standoffish, or madder than a wet hen. Neither would be a whole lot of fun.

"L-Lincoln could have told him."

"And he probably did. Don't you worry none. No one's going to kick you out of *my* home."

But this was Jackson. No one had a better cause to be angry and hostile. Even Mima barely spoke a word to Eve right after she'd humiliated Jackson. Then Mima heard what happened to Eve while away at college, and her heart was big enough to forgive.

Just as she put the last of the finishing touches on the large farmer's dining table that seated twelve, Daisy rushed in.

"Sorry I'm late! There was traffic in Kerrville that slowed me up some."

"Get washed up for dinner," Mima said. "Jackson is on his way. Ought to be here any minute."

Crowding Eve at the sink, Daisy elbowed her. "Bet *you're* nervous."

"You could say that."

"Don't worry, I won't let him kill you." She put her hands out, karate chop style. "If he tries, I'll git him for ya."

"Ha, ha. That's funny." Eve hip-checked Daisy.

Daisy was one of several auto mechanics down at Lou's Auto forty minutes away in Kerrville. With a shortage of jobs in Stone Ridge, most taken up by the men in town, some women moved away. But Eve moved back after college and she and her partner, Annabeth Dantzer, were the only vets in the area.

Eve would have preferred fading into the background, but the men of Stone Ridge made that difficult.

# CHAPTER 2

Minutes after the plane taxied to a full stop, Jackson Carver unbuckled, pulled the brim of his black Stetson low, and stood to grab his carry-on from the overhead compartment. Lincoln would pick him up in baggage claim and drive him the sixty miles home.

Two weeks before the wedding day, time he planned to use unwinding. Fresh off a fifty-city tour, he needed a long break. More like a hibernation. His last recording contract fell apart in a mix of creative differences and management issues. The producer they'd hired walked off, and all contracts were dissolved.

"Welcome to Texas," the pilot said over the intercom and then went on to offer today's temperatures.

Ah, Texas weather. There were only two seasons in Texas: winter and summer. They both often happened in the same week. To hear the pilot describe it, today was winter even if the calendar said June. Tomorrow, eighties were forecasted. No, Jackson wasn't exactly a *stranger* to Texas, but for the past several years he'd resided both on a tour bus and in Nashville.

But he would have preferred a vacation on a deserted island. He wasn't thrilled to be going back to his hometown and there was little else that could have brought him back other than Lincoln's wedding. He would have preferred to return once his career took off but that hadn't happened in eight long years. It was said that an overnight sensation took ten years, so he should be in the seventh inning stretch. Right.

He'd come home for the wedding, but it was also a good chance to unplug. With little to no cell phone reception on their ranch and spotty downtown, he'd be relegated to the home landline. He'd left the number with his manager and musician friends, for emergencies only.

The bright June sunshine pooled over the brim of his hat, casting his view in shadows. His boots thudded across the cement tarmac toward the small building of the regional airport. He followed the crowd to baggage claim, grabbed his guitar case and one other bag, then walked to the curb and scanned the horizon.

Lincoln stood just outside the driver's side of his truck, wearing a dark leather jacket, Stetson, his long legs spread in a stance. Arms crossed. Big brother smirk firmly in place. Jackson might be known as Nashville's cowboy among his friends and band members because of his ranching roots, but Lincoln Carver was the real deal.

Jackson stopped short of the truck, his gaze sweeping over the red four-wheel drive glimmering in the sun. Lincoln must have taken it through the car wash recently, because new or not, a truck that lived on their ranch was never this clean. He slid his hand down the hood in admiration.

"You dare pick me up in this piece of shit?" Jackson asked, sarcasm heavy.

Lincoln burst into loud peals of rich laughter and a moment later, he hauled Jackson into a bear hug. A bear hug because the man *was* a bear. Huge, even to Jackson's six feet. He'd put on weight, too. And this *before* his wedding day.

"Missed you, little bro," Lincoln said.

"Same."

Jackson wasn't much of a hugger anymore. He regularly hugged three people in his life: Lincoln, their younger sister, Daisy, and their grandmother, Mima.

"Guessing Sadie's still a real good cook. You've put on a few since I last seen you."

Linc pulled back to pat his belly. "Guessed right. Enjoyed every last minute of it."

"Heard you were supposed to gain weight *after* the wedding." He snorted.

Lincoln cleared his throat. "Lookin' on the thin side yourself."

"Mima will fix that in no time, I'm sure."

Jackson expected a laugh, but when he didn't get one, the small icicle that slid over his heart the second he'd heard who the maid of honor would be spread like tentacles. His family, doing their "Carver thing." Keeping him in the dark like a mushroom. Feeding him just the same. Something was wrong.

"Yeah," Lincoln said without looking at him. "Uh-huh. She will."

They grabbed his luggage, threw it in the back, and climbed into the truck for the drive through Texas Hill Country to the small town of Stone Ridge. Their town was unique for a handful of reasons, one of them being that they were so far removed from everything that they tended to rely on each other. Now that he'd traveled all over the country and seen his share of mountain peaks and valleys, he appreciated the big Texas sky far better. The view was at times so open and unobstructed you'd swear the land went on forever. But it only seemed that way.

Jackson's mind worked overtime with every passing mile.

There surely couldn't be anything *worse* than informing Jackson that Eve would be the maid of honor while he'd be the best man. He'd received the news several months ago, and with time, digested the idea. Time to tuck in the anger and hostility, all he had left for Eve. He'd get over his damn self. There could be nothing worse than facing the woman who'd ripped his heart out and stomped all over it, humiliating him in front of a full church. Nothing worse than having to face her after eight years of struggling, and too many record deals that fell through. Nothing worse, other than maybe…

"Shit, Linc. What the hell's wrong? What did Daisy do? Is it Mima? What are y'all keepin' from me now?"

"Daisy's fine. Still fixing engines down at Lou's. Still got her eye on the rodeo cowboys." Lincoln kept driving on the main highway headed south. "And Mima…well…she's alright."

Carver code for, "It was bad there for a while, cowboy, but we made it through." In other words, Jackson heard a "but" coming. "But…?"

"She had a little…fall."

Jackson pulled off his hat and shoved fingers through his hair. "Why didn't anyone tell me?"

"Said she's fine, didn't I? Stubborn woman tried to climb a ladder in her bedroom closet, determined to find something old for Sadie to wear in the wedding. Broke her arm in three places. She had surgery, and—"

"Surgery! Why didn't you think to call me?"

"You were on tour."

"My cell phone works all over the country, you know."

Lincoln blew out an exasperated-sounding sigh. "Nothing you could do. Except worry. Spared you that, and now she's fine. She's recoverin' at home, with some hired help to make sure she doesn't try to overdo it."

Jackson allowed his shoulders to unkink. "Smart. That's… that's good."

"Glad you think so." Linc cleared his throat. "Got her a great companion, and Mima loves her. She does *now* anyway."

"Took a bit to grow on her, did she?" Jackson grinned.

The octogenarian did not "suffer fools," or at least that was one of her favorite southwest sayings, of which she had an entire catalog.

"Somethin' like that."

"Let me know how much she's charging, and I'll help pay for it." Jackson reclined his seat and settled in for the long drive. He might catch a wink or two since he hadn't slept well on the plane. "Where am I stayin? The main house?"

"Yeah, if you don't mind."

Mima lived in the main ranch-style house on their land where she'd raised two generations of Carvers. Raised a son, watched a daughter-in-law walk away from her family, and subsequently helped raise another generation of Carvers. They'd lost Pop a few years ago.

Their father, Hank, resided in the smaller house up the hill near the lodge and Linc should know that Jackson would rather not stay with him. Hank still controlled most of the cattle operations, Lincoln his right-hand man.

"Why would I mind stayin' at the main house?"

"You might after I tell you what I have to next."

"Ah, there it is." He did know his family. "What are you holding out?"

"I don't want you to get upset."

"Why would I get upset?" Every muscle in him tensed to the consistency of granite.

"Maybe because you got off that plane already lookin' like you wanted to throttle someone."

"Not true."

"Look, I can't help that Sadie and Eve have been best friends since high school. You should know better than anyone how close they are. How can I tell my future wife that she can't have Eve as her maid of honor because it will royally piss off the best man?"

"Can't. I got over it. I'll deal."

"You sure?"

"Got over Eve years ago." He clasped his hands behind his neck. "After my joke of a marriage to Winona, I'm never even thinkin' of settling down again."

"Oh. Well. That's good to hear," Lincoln said with the hint of a smile. "I'm relieved."

"Glad to relieve you."

"Because it's Eve been staying at the house for a few weeks now, taking care of Mima."

At first, Jackson thought he'd heard wrong. But then the roar in his ears grew louder, brighter, taking up every empty space, taking up everything, and he realized he'd *heard* right.

Eve, who humiliated him by making him a laughingstock, living in his family home.

His.

Family.

Home.

"Tell me I *heard* wrong." Jackson spoke between gritted teeth. "Tell me Eve isn't staying at the house."

"You *said* you're over her."

"That still doesn't mean I want her living in my family's home!"

"Shoot, she was the best person for the job."

"Why? She's a large animal veterinarian, not a *nurse*. We

could have hired someone. A *real* nurse, hell, why not a doctor on call twenty-four seven? Only the best for Mima."

"She's got the best, far as she's concerned. Mima loves her again, you know, after she got past all the, uh...the..." Lincoln struggled for words.

"The leaving her grandson at the altar shit?"

"Uh, yeah. That." Lincoln had the decency to wince. "It was eight *years* ago."

"Thanks, I'm fully aware of how long it's been."

"You haven't been back home since then, so you don't know what went on. Eve came back and eventually she and Mrs. Hollis's niece took over her practice. But hell, apparently vet school is pretty damn expensive. Mima figured she'd give her free room and board, help her get back on her feet paying back some of those loans."

"She's got loans to pay off, then we can all pitch in and help. I don't want her at the house while I'm there. Fire her, or I will."

"Boy, you must have swallowed a bottle of crazy if you think Eve will take our *charity*."

"Not mine, but she'll take Mima's?" Fire churned in Jackson's gut.

Years traveling the country, playing in Nashville honky-tonks and wherever else he could book the band. Then getting that elusive recording contract, losing it, getting another one, also losing that one. Still he pulled himself up night after stinking night. He'd been a mess after Eve stood him up. Left town for Nashville the next day, and the rest was history. So was Eve. His very unpleasant history.

"That's different. She's paid for all she's doing to help out around the house. Cookin' for the ranch hands, all the stuff Mima used to do. She doesn't get a salary. Wouldn't take one. Just the room and board."

"Why can't she stay with Brenda? Doesn't she still work

for the Trueharts?"

After her father had left their family, Eve's mother, Brenda, took work as a live-in maid and cook on the horse ranch that abutted the Double C Ranch. It would be a long walk and a short ride.

"Mima wouldn't hear of it. That cottage is so small for the two of them and Eve hasn't lived there for years. But Brenda's over now and again, to help out and visit with Eve."

"I'll get a room at the Lone Star Old Motel."

"Closed down two years ago." Lincoln shook his head. "Went the way of the gym. We knew it wouldn't last."

Jackson cursed. He could stay with his father in the home up the hill and get to hear cattle talk all the livelong day and night. Hank Carver would no doubt take pleasure in reminding Jackson that he wasn't just a Nashville cowboy but a real one. He'd then make his passive-aggressive jokes about what Jackson did for a living. No, thanks. It was rough enough to come back without much success to speak of, but another to have his father remind him daily that he'd made a mistake.

As Lincoln drove them into town, Jackson was treated to the town limits sign which hadn't changed in years:

Welcome to Stone Ridge, established 1806 by Titus Ridge
Population 5,010
*Women eat free every night at the Shady Grind*

Jackson chuckled. Yep. There was no town in the country quite like his hometown. Following the city limits signage was a newer-looking one that read:

*Women are especially welcome*

"THIS IS GETTING RIDICULOUS," Jackson said as they passed the new signage.

"We passed ridiculous a long time ago. Beulah Hayes is trying to put together a good old-fashioned email-order bride service. Plus, you know, we got to plan for the future. Ever since we got engaged, Sadie's mother has her drinking a concoction of garlic, spices, and pickled pig's feet that's supposed to favor her having a girl."

"Yeah, that's not ridiculous at all."

Lincoln shrugged. "I'm good with a boy or a girl."

"Wait. She's not...?"

"Nah, we're not pregnant. Just want to marry her."

"Yeah? *Why?*"

"Why does anyone want to get married? I love that woman. I almost lost her because I didn't notice her soon enough. I'd pretty much given up on ever getting' married unless I met someone from out of town."

"You can love a lot of people, women included. Doesn't mean you have to marry *any* of them. Think about it."

"Thought about it. Once I noticed Sadie, I couldn't un-notice her. Know what I mean?"

"Yup. She got under your skin."

He understood. At one time, he couldn't have conceived of a life without Eve. Now he'd lived several years of a life without her and it worked. Mostly. It was hard to have a relationship on the road anyway. With plenty of women to pick from, he couldn't discern whether a woman wanted him, or just had a hankering to be with a musician. He didn't have room for a real relationship in his life. He'd been jilted once and divorced once. No, thanks.

Lincoln patted Jackson's shoulder. "Take it easy. Two weeks is all. I'll be married to Sadie and you can take off again. You'll be in and out of here like a Texas windstorm."

"Well, brother, that's the plan."

# CHAPTER 3

Eve heard the front door open, slam shut, and seconds later Jackson Carver stood in the doorframe of the large kitchen. He was, as always, bigger than life to her. Tall and imposing, he looked thinner than some of the more recent photos she'd seen of him online. Lankier. He wore what looked like a day's worth of beard growth dusting his jaw and chin. His hat partially shaded his face, and thankfully, kept her from those always deep blue and penetrating eyes. Her heart gave a powerful and unwelcome tug.

"Hiya, buddy!" Daisy was the first to hug her big brother.

"Hey, Daisy."

Oh my Lord, that voice. As always, deep and gravelly and scraping the edges of her girly parts.

Daisy moved aside, and he went for a hug from Mima.

"Why, it's nothing other than my favorite *Nashville* cowboy!" Mima teased him.

"Woman, funny enough, you're still my favorite grandmother. Even if you won't tell me when you're hurt."

"Now, I didn't want you worrying about me. I've been just fine. And Eve here, well, she's been helpin' me get along."

Everyone's eyes turned to Eve, the runaway bride. She could feel Jackson's eyes on her, sharp enough to pierce her skin. Eve took a step from behind Mima, and heart seemingly thumping in her eyes, she found words.

"Hey, Jackson."

"Eve," he said, his voice sounding as warm and fuzzy as a glacier.

No surprise. He was still angry. She could tell him a few things that had happened to her between now and that day when her stupid twenty-year-old self left him at the church. She hadn't been the wisest woman on the planet at the time, but now realized she hadn't been much different than any other twenty-year-old. Or, at least any twenty-year-old that grew up in a lopsided town like theirs. Maybe it gave her illusions of grandeur to be so special, one of few women. And she'd thought she deserved better than a man who would only marry her because he couldn't figure a way out.

"Supper is served," Eve said, and turned her back to him.

"Hope y'all made enough for me. I'm so hungry I could eat my left arm," Lincoln said. "Sadie's away at a teacher event in Kerrville, so I'm on my own."

"Got plenty. Your father said to eat without him," Mima said. "Let's go in the dining room."

"Need to talk to you, Eve." No sooner were the words spoken by Jackson that it seemed all the air was sucked out of the room. "Now."

No one spoke. It sounded as though they'd all stopped breathing, too.

"Outside," he said and then headed out the back door without waiting.

Eve turned to Mima, who gave her an encouraging smile.

*Seriously?* The woman was the eternal optimist. Anyone in their right mind should be fearing for Eve about now. Like Daisy. She was shaking her head "no." Lincoln was simply studying her, like he would love to be able to place a bet right about now. Mr. Former-Rodeo-Star was still a gambler at heart.

"Be right back," Eve said and followed Jackson out the door.

Because she'd now faced far worse in her life than the wrath of Jackson Carver. Having met evil face to face, she understood who she should fear and who she should not. And though she was still a work in progress, she was slowly getting back to her feisty old self. Baby steps, her former therapist had said.

She tilted her chin and walked to where he stood several yards away next to the stable of family horses. Thimble, their oldest mare and Eve's favorite, canted her regal head over the partition and seemed to be appraising Jackson.

Jackson turned to Eve, arms crossed, his eyes now clearly visible due to his tipped hat. They were narrowed and simmering with resentment. "You're fired."

"Wh-what?"

"You heard me."

Eve drew in a shaky breath. The words were a punch to the gut. *You heard me.*

But she understood why he wanted to fire her. Much as she appreciated living on the ranch, it would be easier not seeing Jackson every single day. The wedding *was* going to be bad enough. And this was the Carver family home. *His* family. She was the intruder here, no matter how much Mima tried to make Eve feel welcome.

"Okay." She turned to go. "That's f-fine."

Eve turned to head back to the relative emotional safety of the house when a sudden thought wrapped around her so quickly that she whirled around to face him.

"W-wait a minute. You *can't* fire me. I don't work for you."

"The hell I can't. We'll hire a nurse or a doctor for Mima."

"I *am* a doctor."

"You're a veterinarian."

"So? There's a lot I also know about the human condition. We humans aren't wired all that differently from some mammals. Hearts, circulation and nervous systems, bones. Besides, Mima broke her right *arm*. We don't exactly need a specialist to look after someone who needs help cooking and driving meals out to the ranch hands."

*Breathe, breathe, breathe.*

She had rights, too. He couldn't just kick her out. She'd given up the cabin on Lupine Lake, and someone else was already moved in. There was no place to go now. These plans were hatched before Jackson showed up. He couldn't just come in now and change everything.

Thimble whinnied and stomped. In tune with Eve's emotions, Thimble would be feeling anxious, too. Before temporarily moving in with Mima, Eve took care of the Carver horses just as she'd done for the horses on the ranch where she'd grown up, doing the job of a groom for some extra cash. She'd also ridden Thimble for the exercise, and the therapy was exactly what Eve needed. Thimble basically started the healing process for Eve. And if she wasn't quite all the way there, well, that wasn't Thimble's fault.

"I'll talk Lincoln into hiring her a cook," Jackson said. "Between the three of us, we can manage to pay."

"If that's what Mima wants, I won't argue with you." Eve crossed her arms, which she couldn't help notice were shaking. "But it has to be her decision."

"This is what *I* want. You can't expect me to stay here with you in my way. Every meal. Everywhere I look."

She was about to suggest that he could stay anywhere he wanted. But she knew Mima wouldn't have that. She wanted Jackson home.

"Two weeks. I'll stay out of your way except at the church. I have to meet you there."

"Yeah, *that* will be a first." He scoffed.

For her, the day would be revisiting the worst mistake of her life, one that led to so many others. But no matter what happened, she was going to this wedding to stand beside Sadie.

Even if it killed her. "Look, Jackson, I never got a chance to say this. But I'm *sorry*."

"Oh, you're sorry. That's good. And here I was worried all this time that you *weren't* sorry. I guess that's it, then? You're sorry, and we're good?"

Behind him, Thimble was gathering steam. "Calm down, Thimble," Eve said. "I'm okay. We're okay."

"Still talkin' to horses, yeah?" He pointed to his chest. "Talk to me, Eve. How are we going to do this? Do you leave, or do I?"

She stared over Jackson's shoulder, gathering strength from Thimble. "Neither."

"Girl, you are not hearing me."

The comment sliced through her, hurting her in new places. But he didn't know. He couldn't know, or he wouldn't have made the comment because Jackson couldn't be that cruel. It just wasn't in him.

"I *heard* you loud and clear," Eve said softly. "You forget that I *know* you. Maybe better than anyone else, and you hate that, don't you? I'm the only one who realized that you didn't want to marry me."

"*What?*" This was said between gritted teeth. His hands were fisted, his eyes flashing heat.

"N-now who's not listening?"

She hadn't spoken to anyone like this in years and the heightened emotions and fear made her breathing ragged and strained. But she'd gathered strength from the true fact that she *did* know Jackson. He might storm out in a rage or at worst kick a chair, but he'd never, ever lay a hand on her in anger.

The back door to the kitchen creaked open and Mima's voice could be heard both loud and almost roaring like the Mama Bear that she was.

"What is this mess?" She stood, left hand on hip, looking ready to go grab herself a switch.

"We're talkin' here," Jackson said.

"You done talkin'. My chops are a' getting cold and I'll have none of this. Eve is stayin' with me because I don't want a stranger in my home. Don't care if he's a doctor and handsome to boot. Not happenin'. Y'all get inside now before Lincoln eats up all the chops. He's already started and the boy's big enough already."

Jackson growled in frustration, but he stalked past Mima into the house.

"I'll be right in," Eve said, turning toward Thimble.

Mima shut the door and Eve walked to Thimble, who strained to get closer to Eve. She pressed her forehead to Thimble's nose and gave her forelock a rub.

"I'm okay. I'm going to be okay. We're going to be okay."

Eve didn't know if she was saying this to reassure herself, or Thimble.

# CHAPTER 4

For Jackson, dinner was a reminder of some of his first shows in Nashville, where nobody had any idea who this *Jackson Carver* guy was. Little enthusiasm from the small crowd, no matter how well the band played. Tonight, it was so quiet he could literally hear the sounds of Lincoln's chewing. But they'd all eaten together, like his grandmother wanted, because she was a good woman and Jackson was trying like hell to be a good grandson.

But Eve hammered on his last nerve.

"Let's head over to the Shady Grind, yeah?" Jackson suggested to Lincoln after dinner.

How many more nights like this would there be, after all, before Lincoln was tethered to the ball and chain? There was the fishing trip/bachelor party coming that Jackson planned. It would be a day filled with worms, fish guts, and beer and then it would be all over for Lincoln. Tied to Sadie. Forever.

Jackson wished him good luck with that.

"I'm in," Lincoln said, grabbing his keys. "You need to cool off."

Cooling off was a damn good idea. He'd been in town an

hour. How was he going to get through two weeks of this fresh hell?

*He* didn't want to get married? Who the hell showed up at the church? Even though a week before their wedding, the band he'd played with on and off for years was suddenly headed to Nashville that summer. Jackson would stay behind. Get hitched. His twenty-one-year-old self didn't know any better. And yeah, he'd loved Eve, like he imagined everyone did their first love.

She'd looked different tonight. Her coffee-colored hair was still wavy and long. But her hazel eyes...he couldn't quite put his finger on it. They were *different* somehow. No shimmer. They were almost...hollow. Empty.

When he'd tried to fire her, it shocked him to the marrow that she'd backed off. Definitely not the girl he'd fallen for. That woman would have fought back immediately. Giving him hell. True, he didn't know Eve anymore. Over the years he'd been sent a family photo or two with her in it. Always with either Sadie, or Lincoln and Sadie. Mostly his family knew better than to bring her up. She was still a sore subject.

Lincoln pulled into the bar and grill's parking lot. Jackson knew even before stepping inside that the large dance floor would be empty and there would be mostly men in here, nursing away their sorrows over a cold beer. Far too many love stories in this town gone south.

He tipped his Stetson low as he entered behind Lincoln. Priscilla Longmire, the owner and part-time bartender was still behind the bar. She'd owned this place for decades and given Jackson his first chance at performing before an audience. She'd be around sixty now and still wore her dyed platinum blond hair teased out nearly two feet on either side of her head.

"Hey ya, 'Cilla," Jackson called out.

"Oh my gawd, it's you. Our hometown boy returns."

Jackson accepted her hug across the bar and took in the strong smell of aerosol mixed with the scent of stale beer. He was fond of Priscilla, who'd allowed him to play every other Friday night when he was starting out.

"Missed you around here, Mr. Nashville. We lost the best man of all when you left town."

"Still the best man," Lincoln joked. "This time the best man in my weddin'."

"I didn't think anything would bring you back to our neck of the woods, after…" She blinked quickly, as if she'd accidentally stumbled upon a sticky spider web. "Uh, well, you know. Tell ya, some girls don't got themselves a lick of sense."

"Maybe she had the only sense out of any of us," Jackson said, realizing he was being generous. "I realize now there's a whole world out there, with plenty of you beauties around."

"Aw, now, ain't you sweet. *And* slick." She threw a towel over her shoulder and eyed him from under obviously false eyelashes. "When'd *you* get so slick?"

"Two drafts," Jackson ordered, not willing to indulge any further conversation into his slickness.

Hard-won, that's what. He'd been considered a country bumpkin his first years in Nashville. Not anymore.

Priscilla poured, then nudged her chin to the direction of the far wall nearest to the dance floor and mock-stage area. "See there. Still got your first ax."

Jackson's first guitar still hung from the wall in a place of honor on 'Cilla's Wall of Fame. It was a cheap secondhand he'd found at a thrift store when he was sixteen. He'd long since upgraded. Still, Jezebel was special. Gratification pulsed through him to see she hung just above framed and signed photos of Johnny Cash, who Priscilla claimed crawled in one night many years ago and performed for a small crowd.

"Hey, I'm somehow above Cash. Can't complain."

One of the Henderson brothers wandered over on their way out and clapped Jackson's shoulder, welcoming him back to town. Jolette Marie Truehart seemed to be one of two women in here tonight.

Jackson paid for their drinks and he and Lincoln settled in at two of the stools. A few down from them, two men sat talking. Jackson didn't recognize either one of them.

"I don't know what I did wrong," one of them said. "Treated her right, never cheated."

The other man clapped him on the back. "We need to move out of this town."

Seemed nothing much changed around here, which should not surprise him. The only work was ranching work, and hobbies included hunting and fishing. Didn't bring a lot of women into town.

"I'll tell ya. I promised I wouldn't come back until I'd made a name for myself." Jackson waved the beer in Linc's direction. "Only came back for you."

"I thought things were going good for you in Nashville."

That was pretty much the party line he'd sent home because no one wanted to hear him whine about his problems when there was a cattle ranch to be run. But truthfully, he'd been writing songs for other musicians because that was the most lucrative. Fans loved his songs. Eventually, he'd get another recording deal but so far, he managed a living writing songs for much bigger artists and playing honky-tonks and some larger halls as an opening act.

"I'm only as good as my last performance."

"You're pretty special around here. Every now and again we see you in the 'out and about' section of the tabloids with some beautiful lady. You're practically a legend at the General Store."

"I'm no one special. Just a hard-working musician."

"Whoowee." Lincoln whistled. "Don't say that around Pops."

When compared to the back-breaking work of a rancher, yeah, not so much. Traveling from city to city, losing his voice because of singing all night in often smoky clubs, and enduring sleepless nights wasn't hard work. Never would be to their father, or Linc, though he was kind enough not to say so. Were Jackson being honest, it wasn't his definition of work, either. Punishing work was mucking a horse stall. Mending fences till your hands bled. Getting kicked in the ass by a pissed off bull. He was no stranger to any of it.

"I'm a songwriter and performer. That's all."

"Gotcha. But hey, you don't mind me saying, you didn't do such a great performance tonight of a man who's over a woman."

Anger flashed through him. "I am over her. She just happened to piss me off because she's talented that way. She's got a hell of a nerve saying I didn't want to marry her. Like she did *me* a favor."

Lincoln's eyes widened. "She *said* that?"

He cocked his head. "Guess I should be grateful."

"Gotta say, I'm a little confused." Lincoln scratched his chin. "You just explained how you never want to be tied to one woman again, but you don't agree Eve did you a favor. Both of those statements seem to be at odds."

"They're not. It's got nothing to do with her. I just wised up, is all." He chugged the rest of his draft and set it down. "And if she didn't want to get married, she could have told me the day before. Hell, the *night* before."

"Amen, brother. Amen. I agree." Linc raised his mug. "But would you have listened to her?"

"It wasn't as if I wasn't nervous about it, too. Our wedding was the only thing keeping me from Nashville. But I showed up. More than she can say."

"Alright. Just saying. If Sadie doesn't show up at the church, I'll go find her and drag her there. One way or another she's marrying me. It's a done deal."

Just the idea made Jackson's stomach pitch and roil. "She *better* show up, or I'll be the one come lookin' for her."

"Guess we both would." Lincoln laughed.

Jackson didn't think this was funny. If he'd been embarrassed to be left at the altar by someone who was arguably the most beautiful woman in town, he'd be outraged to see it happen to his brother. It terrified him to see the gobsmacked look on Lincoln's face when he spoke about Sadie. He was deeply in love with her.

Jackson cleared his throat. "But you two are fine, right? Solid."

"Solid as a boulder." Lincoln set his draft down. "I've dated plenty as you know, if you can even call it that. I know what we have is real, and not just due to convenience's sake."

Just then Becca Smith threw open the door and waltzed inside, a baby on her hip. "Homer, you get on home right now. You have a family waitin' for you."

"Be right there, baby," Homer said.

Jackson immediately recognized Becca, a few years ahead of him in school, and Miss Homecoming the year she'd graduated.

"Oh, hey there, Jackson." She waved and smiled. Still the same pretty blonde he remembered. The baby was cute, too.

"Good to see ya."

Then she turned back to her husband, who happened to be the guy comforting his buddy. "Let's go now."

Homer clapped his buddy's back, paid up, and was out the door within seconds. "Comin', baby."

No one laughed or snickered. If a man wanted to hold on to his woman around here, he best not make the bar his second home.

"You ready for that?" Jackson snorted.

"She's found a way to keep me home. Then again, I don't think I'll hang at the Shady Grind getting drunk after we're married. Why would I?"

"Right."

In Stone Ridge, not only were the few women here chased, but they were also revered. There might have been a few runaway brides over the years, not sure if they should settle down with so much on the menu. But the last man to hit his woman was run out of town by her brother and his friends. They took care of their own around here. Women were protected and isolated from harm.

Because if a man didn't protect and love his woman, there was always someone waiting in the wings to do it for him.

AFTER CLEANING the kitchen with Daisy's help, Eve retired for the evening. In the privacy of the spare bedroom, she undressed, brushed her hair into a ponytail, and pulled her hearing aid out. The aid transmitted sounds from her bad left ear to her right good ear. She'd dealt with SSD, or single-sided deafness, for a few years now and adjusted to the fact that at times she'd miss parts of a conversation or be unable to determine the exact direction of a sound. Thankfully, she still had one hundred percent of her hearing in one ear.

She crawled under the soft cotton blanket now, tried not to think about Jackson, and instead counted her blessings. Despite what she'd been through, there was plenty to be grateful for. Though it took longer and had been far more expensive than anticipated, she'd achieved her dream. She loved being a veterinarian even if it involved long hours and was at times physically taxing. Her mother, Brenda Iglesias, tried to help Eve some with the tuition, but in the end, she'd taken on enormous student loans to get through.

She jerked as through her cracked window she felt more than heard a door slam outside and turned her right ear toward the sound. Probably the men were back. A few moments later she heard a door open and shut. Jackson. The heavy sound of boots thudded down the hallway and Eve stopped breathing when it seemed that the sound stopped just outside her bedroom door. She sat up straight and pulled the covers up to her neck.

Was Jackson back to have it out with her again? Because she couldn't take any more tonight. They'd never talked honestly about why they couldn't be happy when he wanted to go to Nashville with the rest of the band.

It was a talk they *should* have had long before their wedding day.

She'd been accepted into the Texas A&M veterinary program, and one week before their wedding, his band heard interest from Nashville. The band members were moving to Tennessee, but Jackson was getting married. He'd told Eve that he would keep playing the local bars, and, of course, there was also the family cattle business. Ranching wasn't Jackson's first love, but he loved horses and animals nearly as much as she did. Jackson didn't mind staying behind. Or so he'd said.

But on her wedding day, Eve peeked through the garden trellis outside Trinity Church to spy on her handsome groom (her reasoning being the rule was *he* couldn't see *her* before the wedding, not the other way around). Her heart nearly stopped at how gorgeous he looked in his dark tux. She'd never loved anyone or anything in her life like she loved Jackson Carver. In that single moment, all her doubts faded to black.

But he'd been on his phone, and she'd heard the tail end of his side of a conversation.

"Y'all hit me up when you get rich and famous." There

was a strained laugh from him. "Maybe I can come out and visit sometime."

The sound of his voice seemed despondent but accepting of his fate. Resigned. Minutes before their wedding which should have been the happiest day of his life. He'd turned, jammed his hands in his pants pockets, and, shoulders hunched, walked toward the church like a cow to the slaughterhouse. Her future husband.

The knowledge she could no longer avoid slammed into her heart. Just like their town, their relationship was lopsided. She loved *him* more than he loved her. Maybe he thought he owed her a wedding day. He didn't *want* to get married, but it was too late to back out one week before the wedding. They'd made wedding plans for a year before Nashville even came up. He was trapped like a caged animal. Sooner or later he'd eat his arm off to get away from her.

She swallowed the golf ball in her throat. Held back the sting of tears already wetting her eyelashes. Tried to calm her racing heart. There were so many people in the church waiting.

"Hey, there you are," Sadie said from behind Eve. "Better get in here before he accidentally sees you or it's bad luck."

She'd turned to Sadie, the tears finally spilling.

"What's wrong?"

"I-I c-can't do this." Eve handed Sadie her bouquet of wildflowers. It was beautiful, and exactly what she'd wanted. No roses for her. No lilies. Give her the Bluebonnets of Texas.

Sadie pushed the bouquet back. "Don't you dare. I plan to catch this. I'm getting married next, when Lincoln notices me, but this way is cheating. I want to earn it fair and square."

"You can have it now. It's not getting thrown because I can't get married."

Sadie's eyes widened. "Oh my God! You're *serious*."

"Jackson doesn't want to marry me. He wants to go to Nashville."

"Is that what he *said*?"

"He didn't have to say it."

Sadie's gaze started to take on a wild and shifty-eyed look which felt like a mirror to Eve's.

"Eve, there are *a lot* of people here. You can't just *leave*."

And she couldn't walk down that aisle, either. Marrying Jackson or jilting him. Both options made her blood pump ice-cold to her heart. She was going to hurt Jackson by not showing up. There hadn't been a runaway bride since Tracy Presley, who'd been cheating on her groom and couldn't go through with the marriage in the end.

Jackson might never forgive her for this. But she would also hurt him by tying him down to their small Podunk town. He might eventually thank her…someday.

"It's either make him miserable now or make him miserable for the rest of his life by tying him to this town. And me."

Sadie tried, oh how she'd tried to talk some sense into Eve, but she was having none of it. Sadie then sneaked Eve out and drove her home to the cabin they shared at the time. Both of them were sobbing so hard that it was a wonder Sadie could see the road in front of her.

Sadie made some calls and stayed with Eve while she fell apart. Eve's mother showed up, tried to tell Eve this was just a bad case of cold feet. Convinced Jackson would soon be at their door, demanding to be let in, her mother prepared. She cleaned. Sadie baked cookies. Both of them were sure the wedding would go forth anyway, but simply get started a little late. Or maybe they'd have to reschedule to another day. People would be disappointed, but they'd make up some lame excuse. The wedding would go through.

She *should* have talked to him first. Like a coward, she'd cut and run. Or maybe, she thought later, some immature part of her wanted Jackson to come after her, reassuring her once and for all she was all he'd ever wanted.

But he'd never called.

Never shown up.

If he knew the course her life took since that moment, he'd feel sorry for her. Good thing he didn't know because she refused to be pathetic. She hadn't exactly been a martyr when she'd walked away from Jackson so that he could have his dream. She'd walked away because of having been raised to believe that she didn't deserve anything less than a man who *wanted* to spend the rest of his life with her.

A slice of a moment later that felt more like a decade, Jackson kept walking past her bedroom door. Eve relaxed again and started going over the list of things to do in preparation for the wedding. She had a working list on paper, of course, but there was also the one in her head. This was because, as usual, some of her best ideas came when it was time to sleep.

Tomorrow, she'd get up early and finish decorating the rest of the lodge for Sadie and Lincoln's wedding shower. Daisy said she would help and between the two of them and Mima's constant direction, they'd get it done. The food was being catered by Caroline, and they'd already discussed the platters. Also, there was… From a distance, Eve thought she heard a faint sound and turned her good ear closer to her cracked window. The music seemed to be coming from right outside her window.

*Jackson.* He was playing chords, the same pattern over and over again. No singing that she could hear as she strained even closer. She'd always loved his singing voice, a deep and emotional tenor, but hadn't heard him in years. Jackson hadn't been on the radio, but Lincoln owned a copy of a demo tape and she'd last heard his voice a couple of years ago. She sat up and moved closer, listening with her good ear for words when they came so that she could catch every single one wafting through the clear night air.

There were no words but eventually there came the single notes of a melody picked out on the guitar. The song sounded like a ballad, one that gave off a lonely timbre.

And Eve couldn't help wondering now whether maybe she wasn't the only one hurting.

# CHAPTER 5

*E*ve was up the next morning before the sunrise as was her custom. For the next two weeks, Annabeth would take coverage so that Eve could focus everything on the last-minute wedding errands for Sadie. The wedding errands, and making breakfast, lunch, and supper for the family *and* any hired ranch hands as Mima normally would.

She started the coffee for the household, dark and stout like Mima liked it, then made her way to the horse stalls. The Carvers kept their family horses separate from the cow ponies which were all stabled up the hill with Hank. Thimble was already awake. Taco, the male quarter horse who loved to bite grooms, refused to acknowledge Eve. Again. When she approached the stalls, he turned and literally gave Eve his generous backside.

"That's okay, boy. I'm sure eventually you and I will get to liking each other again."

Eve refused to give up on him. He'd liked her once, and Hank swore her voice soothed Taco. She groomed him on the rare occasion, but Hank was afraid Eve would be injured and much preferred to let the newly hired groom take care of Taco, who'd belonged to Jackson. But Thimble was special. She'd been originally purchased to be a cow pony, but a freak barn accident injured her hind leg which meant she couldn't work with the cowboys any longer.

Eve carefully led Thimble out of the stall. She grabbed the groom's bucket and spoke to her gently as she brushed her golden mane.

"I'm coming behind you, Thimble," Eve announced as she walked behind and lifted first one shoe and then the other. "How about a ride this morning? I know I could use one."

Nothing calmed Eve quite like riding Thimble, and she needed the serenity this morning. The quiet. She hadn't slept well, because Jackson was mere feet away from her. The same maddening pull to him still existed despite all their time apart. It made no sense at all.

She'd been an idiot to think she could live this close to him for two *weeks*. And if he made her squirm and sweat while outside her window, or down the hall, how would she walk arm in arm with him down the church aisle? She would not run out this time. This time he wasn't going to get what he wanted. She wouldn't make this easy for him. This day was about Sadie and Lincoln.

After taking Thimble for a ride as the sun rose over the plains, a beautiful burst of orange and red, Eve made her way back to the kitchen to start breakfast. While Eve thought the hands would have been happy with instant oatmeal the word "instant" was a four-letter word in Mima's kitchen. During the entire time she'd stayed at the ranch, breakfast meant bacon, flapjacks, sausage, toast, grits, and eggs.

"Good mornin'," Mima said as she wandered into the kitchen an hour after the sunrise. "You sleep well?"

*Why would I? Jackson is in the house. He tried to fire me.*

*You're crazy to think we'll ever be friends again. He hates me and I'm beginning to return the favor.*

"Perfect," Eve sang, turning a flapjack.

"Now, see? I told you everything would be fine." Sha patted Eve's back as she brushed by on the way to the coffee carafe.

"It's not exactly *fine*," Eve said, intercepting Mima as she tried to pour with her left hand. She poured coffee into a mug and handed it to Mima. "Last night he fired me. He wanted me to leave."

"And what did you tell him?"

Eve pursed her lips together as she recalled the way she'd almost caved and allowed him to intimidate her. It tended to be the norm for her these days. She would keep working on that.

"I reminded him that only you can fire me."

"That's my girl. Is Brenda having supper with us today?"

"She said she'd try to stop in." Eve dried her hands on a dishtowel. "I'm sure she'd like to see Jackson."

Eve hadn't lived with her mother since graduating high school. The little cottage provided by the landowner wasn't much and though Brenda would have welcomed Eve back, she wanted her own place. When Eve got back from veterinary school, she moved into one of the cabins that Sadie's father rented out on Lupine Lake. The rent was cheap, but between her student loans, rent, and buying into a partnership with Annabeth, Eve ate ramen noodles most days. Then Lillian asked for her help and it seemed a perfect solution and a chance for Eve to get back on her feet financially.

"It's not going to be a whole lot of fun around here for these two weeks. He's still pretty angry."

"It's not such an easy thing to forgive, honey."

With her shaky non-dominant left hand, Mima opened the fridge and took out the creamer. Eve was forced to intercept again when Mima tried to pour with her left hand. The woman was a disaster waiting to happen. She desperately needed Eve to save her from herself.

"This isn't going to be easy for me, either."

"I know that," Mima said. "Just give him a little time and he'll come around. Why, I bet by the time you two walk down the aisle for Sadie and Lincoln in a couple of weeks, you'll be the best of friends again."

"Don't get your hopes up."

"Child, I was so mad at you I thought my eyes might stay permanently crooked. And now look at us!"

Having helped raise Jackson and his brother and sister, Mima was quite protective. It didn't matter that Jackson left town, going after what he'd really wanted. For a while, Mima *blamed* Eve for not managing to keep him home.

"I think maybe you have a more forgiving heart."

"Where's the coffee?" A deep and grumpy voice said from behind her.

Oh. My. God. Had he heard? How much? Eve couldn't look at him.

"Sit down and let us serve you breakfast," Mima said from her seat at the kitchen table.

*Translation: "Let Eve serve you."*

"No need."

Reaching for the carafe, he accidentally brushed against Eve and her body buzzed with desire. *Stupid, stupid body.*

"Going to ride Taco up the hill and go see the old man."

"That's why you're up early," Mima said.

"Couldn't sleep," he said gruffly.

"He'll be glad to see you. Tell him that calving doesn't mean he gets away without ever seeing his Mama."

"Yeah. Don't count on it. You know Hank. Gives him a good excuse to hide up there and avoid everyone."

"Don't call your daddy 'Hank,' son. Not respectful. And

try to make it to the wedding shower later today. Eve, Daisy, and I will be decoratin' the lodge."

"*They'll* be decorating." Jackson pointed to Mima. "You'll be sittin' in a chair supervising if you know what's good for you."

Temporarily forgetting herself, Eve piped in. "Oh, she will sit still. I'll make sure of it. Don't you worry about it."

He turned to her. She saw he still hadn't shaved which gave him a sexy, just-rolled-out-of-bed tousled appearance. But he wore a clean, pressed flannel shirt and blue Wranglers that fit him extremely well. Loose and tight in all the right places.

She wished she wouldn't notice such things.

Jackson slid her a look you'd give to a flea on your prized stallion. "Not worryin' about it. That's your job. Do it well or you're fired."

Eve swallowed and bit her lower lip. She would *never* do any job poorly. The Iglesiases worked hard for years. There was a certain amount of self-righteous indignation simmering in her gut on a low flame. She would respond but what would be the point? Avoiding confrontation was her middle name.

"Now, now. Only I can fire Eve."

"We'll see about that." With that, he turned and strode out of the kitchen.

"Don't let him bother you," Mima said from the kitchen table. "I know my Jackson. He was always the sweetest boy. He'll get over all this anger."

But Eve wasn't so sure about that. If he'd held on to it for years, how would two *weeks* make a difference?

"I need to put in a few hours today over at the clinic, then I'll be yours and Sadie's for the next two weeks."

"I'm so excited! What a wonderful time we're all going to have."

Yeah. *Wonderful.* Eve pulled out a pan and flipped on the gas stove.

There were cowboys to be fed.

# CHAPTER 6

Eve drove her pickup truck straight from dropping breakfast burritos off for Hank and his ranch hands over to the Lone Star Veterinary Clinic where she worked with Annabeth. Her partner at the clinic didn't have nearly the same affection for Stone Ridge that Eve did. The only thing she loved about Stone Ridge was the abundance of men. They were two very different women, which might be why they worked so well together.

Eve was organized, loved routine and schedules, wasn't dating anyone, and understood the coffeemaker. She talked to horses and was generally far more intuitive with animals. Annabeth loved details, men, and had a take-no-prisoners attitude with both pets and their owners. She was tall, thin, and wore her spiky, short hair with a streak of purple. She also preferred working with small animals. Eve worked with the large animals mostly, taking the truck and supplies out to the ranches that often called on them.

As soon as Eve made the coffee, Annabeth cornered her. "Are you still going through with this?"

"Sadie's wedding? Yes."

Eve was going to enjoy doing one job for a while instead of two. Juggling Mima's job and hers was beginning to wear on her.

"You should have just kindly bowed out months ago, when you had a chance."

Disappoint Sadie and make things easier for Jackson? Not a chance. "Sadie's my *best friend*."

"And the best man is your ex-fiancé. That's just crazy-times, girl. You'd never catch that kind of thing happening in Austin."

Annabeth continually compared the two towns to each other. No surprise, she was originally from Austin, and Stone Ridge always came up short.

"If you're worried about me, don't be. He just came in last night and we agreed we're going to do our best to stay away from each other. It shouldn't be too hard."

"While staying under the same roof, even?" Annabeth went all squinty-eyed.

"It's a big enough house."

"You two are going to shack up while he's here. He's going to leave after the wedding, and this time you'll be one more woman tossed to the side. You better quit while you're ahead. At least you left him."

Eve wouldn't be falling into bed with him anytime soon, or he with her. They were barely going to tolerate being in the same room together.

"You wouldn't make such a ridiculous statement if you'd seen how mad he is with me. He tried to fire me. He can barely stand to look at me."

"Good. Keep it that way."

Eve sighed. "Okay, let's get on with our day."

Annabeth rummaged around the desk that would belong to a receptionist, if they were able to afford one, and handed Eve a piece of paper. "There was a message from a Mr.

Mansfield."

"*Mr.* Mansfield?"

"He's the new foreman over at Maddox Ranch. Leroy retired." Annabeth lightly touched Eve's shoulder. "Are you going to be okay? I could move some appointments around and go with you."

"No, I'll be fine," Eve said, folding the paper and tucking it into the back pocket of her Wranglers.

She'd been out to the Maddox ranch dozens of times. And it wasn't the first time she'd gone out on a call alone. It's just that usually she already knew the men. Had known them most of her life and they were like fathers, uncles, brothers.

*You have to get past this. Don't be pathetic. Be brave.*

"He thinks a cow pony has colic."

Colic was about the worst thing that could happen to a horse and it was far too common. Eve had treated it many times and lost a handful of horses to it. Colic was always painful for the horse and frightening for the owners.

"Go home after this call," Annabeth said. "I'll hold the fort down."

Eve grabbed her bag, analgesics, and the tubing she would need and packed the mobile unit with Annabeth's help. Annabeth pointed to Eve. "And no matter what, don't hook up with the ex-fiancé!"

A few minutes later Eve set out for the drive to the outskirts of Stone Ridge and the midsize Maddox cattle ranch. She sent up a silent prayer that the new foreman was just being overly cautious. Colic was so difficult to treat. It was the only part of the job that she hated. Sometimes, no matter how hard she tried, she couldn't make a difference in the outcome. Animals suffered, and she was forced to stand by helplessly.

She parked near the barn and in the distance spotted a large man walking down to meet her. He was at least six five and looked like he bench-pressed in his sleep. He could barely keep his arms down. She gripped the steering wheel.

*I can do this. I'm not a coward. I hate cowards.*

Forcing a deep breath in her lungs, she climbed out of the truck and walked to meet him.

*Not a coward. Not a coward. Not a coward.*

She looked past him to the stables when he unexpectedly stuck out his big ham hock of a hand. "Jeff Mansfield."

Eve flinched but thought she may have recovered quickly enough that he didn't notice. She should have expected the handshake, but his hands were large and his grip strong. A small pebble threatened to close up her airway. He seemed otherwise harmless, but Eve knew that didn't mean a damn thing.

She got busy pulling on her gloves. "I'm Dr. Iglesias. Y'all have a cow pony with colic?"

He led the way to the stall. "Holly's been acting up for days now. Finally pulled her from duty yesterday. But need to get her back out there workin'."

Days? He'd waited *days*? Colic should be treated immediately. It was highly irresponsible for him to have waited that long. But if she told him this, they might start their relationship off in a confrontation. She didn't *do* confrontations anymore. The one with Jackson was the first in years, and she'd need a few more years before she had enough energy or nerve for another.

"I'll see what we've got going on here then." She gave him a slight smile which she hoped looked friendly and not as shaky as it felt on her lips.

She had confidence in her abilities and realized she was good at what she did. But men like Mr. Mansfield were intimidating. Even his voice was gruff and off-putting. None of this would bother Annabeth at all. If only Eve could channel some of that Annabeth "Austin" attitude and vibe. Easy and breezy. Hipster.

*Focus on your patient. It's what you do best.*

The mare was clearly in misery, pawing at the ground, head down. Eve got to work immediately, trying to find the blockage in the intestines by pulsating with her hands. Because of her hearing loss, she only partially relied on the stethoscope.

"I'll need you to help me," she said. "We can't let her lie down or she'll try to roll and injure herself."

"This isn't my first rodeo, doc."

He gave her a funny look as he held on to the mare and she continued with both the stethoscope and her hands. Softly so that Mr. Mansfield wouldn't hear, Eve spoke to the horse. She reassured her that she was only trying to help take this pain away. Quietly whispered she'd at least get a few days off from work.

"Well hell, didn't know I got myself a horse whisperer," he joked.

Eve ignored that, or tried to, anyway. Once, Jackson appreciated that she talked to horses. Now he, too, was making fun of it. She didn't care about him, or Mr. Mansfield. Okay, maybe she did care but she wouldn't let that stop her. Her patient always came first.

"I'm sorry about this, girl." She turned to Mr. Mansfield. "She's bad. I think I can help her, but—"

*Next time call sooner. You could have lost her.*

The words stayed stuck in her throat. She went over what she was about to do even as he rolled his eyes. Yeah, right. Not his *first* rodeo. He held on to the horse as Eve gently put tubing down Holly's throat and poured castor oil down.

The horse resisted and reared back but Mr. Mansfield held her tightly. "Whoa, girl. Whoa. Tryin' to help you here."

Eve hated this part. The pain she would cause to get Holly

well again. There was no other way but through it. The next time Eve came toward Holly, if there was a next time, she'd probably shy away from Eve because of this experience. She spoke soothingly to the horse as Holly fought to get away, her eyes wide and wild. As the last of the castor oil was poured through the tubing, Eve slowly began to remove the tube but lost her footing.

She wound up flat on her back on the stall's floor, Holly above her, pissed, snorting, and ready to trample. But it wasn't the horse Eve feared at the moment. It was the man coming at her. She was suddenly back in her dorm back at College Station, where she should feel safest, with a man's large hand before her to…help.

*He's trying to help you.*

Eve shook her head clear of the memory.

Mr. Mansfield singlehandedly pulled her up with one arm while still hanging on to Holly with the other. "Okay there, doc?"

"Y-yes, I'm sorry. Lost my footing."

He glanced down. "Sure did. But the good news is this blockage is gone."

And, there at her feet, was said evidence of Holly's immense relief. It was a rancid steaming brown pile. Good thing she'd worn her old work boots. This smell might never come out of them.

Later, after Eve cleaned off her boots, made sure to walk Holly around the corral a few times, and packed her truck, she met Mr. Mansfield in the foreman's office. He sat behind his desk cutting her a check and handed it over.

"Gotta hand it to ya, doc. You're a little skittish around horses but you did good."

He thinks you're skittish around *horses.* She almost laughed. Almost.

"Thank you. I'm glad I could help."

"I'll call you next time there's a problem around here. Looks like you could use the experience."

Eve stiffened. It started at her spine and traveled south to her legs. She feared there was about to be some mansplaining following that statement. And maybe he was right. She could use more experience.

In learning how to stand up for herself.

*Coward. Mami didn't raise me this way. She taught me to be strong and work hard. The Iglesiases are hardy. Tough.*

Except for her Papi. He was apparently made out of lint.

"My advice is to keep her quiet and let her rest for a few days," Eve said.

"Huh." He leaned back in his chair as if he was considering it. "For you, doc, sure."

"Thank you." There was so much more she wanted to say to Mr. Mansfield.

*Never wait this long to call me again.*

*Do you realize how easily this could have gone sideways?*

But the words felt stuck in her windpipe and that old stone had lodged itself in her trachea.

# CHAPTER 7

*I*t was official. Jackson had heard enough talk about bull sperm to last him a lifetime.

"That damn bull," Hank said, removing his hat and scratching his temple. "Of all the lousy luck. Got himself a libido problem. Nothing wrong with him otherwise. He's got the goods. Just won't give 'em up."

"Go figure."

Both he and Hank were riding side by side like they hadn't done in years. The last time was well before the wedding-day fail. He'd stopped spending time with his father when it was clear that Lincoln would take over the family business. And he was the right choice. Jackson could have worked the ranch as well, but he'd found something else to do. Unfortunately, Hank didn't particularly like the idea of his second son playing music for a living. It didn't sound "honorable."

And at times, it was less than honorable. That suited Jackson just fine.

"Glad you finally got yourself back home."

"Didn't think I would?"

"Must admit, had my doubts."

Jackson spoke through a tight jaw. "Lincoln is my only brother and I'd do anything for him."

"Good, good. Family *is* everything."

But if that was true, why hadn't Hank ever been to one of Jackson's performances? The entire family had at one time or another, but Hank was always busy. Always. Sometimes Jackson couldn't reconcile the loving father to the man who often withdrew from the family. Who answered the simplest questions at times with unwarranted hostility.

*"How are you, Dad?"*

*"Who the hell is askin'?"*

At one time, Jackson told himself that it was Hank's deep anger at his wife having left the family. And, after Eve left him at the altar, for the first time Jackson understood. To be abandoned by the one person you loved most in the world was devastating. But while Hank was abandoned once, for Jackson it was *twice*. First, his mother, Maggie Mae Carver. Then Eve. It was difficult to believe that wasn't what he deserved.

Jackson's anger was so big it didn't fit anywhere. No place large enough, so he'd buried himself in the bottle for a while. The bottle might not be wide, but it was deep. He might have stayed in there longer, if not for his music.

For that reason alone, he wished that Hank would have a little more respect for how hard Jackson worked. And a musician, while maybe not the noblest profession in the world, could change people's lives. But Hank didn't want to hear any of that. He wanted to talk sperm.

Hank stopped his stallion at the top of the hill that over-looked the entirety of the Carver ranch. One hundred and fifty acres of rolling hills to the north ending at the Truehart horse ranch. A tiny cottage sat at the back of the Truehart ranch, the place where Eve used to live with her mother.

Hank pointed in the direction of the home Lincoln was having built for his family. It seemed far enough away for some privacy and near a creek that ran through the Carver and Truehart properties.

"Over yonder is where your brother will live, and the family he'll have soon enough."

Jackson braced himself.

"When you think you'll settle down and have some children?"

Straight from bull sperm to Carver sperm. "Not in any hurry, Dad."

"I don't know about the women out there in Nashville, but I know here we grow 'em strong and beautiful. Like Eve. But, guess you know that better than anyone."

"Right. Beautiful women in Stone Ridge. Though not plentiful, that's for sure." Jackson diverted from the subject of Eve.

"True enough. Wish we had more like Eve. Looks just like her mother. Prettiest women in all of Stone Ridge. Hell, maybe even Texas."

Always like Hank to point out the obvious. Jackson resisted reminding him of just who'd left whom at the altar. But there was no point. His father favored Eve from the day he discovered she loved talking to horses. The fact that she'd not only become a veterinarian, but come back to Stone Ridge to practice, was sort of the blue ribbon on that deal.

"Right."

"Got to be tough for you," Hank said as they crested the hill that faced their farthest pasture. "Eve's got no need for you."

"Good," Jackson said, his throat tight. "Got no need for her, either."

Hank snorted. "Just keep tellin' yourself that, son. Might someday believe it."

Jackson resisted leaving Hank and his slow horse in the dust. Taco was up for anything.

"What was I supposed to do? I know you loved her, too, but she walked out on me, case you forgot."

"Nerves. That's what Brenda told me."

"Hell, I was nervous, too. But I showed up."

Hank nodded. "Yup. And left the next day."

"Because *she* didn't show up."

"Like I said, it was nerves. Should have gone after her, calmed her down. Talked to her. You'd be married to the most beautiful veterinarian in Stone Ridge, more like the entire county, and happy as a pig in shit."

They'd talked about this before. About once a year. Hank even met one of Jackson's old girlfriends when he'd been out to Nashville with the rest of the family. All beautiful women, though none exactly pierced Jackson's heart with an arrow. Especially not Winona James, his ex-wife and a fellow country musician. He'd been married to her for about three months. And if Eve soured him on the idea of marriage, Winona finished the job.

At first, she'd been exactly what he needed in his life. Winona hated Eve on his behalf, without knowing her. Hated Eve for the pain she'd caused him. She became his friend and drinking buddy, and one night they'd made the mistake of getting married. No plans or invitations. Just one long night of drinking and partying, waking up married. Biggest mistake of his life.

Now, he wasn't looking to be tied down. He was fine with relationships lasting six months or so, and then everyone moved on. Being on the road, it was best not to form deep attachments to one woman.

But according to Hank, he'd never find anyone like Eve again. Period. It was damn annoying. Of course, Hank valued far more than Eve's looks. She was the whole package: smart, kind, and beautiful.

He had a point.

Jackson dated his share of beautiful women. Toned bodies and perfect hair. Eve wasn't perfect. Her long hair a little wild and untamed, and she didn't seem to care. Rather than toned, she sometimes carried a little extra weight around the hips. But then there were those long legs and a smile that could knock a man out cold.

Hank loved her like a daughter. When Eve's father, Ricardo, left his family, it was Hank who found Brenda work as a live-in maid for the Trueharts. Jackson figured the old man's long friendship with Brenda somewhat clouded his judgement for Eve being anything less than the ideal young lady.

Rather than continue to argue, Jackson took another tactic. Agreement. He only had to get through this wedding. Then he'd be back to Nashville and a sense of normalcy again. His chest would stop being so tight, and he'd be able to breathe again. Deep, cleansing breaths, instead of the shallow ones he managed around Eve. He should get away from her before he said or did something he'd regret. No two ways about it.

"You're right. I screwed up." It was a cowboy's job to take the blame, according to Hank.

"I'll be gall darned. The first step is admitting it." Hank turned his horse around. "Best get back. Got one heifer about to drop. It's her first and Lincoln might need my help."

Jackson turned Taco to follow. There was still so much he wanted to ask Hank.

*Why are you still so angry? Am I doomed to wind up just like you?*

Those questions would have to wait. First, they all had a wedding to attend.

. . .

Tables were covered in burnt orange cotton cloth with adorable centerpieces Sadie's mother, Wanda, had created. Small pieces of redwood were surrounded by pinecones, and little glass-enclosed white candles sat atop each piece of cut wood.

At the very center of the room Eve caught sight of a gigantic big-screen TV that was obviously Jackson's gift, delivered late morning by an irritated UPS guy. Since it wasn't wrapped, Eve slapped a big red bow on it. *Someone* was thinking more about Lincoln than he was about Sadie though she supposed Sadie would also enjoy the new TV. Especially during their marathons of *Chicago Fire*.

They expected a large group of women to descend on them shortly, every parent from the school where Sadie taught, carrying all manner of household appliances.

One thought kept running through Eve's mind over and over again. The memory of having to send back all of the presents from their wedding shower *and* her non-wedding day. A food processor, a state-of-the-art espresso machine, a twelve-person serving set, a crap ton of lingerie she *couldn't* return and much more. Eve, her mother, and Sadie sat for hours composing "thank you, anyway" cards which they'd attached to the gifts as they were each returned.

The pain of that time still managed to render her nerves a quivering mess. But it was simple enough not to dwell on it all these years later, until Sadie and Lincoln announced their engagement. Then, memories rushed in, and Eve forced them back. She'd been thrown into all of the planning and anticipating. Everyone around her seemed to assume she'd long ago gotten over the fiasco of her wedding-day fail.

Eve thought so, too, until she began to help Sadie in the same way Sadie had helped Eve years ago. Then a strange sense of déjà vu covered her, with memories about the moments they'd spent together dreaming of the perfect day.

"Everything looks beautiful." Sadie arrived with her mother, Wanda, with Lincoln bringing up the rear.

While Lincoln and Wanda headed in the direction of the buffet, Sadie headed straight for Eve and pulled her behind the huge plasma TV.

"I have a problem. You have to help me."

"What's wrong? Is it your dress?"

"Eve, I…" She hesitated. "I'm worried."

"Why?"

She grasped Eve's hands. "The wedding. Something could go wrong."

"Something is bound to go wrong. But it won't matter because you're marrying the love of your life. Right?"

"Yes, true," Sadie said, and bit on her lower lip. "But some-times…unexpected things. Unplanned…"

"It's all good. Nothing will ruin that day."

When Sadie's gaze lowered to her belly and a single tear rolled down her cheek, Eve was caught between emotions. She'd be happy but Sadie looked scared. "This might."

Eve sucked in a breath and squeezed Sadie's hands. "Did you tell him?"

"Not yet. And I haven't told you, either. You just guessed. I'm supposed to tell him first. But…Lincoln didn't want to have children right away."

"Well, this happens. He's just as much a part of this as you are."

"I hate to spring this on him, right before our wedding day."

"Honey, you should be happy. He'll be fine. Hey, at least you know he's not marrying you just to do the honorable thing."

Sadie didn't laugh. "I'm six weeks pregnant, Eve. I've been feeling sick every morning and chances are I'll be sick on our honeymoon."

"What can I do to help?"

"Nothing. I'm *not* going to tell him. Not until we get back from our honeymoon."

"Sadie, I don't think…"

"I just wanted to tell *someone*." She pointed. "But remember, I didn't tell you! You just guessed."

Wanda came around behind the plasma TV. "There you are! Oh, hello there, Eve. My goodness, Sadie, what on *earth* are you doing behind a TV? It's time to get started."

A few minutes later, the crowd of women slowly trickled in, carrying enough presents to open a department store. Lincoln stood behind Sadie as she sat on the chair of honor at the head of the folding table and tried to make himself useful by occasionally rubbing her shoulders. But he disappeared shortly after a pair of edible panties was unwrapped. Gifted by none other than Pastor June Marie, scheduled to marry the couple.

"*Edible?*" Mima elbowed Eve.

"You can eat them," Eve hissed, wondering why no one thought to gift her a pair at *her* wedding shower.

"What, now?" Mima asked, straightening.

Sometimes Mima acted much older than her eighty-something self. "Use your *imagination*." Eve certainly was doing so now.

Except that an image rose, unbidden, of Jackson nibbling her panties off. Lord! Eve shook her head. What was wrong with her? Finally, what seemed like hours later, every present open and every dish licked clean, they all helped pack Lincoln's truck to the brim with presents. And still they didn't all fit.

"I'll come by for the rest tomorrow," Lincoln said.

"Take good care of my bounty." Sadie tenderly petted the box containing an espresso machine.

"Hey, woman, you got your bounty right here," Lincoln

said, wrapping his arms around Sadie. "Already taking me for granted?"

"Oh no, baby, of course not."

Then they kissed for what seemed like an eternity until they finally got in the truck and drove away.

Eve finished cleaning up alone since Daisy ran off somewhere, probably to drool over some of the ranch hands. Every now and again some cowboys came off the rodeo circuit and worked the calving season, adding even more men to the mix. After letting all the dogs and barn cats back inside their abode, Eve locked up the barn and went to check on Mima. She was curled up on her leather recliner in front of the beautiful rock fireplace hearth, her laptop open.

She glanced up at Eve, jaw gaping. "Good Lord almighty, I just googled edible panties!"


Eve didn't see Jackson for two days. He was probably putting finishing touches on the bachelor party. One of her jobs was to plan the bachelorette party. Another was to help with the wedding favors. And possibly attend yet another dress fitting, because Lord help her, she was probably an inch wider around the hips. She was officially back to the weight she'd been at twenty, when she'd been healthy and happy.

Today, she and Sadie were occupying both the island and the table in Mima's kitchen. Small mason jars filled with the popular jam that Sadie's mother, Wanda, sold covered the table. There were at least a hundred of them. Eve was in charge of placing the pre-printed labels on that read:

June 16
"Spread the Love"
Lincoln and Sadie

SADIE TOPPED them with a patch of short burlap and tied each with a matching string. Definitely a production, and they could have used Daisy's help, but she'd taken off. Mima, who would be of little help at all other than supervising, was out shopping with Wanda for comfortable but stylish shoes. They'd gone to Kerrville and likely wouldn't be back till much later in the day.

"Still fightin' with Jackson?" Sadie said.

Talk of the pregnancy was off limits when anyone could walk in on them. Eve knew better than to ask whether Sadie had told Lincoln yet.

"I'm avoiding him."

"You know why he's so angry, don't you?" Sadie slapped the burlap over the top of a jar and moved it around to make it fit. "He was so hurt when you stood him up."

"Hmm. I don't know about that."

"Eve, you didn't see him."

"Neither did you." In fact, he left town like a streak of lightning and it was a wonder anyone saw him.

"No, but…well, look, I'm sworn to secrecy, but you are my best friend. And you're doing all this for me, which I know can't be easy. I know how he was because Lincoln told me. When Jackson got home from the chapel, he changed and took Taco for a ride. He didn't come back for hours." Sadie moved to the next jar. "Mima was about to send for the law, but Lincoln made her wait. He went looking for Jackson himself, terrified when he couldn't find him. But sure enough, he came back hours later, stormed into the house, and proceeded to wreck his room."

"That doesn't make me feel better." Another stone slid down her throat.

"Lincoln made everyone just wait it out and an hour later,

Jackson came out with his bags packed. Said as long as he wasn't getting married, he was going to Nashville with the band." Sadie looked up, remembering. "And then it was Mima's turn to get mad."

"At me."

"That's right," Sadie said. "Well, both of you. Because of you standing him up, her Jackson left town. He couldn't show his face again because he was heartbroken."

"I don't want to talk about this anymore."

Sadie covered her mouth. "Listen to me. I'm sorry to bring up bad memories, but I think if he was that upset, he must have really cared. He loved you, Eve. A whole lot. You were his world."

Eve swallowed. "And he was mine."

"I just think a second chance wouldn't be so out of the question. Would it?"

"Sadie, don't look now but your incurable optimism is hijacking your brain." Eve slapped a label on a jar with a bit more force than the previous one. "Weren't you the one that told me Jackson moved on and I should get out there and date again?"

"I tried that, and you don't seem to want anyone else."

"So? That doesn't mean I'm goin' to go running back to Jackson just because he's come back home. He came back for Lincoln, not me."

A car door slammed outside, and both Eve and Sadie turned to the large picture window giving them a clear view of the top of their long circular driveway. Jackson leaned into the driver's side window and braced arms with an ease and familiarity you'd see between two lovers. When he straightened to his full height, Eve got a clear and unobstructed view of Jolette Marie Truehart behind the wheel. Jolette Marie was a three-time runaway bride and a buckle bunny. The only daughter of the wealthy man who owned the second largest horse ranch in Stone Ridge. Her mother's employer. Jolette smiled up at Jackson, winked, and blew him a kiss before she drove off.

Afraid to be caught in the act of noticing this, Eve quickly looked away. She met with Sadie's rounded hazel eyes, filled with pity. If there was one damn thing Eve couldn't stand it was pity. She bristled, her stomach a quivering mess.

"I don't care," she said.

Jackson strode into the kitchen, a big grin on his face. He tipped his Stetson. "Ladies."

"Hey, Jackson," Sadie said. "We're just working on the weddin' favors. I hope we're not in your way."

"Don't mind me." He opened the fridge, took out a bottle of water, and uncapped it.

There was no way they couldn't pay attention to the cowboy in the room. He took a seat next to Sadie and observed their process.

"Aren't these cute?" Sadie said. "It's from my mom's label."

"I love your mama's jam," Jackson said, picking up a jar and leaning back as he read the label. "Very funny. Spread the love."

But Sadie's wide smile was wiped right off her face when Jackson put his big finger in an opened jar and swiped a big dollop. He licked it off his finger and met Eve's gaze.

She swallowed. "Um, Jackson? Don't you have something to do?"

"Yup. And I'm doin' it."

"This jam is for the weddin'," Eve said.

Jackson reached in his back pocket, pulled out his wallet and took out a bill which he slapped on the table. "There. I get my jam now."

"I do have extras. You don't have to pay—" Sadie said.

"Yes, he does," Eve interrupted.

"Not that it's any of your business, but I'm here to talk to

Sadie," Jackson said.

"What about?" Sadie straightened.

"Now, I know you love my brother—"

"Oh, I do, Jackson. I do *so* much."

"But you'll have to excuse me for having my doubts. You are best friends with a woman who doesn't follow through with her commitments."

"Are you *kiddin'* me?" Eve whispered.

He ignored her. "Not that I expect this, but just know that if you stand my brother up, there'll be hell to pay."

"Jackson." Eve stood.

Sadie seemed shocked to silence, staring from Eve to Jackson and back again.

He also stood, nearly knocking over the chair. "You got something you want to say to me?"

"Yes," Eve said. "But I can't say it here. Sadie doesn't like it when I swear."

"Outside, then." He strode toward the back door.

# CHAPTER 8

*Here we go again.*

Jackson followed Eve out the back door, but they hadn't gotten far when she turned to him, her hazel eyes flashing anger.

"S-say what you want about me, but you lay off Sadie."

"This is a conversation I'm about to have with Sadie and you need to stay the hell out of it."

"You can't blame Sadie for what I did. She's my only friend and I can't let you. I just can't." She crossed her arms.

He didn't know what the hell was up with the women in this town, so he couldn't be sure that Sadie should be trusted any more than Eve. He'd just been dropped off by Jolette Marie, who held the runaway bride record. Best as he could surmise, the women here had their pick of men so they often couldn't make up their minds who would be best.

Yes, Sadie claimed she loved Lincoln. Eve said she'd loved Jackson and look what happened there.

"She's been after my brother for years. She has her choice of men. Why? That's what I want to know."

"Why? She *worships* him. And she's loved him for years. You've got to have seen it."

"All I see is two people headed in the direction of what could be a lot of heartache. And I can't stand by and let it happen to my brother."

Eve's gaze softened. "They're not as young as we were. They know what they want and they're ready to commit to each other. They've both dated other people and they know what they have is special. You can't compare them to us."

"They practically *are* us! She's your best friend, he's my brother. It doesn't get much closer than that."

He'd been thrown back eight years to all the same type of wedding shenanigans that he'd been through with Eve. Lincoln had been his best man and now Jackson would return the favor. His first order of business was to make sure the bride showed up.

"It's different," Eve said now. "Why can't you just believe me on this?"

"That's rich. Because you're so trustworthy?"

"Please." She closed her eyes and took a deep breath. "You have to let this go. We need to get along."

She was right, but he'd been home two days and every time he laid eyes on Eve he didn't like all the feelings she stirred up in him. She was impossible for him to ignore.

"I'm still so damn mad at you."

"Don't you think I know that? But anger is a *useless* emotion. Trust me, it won't get you anywhere. It will simply eat you up alive. Anyway, you certainly recovered quickly enough. And now, you've got curbside service drop-off from none other than Jolette Marie. I know how long *she's* waited to get your attention."

He felt the right side of his mouth tip and yeah, he just might be smiling. "Careful. You sound kind of jealous."

"Not at all. It's just that Jolette Marie is such an obvious choice."

"Because she's tall, blond and beautiful? Yeah, all men *hate* that."

"Jolette Marie just likes *men*. All of them."

He laughed. "You're right, that's too obvious."

Eve went palms up like she surrendered and turned to give him her back. She took two steps away from him before he grabbed her wrist.

"Don't you walk away from me. We're not done here."

He hadn't exactly wanted, nor expected, to enjoy touching her. It took him a minute to realize that he hadn't let go of her wrist even though she was no longer moving away from him.

"I don't know what you want from me," she whispered.

She probably couldn't give him what he wanted. He needed to stop feeling anything at all for her. He wanted her to stop walking around, being Eve, making him look and yearn and want. It shouldn't be happening. He should feel nothing, or at least next to nothing. Should be able to simply appreciate that she was a beautiful woman, the same way he appreciated Jolette Marie. Detached. As when he admired a beautiful sunset from a distance. And to feel *nothing* more.

"I want you," he said, knowing that there was more truth in those three words than he cared to admit, "to make sure that Sadie shows up to the church. Because if she doesn't, it's you I'm coming after. *You* that will have hell to pay."

"She'll be there."

When Eve walked back into the kitchen she was still shaking. The most unsettling part of the shaking was its reason. Because this didn't feel like fear. Instead, she recognized the pulse and thrill of intense desire. Lust. Animal magnetism.

Chemistry. She hadn't felt any of those sensations in such a long time it was a wonder she didn't confuse them with actual terror. But the connection with Jackson was still alive and crackling with sexual tension, making him difficult to ignore.

"He's still so angry. What did you do to him now?"

"Nothing! I'm just here." She held her arms out. "That's bad enough."

"That was…incredible."

"I don't want to talk about it." She reconsidered and held up a finger. "Except to say that I'm sorry he said those things to you. He shouldn't have."

"I thought he was going to swipe every jar off the table and, like, *do* you, right here." She pointed to the kitchen table.

"Sadie!" Eve found herself laughing at the brutal honesty.

"Why on *earth* does he think I won't show up to my own wedding?"

Eve deadpanned. "I believe he thinks you and I are far more alike than we actually are."

"That's just crazy. Lincoln and I took years to get to this point. How could I ever walk away?"

"The same way I did, *he* thinks. Don't worry, I handled him."

Sadie batted her eyelashes. "And how exactly did you handle him?"

"I assured him, on pain of my own death apparently, that you will be there. And I'm not worried."

"It's actually so sweet that he loves his brother so much. He's protective of his heart." She grinned. "You guys still have sparks. Watching you two is…well, it makes me want to go find Lincoln, if you know what I mean."

"Yes, I believe I do. And those sparks are bound to put my eye out at some point."

"Now that you're older, and both more settled, maybe it could work this time. There's still something there."

"No. It's too late. He'll never forgive me, and he's got a life in Nashville. My life is here and always will be."

"There's surely a need for vets around Nashville, too."

"Stop. My mother is here, Mima is here, and last but not least, you're here. I'm going to watch you and Lincoln have those Carver boys you always dreamed of having." She winked, knowing one could already be on the way.

"But what about you?" Sadie stuck out her bottom lip.

"I'm going to be Auntie Eve, of course."

"Eve, you just can't…you can't let what happened to you dictate the rest of your life." Sadie's voice broke.

The attack left her deaf in one ear but hadn't defined her entire life. That gave the man who'd hurt her too much power. She'd gone over and over this in counseling, but when (and if) she was ever ready for an intimate relationship again with another man, it would have to be someone she'd trust implicitly.

Simply trusting in a man's good intentions felt overwhelming. She'd dated Jackson from the time they were both sixteen, and no one else until college. She supposed that the wedding reception would be a perfect and safe place to practice flirting with a man and she'd already devised a plan to at least try.

"I won't let that happen, honey. I swear." Eve squeezed Sadie's hand. "They might not be Carver boys, and who knows, they might even be girls, but someday you and I will take our children to the park together. Do birthday parties together. Just like we planned."

"Promise?" Sadie sniffed, squeezing back.

"I promise."

# CHAPTER 9

When Eve arrived at Texas A&M to begin her veterinary studies, it was like she'd crossed into a brand-new sparkling world in another dimension. There were young and handsome men everywhere, but there were just as many beautiful women. On campus. In her classes. Eve's roommate, Marisol, was elated that men were so interested in Eve. She regularly got asked out and Marisol hoped Eve would give her the "castoffs."

At first, heart bruised by Jackson's explainable but abrupt exit out of town, she'd stayed to herself. The fact that Eve turned down all the men asking her out seemed to make her interesting, somehow. But it was what she'd become used to, in Stone Ridge. Men were always chasing the few available women. Marisol eventually became quite popular, dating all the men who'd first asked Eve out and been turned down. That's when she figured out what Marisol meant by "castoffs."

Eventually Marisol talked Eve into going out on a double date with her current boyfriend's (they seemed to change weekly) roommate. After much prodding and reminders that she'd already been in school for three years but dated no one, Eve agreed. It was time to get out there. She'd heard nothing from Jackson, not that she'd expected to. His pride would have prevented him from reaching out, and her shame and regret kept her.

There would be no point, because they couldn't ever come back from a public breakup like theirs. Once in a while Sadie would come to visit and report back on town happenings. Never a word about or from Jackson, but then again almost no one talked to Sadie anymore, either, knowing she was still close with Eve.

Bobby Butler, the first man she'd dated, was so kind and sweet and he eventually became Eve's lover. Not quite like her and Jackson, there were never any sparks or crackling chemistry. And no fighting, because every time she argued about something or spoke her mind, Bobby laughed and agreed with her. Eve chalked up their lack of chemistry to differences in people. Bobby was a great and loyal friend. But she was only a little bit sad when after a few months he switched majors and dropped out of the program.

Not long after, she'd met Matt Friedenbach. He was nothing if not persistent, and Eve was flattered by his attention. Part of the football team, he was incredibly popular, handsome, and athletic. Everyone seemed to like him. She still didn't want to go out with him and told him so. He seemed shocked, but instead of backing down became even more persistent. He was an athlete, after all, and Eve figured that she'd become a kind of challenge.

But one Sunday at the Piggly Wiggly, she'd spied the cover of *Nashville Up-and-Coming*. There in splendid, bright color inside the pages of the tabloid was a picture of Jackson walking down a sidewalk hand in hand with a breathtaking blonde. The paper referred to Jackson as the new husband of CMA Award–winning star Winona James.

She nearly got sick right in the check-out line, a stone sliding over her throat to close off her airway. Her legs were weak and trembling. She'd wanted to get out in the world and experience life outside of Stone Ridge, but she'd been the one to remain stagnant. Maybe because some part of her still believed with all her heart that she'd always love Jackson Carver.

But Jackson clearly moved on.

"Are you gettin' that?" The check-out girl asked, reaching to ring up the magazine.

Eve was still holding on to the paper like it was welded to her hand. "N-no. I don't want this." She tucked it back into the rack with all the others and somehow managed to pay for her groceries and get out to the safety of her car.

Hands shaking, Eve gripped the steering wheel but that was as far as she got out of the parking lot. She kept seeing the photo of Jackson and his wife. His *wife*. Lord, she was so stupid. *Why* hadn't she moved on? She'd decided to let him go, and he'd moved on, which made all the sense in the world. No one would blame him, and neither should she.

It occurred to her at that very moment that she'd been waiting all this time for him to come after her. To fight for her. To assure her that he wanted her just as much as he wanted music. But if he hadn't done any of those things by now, he never would. He'd gotten what he wanted after all. To be free of her. His teenage sweetheart.

Eve searched for the phone in her backpack and pulled it out. She went to one of Matt's many missed calls and pressed the call back button.

"Hey," Matt answered.

"Do you still want to go out with me?"

. . .

IT ONLY TOOK two dates for Eve to realize that Matt was not the man for her. He'd behaved himself fairly well on their first date. They'd gone to the local grill and hangout, where among his entourage of friends he made her feel like the only woman in the room. Held her hand, pulled her close and tucked her next to him. Tenderly pressed a kiss to her temple. He'd laughed when she spoke up and told him he was wrong about this or that, as if shocked anyone would disagree with him. Eve could feel every woman's eyes on her, and she kept thinking of Jackson, wishing he could somehow see this display. Look at her, the modern, liberated woman getting out in the world. She took a selfie with Matt and texted it to Sadie, hoping somehow through the magic of the internet, mutual connections, and social media it might eventually get back to Jackson.

On their next date at a frat party, Matt became very drunk and very gropey. She yelled at him to settle down and keep his hands to himself. But because she was so worried about him on the road, she drove him back to his dorm. He expressed his gratitude by unzipping his pants and inviting her to go down on him.

"Are you *kidding* me? Get out of my car. You're stinkin' drunk."

She went to find one of his friends to help get him out of her car, and loudly declared that she didn't date creeps. When Eve got home, she texted Sadie to please delete the photo she'd sent of the handsome football player. She would never be seeing him again. Matt sent flowers in apology the next day, called and texted, even bugged Marisol to put in a good word. A small part of Eve was flattered. Another, much bigger, part was annoyed.

"You're just the kind of old-fashioned girl I need in my life. Please give me another chance," he'd said.

*Old fashioned?* Because she wouldn't go down on him on

the second date? She informed Matt that she'd decided to take a vow of abstinence for the rest of the year and concentrate on her studies.

This wasn't a lie.

Matt didn't listen.

When the texts and voice messages got nastier, Marisol sat Eve down and leveled with her. "Honey, he's stalking you."

It wasn't easy to frighten Eve. She'd grown up in a town filled with strong women who taught her a thing or two about standing her ground. With the kind of men who would never hurt a woman.

"He's just mad and not used to hearing 'no' from a woman. Soon he'll find someone else."

But according to the grapevine, Matt had already found someone else. Still, the nasty calls and text messages continued. One particularly threatening text finally frightened Eve enough that she agreed with Marisol's advice. She'd have to report Matt to the campus police. On an early spring afternoon, Eve had just finished eating lunch when someone knocked on her door.

She opened it to find Matt, his blue eyes nearly black with fury, his lips curled into an unnatural sneer. Her last memory was of Matt's huge fist before everything went black.

When she woke up in the hospital, Eve was surrounded by her mother, Marisol, and Sadie. Eve got the rest of the story in small bits and pieces. Marisol interrupted the attack, chasing Matt off. He'd been arrested hours later. Eve was brought to the hospital unconscious. She'd suffered a severe concussion and several broken ribs. Two black and swollen eyes.

Eventually, she would come to find out that the hearing loss in her left ear was permanent.

But she'd survived.

Eve lay on that hospital bed for weeks healing, receiving the kind of encouragement and support everyone who'd been the victim of a vicious and unprovoked attack should receive. Teachers and classmates rallied around her and organized crowdfunding for her medical bills. Even Bobby drove up to see her. The room was filled with cards, colorful flowers, and bright balloons. Marisol and Sadie took turns reading out loud to her. Her mother wouldn't leave her side, night or day. But crazy though it was, and even though it had been years since she'd last laid eyes on him, one thought ran through her mind and heart like it was on a time loop:

*Jackson would know what to do.*

*Jackson would know what to say.*

*Lord, I miss Jackson.*

# CHAPTER 10

Sunday was filled with last-minute wedding errands. Eve, Sadie, Brenda, Wanda, and Mima drove into Pleasanton for some serious shopping. Sadie had bridesmaid gifts to buy, and Brenda was still searching for the perfect tea-length dress to wear to the wedding. They split up into groups and divvied up the tasks.

"How about this one, Mom?" Eve held up a beautiful magenta dress with a ruffle near the hem of the skirt and a sweetheart neckline.

"That would look wonderful on you."

Eve frowned, looking from the dress to her mother. "I'm a *bridesmaid*. We're shopping for you. Remember?"

"Oh, yes, I know, but you could wear it another time. It will flatter your complexion."

"But what about for you?" Eve twirled the dress. "Don't you like it?"

"When I was younger, I might have worn that dress." Brenda waved it away.

Eve sighed. This was a problem every time they shopped. Brenda didn't believe in spending money on herself. A youngish fifty-two, she'd be happy living the rest of her life in a pair of Wranglers, boots, and a flannel shirt.

Round and round they went from one store to another, Brenda always finding a dress for Eve. Nothing that seemed "appropriate" for Brenda, a "woman of a certain age." The requirements were lengthy and a tall order for a single dress.

"Maybe I'll wear the same—"

Eve held up her palm. "Oh, no you don't. We don't need anyone jinxing this wedding."

Brenda laughed. "Mija, a dress is just a dress. It won't jinx Sadie's wedding."

"No." Eve went hands on hips. "I refuse to allow you to wear the same dress you wore to my wedding."

"But I'm still the same size. I wore it once. Once! There's no place else I can wear such a fancy dress. Such a *terrible* waste."

Finally, by the grace of God, Eve found a suitable dress for her mother. Best of all, it was discounted enough that Brenda agreed.

"I could wear this to church on any Sunday. It will get mileage. Good find."

"Glad I could help." If only she could get her mother to agree that she was worth more than a discounted dress.

But she supposed her wonderful father internalized that belief. A few hours later, all five reunited at the food court for a long lunch, then piled in Eve's truck for the drive back to town. By the time they got back, the sun was slipping down the horizon.

Once home, Brenda gathered her bag and excused herself. After Sadie and Wanda headed home, Eve and Mima retired to the main house.

"You need anything?" Eve asked Mima, who was settled on the couch.

"We'll eat leftovers tonight, sugar, you've done worn yourself out today. We all have."

"I'll warm them but first I'm going to go take Thimble for a ride."

"Haven't seen much of Jackson. With any luck, he's helping with the calving and remembering who he really is at heart."

Eve snorted. "And who is that?"

"A cowboy who belongs on the family ranch."

Lord almighty. Was Eve the only one who didn't see that happening? Jackson left small-town life behind. And she didn't think he'd been avoiding the house due to his interest in spending time with Hank and cowboy chores.

*He's simply trying to stay away from me.* She didn't exactly blame him. But for Jackson to spend another day with his father made a gigantic statement of how much he needed to get away from her. Jackson and Hank did not usually get along. He greatly favored Lincoln in a way that used to be painful for Jackson. She had no idea how he felt about his father anymore. For all she knew, the two would now be best buddies but probably not. She'd become well acquainted with how long Jackson could hold a grudge.

Eve changed into her Wranglers and a flannel shirt pulled over a long-sleeved tee and pulled her hair up in a regular ponytail. Then she looked in the mirror and brought her hair down again to cover her ears. Not that she was ashamed of the hearing aid, but she didn't want to invite any questions from Jackson. Not yet. He'd find out soon enough because everyone in their small town knew. Most didn't know *how* she'd lost her hearing, and for the sake of those who cared about her, she hoped they never would.

She pulled on her boots and denim jacket and strode outside into the now-dark night, wondering if the quarter moon gave off enough light for a night ride with Thimble, or if she should just take a walk instead. The summer night was mild and cool, so she decided on that walk.

There were five acres between the two properties but the Carvers owned more than a hundred acres, most of them used for cattle grazing, though Lincoln was building a house for him and Sadie on a five-acre parcel.

Maybe she owed Jackson more of an explanation. She wasn't sure how to explain the ramblings of her then-twenty-one-year-old mind to anyone, least of all Jackson. She hadn't been exactly mature. She could try to explain, but he might not have the patience or desire to listen. Still, the level of his anger was such that she wondered what she could ever say for him to forgive her.

But there were some people Eve would never forgive, either, so she understood.

Grateful for the patch of moonlight, she continued on. She never took walks in the dark anymore, but the Double C Ranch was her safe place. She'd been attacked and beaten in the middle of the day when she lived near College Station, a large city completely unlike Stone Ridge. But every now and then a certain smell or a tiny sound could take her back. The doctor called it post-traumatic stress, which Eve thought should be a term reserved for battle-scarred soldiers.

But here she was, a twenty-eight-year-old educated woman, a veterinarian and a businesswoman, and sometimes just the sound of a man's whistle could reduce her to a pile of raw nerves. She shouldn't be thinking about any of this right now. Thinking caused her to dwell too much on the past and then it became this living, breathing thing that wrapped its hands around her neck and squeezed.

Her life was good now. Calm. She spent all her time with animals. Living her dream. Sure, the hours were long and the work not as satisfying as she'd once imagined it would be.

She hated seeing any animal in pain, and there were those terrible times when there was nothing she could do to help.

But she'd settled into a routine and her main concern at the moment were her school loans. Then there were the health-care premiums of a self-employed woman and the hearing aid that went out on her now and then, giving waves of feedback. But she'd take care of all her bills, one by one, just like she had eventually repaid her mother and Hank Carver for the wedding that never was. Jackson tried to also, she'd heard, but his money was refused.

Eve's gut churned, and that old, and now-familiar, emotion rose from her tight chest to her neck. Overwhelming guilt. Regret. Fear. Everyone and everything around her seemed to be forever changing. Jackson. Now Sadie. Everything would be different once Sadie and Lincoln were married. Lincoln, and the family they would raise together, would have to be Sadie's priority. Not Eve, her single friend, and whatever old and tired memory made her weepy that week. They were supposed to have done everything together. Marry the two Carver men, have little cowboys that would play together, and go to school together. Sadie would live that part of her life without Eve. And there was no one to blame but herself.

The sudden and unexpected sound of a horse's hooves behind her startled her and she whirled around, heart pumping. Since she only had half of an average person's hearing, she always worried she'd heard something too late.

The figure of a man sitting atop Taco moved into the moonlight.

*Jackson.*

She took a breath. Both he and Taco looked pissed.

His eyes narrowed, jaw tight, he almost spit the words out. "What's wrong with you?"

*J*ackson noticed the lone and slight figure of someone walking in the distance and rode Taco to catch up to who he assumed was a night ranch hand who might appreciate a ride. He'd spent all day with the old man checking on the calving every two hours along with the day hands, and the night help would now take over.

When Eve whirled around, a wild-eyed look of terror in her eyes, it stopped him cold.

"Are you seriously *afraid* of me?" he managed to grind out.

No matter what went on between them, no matter how pissed he'd been, she knew he'd never lay a hand on her. Just the implication insulted him.

"No!" She still held a hand to her neck like a pearl-clutcher. "I thought you were someone...I didn't hear...I just...I got startled."

He'd believe that if she didn't look like a beaten animal, a wild look in her eyes. Far more than startled, she seemed terrified. Horrified.

What the hell.

"Thought you were a hand who might want a ride. What are you doin' out here anyway?" He hopped off Taco and gathered the reins.

She should be inside about now, cooking supper for his grandmother. Doing the job he couldn't fire her from. So, he was going to have to go on watching her walk around in those very tight Wranglers. Always been curvy, now she resembled a 1950s pin-up girl. He sure in the hell didn't appreciate noticing this. It was only making him meaner.

The anger made sense, but she could make him irrational, too, and that's not how he normally rolled. He needed to get a handle on his emotions. Let the anger go.

Some of his bandmates thought he should tell Eve how he'd managed those first few weeks in Nashville. To share how low he'd come after she'd jilted him. But he hadn't seen the point of letting her hear how pathetic he'd been. Except for now, when it seemed that everything unsaid *was* being said anyway, loudly, and in ways which didn't make much sense.

Naturally, he believed that Sadie would show up to this wedding because *she* wasn't Eve. And Lincoln wasn't Jackson.

They would have a different story.

"I'm takin' a walk. We're having leftovers tonight." She jammed her hands in her jean pockets and could barely fit the tips in they were so tight. "Anyway, you should be happy to have me out of the house."

"Not out here alone in the dark I'm not. Hank and I heard a coyote earlier."

He realized the implication meant he cared about her well-being. But who would want to find a young woman attacked by a coyote? A monster.

"That coyote is probably miles away. They're just loud and sound like they're much closer."

This was the Eve he remembered. She'd never been afraid of an animal. Even wild ones.

"Walk with me," he said, as he led Taco toward the stable. "That coyote sounded a hell of a lot closer to me."

"Oh," she said and looked stricken. She played with the hair on the left side of her face.

He stopped moving when he realized she wasn't following, and Taco halted beside him. "I'd rather not leave you out here alone."

"I'm okay. Really."

"I don't believe you."

"What? Why *not*?"

"Because…"

*You don't look like Eve anymore.*

"Maybe it's not you, but something is going on around here. I'm sick of my family keepin' stuff from me. First, they don't tell me Mima broke her arm and needed surgery—"

"You were touring."

He ignored that. "Then Linc forgets to tell me you're livin' here until he picks me up at the airport."

"And I'm sorry about that. I wish they'd told you soo—"

"But there's something else they haven't told me. I can't put my finger on it, but something is *different* around here. I don't like it. I spent all day with my dad, hoping he'd be the one to slip up and not even know he was doin' it. But all I got was sperm talk and complaints about the prized bull he bought with a loan against the ranch. He apparently has a libido problem."

And if he never heard another word about so-called prized-bull sperm for the rest of his life, he could die a happy man. But something told him he would not get that lucky.

"Hank had me check him out to make sure there's nothing physically wrong."

Jackson quirked a brow, trying to picture Eve examining

a bull for sperm count. "That bull weighs fifteen hundred pounds."

"I didn't do it alone."

He shook his head, clearing it of the picture of Eve, being trampled by an angry bull. Being a large animal vet could be dangerous, not that she'd ever admit that.

When she started walking, he did, too, leading Taco. "Do *you* know what else's going on around here?"

"A wedding. That's all."

"No, there's something else."

"Why isn't that *enough*? Weddings are huge deals and make everyone nervous and anxious. Especially given our history. That could be what you're sensin'."

He grunted. "Not my favorite thing in the world, talking to you about weddings."

"It's not mine, either. But we have to do this for Sadie and Lincoln. We both agreed."

"Doesn't mean we have to *talk* about it."

"You started it. You *asked* me if I knew what was going on."

Frustration bubbled up. She was keeping something from him, too. They reached the stable, and he removed Taco's saddle, hung it up, and grabbed the brush. She stood by in silence for a few minutes, but then began to help, taking a spare brush to get Taco's other side.

Jackson led Taco into his stall, then turned to Eve. "I obviously didn't mean the wedding. Something else is going on."

"Well, I don't know then. Guess I can't help you." She studied the ground. "B-but while I have you here...um, Sadie said something today."

"Yeah?"

She wouldn't look at him. "Uh, she said that you and I never got...closure."

He snorted. "Closure's for doors."

"But…you and I…" She studied the ground, one boot kicking at a small pebble. "One minute we're gettin' married, the next we aren't even talking."

"Yeah. I was there." He simply stared until she finally met his gaze, that dark and stormy gaze of unreadable emotions.

A coyote's wail burst through the night air, wrapping around him, sounding much closer than a mile away. Eve might have a heart for all animals, but he hated coyotes.

"Get in the house," he ordered. "I'm right behind you."

"Don't you fight me on this," Jackson said, his gaze locking with Eve's.

She didn't want to fight him. Instead she let the knowledge that Jackson cared just a little bit wash over her. More than any man she'd ever met, Jackson straddled the fine line between protective and possessive with true skill.

"I'm going to make sure all the dogs are in the barn first," Jackson said, echoing her thoughts.

The family stable was always safe and guarded from the elements and any predators. Wanting to help Jackson with the dogs, she reluctantly went inside simply because she didn't want to push her luck.

"Are you ready for some supper?" Eve said as she walked into the living room, where Mima sat watching *The Pioneer Woman* on the cooking channel.

"Looks like it will just be you and me tonight after all."

"Actually, Jackson will be inside in a minute. He heard a coyote."

Alarm flashed in Mima's eyes. "Did you hear it?"

"I did but I didn't think it was close." She could have been wrong. It bothered her more than she'd want to admit. By now, she should be used to having less than perfect hearing.

"Matter of fact, I'm not hungry. Why don't you two go on and eat without me."

"What?" Eve froze halfway to the kitchen and back-tracked. "Wait. Mim—"

"Don't argue. My arm needs restin'." Mima waved with her good arm and disappeared into the back wing of the house in the direction of her bedroom.

So much for talking the stubborn woman out of anything she didn't want to do. Eve quickly pulled covered dishes out from the refrigerator one after the other. If she was fast enough, she could make it to her own bedroom with her dinner and just leave Jackson to fend for himself.

But he walked in the door just a moment later, Winston with him, the white border collie he'd raised from a puppy. Winston was an old guy now with arthritis, and Eve would be lying not to say she occasionally snuck him in with her on a particularly cold or rainy night. She figured he'd earned his keep over the years doing his part for the ranch. Two years ago, he'd retired to be a family dog but Mima still believed he belonged outside in their perfectly good barn with all the other pets.

"He's sleeping with me tonight, and I don't want any guff about it," Jackson said without looking up, clearly believing he was speaking to his grandmother.

"She's…she went to…" Eve stammered and then promptly dropped the glass covered dish filled with the leftovers of last night's pork chops.

It shattered into pieces at her feet and within seconds Winston was salivating at the entrance to the kitchen headed straight for the meat.

"No!" Eve and Jackson yelled at once.

Jackson ordered him to sit and Winston obeyed, knowing that they were both deadly serious. He whined in desire to gorge on a chop, but he stayed put.

"What on earth is going on out there?" Mima shouted from her bedroom.

"Don't worry," Jackson shouted back. "Eve managed to duck just in time. She'll be fine."

Eve met Jackson's gaze. She studied penetrating blue irises that shimmered with humor. His lips twitched, and a second later Eve burst into laughter. The thought of Jackson being angry enough to throw a plate at her struck her with the humor he'd obviously intended.

Still at the edge of the kitchen entrance, Winston cocked his head in curiosity.

"Do you think she believed you?" Eve said.

"We'll know in a minute."

Eve bent and started to pick up the holy mess she'd made. There were pieces of glass everywhere on the tile floor, the chops lying in the middle of it all. A real waste. Even Winston couldn't benefit from this disaster.

"Let me do that," Jackson said, staying her hand. "You'll cut yourself."

A sliver of electricity pulsed through her at his touch and she wouldn't look at him, worried he'd see a flash of exhilarating desire in her eyes. She let him take over, and he found the broom and picked up large pieces.

"I'm sorry I ruined your dinner," she said, getting the trash can from under the sink.

"My personal trainer says pork isn't fit for human consumption. But hell, don't tell Mima."

"You have a personal *trainer*?"

It was something you didn't hear much about in their area. A couple of years ago, a couple moved into Stone Ridge and opened a gym. It closed down within two months. Physical activity was part of daily life on a ranch.

Jackson threw the last of the glass and chops in the trash. "We hire one for the band. Being on the road means a lot of inactivity driving from city to city. The performance is my only real exercise. Not exactly what you'd call effort."

"But what about bacon?" Eve asked, more than a little shocked. "You don't eat *bacon*?"

"Don't be crazy, girl." He stood and slid her a smirk. "'Course I eat bacon."

"Oh," she said on an exhale. "That's good. I was beginning to wonder if you had anything in common with the old Jackson."

"I have a lot in common with the old Jackson. Happen to *be* the old Jackson." He said this a bit abruptly, his jaw tightening.

Apparently, he was sensitive about having changed so much throughout the years. She saw little of the man she'd loved. Leaner now, he carried a tension in his shoulders he never had before. He'd smiled only once since he'd arrived but then again, she might have something to do with that. She wasn't exactly his happy place.

They stood nearly toe to toe, the air pulsating and crackling between them.

Two years into her life at Texas A&M, she'd discovered that what she'd felt for Jackson was *not* common. There were many handsome men at A&M. She'd met a few of them. Dated two. But not one of them was Jackson Carver. Had she known that truth on the day of their wedding, she'd have likely swallowed her pride and gone through with it. But she hadn't been gifted with wisdom at the time. Or with psychic abilities.

Not then, and not now.

And she couldn't help wondering where he'd be today if they'd married. Maybe ranching with Lincoln and Hank, hating his life. Hating her for keeping him here. Or maybe he'd be happy enough playing in local honky-tonks. Raising a family with her. There was no way of ever knowing.

"Did you hear me?"

She shook her head clear of the past, a dangerous tunnel she couldn't afford to get sucked into. No, she hadn't heard him. She watched as he used the broom he'd grabbed and bent to scoop the entire mess into the trash can. Wonder what his fans would think to see him now. To be fair, he looked just as irresistibly sexy sweeping as he did playing a guitar. Or riding a horse.

"Mima wants you to stay and I don't like denying her what she wants. I think we can be at least civil to each other. You think?"

"Yes, of course. I don't have a problem with that."

"I noticed. And *that's* a problem."

"What do you mean?"

"The way you let me talk to you. You're not fighting back, and that's not like you. Want to talk about people who've changed? I'd say you have."

The words kicked her in the gut, the pain hard and swift. "I d-don't even know what you're talkin' about. I'm the same old Eve."

"Yeah. Try again." He gave her a sideways look before he went back to the trash can.

"Maybe I'm older and wiser. I know everything can't always be my way. After going away to school, I know what it's like to be one of many."

"Doesn't mean you change your personality. You're skittish, like a scared barn cat. Half the time you won't look at me. You're not…not…"

"*What?*" she pressed, almost afraid of what he'd say. She didn't much like the trajectory of this conversation.

He tilted his head for a moment as if considering it. "Difficult."

She snorted. "You *want* me to be difficult?"

"I want you to be yourself, so, yeah." He shrugged.

"I'm *difficult?*" She crossed her arms, feeling an old flame of anger flash.

That wouldn't work for her and she tamped it down quickly. She'd left all her anger behind. Too much anger had a way of spreading into every conversation and infecting every thought. She refused to go there again.

He slid her a half grin, dimples flashing, and he pointed. "Now see, that's much better."

She huffed, not taking the bait. They finished cleaning up the kitchen and Winston was allowed past the threshold. He busied himself trying to follow the smells that they'd wiped away.

"You do see what she's done, don't you?" Jackson threw a look in the direction of Mima's bedroom. "We're alone for a reason. Talk to me."

"About what?"

"Oh, I don't know. How about that time you didn't show up at our wedding?"

After a stunned second, she found her words. "I...don't have anything more to say. I said I'm sorry that it happened."

"Then I'll talk. And you can listen."

She may have conquered anger, but fear and anxiety were still sidekicks that showed up often. It helped to do something routine, but this was far from business as usual. So, she pictured her bedtime process. Brushing her teeth, flossing, taking out her hearing aid, putting on her PJs, brushing her hair...

He leaned on the broom. "Want to know what happened my first few weeks in Nashville? I drank."

"I-I don't think I want to hear this."

"For about two weeks straight. Morning, noon, and night. I was such a mess the guys threatened if I didn't shape up right quick, I was out of the band. And they were all I had left, so I sobered up and picked myself off the floor. You wrecked my heart, Eve. You *broke* me."

The ugly truth slammed into her like a punch and whether deserved or not, she couldn't take it. "Please. Please stop. I can't hear any more of this."

"Why not? Remember? We don't have closure." He half sneered at that. "Let's get it."

"This is not the time or the place to talk about this. I can't do this with you right now."

"When is the time or place? You tell me."

"How about n-never?"

"Try again, baby." There was the same edge in his tone when he'd fired her. "Because I have a lot of questions, too, and you're going to answer them."

Why couldn't she face him and stand up to him like she used to do? The old Eve would have engaged him better than she'd been doing this past week. She'd certainly never run from him. She'd always ended the argument with a witty remark. She used to love to fight with him because of all the making up. Now, she was empty and fighting simply reminded her that she didn't always win.

And losing could sometimes be devastating. Life altering.

"You never backed away from a fight before. Gave back as good as you got."

She crossed her arms. "Maybe I'm tired and not in the mood to be reminded what a horrible person I am."

"I'm not doing that. But how about givin' me an explanation? Don't you think you owe me one?"

"You want an explanation? You wanted to go to Nashville and our wedding day was standin' in the way."

"*I* wanted to go to Nashville? Is that why I showed up to my weddin' and you didn't?"

"I did you a favor."

"Don't do me any more favors, will ya?" His voice

sounded gritty and low. In the quiet of the house, it seemed to reverberate all around her. "Look at me."

She did, blinking back tears. The old Eve would have told *him* to look at her *ass* on the way out the door.

"What are you thinking right now?" he said, far more softly, reaching for her hand and squeezing it. "Tell me."

"That…I don't know what you want from me."

"Just the truth, Eve. What did I do wrong? Please. I have to know."

The knowledge that all these years he'd believed that *he'd* done something wrong squeezed her heart. She should have realized that he would blame himself, but she'd been too selfish and caught up in her own regrets. He might be angry with her for walking out on him, but Jackson would have wanted to fix it. Make things right. He couldn't do that now. Not with this.

"What makes you think *you* did anything wrong?"

"Because you stopped loving me. Why else would you walk away?" He met her eyes. "And don't tell me it's this self-sacrificial bullshit of wanting me to have my big break. That wasn't you, Eve. I don't know what happened to you, but you were a *fighter*."

Past tense. But now she was trying, damn it, trying like hell to get herself back to the woman she used to be. But when she'd pressed down the anger she'd felt for years, depression followed in its wake.

Jackson had reminded her that she hadn't made nearly enough progress.

And he was still holding her hand.

She squeezed his hand back, unable to stop herself from wanting the contact. She forced herself to meet his gaze. "I *hate* that I hurt you. Mima forgave me but I don't deserve her kindness."

"Don't say that. Of course you do." He tipped her chin.

So unexpectedly tender, the gesture so sweet, that her lower lip quivered uncontrollably. "I wouldn't blame you if you hate me for the rest of your life. I—"

"Stop."

And then, hand on the nape of her neck, he hauled her to him and kissed her. The shock and pulse of desire reverberated and crackled through her body. She reciprocated the kiss and clung to his shoulders to steady the rocking of her world. His was not a soft kiss but its tenderness reached all the way to her heart. That same heart cracked open. His lips were moving over hers, not insistent, but tentative. Exploring.

When he broke the kiss, Jackson pressed his forehead to hers. "God, Eve. You still drive me crazy."

"You…you kissed me."

"You kissed back." He yanked a hand through his hair. "I'm sorry. Look. I don't know why I did that. No. Wait. I'm lying. I know exactly why. I wanted to."

"Th-that's okay."

"Yeah. Know what's not okay? The way I've been treating you since I got here. The way I talked to you. I'm sorry, Eve."

"Okay."

He touched her nose. "I promise that I won't ever make you cry again."

"Since we're being honest about everything now, I should tell you something. I heard you on a phone call before our wedding. You didn't think I made it to the chapel, but I was there before you were. Ready to start our lives together. But you sounded so miserable. You walked like someone headed to the brig, not the happiest day of your life. You wanted to go and I thought…I thought I deserved someone who wanted to stay. I thought the only reason you were going through with it was because there was no time to postpone the wedding."

"Eve, I was nervous. I wasn't miserable, just confused. That's what happens when you want two things more than anything else in the world."

"I should have talked to you. We could have postponed the wedding. But I was too proud for any of that. I wanted you to come after me. I needed you to show me that I was all you wanted."

"And I didn't."

"It wasn't fair to hope for that, I know." She nodded, biting back tears. "When you went away, you showed me what you really wanted."

"Or maybe I went with the only thing left to me."

She'd never thought of it that way.

*You broke me.*

*And somebody else broke me.*

"I was always yours." His blue eyes were shimmering with heat and he brought her hand to his lips. "What am I going to do about that?"

"I don't know, but I don't think we should do that again. The kissing."

"You didn't like it?"

That was irrelevant. Of course, she'd liked it. No one kissed like Jackson. "I'm too fragile for any of this right now."

"I can see that, and I don't understand why. But I'll leave you alone. Promise." A beat later, he spoke again. "As long as you answer one question."

"What's that?"

"What happened at A&M? I know something must have."

A stone of anxiety lodged itself in her windpipe and she would swear her oxygen had been cut off. "I'm not ready to talk about that."

"When do you think you will be?"

"I…don't know."

"That's all right. We have time. I'm not going anywhere."

She sucked in a breath. "I thought you were going back after the wedding."

"Maybe I'm not leaving until we resolve this between us. It's gone on long enough."


LILLIAN HEARD LAUGHTER from the kitchen, and then the muffled sounds of two people talking. Good. Talking was good. Progress.

*Enough spying on those two for now.*

"Woman, what in tarnation are you up to now?" a deep and crotchety voice said from behind her.

Oh no. Not her dead husband again. She used to write him letters before he'd appear. Now, her arthritis was too bad, and Albert only showed up to haunt her when he sensed she was about to step into a little bit of trouble. But it wasn't as if Lillian saw *ghosts*. Just Albert. He'd been dead for years, but the old cowboy just couldn't hang up his spurs. The therapist she'd visited shortly after she'd first started seeing Albert, wondering if life on the range had finally driven her completely insane, assured her that she wasn't *crazy*. As long as *she* realized that Albert's visits were a figment of her active imagination, and served only to bring her comfort, all was well.

However, the jury was still out on *comfort*.

Albert sat on her reading chair, booted feet propped on the edge of their bed.

"What are you doin' here? Haven't seen you in weeks. Still haven't found the light? I've told you over and over again: go into the light." She waved her arms, as if pushing.

"And I've told you: I can't find no dang light."

"Oh my Lord, as usual, you're too lazy to look for it. You put the 'tub' in stubborn! Just leave me to my plans. I'm still among the livin' unlike you, and when I want your help, I'll ask for it."

"I can see what you're up to now. Leave them two alone. I mean it. Haven't they both been through enough? Jackson and Eve will find their way back to each other if it's meant to be."

She sighed loudly. "That's easy for you to say."

Albert hadn't been alive to witness Eve return to Stone Ridge, as broken as Lillian ever saw anyone. And she'd witnessed plenty in sixty-plus years on a ranch. Life had kicked Eve something fierce. Someone literally beat all the hope out of that beautiful girl and Lillian wouldn't stand by and just watch her suffer no matter what she'd done to her grandson. Call her foolish, but the good Lord put her on earth to be useful. And she was going to be just that until it was time to join her ornery cowboy.

"You got lucky with Lincoln and Sadie. That don't mean you're a matchmaker."

"Ha! Lucky? You call that luck? I call it incredible skill and a little bit of good timing."

Feeling responsible for his younger siblings hadn't left Lincoln a whole lot of time for serious relationships. It wasn't until Lillian started Phase One of her attempts to get those two together that he noticed Sadie had grown into a beautiful young lady. Now he wouldn't know how to live without her and there would soon enough be Carver babies. Hopefully girls.

And it was all thanks to her.

Next up, Jackson and Eve. Those two had been apart far too long. Last, she'd take care of finding the perfect man for Daisy. No more of those no-good rodeo cowboys intent on leaving a young woman a widow. Her ornery granddaughter would need a strong man.

"Gettin' a little too cocky, you ask me," Albert said.

"I didn't ask."

He held up his arms in an "I give up" gesture and in the next moment he vanished from Lillian's imagination. Good thing. Her occasional flights of fancy with Albert were distracting.

Her plan was put into place the moment she'd realized that Lincoln and Sadie announced their marriage. Originally, her grand plan involved asking Eve to help her with various chores for the wedding, keeping her at the house often so she'd be forced to run into Jackson over and over again. She didn't actually *plan* on breaking her arm in three places, but what a godsend that was! It gave her the perfect excuse to move Eve into the house and help that girl pay off some of her loans without having to straight out give her the money.

Time and forced proximity would do the rest.

And if it didn't, well, that's why God invented shoves.

# CHAPTER 12

*E*ve tried her best to avoid Jackson. She hadn't been able to stop thinking about that kiss since the night it happened. And since all she wanted was to feel that way again, held tightly in his arms, she should stay away from him. Being an early riser helped, since Jackson wasn't. She'd sometimes hear him late at night after she'd gone to her room, poking around the house. Strumming his guitar, talking to Winston, who as far as she could surmise now spent every night in Jackson's room. And even though it went against her survival instincts, she'd lay with her good ear pressed against the mattress after removing the hearing aid. She could only drift off to sleep when she couldn't hear him walking around the house at night or passing her bedroom door.

But it just wasn't enough. There were times when she couldn't avoid him. Breakfast. Lunch. Supper. Each time Mima asked her to go find him because she needed his help with this or that. At those times she'd catch herself watching him, unable to look away. Supremely embarrassed when he'd catch her in the act. He'd smile easily and quirk a brow in question. She'd then quickly find something else to do.

But today Eve had maid of honor duties. She'd be accompanying Sadie to a meeting with the Society of Reasonable, Respectable Orderly Women (SORROW). The society was founded during World War II when women wanted to do something to help the war effort. They'd started by knitting baby blankets for expectant mothers. All good stuff.

The problem began when all the babies born that first year were boys. Pink blankets went unused. Once the war was over and some of the more fortunate men returned, nine months later there were more boys. And then more boys, with a lucky one or two girls born to amazed and grateful mothers. Encouraged, and searching for another way to help, the founding members decided that they'd put together a primer: *The Men of Stone Ridge*. They were determined for word to get out about how lucky the women of Stone Ridge were, with such handsome and plentiful men to choose from. And somehow with false promises of handsome cowboys and romance, lure women back into town.

There were rumors of plans to use the *Men of Stone Ridge* primer and start an email-order bride service. Sort of a pamphlet of "here's all you'll have to choose from." A bit disconcerting.

Beulah Hayes, the current president, still liked to gather the group and give a bride a few pointers before the wedding day. It was now a tradition in Stone Ridge. They'd offered Eve advice, too. Advice that to this day Eve found offensive, but heck, there was something to be said for tradition.

Besides, she hadn't been able to talk Sadie out of it. Her mother was a big supporter of the group. Then again, Wanda was a character. She claimed to have devised a concoction that led to giving birth to a healthy girl. She believed it was how she'd given birth to Sadie in addition to Beau, when all of her sisters had sons.

"Are you really drinking that vile stuff?" Eve asked now as she drove them to town. She'd seen the drink, or rather, smelled it. The thing smelled like sulfur and onions. You couldn't pay her enough to drink it.

"Am I crazy?" Sadie asked. "Of course I'm not drinking it. Too late anyway, but it makes my mother feel better. Like she's helping, and there's no harm. But I don't care if we have girls or boys."

"That's because you both have good sense." She paused. "Did you tell him yet?"

Sadie hesitated and Eve had her answer.

"Why not, honey?"

"I'm waiting for the perfect time. There hasn't been one yet. He's been coming in so tired from a long day and I just can't do that to him."

Eve heard the fear in Sadie's voice. "He's going to be happy even if it's sooner than y'all planned."

"I don't know about that."

"Well, I do."

"We were going to wait."

"Tell him tonight. After you bring the quilt home and talk about how much you learned." Eve turned onto Miller Road and hung a left at Trinity Church. "I did prepare you enough for this, didn't I?"

"Yep. You and every other woman my age who's been through this. I know I'm going to listen to a bunch of old-fashioned mumbo jumbo about keeping a happy home and if I'm lucky enough to have them, raising strong daughters."

"Yeah, it's just going to be a lot of silly talk that, if you can stand, can be kind of funny. I managed not to laugh during mine, but it took biting my tongue. Jackson said if I ever did anything like the women suggested, he'd think aliens hijacked my body."

And there went another memory.

"Our town is quirky, but I love it," Sadie said as they pulled into the Trinity church parking lot where Beulah held her SORROW meetings. "I doubt there's any small town in America quite like ours."

"Let's hope."

Beulah opened the door and greeted Sadie with a hug and an air kiss. "Welcome, sugar. Welcome."

"Hello there," Eve said, not expecting a great reception.

"There she is," Beulah said, clucking. "Lawd have mercy. You didn't listen to a thing I said, or you wouldn't have chased a Carver man right out of town, that's what. All water under the bridge. Don't worry none, I've got my sights on the last Carver boy and he ain't a leavin' town without wanting to come back."

"Good luck with that," Eve said and took a seat.

Thirty minutes later, after sweet tea and sugar cookies, Beulah led Sadie into the center of a circle. The five members of SORROW surrounded her, Eve on the outside as a special guest. A special silent guest, if she was to go by the members' puckered, red-painted lips.

Clementine Rogers read from the mission statement which was boiled down to one sentence: find good women for the men of Stone Ridge. Whatever it takes. Eve listened to twenty minutes of "advice" from the members, which included admitting a man is always right, and never to be challenged.

"But what do I do when I know *I'm* right?" Sadie dared to ask.

Eve muffled a laugh.

"Oh, honey, you are *always* right," Beulah said.

"Uh-huh. That's right," said Clementine.

"But I don't understand," Sadie said, honestly sounding confused.

"Well, now, there really isn't any trick to this. You are always right, but he has to *think* he's always right," Beulah said, shaking her head. "Even if you have to leave the house, honey, just to keep your composure."

"Sometimes I write in my secret diary," Magnolia Smith offered. "I keep it under my side of the mattress. It's got little letters that I write to the insufferable fool. Explaining how he's so wrong about…well, everything. Oh, he'll never see them. I've been married forty years and no one can say I chased *my* man out of town."

With that, all biddies sent a significant look in Eve's direction. She snorted and looked away.

"This doesn't sound healthy," Sadie dared to say. "I think I should tell him when I'm mad."

This brought about a general tittering from the circle of "bless her heart," "oh my," "she's just a baby," and "these young'uns don't know a thing, do they?"

"Want to know what's healthy?" Beulah said. "Having a town with an equal amount of men and women. Then we can all enjoy the fruits of our labor. Until that time, I'm afraid we're all going to have to swallow our pride. And be wrong. In theory."

Shortly after that, the meeting was concluded, and Sadie was showered with presents: A print copy of the bound book, *The Men of Stone Ridge*, created by their founding member, Wimbreth Williams; a pink knit baby blanket; a beautiful quilt with the date of their wedding embroidered on it; and a carved wooden sign which read "The Carvers: Established June 16th."

By the end of the meeting, Sadie was crying real tears. The presents were packed up in Eve's truck for the ride back to her home.

"That wasn't so bad," Sadie said, buckling her seat belt. "I can ignore the stupid stuff."

"Guess you're right. I'd forgotten it's like another wedding shower."

"With heartfelt gifts." Sadie clutched the quilt. "Did you get one of these?"

"I did," Eve said, the pebble sliding its way over her throat again. "It's either still at your cabin or packed in a box, now in Mima's house…somewhere."

"You've moved a few times, but you kept the quilt."

"Who else could use a quilt with mine and Jackson's names and our wedding date?"

"You kept it," Sadie said, with a wistful sound in her voice.

"Don't read too much into that. It's a beautiful quilt. It would be silly to give it away." But Eve's hands were tightening around the steering wheel to the point where her knuckles turned white.

All her life she'd wanted a quilt like the one she'd seen other brides receive. Her mother owned one, too, and she'd kept it. Mima still had hers. It wasn't something you gave away.

Chalk it up to yet another memory brought about by Sadie's wedding.

Another sentiment, another buried emotion that she just couldn't afford to take out and reexamine.

The next morning, Jackson woke before Winston even stirred. He'd been getting up every morning to let Winston outside, then mainlining the coffee to get on with his day. But today, his eyes popped open before the first rays of dawn filtered through the shutters.

And his first thoughts were of Eve.

He clasped his hands behind his neck and stretched under the sheets. He felt as if someone let all the hot air out of him. The anger that he'd carried for the past few years had stoked his fire far too often. Revenge kept him going when times were tough. When he wanted to give up. Revenge might have been the reason he'd agreed to marry Winona when he'd known it was a bad idea. But he wanted Eve to hear about it and see that he'd moved on.

He wanted to be a success because one day he'd *show* her. Damn it, one day he'd make her sorry. She'd regret abandoning him. But even though he'd only achieved half of what he'd planned and dreamed of in his career, one thing became clear. Eve had regrets, too. He could see them in her eyes.

He wasn't sure where that left him.

After dressing and pulling on his work boots, he wandered into the kitchen. No one seemed to be around, but there was a steaming pot of hot coffee and he poured himself a cup. Flapjacks, bacon, eggs, and grits were warming on the stove. The table was set for four.

Nabbing a piece of bacon, he looked out the big picture window that faced the corral. Levi, one of the ranch hands, was running a cow pony in a circle, probably one that either wasn't cooperating or was treated for colic. From time to time, their cow ponies required remedial lessons, and this might be one of those times. Perched on the edge of the corral watching them was Eve. She threw back her head, laughing at something Levi said.

He did not welcome the roiling pitch of jealousy simmering in his gut. He didn't have any claim on Eve. No reason to object to her spending time with a single man. She had every right, just as he did. They were both single and unattached. Jolette Marie Truehart was certainly interested, but when she'd suggested they get together, Jackson hadn't felt the slightest flicker of interest.

This frustrated him, because Jolette Marie was a beautiful woman, and she'd come on strong. Then again, she held the dubious distinction of being a three-time runaway bride, a record. But he wouldn't exactly be worried about any of that with her.

He'd run into her after he'd hitched a ride into town with Daisy and dropped in to visit with Priscilla before the Shady Grind opened for lunch. But Priscilla ran off to an appointment in Austin she said she couldn't miss. She'd no time to drive him back to the ranch and Daisy had already left for her job at the auto shop in Kerrville. Jolette Marie was more than happy to oblige.

"You're single and I'm single," Jolette Marie said inanely as she drove him back to the Double C.

"You're still single, Jolette Marie? How's that possible, now?"

"Plenty of choices, but I'm picky." She pouted, then boldly reached over to palm his knee.

"You deserve the best."

She'd slid him a sly smile. "We're both on the same page there. I do deserve the best."

"I'll see what I can do."

He'd flirted and flattered and laid the compliments on thick as Mima's gravy. But when she'd asked him on a date, he explained that he'd be too busy with the wedding.

Still, he'd asked Jolette Marie to drop him off in full view of the front of the house. A few minutes later he'd proceeded to make an ass out of himself with Sadie. He still wanted to apologize to her. No matter how angry he'd been with himself for still lusting after Eve, he couldn't take that out on Sadie, an innocent bystander in their dysfunctional mess.

He continued to watch now as Eve walked alongside Levi, Eve now leading the horse out of the corral. They both seemed to be headed back up the hill toward Hank's. Suddenly and inexplicably, the horse reared and knocked Levi down. It took off at a gallop, but Eve kept hold of the reins, half running, half being dragged alongside.

Jackson tore out of the house. He reached Levi, who was struggling to stand, and helped him up. "You okay?"

"Yeah. Didn't see that coming." He scanned the horizon and they both watched as a few hundred feet away, Eve struggled for control of the horse, not letting go.

She'd managed to slow him down and get his attention as they both spun in a circle. She appeared to be talking to him, trying to calm him. Didn't seem to be working from where he stood.

"Shit fire," Jackson muttered, heading after her at a run. She was going to get herself killed by a mad horse. "Eve!"

If she heard him, she didn't listen, and in the next second she face-planted on the hard ground, losing the reins. The horse galloped away.

Jackson ran the rest of the way to her, cursing the entire way. He squatted beside her, afraid to move her and cause more injury. "Are you okay?"

She rolled over on her back, spitting dirt and hair out of her mouth. "Peachy. Why do you ask?"

Giving her a thorough look, he noticed no blood. He gently slid his hand down her stomach. Her arms. No bones sticking out. He pulled her to her feet. "That wasn't smart."

She brushed some loose dirt from her knees and then pushed the wild hair out of her eyes. "I *had* this under control."

They both scanned the horizon as in the distance the horse met with the fence on the first pasture. Nowhere left to run. He turned and trotted down the fence line.

"Almost isn't good enough when it comes to a horse." He squeezed her shoulders, feeling worry and concern pulse through him.

She pulled away and tugged on her left ear. Turning in circles, she searched the ground. He followed her gaze. Something metallic shone in the dirt a few feet away from them which he assumed was an earring she'd dropped, and he reached it first.

"What's this?"

"It looks like a hearing aid," she said, patting down hair on her left side.

Jackson's stomach took a hard dive and he stood stone-cold, locking eyes with Eve. Her eyes were wild, shimmering, and completely unreadable to him.

"Give me that, please." Eve snatched it out of his hands.

She stomped away from him, headed toward the stable,

hips swinging. "I'm getting Thimble and bringing that cow pony back."

"Let me do that," Jackson said.

She faced him. "Why? Suddenly don't think I can *handle* this?"

"It'll keep. He's not far."

"He needs to remember that he's a cow pony. We may need to take him to the Truehart's for some serious remedial training if he doesn't get in line. No freedom for him." She huffed. "Not yet."

"Wait. You and I have to talk." While it might be none of his business, he couldn't ignore this development.

*When?*

*Why?*

*How?*

*Was this what everyone had kept from him?*

She continued to walk ahead of him, not turning once to acknowledge him.

He caught up to her and, hand on her shoulder, spoke softly into her right ear. "A hearing aid? Since when?"

She turned to meet his eyes and hesitated only a moment.

"Since I have single-sided deafness. It's not a big deal. I'm not completely deaf. I just can't always catch the flow of conversations and sometimes I don't know exactly which direction a sound is coming from. The aid sends signals from my left ear to my right." She self-consciously pulled at her earlobe. "When it works. But it's hardly perfect. Guess I'll need a new one now."

When he didn't speak for several seconds, staring at her dumbfounded, she added, "I meant to tell you. Just waiting for the right time."

"When did this *happen*?" He managed to keep his tone low and even despite the coil of emotion that burned in his gut. In his heart.

"Um, I got very sick my third year away at Texas A&M. I was hospitalized for weeks."

"Jesus, baby."

"Yes, Jesus did help." She gave him a half smile. "I'm alive, after all."

"I wish someone told me."

"Oh, your family didn't know when it happened. Sadie did, but y'all were barely speaking to my family or Sadie."

"Everyone knows now?"

"Yes."

For a moment, he couldn't speak. "I'm sorry."

"Don't you dare feel sorry for me, Jackson Carver. That's *why* I didn't want to tell you."

"What do you want me to do? Act like I don't care that you lost your hearing?"

"I want you to act like I'm the same old Eve. Because I am, except for this."

That wasn't true, not by a long shot. Something *else* happened. Simply losing her hearing in one ear, while bad, wouldn't have her this fearful. But he hesitated, unwilling to fight. This wasn't the time or the place. He almost couldn't accept that this happened. To think he'd asked whether she could *hear* him. Accused her of not *listening*.

"I wish I'd known because maybe I could have helped." He took her hand and stroked the palm tenderly.

"There wasn't anything you could do." She didn't pull her hand away but glanced at the ground and kicked at a pebble with her boot.

"Now? Is there anything at all I can do?"

"Like what?" She met his gaze.

He shrugged. "New hearing aid?"

She blinked, then shook her head. "That's kind of you, but I have health insurance."

"Okay, but if you need anything. Anything at all."

"No, that's okay. It's all right."

"It's not."

He stepped toward her and pulled her into his arms. She didn't protest, but simply wound her arms around his waist, clasped them on his back, and laid her head on his chest.

"I hate this for you, Eve. Hate it."

His head fit neatly over the top of hers and he bent to kiss the top of her head.

And they stayed that way for a very long time.

Now that her cabin on Lupine Lake was stuffed to overflowing with wedding shower presents, Sadie still needed to find one of Eve's boxes in this holy mess. But not only did she have Eve's boxes to go through, she would have to wade through some of Lincoln's stuff. He'd moved in about a month ago. They'd decided to stay here until their home on the Double C Ranch was finished. Good thing he was the love of her life because he owned a lot of *junk.*

But Sadie *needed* to find Eve's quilt.

She'd phoned Lillian immediately after learning that Eve had kept her quilt. Like Sadie, Lillian believed this quilt could be the push Eve needed to run right back into Jackson's open arms. She only had to accept the possibilities. Jackson would take her back. His anger was nothing but displaced passion. He'd been devastated to lose Eve.

Besides, when Sadie had this task on her mind, she couldn't think about the fact that she still hadn't gathered up the nerve to tell Lincoln about the baby. Half of her wanted to wait until their honeymoon, the other half understood she couldn't keep something this big from him. Eve was the only one who knew, and she'd guessed. The father should be the second one to know, and Sadie wanted to tell him.

She and Lincoln didn't want children right away. Well, Lincoln didn't, and Sadie agreed because she couldn't blame him. He'd raised his younger brother and sister and wanted to wait for children of their own. Sadie knew this, agreed, and yet… She lowered her hand to her womb. They'd had a plan. But their baby wasn't a mistake. And yet she couldn't bring herself to tell Lincoln. Maybe she *should* wait to tell him on their honeymoon, where he would be the most relaxed and happiest in his life. Surely, he'd be happy after getting used to the idea.

She hoped, because it would kill her to see any hint of fear or disappointment in his eyes.

Finding the second box filled with nothing but clothes and books, just like the first, Sadie closed it back up and put it in the "done" pile.

The front door swung open and her cowboy walked inside. "Hey, baby."

"Linc! What time is it? I lost track." While she loved long summer days, they wreaked havoc with her internal clock. "I didn't make dinner."

"I'll grill burgers." He walked toward where she sat in the midst of a tower of boxes and set a box aside. "What are you lookin' for?"

"The quilt."

"It's over by the bed."

"Not *our* quilt, silly."

"There's another one?" He took a closer look. "Wait. Aren't those Eve's boxes?"

"Yes, I'm looking for something that belongs to her."

"Why isn't she looking for it?"

Sadie blew out an exasperated breath. Lincoln asked so

many questions. He believed that Jackson had long ago moved on, but he hadn't seen the look in Jackson's eyes. He couldn't take them off Eve. She recognized that look because she saw it in Lincoln's eyes every day. Longing. Desire. Jackson just didn't know how to forgive Eve, but he wanted to.

"Because…she doesn't *know* she needs it."

Lincoln tipped his hat and scratched his temple. "I used to be smarter than this. Why doesn't she know she needs it?"

"It's going to remind her. Eve's quilt. She kept it, all these years." Sadie's voice broke and she covered her face. "She still loves him. Don't you see it?"

"Hey, hey." He pulled her into his arms. "Baby, don't cry. You sure cry easy these days. I believe you. But I'm just not sure he feels the same way. I mean, he's pretty angry. Rightfully so. We should just leave well enough alone."

She buried her face in his warm neck. "Remember when you thought I could do better than you? When you broke up with me?"

"Now, I came around, didn't I? I know you couldn't possibly do any better than this cowboy."

"And I know Eve won't ever do better than Jackson."

"Not if she doesn't try."

"That's just the thing. She's never even going to try." The thought made Sadie ache for Eve. "I don't want her to wind up alone for the rest of her life."

"She won't, baby."

"How can you be so sure?" A single tear rolled down her cheek. All the books were sure right about all this hormone stuff.

She wished she could already be on her honeymoon where she'd find the perfect time to tell Lincoln about their baby. When they were relaxed and alone. Not when they were so stressed over the wedding, Jackson, and Eve.

Lincoln wiped the tear away with his thumb. "Okay. I'll help. I don't know how I can, but I'll sure try."

THE NEXT MORNING, Jackson woke before dawn for the first time in weeks, got dressed, and pulled on his boots. Winston, who'd been bunking with him every night, hovered at his feet, desperate for rubs and pats.

"Hey, old boy." He scratched Winston's ears until he made a happy moaning sound. "Let's go."

He'd slept little, not assisted by memories of Eve, the girl he'd known and loved. She'd always helped both animals and people, and sobbed when she saw an animal injured. He'd once asked her how she'd planned to be a veterinarian if she didn't toughen up, and she'd removed her boot and thrown it at him. By then he'd become great at ducking. Eve had a fiery furnace of a temper just as warm and deep as her heart.

"Just because I cry a little doesn't mean I'm not strong, Jackson Carver! And I'll do it, you just watch."

He smiled now at the memory and wanted that girl back. He wanted to see the same light in her eyes return. The fierceness. She'd obviously had it when going through school, until her illness took it out of her. As a musician, he couldn't imagine being deaf in one ear, so maybe it hit him harder than it would others. But he ached for Eve, because she'd always worked so hard.

He walked out to the stables where he'd probably find her. Her normal routine, he'd determined, was to take Thimble for a ride before making breakfast for everyone. That girl loved horses, even if she'd never owned one. Still, Thimble thought of herself as Eve's, and the feeling seemed mutual. Not surprisingly, Thimble was missing from her stall. Taco whinnied.

"Want to go find those two?" Jackson reached to rub his mane. "Yeah. Me too."

Now *he* was talking to horses. That was usually Eve territory. Had been ever since at the age of eighteen his father discovered that horses loved the sound of Eve's voice. She soothed them. Once, the sound of her voice calmed Taco, too. But Jackson knew the moment all that changed. He saddled Taco and hooked the lead to him, helping him out of the stable.

As he rode, he remembered the day he'd taken Taco for a devil of a ride after Eve stood him up. He'd ridden across the hills fast and hard. Stopped once, only to give Taco a break. Anger, pain, and loss fought for top billing in the chaos of emotions that rolled through Jackson on that day. Eve abandoned him, plain and simple. Same way his mother abandoned her family when Lincoln was ten and Jackson eight. Little Daisy only three.

For hours he'd wrestled with his demons. In his mind, abandonment was unforgiveable. If he hadn't forgiven his mother, whom he'd adored, he *couldn't* forgive Eve. The day before the wedding, she'd texted him a simple message:

I can't wait to be your wife. xoxo

Then, with no explanation, she didn't show.

He'd ridden Taco to the fence line dividing their property from the rear of the Truehart ranch, on which sat the small cottage where Eve's mother Brenda still lived. He watched long enough to see her arrive at her home, run inside, then right back out again. No sign of Eve.

Disgusted, he'd pushed Taco to a trot, the sound of his pain turning into a loud guttural yell. He'd yelled at Eve. At Hank, who didn't think he'd ever be a good enough cowboy until he put away that "sissy" guitar. And he'd yelled at his mother, who'd left after telling him how much she loved him.

"Good riddance, all of you!"

Taco bucked, then threw Jackson off. Skilled at falling through years of practice, Jackson rolled and avoided serious injury just feet away from a sharp rock. He'd brushed himself off and stared in confusion at Taco, who'd locked eyes with him for one interminable moment. Whoever said horses couldn't talk never looked into the eyes of a frightened one. Taco turned and galloped off in the direction of the Carver ranch...without Jackson.

The sound he made, the pounding of his hooves against the red dirt, forever changed Jackson.

"I'm done being left behind. From now on, I'm the one who leaves. You hear that?"

Until today, the first and last time he'd talked to a horse.

On the long walk back to the ranch, Jackson made his decision. He would go to Nashville and forget Eve. This could be the only chance he'd have to change the trajectory of his life to this point, and he'd take it. He'd forget the stupid town of Stone Ridge and shake the dust off his boots. Make a name for himself so that someday Eve would come to regret her decision in a stellar way. Years from now she'd sit next to her bald and fat husband and say, "I was once engaged to that guy." And she'd regret leaving him, same as his mother would if she ever happened to hear his name announced over the radio and recognize him as a full-grown man.

Now, Jackson rode across the plains searching for Eve and Thimble, much calmer and centered. He was no longer the boy abandoned by his mother or the young man left at the altar. He was beginning to see that it wasn't always about him. No one made a decision in a vacuum. They made them from life experiences and beliefs which weren't always true but were always true to them.

He tried talking to Taco once more, just in case the emotions Taco could sense flowing out of Jackson were clouding their communication. This time not anger and grief, but remorse.

"Easy, boy. I just need to talk to her."

She and Thimble were headed back when he caught sight of them. Eve did, too, slowing Thimble, and turning toward him.

"Is something wrong?" she asked, once they were within a few feet of each other.

"Wanted to ride Taco."

As good of an excuse as any other, though he'd really wanted to talk with Eve. Ask her how he could make her life better. Easier. Whether maybe he could pay for the hearing aid. Maybe some of her student loans. He wasn't wealthy, but he did all right for himself with song royalties. He'd have to tiptoe around that suggestion, because she might believe this was based on pity for her.

He didn't pity Eve but felt only admiration for her. And a brand-new understanding. He needed her to realize that he didn't see her any differently, and that no one should.

Jackson hopped off Taco, and holding the reins, walked a few feet to face east and the slowly rising sun. Eve did the same, but she kept a healthy distance between them.

Damn, how he wanted to hold her. He took a tentative step closer and simply reached out to squeeze her shoulder. "Look at that sunrise, Eve."

She didn't flinch or move away. "Nothing like a Texas sunrise."

"You get to see one every mornin'?"

"If I'm lucky and don't oversleep."

Guilt coursed through him. She was in his family home, pretty much a servant. Just like her mother, Brenda, over at the Truehart horse ranch. He'd once promised Eve she'd have a different kind of life than her parents. She'd kissed him, and then assured him this would be true, but she would be the one to take care of that.

Eve. Always independent. Always confident. Fearless. And even though he told himself that cooking in Mima's kitchen was temporary, he didn't like her slaving away for the cowboys. For him.

"Why are you here?" she asked quietly. "This early, I mean."

He cleared his throat. "I wanted to see the sunrise."

*And you. I wanted to catch you before you were off on whatever wedding errand you're running for Sadie today. Maybe steal another kiss if I'm lucky.*

"There's one every day," she teased, and he glanced over to see that she was smiling at him. "Just get up early enough."

He grinned back at her. "Is that an invitation?"

"To the sunrise?" She gaped at him, then threw her head back in a laugh. "It's available to everyone."

"Not this view," he said, and this time he made a slow appraisal of her body.

She bit her lower lip, then looked away shyly. That also wasn't Eve. She was proud of her body. Proud he'd wanted her every day and couldn't get enough.

He stepped closer to reach for her hand this time. "Forgive me for being an idiot. For trying to fire you."

"That's okay," she said. "I understand what you must have thought, walking in and finding me here in the family home. I wanted them to warn you but Mima and Linc said it would be okay. That I shouldn't worry. But I *was* worried."

"You know me best." He squeezed her hand. "Guess I forgot I've been taught to put other's needs first. I think I've been gone too long."

Surprising him, she squeezed back. "We all missed you."

While he wished for a little more personalization than that, he wasn't going to complain. With their horses behind them, Jackson stepped behind Eve and slowly and deliberately pulled her to him, her back to his chest, his arms wound tight around her waist.

"Is this uncomfortable?" he murmured against her temple. "Too much?"

She hesitated only a second. "No. I'm good."

"Then let's just stand here and watch the sunrise."


THE NEXT MORNING before daybreak Eve walked to the stables to find that Jackson was already there. He carried two mugs of coffee, one for him, and one for her. Without words, he set his mug down, led Taco out, saddled, and groomed him. She did the same with Thimble, side by side. They didn't speak much, except to talk about the weather.

It happened again the next morning, Jackson there as if planned. They'd then taken both horses out for a ride together.

On the second morning, he'd kissed her tenderly as the sun rose behind them. She'd lost interest in the beauty of the sunrise. And he was far more interested in holding her hand and kissing. She couldn't complain about any of this. It was nice just to be together and not talk about the kiss, or what it meant, if anything at all. She reminded herself that, as he'd told her in the kitchen, he'd kissed her simply because he wanted to. And she'd kissed back for the same reason. Best to keep it simple.

There had been more kisses, plenty of hand holding, more hand caresses, and warm hugs. There were looks and genuine smiles that made her heart ache in a sweet way. Eve hadn't been this treasured by a man in a long while and the sensation was addictive.

This morning, they talked about the ranch, Winston and all the working dogs, Hank and the bull, and Mima's health.

"Thanks for taking such good care of her," Jackson said, and Eve could hardly believe she'd heard the words.

"I'd do anything for Mima. She's like my own grandmother."

"Does Brenda get jealous at all, with you spending so much time over here?"

"No, and in fact she's actually spent more time over here lately. She and Hank are such good friends. And she loves your family."

"Well, we all love her. Especially her daughter." As if realizing what he'd just said, he corrected himself. "You know that Hank is crazy about you."

"To him, I'm the horse whisperer." She laughed, leading a saddled Thimble out.

"We all have our gifts." He came up behind her, leading Taco, and paused to tip his Stetson. "Apparently I'm the Nashville cowboy."

"Long as you're still a cowboy, you fit right in." She pulled herself up and mounted Thimble. "See ya, cowboy."

With that, she took off and left Jackson and Taco in the dust, laughing as she did. But one look behind her, and she could see that Jackson and Taco were quickly gaining on her. In no time flat, they'd caught up. Taco was always the fastest horse. They raced to the first pasture, Taco winning handily, then slowed to head back, giving the horses a break.

"What's it like in Nashville?"

"Loud and bright. Busy. The music business isn't what I'd thought it would be."

"Why not?"

"It's not always about the music. It's about the almighty dollar. What will sell, what won't. Branding. Messaging. Don't get me wrong. The people there are kind. Hard working. It's just...not like home."

Life was probably simpler here and he missed that. Hope swelled in her.

"Do you think…you could stay? For good?"

"I want to, but I started something I should finish."

"Right."

"It's just…since I've been there, I've sold my best songs to other artists. I needed the money. Plus, it was flattering when big names wanted to record my stuff. But I'm not going to shortchange myself anymore. My next song is for me to record. Hopefully people will still buy the song when it's me singing it, and not Keith Urban."

"Oh, I'm sure they will. You just need that chance."

Jackson reached with his big leather-gloved hand and covered hers. She smiled back at him, enjoying his touch. Reveling in the warmth that pulsed through her every time he so much as glanced in her direction. As the orange sun crested over the horizon, and Jackson continued to hold her hand as their horses walked slowly back, she counted her blessings.

*I used to feel sorry for myself, but I do have a lot to be grateful for. For a long while, I never thought I'd smile again. Life got so ugly and dark that some days I just wanted to die. Then I came back to Stone Ridge and Mima said I could ride Thimble whenever I wanted to as long as I'd help with the groom's job. The first time she smiled at me I thought I was seein' things. Horses don't smile, some say, but I know they do. She's one of my best friends even if she can't talk back to me.*

*And I know it's going to hurt when Jackson leaves, but if I can survive what I did, I can survive anything.*

They dismounted at the same time and led their horses back to the stable. Jackson took Thimble's reins. "Let me."

"You're going to unsaddle and brush 'em both?"

"Yeah, I am. I guess you're needed inside."

That was true and she appreciated the help. The groom wouldn't be around today. "Don't forget to clean their shoes."

He cocked his head and slid her his dimpled grin. "Eve, I know what to do."

"Of course you do." She stepped away, but then stopped and turned. "Jackson?"

On her mind were many things she wanted to say to him. She wanted him to kiss her again because just being held in his powerful arms wasn't enough anymore.

*Please be patient with me. When I tell you everything, and I will, I need you to understand. I don't want you to dissolve into anger and revenge. I've done that myself, and it doesn't help a thing. I know.*

"Eve?" Jackson was studying her, his blue eyes intent, brow furrowed. "What is it?"

"Um, thank you for the help."

He nodded, his eyes smiling teasingly. "You work too hard."

She laughed and shook her head, removing her gloves as she walked away. "No, I don't."

By the time Eve reached the kitchen, Mima was already up.

"Mornin'."

"Already been out for a ride?"

"Every morning before sunrise."

Eve cooked up the usual breakfast burritos for the hands, then packed them up for the short drive up the hill. "I'll head out and drop these off then be back for your breakfast."

"Am I working you too hard, sugar?" Mima asked.

"Funny, Jackson just told me I work too hard." She waved the thought away with one hand while the other carried the box of food. "Y'all stop worrying."

Keeping busy helped to push dark or negative thoughts away. Between the ranch and her work, the dark thoughts only chased her at night when it was time to sleep. Only then did she remember that the world wasn't always a safe place, that sometimes when you least suspected it, you could be flattened by life. That moment could come along at any time, without notice, unless you were always on alert.

But for several days she didn't have a single dark thought or memory to push away. She thought it might be because of Jackson. He'd brought a certain kind of sweetness back into her small world. Some part of her would always love him, but she could accept what they had now. There was no need to hurry a thing.

If, with time, something more developed, she'd be open to it. She just needed more time to be ready to feel close to someone again.

As she drove her truck past the stables, she waved to Jackson, who was just making his way back to the house. She drove the quarter mile up the hill. The cowboys were ready for her when she arrived, barely waiting for the truck to come to a full stop. She handed out breakfast to grateful men, then caught sight of her mother nearby.

"Mom?" Eve asked in surprise. "What are *you* doing here?"

Brenda did something that Eve never saw her do before. She blushed. "Hey there. I just came by to see you."

As far as Eve knew, this was the first time her mother ever lied to her. "So early? The sun just came up."

"Did you forget I'm an early riser, too?" Brenda came close, tugging gently on Eve's braid. "Your hair looks so pretty."

"In a braid?" Eve blinked. "Um, okay. Thanks?"

"I've been meaning to ask you about the wedding preparations."

"We have the bachelorette party this weekend. We're going to a spa in San Antonio."

"A spa!"

"I'll tell you all about what it's like when I get back. Maybe I'll take pictures with my phone." Neither one of them had ever been to a spa.

"And…everything else? How is Jackson?"

"He's…he's actually being very nice. He insists on helping me most mornings and thinks Mima's working me too hard. We went for a ride with Thimble and Taco. It was…nice."

"I've always envied your connection to horses."

She shrugged. "Well, I did pretty much grow up on a horse ranch."

"Did I ever tell you how sorry I am that we couldn't buy you a horse of your own?"

To Eve's horror, her mother's eyes filled with tears. "Oh my Lord, Mami. That's not a big deal. You helped me in so many other ways. And with veterinary school."

Eve wasn't even going to mention the breakup with Jackson, when her mother literally brought her meals to bed for a week without complaining. Or the way she'd come to the hospital and wouldn't leave her side. They'd never earned much money, but somehow they always had access to everything they needed. Thanks to Brenda, who worked so hard for the Truehearts. She had no 401(k) plan. No IRA. She'd saved, but not enough. Long ago, Eve determined she would take care of her mother in retirement. She'd be Brenda's 401(k).

"I didn't help enough. You still have too many loans to pay back."

"But so does everyone else I know. I'll be fine. Annabeth and I have a plan. It's a five-year plan."

Brenda cupped Eve's face. "Just make sure you make time for a man. To plan to fall in love again."

"There she is." Hank walked up to Eve and Brenda. "Brenda, didn't expect to see you here."

"My daughter's so busy, and I know where I can find her every morning now," Brenda said.

"Heard you've got three new heifers," Eve said to Hank.

Usually the cows didn't need assistance to give birth, but once in a while one who'd never given birth needed an assist. Hank and his hands were well-trained in pulling calves and Eve would only be called in the case of a breech birth.

"Since you're here, mind taking a look at one of my calves?" Hank turned to Eve and hooked a thumb in the direction of the barn.

"Of course," Eve said and looked at Brenda. "I'll come by soon. We'll go out to lunch."

"Yes, let's do that." With a wave, Brenda turned in the direction of the Truehart ranch.

"Good seein' ya, Brenda," Hank said, holding up a hand in a wave even if he'd already turned toward the barn.

She followed Hank into one of the pens containing a newborn calf. Lincoln was nearby, cleaning up the pen. The equipment he'd have used to pull the calf out was nearby.

"Hey there, Eve," Lincoln said.

"Hi, Linc."

The calf lay on the ground, the mama not far, but seemingly also not doing her job. Usually instinct took over and the cow would lick the afterbirth off her calf, which served the dual purpose of helping it to become more alert.

"She just needs to be left alone to get acquainted," Lincoln said.

"Sometimes they're a little slow to show interest and do their job when you have to assist the birth," Eve said, but after bending down to give a cursory check on the calf she found the heifer to be responsive with good color. "She's just a little dazed, huh, baby? Welcome to the world."

Eve loved this part of her job and she wasn't often privileged to witness a natural birth. She was called to the calving when there was a problem. A breech birth or, worse, a still-born. Always so horrible. But this new life before her was beautiful to witness. Maybe it was true, as her therapist used to say, that there was far more good in the world than evil. She wanted to believe that. After a few more minutes of watching the two together, Eve agreed with Lincoln. They should leave those two alone to do what came naturally.

"Just check on her after a while," Eve advised. "Make sure she's taking care of her baby. I bet it doesn't take her long once she loses an audience."

A few minutes later, everyone dispersed to other tasks. Hank thanked her and went off to do something else, but Lincoln pulled Eve aside.

"I owe you an apology."

"For what?"

"For not ringing my fool brother's neck. I don't like the way he spoke to you, and I should have stopped it." He tipped his hat. "It's just that…it seems like Jackson wanted to get something off his chest. I figured he'd be better after that."

"Well, thank you." Eve shoved her hands in the back pockets of her Wranglers. She didn't like the idea of coming between the two brothers who'd always been so close. "But this is between me and Jackson."

"And how are things between you?" He cocked his head, appearing honestly interested.

She didn't know why she was surprised. Lincoln was just as solid a guy as they came. But despite that, Eve wasn't quite comfortable sharing the details.

"We're not fighting anymore." She kicked the ground with the heel of her boot. "I think we'll behave ourselves for your weddin'. No worries there."

"I wasn't worried."

"In fact, he's been helpin' me. Getting up before daylight lately."

"Jackson?" Lincoln chuckled.

Eve nodded. "This mornin' he had coffee waiting for me. We've been goin' for rides with Thimble and Taco."

And a lot of kissing but she wasn't going to mention that. Good thing, because the grin on his face made Eve think he'd read her mind.

"Well, well. That's good news."

"I better get back to it. Sadie and I have a few last-minute things to do before we head out for San Antonio tomorrow."

Lincoln pointed. "Okay, y'all have fun and take care of my bride."

"Will do."

It was finally time for the bachelorette party, the one she'd planned for months. Just a weekend of pampering, girl talk, junk food, and rom-coms. No men or talk of men.

Good thing, because as much time as Eve was spending with Jackson lately, she needed a moment to sort out her feelings. To take a break from the intensity of emotions that washed over her every time he was in the room.

Waving to Lincoln, she hopped in the truck and headed back down the hill.

# CHAPTER 15

*E*ve had quite possibly never been this relaxed in her life.

Then again, neither she nor Sadie had ever been to a spa. It was one of those luxuries they'd never allowed themselves. Besides, Eve was always more comfortable on the back of a horse, and ranch living wasn't conducive to such pampering. Still, she would agree there was a time and a place, and right before a wedding seemed a good reason for such pampering. It also became the perfect way to host a small bachelorette party.

The bachelor and bachelorette parties were occurring a week before the wedding, to give the groom enough time to get over the hangover he'd be likely to have the next day. They'd all heard horror stories about grooms who were late, sick, and hungover. One of Linc's friends threw up on the altar. Not an auspicious beginning.

Eve was salt scrubbed, exfoliated, and deep tissue massaged with aromatherapy essential oils until she nearly fell dead asleep. Keeping her from falling asleep was Daisy's nonstop talk about Wade. Wade this and Wade that.

"Do y'all think Wade will ever get married?" Daisy asked.

Eve was lying on a cot between Daisy and Lucy, Sadie's friend and a part-time waitress at the Shady Grind.

"I don't know," Lucy piped up. "He's a bit of a loner. Why do you like him?"

"He's a good guy deep down," Daisy said. "With a big heart."

Eve and Lucy shared a smirk. That sounded like wishful thinking.

"I know he must have a big something," Lucy muttered under her breath and Eve swatted her.

"All I know is I'm marrying the most handsome man on earth, y'all," Sadie said from under a towel placed at strategic points to cover all the naked. "He's mine. And he knows how to give his woman some good lovin'."

"Eww!" Daisy rolled over to her side, turning away from Sadie.

"A little tact?" Lucy snort laughed.

"What? I'm just talking about his kisses." Sadie winked.

"Yeah, right," Eve said.

"I'm sorry, girls. I'm just so happy," Sadie said. "It's kind of like trying to hide a bush fire under a basket. It's not going to stay under there long."

"You have every right to gush." Eve then hushed her voice. "Just don't brag about his sexual prowess in front of his sister."

"Alright, then." Sadie waved a hand dismissively.

A while later, they'd all made their way up from the hotel spa to the sixth-floor three-bedroom suite, still wearing their hotel spa bathrobes and sandals. The suite contained a separate living room with a plasma TV, a sofa, and a mini fridge. A sunken whirlpool tub sat in the two-vanity bathroom.

Sadie's parents wanted to spoil their only daughter. They told Eve to spare no expense, and she hadn't.

"Are you sure about this?" Eve perused the room-service menu. "This food is way too expensive. We could get dressed and go find a diner somewhere. Look at the price of the hamburger! Even Hank would be shocked."

"Is it Kobe beef?" Lucy leaned over Eve's shoulder.

Eve shrugged. She handed Lucy the menu and went to find her phone. She'd been pathetically checking it frequently this week, asking Annabeth if everything was going well at the clinic, and whether she should come in to help out. Annabeth kept reassuring her everything was under control, and to try to enjoy herself.

Eve pulled Sadie aside after they ordered meals. "Did you tell him?"

"No, but I will. Tomorrow night."

"I can't believe you've waited this long!"

"No time has been perfect. Something always stops me."

"No time is ever going to be perfect."

"I was thinking on our honeymoon. We're going to be so relaxed and I'll make it special. One night over a candlelit dinner or something."

"If you're okay with not telling him before your wedding day. I'm sure it won't matter. Not like he won't marry you if you're pregnant. That's usually the other way around."

"True. At least I know he's not marrying me for the wrong reasons."

"Exactly. It's going to be fine."

"Sure. Now, help me talk Daisy into staying away from Wade. It isn't like she doesn't have plenty of other choices. The last thing she needs is to fall for Lincoln's best friend. Then 'rodeo-Wade' will drop her, break her heart, and I'll have to intervene so I don't wind up visiting my new husband at the pokey."

"You're exaggeratin'."

Sadie went hand on hip. "Now, he wanted to kill the man

who hurt you. What would he do to someone who hurt his little sister?"

Eve doubted Wade would ever hurt a woman in the same way, but the point was taken. Emotional pain could be as devastating, and Daisy was inexperienced both with men and their rejection.

"Okay, okay. But I don't know how we can talk her into ignoring a sexy rodeo cowboy."

"Follow my lead," Sadie said, beckoning Eve.

Lucy was making herself at home behind the bar. "Anything you want. Anything at all. Challenge me."

"Oh! A mojito," Daisy said, jumping up and down.

"Challenged accepted." Lucy ducked under the bar and came up with vodka. "It's a good thing I dropped by the store to pick up fruit, olives, and mint. It's always such a challenge being the only bartender at a party."

"Is it?" Daisy rolled her eyes. "The weight of the world?"

"Y'all, you know what I was just thinking?" Sadie said, sliding Eve a look. "I'm so glad I waited and took my time to find the right man. It was worth the long *wait*. Lincoln would never hurt me. From the start, when we got together, I knew it would be a forever thing with us."

Eve should follow Sadie's lead. But suddenly she didn't want to play. Because Daisy should know the whole story and not just the pretty-packaged version of love and romance. Daisy should know that not all men were after love, or even sex. Some craved control. Possession. And if they couldn't have you, they wanted to make certain that no one else could.

"I agree," Eve said. "Sadie and Linc are made for each other. But Daisy, first make sure the man you're with isn't just with you because he wants to control you."

Daisy snorted. "Control *me*? Who would even dare?"

"Eve's got a good point." Lucy shook the tumbler filled

with crushed ice. "I myself am done with men. All they want to do is call the shots. 'Wear this, cut your hair like that, don't talk to that man. Is that your ex texting you?' No thank you."

"And our men know better than to fool with that controlling business," Eve said.

"Then why'd you bring it up?" Lucy said.

"You want to see real men, you should come by my daddy's ranch sometime," Daisy said with a wicked grin. "Some of the rodeo cowboys are ranch hands off season. Oh good Lord, the way they fill out them Wranglers."

"Back to what I was sayin'. Eve's right about the control thing, but you also don't want to be with a man that's just going to drop you when the next pretty young thing comes along." Sadie gave Eve a significant look. "Know what I mean?"

This conversation was making Eve's eye twitch. Once, she'd found the perfect man in what might be viewed as a haystack of men. It could happen.

"I think Daisy needs to date some more men to find out whether Wade is as great as she thinks he is. Because you know, he might be, or maybe not. How would you know?" Eve said.

"That's right." Sadie elbow nudged Eve. "Listen to Eve. She knows what she's talkin' about."

Daisy crossed her arms. "Is that why you left my *brother* at the altar? You weren't sure he was the right man because maybe you hadn't tried everyone else?"

The silence and sudden tension in the room was thick and swift. Lucy stopped pouring drinks. All eyes were on Eve.

"It's a little more complicated than that," Eve muttered.

"Let's go have some of those drinks!" Sadie said, moving toward the bar. "I am so thirsty. Whew!"

"Y'all are going to love my mojitos." Lucy started pouring.

No one had yet noticed or questioned why Sadie wasn't drinking with the rest of them.

Daisy stood, arms crossed, more hostile than Eve had ever seen her before. She'd been a teenager then and one of the bridesmaids for their wedding-day fail. She and Daisy never talked about any of this.

"Well?" Daisy pressed.

"I was younger than you are now. I'd never dated anyone before Jackson. I was sixteen when we met. How could I know that I'd met my soul mate in our Podunk town?"

"Aww," Sadie and Lucy said at once.

"And Wade could be my soul mate." Daisy flipped her hair. "How do you know he's *not*?"

"He *could* be. I don't know. Just make sure he wants the same things you do. Just because y'all are soul mates, that isn't always the case," Eve said.

A few minutes later, the other women were enjoying their cocktails. Except Sadie, of course. Eve, too, remained sober as a nun. She'd never been much of a drinker, and in college she hated the alcohol excess she'd witnessed. They ordered off the room-service menu, an impressive presentation of hamburgers and crunchy, warm French fries rolled in on a white cloth-covered cart. It made their junk food look fancy. Lucy and Daisy were staring with rapt attention as Tatum Channing danced on the plasma TV in the first of their marathon movie-night selections. Sadie was alternatively staring dreamily between her sparkling one-carat diamond ring and the TV screen, a dopey smile on her face.

Eve interrupted whatever dream her best friend was caught in. "I lost my hearing aid yesterday and I don't think I'll have a new one in time for the wedding. So just make sure if you have something you want to whisper, be on my right side."

"Oh, okay. How'd you do that?"

Eve explained how Levi was trying to give a difficult cow pony some retraining, how she'd gone after him, and dropped her hearing aid.

"I tried to save it, but it was a lost cause. At least now Jackson knows, and I don't have to find the right time to tell him. Or think about whether he has to know at all."

"What did he say?" Sadie's eyes went wide with anticipation.

"He…he said he was sorry and then he held me. For a long time."

"Oh." Sadie patted her heart. "That's the Jackson we all know and love, isn't it?"

Eve thought back to that moment of incredible warmth and comfort, feeling herself enveloped in his big arms, his tall body dwarfing hers. He'd been so close she could feel his heartbeat. She'd longed for that moment and yet when it came, she hadn't been prepared. She couldn't handle the emotions that came rushing back. The memories. He happened to be a part of her best ones.

"I don't know what I'm going to do. Now that all the anger is behind us, I can't help the way I feel."

"How do you feel?"

"I like him…a lot."

It would be more, were she ready for that. But she wasn't in the position to trust anyone. Not even him.

Sadie grinned. "That's a good start."

# CHAPTER 16

Jackson glanced at his watch. He and the guys were fishing all day, and Lincoln caught enough bass to feed a wife and four children for a year. He hoped Sadie liked a good fish fry.

"Don't know about y'all, but I'm about ready to head back to the cabin and start drinkin'. Maybe hit the hot tub." Jackson hooked one last line and threw it in the waters of Medina Lake.

"I'm going to agree with you there," said Wade. "I'm zero for ten here."

"Stick to the rodeo," said Lincoln. "There's a trick to fishin'. You need the right bait."

"I need the right *worm?*" Wade narrowed his eyes. "What's one damn worm to another?"

"Here, let me show you how it's done," Lincoln said, and spent the next thirty minutes lecturing Wade on hooking a line.

They'd wound up with a warm and perfect summer day. Rain was predicted for weeks but kept passing them. One thing you could say about Texas: if you don't like the weather, wait a minute. The sun beat down and Jackson scrubbed a hand down his face. This was the last fishing trip with Lincoln before he got hitched and he should enjoy the time with his brother. Instead, he couldn't get Eve off his mind.

"Yeah! Uh-huh. That's right!" Wade shouted when he caught one. Reeling it in, he turned to Lincoln. "Give me some more of that bait, yeah?"

"Give the fish a break," Jackson said, annoyed. "We've all caught enough."

The men looked at him as if he'd lost all good sense. Not exactly the words of a rancher's son.

"You gone fish-soft on me?" Lincoln asked through squinted eyes.

"Eat or be eaten," Wade said and everyone chimed in with "uh-huhs" and "that's rights."

He took off his Gone Fishin' cap and scratched his head. "No, I'm just saying give them a sporting chance...or something."

He had no idea what he was saying anymore. His brain had been hijacked by Eve. He wanted this party to be over so he could get back to the ranch and spend time with her. Fortunately, they all thought he was kidding given the raucous laughter that rang out over the shimmering lake moments later. Finally, almost an hour later, they were all back at the cabin relaxing around a plasma TV nearly as big as the wall behind it. Jackson wasn't drinking. He needed a clear head now more than ever.

He had a bone to pick with Lincoln, but he'd wait until they were alone. So far, this week meant back-to-back events scheduled so tightly a sheet of paper wouldn't slide through. But Lincoln, more than anyone, could have told him about Eve. Remembering how she'd been frantically searching the ground for that hearing aid...his chest was too tight. Holding her close hadn't helped. He wanted to do a lot more than hold her.

He wanted to *fix* it.

Wade held up a DVD and wiggled his eyebrows. "Brought a dirty movie or two. And a bunch of cigars."

The doorbell rang, and Jackson rubbed his hands together. "Alright. Dinner has arrived."

Jackson accepted the ten pizza boxes and handed them out.

"Dig in!" Jackson said. "Linc, I hear you like to eat."

"You damn right I do." After all the guys had been helped to slices, Lincoln pulled Jackson aside in the kitchen. "Thanks for not gettin' me a stripper. Didn't want to start my marriage off with a lie."

"Welcome." Jackson took a soda can out of the refrigerator, popped it open and narrowed his eyes. "Speaking of lies. What about Eve?"

"What's Eve got to do with any of this?"

"You didn't think it was important for me to know about her hearing loss?"

Lincoln blinked. "How did you find out?"

"When I found her hearing aid on the ground. It fell out when she was chasing a mad gelding. Crazy girl." He shook his head.

"When she was…what?"

Jackson explained. Tried his best to tell Lincoln about her wild-eyed look, how she'd frantically searched for it. Her obvious embarrassment when he'd located it first.

"She didn't want me to find out that way."

"Well, listen, you don't know what she's been through. And it's not my place to tell ya."

"Thanks for keeping me in the dark. Although I imagine that's how Eve wanted it."

"Wait." Now Lincoln's brow creased. "She *told* you how it happened?"

He nodded. "I wish I'd known because maybe I could have helped. But I'm done talkin' about it."

Lincoln whistled. "Gotta say, I didn't expect you'd take it so well."

"It doesn't make her any less Eve."

"Yeah, but I mean, even I wanted to kill the guy with my bare hands when I heard, and I wasn't the one once engaged to her."

"Wait. What *guy?*"

"What do you *mean* what guy? The one who beat her and put her in the hospital. The reason she lost her hearing."

Jackson heard a roar in his ears that grew louder as he tried to understand. His gut burned with fire. He was beginning to see everything in a haze and his stomach roiled and pitched. For a moment, he thought he would literally be sick.

"Oh, fuck," Lincoln said as he hit the wall with a fist.

There seemed to be a growing buzz in the room that was taking up all the sound. Lincoln cursed once every few years only when the occasion warranted it. The last time Jackson heard him curse was years ago when he'd had to put his stallion down.

"I thought she *told* you. You made it sound like she did."

"She said she'd been very sick and hospitalized for weeks. Why would she lie to me?"

"Because of…this!" Lincoln spit out. "You!"

"Who is this guy? I want to know."

"Calm down. He's in prison where he won't ever hurt Eve again."

"*Why?*"

He knew Lincoln would follow his currently chaotic thoughts. The why didn't matter but he still wanted to know. While he'd been out playing clubs and writing songs, hating her, meeting random women, drinking and chasing his dream, she'd been suffering.

"Did he—" Jackson couldn't finish the sentence.

The thought that she'd been violated was too raw, too horrible to even say out loud. His hands formed into fists.

"No, he didn't." Lincoln grasped Jackson's shoulder, somehow knowing what he'd asked without words. "We didn't even know for a long time. Eve was away at school when all this happened. Sadie was the only one who actually knew. And then Mima found out later, through Brenda. I didn't even know any of this until recently."

That was why she'd taken Eve in and easily forgiven her even when Mima was so bitter about the whole wedding. And he'd been such an asshole when he'd first seen Eve again. Ordering her out of the house. Firing her from a place where she obviously felt safe and wanted. He thought back to when he'd threatened Eve if *Sadie* didn't show up to the wedding. Regret pulsed through him. He didn't think he'd be able to apologize enough in one lifetime.

"What *happened?*"

He couldn't believe anyone would purposely hurt Eve. It might have been a random attack in a large city.

"You need to talk to her." Lincoln grimaced. "I think…*I've* said enough."

Jackson shoved a hand through his hair. "I have to go now."

"Wait. Where?" Lincoln put a firm hand on Jackson's chest in a move to stop him.

"I know where they're staying in San Antonio and I need to go there now and see Eve. Talk to her. Apologize for being such an asshole. You don't know all the hurtful things I said to her. I noticed she was different. Skittish. But in my wildest dreams I couldn't imagine this. "

"No." Lincoln made a move to stand between him and the front door of the cabin.

"Don't try to get in my way," Jackson snarled.

"You can't go like this. This angry." Lincoln grabbed his truck keys. "I know how you feel, you're ready to kill someone for her. But you don't have that right anymore. You checked out of her life. Every time I even mentioned her name you'd go to a dark place. After a while I stopped talking about her. That was the way you wanted it. Tell you what. If you go, I'll be the one who's drivin'."

# CHAPTER 17

The hour-long drive to San Antonio was vicious to Jackson's peace of mind, but necessary because Lincoln was right. Jackson tried to calm down. He couldn't screw this up. First, he wanted Eve to stop keeping the truth from him, no matter how harsh. Despite what they'd been to each other in the past, they were friends again. That meant he'd want to be told from now on whenever she was in trouble. Whenever she needed anything. He wanted to make up for those years when he hadn't been there for her, to support her. She *had* to let him. She would have to let her guard down the rest of the way and let him care. Stop being so damn proud and let him *help*.

What happened was horrible and painful and he didn't want her to have to revisit it. But he did need her to know he was sorry that he hadn't been there when she needed him. Because he should have been. He should have instinctively known that she was in trouble. Should have known that she needed him. Because this was his *Eve*.

"Hey, baby," Lincoln said into his cell phone with a sigh. "I'm on my way to the hotel. No, nothing's wrong. Well, not exactly. Yes, I miss you, too, but this is about Jackson. He wants to talk to Eve. You can guess what this is all about. That's right. Well, I *thought* he knew everything. He fooled me. Yeah, apparently it does have to be now."

Jackson sat quietly and after the first thirty minutes of the drive, stopped mentally flogging himself for the way he'd treated Eve. Suggesting something was wrong and that he could sense it.

*She* was different.

It must have been difficult for her not to take him to task. Not to tell him to mind his own business. Not to let him know that he didn't realize the half of it.

And on the last half of the drive, he came to a stunning realization.

He'd placed all the blame on their breakup entirely on Eve, but for the first time he saw how leaving the next day for Nashville sent a powerful message. In his mind, there was nothing left to stay for. But his twenty-one-year-old self hadn't even considered fighting for her. Obviously, Eve heard his message loud and clear. Because much as he loved Eve, he hadn't been ready to be married, committed fully to the two of them, and give up the opportunity in Nashville. But he would have gone through with the wedding, because he apparently had far less courage than she did.

Which meant he should forgive Eve for leaving him at the altar. He should probably even thank her.

Lincoln pulled into the JW Marriott hotel lot and parked, then turned to Jackson, who'd started to unstrap his seat belt before the truck stopped moving.

Hand on Jackson's chest, he pushed back hard. "I'm going to say this only once. Calm. The. Hell. Down."

Jackson scrubbed a hand down his face. "I have so many questions and don't even know where to begin."

"Just *listen* to her and for God's sake don't make this about you."

He and Lincoln both walked to the lobby, then hopped on the elevator. Lincoln punched the button for the sixth floor and together they walked down the hallway that seemed to never end. Jackson's throat was tight. It was so dry he could hear himself swallow.

Sadie opened the door. "Y'all really *are* here. It couldn't wait, Jackson?"

"This is my fault and I'm sorry, but I need to talk to Eve. Now." He cleared his throat then rolled his shoulders. "Um, please."

"Hm." Sadie quirked a brow. "That's better now."

"And also, I'm sorry about your mama's jam. That was rude." He shoved a hand through his hair. "I shouldn't have taken my anger out on you."

"What'd you do to her mama's jam?" Lincoln asked, looking pissed.

"Never mind. It's all right. You're my groom's brother and I forgive you." Sadie opened the door wide and pulled Lincoln inside first. "She's in the bedroom to the left. Y'all can talk in there."

It seemed as if every vein in Jackson's neck tightened to the point of snapping. He needed to calm down because if he didn't his anger would seem misplaced. Lincoln had a point. With anger, sometimes just its nature hurt everyone around. It could be like a storm, which hit everything in its path. He ought to remember, having more than once been the recipient of Hank's wrath when he'd simply had a "bad day." It too often felt like Jackson was the reason for that bad day. Only now as a grown man did he realize he'd simply been in Hank's path.

Jackson opened the door and found Eve sitting on a

wrought iron daybed. She wore clean Wranglers and a tight long-sleeved Henley-style tee, the top buttons opened.

"Hey, there," she said, arms crossed. Her expression was sober, but her gaze soft.

He didn't speak for a moment because it felt as though he was seeing her again for the first time in eight years. She was so beautiful, more fragile than he'd ever known, and she'd been so hurt. He would *kill* anyone who ever tried to hurt her again with his bare hands.

Unable to rein the emotions in, his hands clenched into fists at his sides, the anger boiling. "If I could have just one minute alone with the man who hurt you, I swear he'd never walk again."

She turned away from him, staring at the wall with pursed lips.

He simply sat beside her, hip to hip. "Why did you keep this from me? Why did you lie?"

"Why do you *think?*" She turned back to him, eyes shimmering. "Because this is exactly what I *didn't* want. You, so angry. You want to fix this, and you can't. Believe me, I've been all the way through this mess. Through it, under it, around it, and all the way to the end. And I know what it's like to be so angry it's the only emotion you feel and it rules your life. You don't want that, Jackson. Don't take it on."

"But I won't ever be able to stop being angry at the person who did that to you."

"You have to. If I did it, you can."

"How…you're not *angry?*"

He couldn't comprehend that. He'd never be able to let this go. Hurting a woman…it was disgusting. Reprehensible.

"I've *been* angry. It didn't do me any good."

"Tell me what happened. Was it a random attack? Were you robbed?"

"No." She shook her head. "I'll tell you, but you have to promise you'll listen all the way to the end."

She held up a finger as he was about to open his mouth to agree. "Without saying a word."

He nodded, planning to squash every word, growl, or grunt down his windpipe.

"I didn't date much when I was at A&M. I had one boyfriend, Bobby, and he was a really nice guy. I think… maybe I could have married him someday if he'd stuck around, but he changed majors and moved away. Afterwards there was another guy, Matt, a football player, who always asked me out. He was too popular for my taste, too loud, too…too much everything. I kept saying no."

A worry line creased between her eyebrows. "But then one day, well, something happened and I…I changed my mind. I thought it was time to move on, to date someone. So, I did. He was nice our first date. Very good manners. Attentive and kind. But on the second date, he showed his true colors. He got drunk. Gropey. I said no."

Jackson tensed, every muscle in his body turning to granite, but he kept his word. He didn't say anything, though he knew where this was headed. He'd certainly met enough female musicians and singers in Nashville who'd been through similar. Some men didn't hear the word "no." Get too much alcohol in them and everything got a whole lot worse.

"I didn't realize it, but he was stalking me. He'd call, begging me to reconsider. But the calls got nastier. Meaner. I'd heard he was already dating someone new, but he seemed to have taken my rejection so personally. I should have talked to the campus police. I *should* have acted sooner. But I hoped he'd get over it and forget me."

She took a deep, shaky breath and every cell in Jackson's

body shook. He took her hand in his and began tracing circles in her palm.

"One day he showed up at my place and knocked me out cold. No more words. No warning. I don't know how long the attack went on, no one really does, but my roommate showed up and stopped it. She screamed for help and Matt ran. He was arrested the next day. I was in the hospital for a couple of weeks. That part was true. And I really was lucky. If my roommate hadn't shown up, if the campus police hadn't acted quickly and firmly…"

Jackson simply squeezed Eve's hand tightly.

"I went through so many emotions after the attack. Terrified, and then *so* angry. I lived with anger for two years, let it consume me, while the DA prepared to take him to trial. His attorney came up with the most ridiculous defense. Matt was raised too privileged, through no fault of his own, so he didn't understand the word "no." They made our relationship out to be much more than it was. We were *never* intimate. They tried to assassinate my character. To claim that I'd pursued him, then changed my mind, and Matt didn't understand the sudden change. Couldn't accept it.

"I couldn't concentrate, and my grades slipped. Worse, I let my anger infect the rest of my relationships. When Sadie called and wanted to talk, I'd say I was too busy and didn't have the time to make her feel better about what happened to me." She grimaced and a single tear rolled down her cheek. "I accused my roommate, the woman who may have saved my life, of conspiring with the defense. All nonsensical but the anger took root in me and spread. I was saved from testifying when Matt took a plea. From attempted murder to aggravated assault, a lesser charge. I didn't like it, but it wasn't up to me. You can guess that I was angry about that, too."

Letting go of her hand, he ran his palm down her spine

and up again in a soothing motion. "How did you get past that?"

"I *had* to. And so do you. You've been angry at me for so long, for good reason—"

"No, it *wasn't* a good reason."

"It couldn't have been healthy. All that drinking."

"In a way my anger fueled me for a while. It gave me a purpose."

"Mine did, too. But that purpose ended. He was put away, and I didn't need the anger anymore. But I couldn't let go. Until I had a little breakthrough. My therapist helped with that. Then the only emotion left was sadness and…fear. I'm still working on that."

He brought her hands up to circle his neck. "I wish I could have been there when you needed me. When you were suffering."

"But I liked that you didn't know. You're the only one in the family who treated me like the old Eve. Not with kid gloves. And I want to be that woman again. Fearless."

"You *are* that woman. That's the way I see you." He nuzzled her neck.

"Only with you. Somehow you bring it out of me."

"I'm talented that way. Pissing you off is my specialty."

She laughed. "No, I think it's because I still feel safe with you. You're one of my last memories of feeling truly safe. And loved."

"I would never hurt you." He hitched in a breath. "But I did, didn't I?"

"No more than I hurt you."

She was being generous, but he was done with excuses. "I *should* have come after you. I would have fought for us, too, if I didn't have my head up my ass."

"Stop. I knew what you wanted, and you had every right

to your dream. Don't think for a minute that I was being all noble and self-sacrificing. I just wanted to be first with you."

The knowledge of that slammed into him. Eve was so proud, it was no wonder that she'd left the church after seeing him appearing less than thrilled.

"But if I'd gone after you?"

"If you'd have come after me, we'd have gotten married. I know it was stupid and I was immature. Too proud. I guess I wanted you to show me that you still wanted *us*."

"That's not stupid or proud. But I guess I showed you that you were right about me, by leaving the next day for Nashville."

She shook her head. "Maybe we were both too young to know what we wanted."

"You mean that we were both too young to know what we had." Jackson pressed his forehead to hers, wanting the contact.

"I can only speak for myself, but I had no idea." She whispered.

DRAINED OF ENERGY, Eve wanted to collapse and take a nap. For six months.

Only a few minutes ago, her plans for a ladies' night was derailed. She'd been warned by Sadie when she'd ended her phone call with Lincoln and turned to Eve.

"I hate to say I told you so. My Lincoln is wonderful but keeping a secret like this from his brother was asking too much. Everything you tried to stop is headed your way. Right now."

Eve understood the time would come when someone would slip up. The Carvers weren't known to keep secrets for long. It was possible with the benefit of distance and geography, but not once back in the cocoon of the family ranch.

Heart racing, Eve had waited for him in a bedroom, and when he'd walked in, his eyes were shimmering with unspent pain, anger, and confusion. The sorrow in them was exactly why she hadn't wanted him to know. Ever. She didn't want his pity, but it only took a few minutes for her to see that Jackson didn't feel sorry for her. He hurt for her, and there was a difference.

Without the filters of anger and fear clouding her thoughts, she could see that now.

"I missed you," Eve said now and tugged on the nape of his neck. "So much."

Eve hadn't been intimate with another man since Bobby, but that wasn't due to a lack of options. There were many men in Stone Ridge. Once, a man who'd been passing through town brought an injured cat he'd found on the side of the road to their clinic. They'd connected over a mutual love of helpless creatures. He'd asked her out and she'd agreed.

On the first date, when he'd unexpectedly tried to kiss her, she'd literally recoiled. It was very difficult to come back after that. He'd been insulted, hadn't bothered to try to understand, and dropped her off without indicating that there would be a second date. The same thing happened a couple of more times, and even when it went past one date, none were at all patient. If she stopped them from getting too handsy, they quickly lost interest. She eventually gave up dating.

Jackson had waited patiently for her to want more. Now, she made the first move with a kiss that wasn't particularly tender. Their tongues and lips slanted across each other as he responded, eager, demanding more. He followed with deep and hot kisses.

They were both breathless when she broke the kiss. "God. Oh God."

"Baby, you are killing me right now. You do know my brother and Sadie are in the next room?"

"And so are Daisy and Lucy."

"I know I should go, but I don't want to. We're supposed to be watching dirty movies, smoking cigars, and getting tanked. I'm afraid I'll go down in history as the worst best man ever."

She snorted. "Hush. Lincoln and Sadie are right where they want to be right now. Together."

"I would say that they've got a lifetime of that ahead, but somehow I don't take anything for granted anymore."

Eve framed his face and studied his lips so she could catch every word. "I'm tired of being afraid. Tired of feeling numb inside when I'm not afraid. Stay with me just a little while."

Every raw emotion had been pulled out of her in the past few minutes. She just needed to sleep. And she wanted him right here with her.

"Come here and let me keep you warm, girl." Jackson took off his boots and his jacket. Fully clothed, he laid on his side, pulling Eve's back to his chest.

She lay there in the circle of his arms, content, drifting off after a few minutes. No waking nightmares chased her sleep this time. When she woke, it was dark, shadows of ambient light in the room. No sound. She hitched in a breath, and stiffened, for one moment not remembering. That old sense of urgency and fear tugged at her, but then she felt Jackson's even breaths on her neck. His arms wrapped loosely around her waist. He'd fallen asleep, too.

The next time Eve woke, it was daylight and hushed voices were at the door. Jackson and Lincoln. She turned toward the sound and concentrated hard to catch every word.

"Bet I'm the only groom in history who spent his bachelor party with his fiancée."

"Are you complaining?"

"Nah, I can never get enough of her, but we do need to get back to the guys. God knows what they've done to the place."

"Be right there." Jackson shut the door.

Eve closed her eyes, pretending to be asleep.

He pressed a soft kiss against her temple. "Bye, beautiful."

She heard him as he made movements sitting on the bed next to her. Then he leaned close again and seemed to hesitate. "I love you."

The words were nothing but a whisper in her good ear, and she caught every single word.

# CHAPTER 18

"Dad, put the tie on, or don't, but don't let me hear another word about it," Jackson said from his father's recliner.

Hank continued to grumble and complain for thirty minutes straight, give or take. He didn't want to leave the cattle. He didn't want to leave his hill. There was work to be done that waited for no one.

But three days from the wedding, it was time for the wedding rehearsal followed by the dinner, on the old man's dime. Jackson had kept busy around the ranch, helping Hank. Helping Lincoln as they both corralled the rest of the cattle to a second pasture and got the ranch ready to be without him while he was on his honeymoon.

Far from avoiding Eve, however, he continued to seek her out.

Sometimes if he woke early enough, he'd find her alone in the kitchen, packing breakfast. He'd come up behind her and put his arms around her hips. She had a great deal of patience with him, treating him to a few more kisses. He'd help her in the kitchen, which would earn him a few more kisses. But when his hand would slip under her shirt, she always stopped him.

"Not yet," she'd whisper, and he was a teenager again, living on hormones, hope, and a prayer.

"Not sure why they picked a fancy place for the dinner," Hank said as he looped his tie around. "Lincoln would have been happy with the Shady Grind."

The Shady Grind was the place where he and Eve had their rehearsal dinner. A very affordable, reasonable bar and grill. But it was also a place a young couple tight on funds might choose.

"We all know everything is for the bride."

"Then let her parents pay for it."

"They're paying for the whole wedding and neither Sadie nor Lincoln would let us help with that."

"How many songs would you have to write and sing to help pay for this dinner?" He actually sounded interested in Jackson's career for once.

"I'd have to think about that."

"Well, sure must be nice to prance around and sing and make money."

"Yup."

It was a little more complicated than that, not that Hank would understand. In Jackson's case, he still hadn't hit his stride as a musician. No matter what he said to Hank, Hank would bring it down to Jackson finding a way to have fun and make money. But it wasn't always fun to see newer artists pass him by with stellar recording contracts because they had connections. Or a better management team who pushed for them. A star-making producer. Or maybe just more talent. There was a hell of a lot of "business" to show business and he'd found that out the hard way.

Sometimes he wished everything could be as simple as life on a ranch, where hard work equaled a direct reward.

"We'll be late if we don't head out now," Jackson said, moving toward the door and grabbing Hank's truck keys from the Longhorn-shaped hook by the entrance.

He'd been tasked to pull Hank away from the ranch and down the hill into town. Mima, Eve, and everyone else would meet them at Trinity Church and after that they'd all make their way to the Wild Rose for dinner.

They arrived in time to see Mima and Eve just ahead of them, walking toward the entrance of the chapel behind Sadie and Lincoln. Eve wore a short dress that hit well above her knees, a tight denim jacket over it, and some fancy cowgirl boots. Her hair was down, and she threw her head back, sharing a laugh with Mima. She saw him walk in, and her grin went even wider.

"Hank!" Eve walked right past Jackson with outstretched arms to his father. The man worthy of her smile. "I haven't seen much of you lately."

Over Hank's shoulder, Eve shared a conspiratorial wink with Jackson. Ha. She thought this was funny making it seem that she hadn't even noticed him.

"If it ain't the most beautiful vet in all of Texas," his father said, giving her a hug. "You'll sit with me at dinner tonight, darlin'. No one else deserves you."

"She'll sit with me, son," Mima said. "I need my right hand."

While that love fest went on, Jackson walked past them to the chapel. It was just his luck that like so many structures in Stone Ridge, the building was exactly the same from the outside. White clapboard building, steeple, and belfry. Big, welcoming sign that spelled out:

Stephens and Carver wedding this Saturday
Sadie and Lincoln

He broke out in a cold sweat as he walked up the steps again for the first time in eight years. There was a memory in each step.

Catching up with Lincoln, he clapped him on the back. "Tell me they've at least renovated the inside."

"No such luck, brother. Same old hard pews which are hell on a rancher's back. All the extra funds go to help the poor. Pastor June is very insistent on that."

"Don't worry, Jackson," Sadie said. "I have a different color theme."

He hooked a finger at his chest. "Worried? Me?"

A different *color* theme. Why sure, that ought to do it. Might make more of a difference if he could remember their color theme, but he'd been far less interested in any of the wedding details than he'd been in his bride. She'd tortured him by making him stay away for a week before the wedding, so their honeymoon night would be special. Ironic.

A few minutes later the pastor directed everyone to their places. Bridesmaids and groomsmen lined up, he and Eve sent toward the very back since they'd come in last just before Sadie and her father.

"This isn't awkward at all," Jackson said as he and Eve waited for the procession to begin. "Everyone is watching us."

"It will be over soon," Eve said quietly, not looking at him.

He rolled his shoulders. "I don't mind being paired with you. Just wish it were anywhere but here."

"That makes two of us."

Each bridesmaid held a fake bouquet filled with bright ribbons and Jackson noticed Eve's hands were shaking. Either that, or some critter was caught in the arrangement.

He reached for her hand and squeezed it. "I've got you, baby."

This earned him a wistful smile.

The line moved, and ahead of him, Sadie's friend Lucy took the arm of Lincoln's best friend, Wade, and they moved down the line.

"Let's do this," Jackson said quietly, and offered his arm.

Eve linked her arm with his and slowly walked beside him in time to the organist. Her arm felt soft and warm. She appeared to be in some sort of trance. Her eyes were staring straight ahead, no smile, walking zombie-like to the altar.

This moment was probably hardest on her. When sides were taken, most everyone rallied to his defense. At the time, he'd appreciated it. Now, not so much. He felt very protective about Eve and on the actual wedding day, if anyone dared say a word to her or so much as snicker, they'd have to deal with him.

He and Eve separated at the altar and she went to the bridesmaids' side, while he joined the other groomsmen. The organist played the wedding march and everyone's attention went to the bride as she prepared to walk down the aisle and join Lincoln. Everyone except for Jackson, who was watching his brother. He had such a gobsmacked, love-struck look on his face that for a moment Jackson thought he'd be sick. His stomach clenched uncomfortably while the rest of the family stared with awed smiles and starry eyes. He should be happy for Lincoln but instead he was terrified for him.

He could lose her. Lose everything. Maybe not today, or on the wedding day, but later. Marriages didn't always work out. His parents were a perfect example. Eve's parents, too. For those that actually made it to the altar, fifty percent of them ended in divorce. He didn't see how everyone else could be so damn hopeful. He looked to Eve, and she was equally starry-eyed as she smiled at Sadie, her eyes shimmering.

That hit him harder than he would have imagined. Eve,

after all she'd been through, believed in love. Believed in forever.

Finally, the ordeal was over, and they all filed out again. At the back of the chapel, he was one of the first to rush through the chapel doors where he could catch his breath. A small crowd dispersed to their vehicles, and Jackson did a fairly good job ignoring the fact that Eve piled into a car with Mima and Beau, Sadie's very single brother. Jackson drove Hank to the Wild Rose, where they'd be having the so-called "fancy" dinner.

He walked in front of Hank, opening the door for him. Then Jackson strode over to the no-host bar and ordered himself a double.

He found Lincoln, already taking a seat next to Sadie at the main table. Others were still milling about, chatting, and finding their seats. Sadie's parents and Beau, the other bridesmaids and groomsmen. All people he knew but hadn't seen or talked to since he'd been back.

"You're really doing this," Jackson said, clapping Lincoln on the shoulder. "Gettin' hitched."

"Can't wait to make this woman my wife." He tenderly kissed Sadie.

"Y'all won't have to wait much longer."

"You okay?" Lincoln asked.

"Sure."

Jackson narrowed his eyes. Eve now had her hand on Beau's shoulder, leaning in to say something to him. He needed another stiff drink. Maybe he'd get his Dad to drive them back.

They'd be eating soon, and Jackson figured he'd get another drink in the meantime. He noticed that Eve had walked over to the bar alone, and it was as good a time as any.

"White wine spritzer, please," Eve ordered and then she

noticed him. "Hi again, you."

"Hey, you." He ordered a single shot this time, deciding to pace himself. "You look beautiful."

"Thanks, and so do you. I mean, handsome. Not...not beautiful."

"I don't know about you, but that was easier than I thought it would be. Walking down the aisle with you."

"Oh, me too. So easy."

"Eve..."

There were a million things he wanted to say to her. He wanted to ask her whether she'd ever consider coming out to Nashville to visit him. Whether she'd ever consider giving them another chance.

He was one sick puppy. Lovesick, and getting way ahead of himself. Eight *years*. They'd spent eight years apart and frankly weren't the same two people anymore. There was no getting around that fact. She was still dealing with the repercussions from her past, and so was he.

"What?"

*I love you.* He wanted to have the guts to say it when she was wide awake.

He cleared his throat. "Nothing. I forgot I already said you look beautiful. I hate repeating myself."

"You charmer." She glanced at the table, nearly everyone seated now. "We better go find seats."

"Wait," he said, getting tired of talking to her back.

He stepped in front of her, blocking her way. "We should sit together."

"I-I have to sit with Mima," she said. "She needs me."

"Then I'll sit on your left side. You don't have to talk to me, but you have to know that everyone here is acting like they're sneaking around landmines whenever we're too close to each other."

"What are you saying?"

"I'm saying we need to show everyone that we're gettin' along fine. At least in private. Might as well let everyone else in on our secret."

"Secret?"

"Face it. You like me." He grinned.

"And you like me."

Sadie rushed up to Eve. "You better come quick. They put a fancy bread tray out and Mima is trying to butter her bread with her left hand. She's already dropped the knife twice and the pastor looks scared."

"Excuse me." Eve gave him the hint of a smile and followed Sadie.

Jackson took a few seconds to get his bearings, and then went to join the family.

*Oh, yeah so easy walking down the aisle with Jackson.*

Frightening what a good liar she'd become. It would have been easier if there were no feelings left for him at all, but Eve obviously still had uncomfortable emotions that she couldn't ignore. Deep feelings that went beyond anger and pain. Love. Desire. They were strings winding themselves around her heart until she couldn't breathe.

He'd whispered that he loved her when he'd thought she was asleep. Some days, it was all she could think about. She didn't honestly believe in second chances, least of all that she would ever be deserving of one with Jackson. But even *she* wanted to believe in true love. In two people who were meant to be together, and no matter what obstacles stood in their way, nothing and no one could keep them from being together.

She'd been hardly able to draw in a single breath inside the chapel. But then she'd seen Sadie walking with her father, so filled with joy that the intensity threatened to blow the ceiling right off the rafters. Eve's heart swelled for her friend, who deserved every kind of happiness. She'd never once taken Lincoln for granted. Not once.

Toasts and their dinner finally over two long hours later, Eve just wanted to go home, get in her jammies, and go to sleep. Morning always came too early at the ranch.

"I'll be right with you," Eve said to Mima. "Just need to visit the ladies' room."

"Go ahead, sugar. I'm fine." Mima waited next to the entrance with Hank.

It was silly that they'd come in separate cars, but she and Mima weren't sure how long it would take Jackson to prod Hank away from the cattle. Turned out to be not nearly as long as anticipated. Washing her hands, she took a glance in the mirror. The woman in the mirror thought she was putting on a good act, but it was all a show. She was a washed-up shell because the attack hadn't just taken her hearing. It took her hope. Her spirit. But she'd been gradually getting her old self back. She was content to spend the rest of her life in Stone Ridge, for the most part, until the moment Jackson arrived.

She'd *thought* there was no passion left in her. No desire. She'd certainly never felt a hint of it in years, even though Beau and many others had been after her for a long while. And Beau Stephens was as classically handsome as Sadie was beautiful, but he didn't do a thing for Eve. She'd tried for a long time to feel something for him, or for anyone else. But she hadn't felt the throb and pulse of desire again until Jackson strode back into the family kitchen and ordered her outside so he could fire her.

Then suddenly she'd experienced every emotion under the sun. Blazing hostility, paralyzing fear, and don't forget deep regret. Desire. Lust. The emotions were too much, too intense, and she wanted to shut them all down. Go back to being numb again. If only he'd *let* her. But no, bit by tender bit, he was making her love him again.

Eve came out to a mostly empty restaurant. No one was where she'd last seen them, Mima and Hank included. What in the world. She was digging for her cell phone when Jackson came walking out from the back room.

"I hope everything was to your satisfaction, Mr. Carver," Shula Velasquez, the manager, said. "Please do come again."

"Thanks. Y'all did a great job." When he noticed Eve, he stopped and slid her a half smile. "You're still here?"

"Have you seen Mima? I drove her."

"I was in the back. Told Hank to wait for me."

"Maybe they're outside." Eve went to open the door, but Jackson beat her to it, holding it open.

The parking lot was empty save for two vehicles, and one of them was Hank's four-wheel drive. Mima's truck, which Eve drove here, was now gone.

"Looks like they left us." Jackson snorted. "Subtle."

"The Carvers have never been known for their finesse."

"You damn right." Jackson scanned the parking lot, then, hand on the small of her back, he led her toward the truck. "Get in the truck, woman. Looks like I have to take you home."

She accepted his hand to hoist herself into the passenger seat. "Clearly, you're a Carver through and through."

Inside the truck, the close quarters were strangely intimate.

She breathed in the wonderful woodsy scent of him and told herself she was only intrigued by Jackson because she hadn't been with a man for so long. To keep her excitement from bubbling over straight into anxiety, Eve employed an old trick. She comforted herself with the smallest of details. She strapped herself into her seat belt and heard it click into place. Adjusted the seat, which had last seated a much taller person. Routine was comfort. Safety.

But Jackson was of no comfort at all as he sat beside her, causing her heart to race wildly. She was alone with him, this time with no one around to interrupt. No one to question what the hell did they think they were doing, jumping right back into a relationship like they had good sense.

Eve didn't even know if she could remember *how* to be intimate with someone. They'd just spent the night together, simply sleeping next to each other, which had been so warm and comforting. And thrilling. But she still felt unnaturally shy around the man she'd first given herself to at age sixteen.

Because she just wasn't that young girl any longer, not even the twenty-year-old that thought she was ready to be married. It took a lot more than good sex and combustible chemistry to keep two people together long-term. Mutual respect, common life goals, and a deep trust in each other.

Jackson plugged his phone in through the stereo system and began swiping through it.

"Sometime tonight?" she said.

Head bent, he fooled with his phone. "Can't wait to be rid of me?"

"No, not at all. I just...I get up early and I'm already tired." She yawned to emphasize her point.

But nothing about Jackson would ever make her yawn. He'd always meant excitement, thrills, and red-hot lust. She couldn't think of a single reason to avoid spending time alone with him, other than fear of what *she* might do.

Dear Lord, there could be no more doubt. She was avoiding *intimacy*. This should not surprise her, because she hadn't been close to anyone since Bobby. And before that, it had just been Jackson. Always Jackson.

He finally, thank you, God, stop fiddling with his phone.

Brett Young sang "In Case You Didn't Know" through the speakers, and Eve's shoulders unkinked.

"This is very convenient for me," Jackson said, as he pulled out of the lot. "They played right into my hands."

She smirked. "Just don't forget there are two of us involved in this plan of yours."

"Of course, and by the time I'm done, it will also be your plan."

"My, you're confident."

"I prefer to call it positive thinking."

"Where are we going?" she asked, as they passed the road that would lead them to the ranch.

"See if you can guess." He flashed her an easy smile, wide enough to display both dimples.

"Oh, you've got to be kidding me," she said a few minutes later when he made another turn.

She'd bet her Texas veterinary license that Jackson was taking her to Holiday Lake. Also known as the most popular make-out spot in Stone Ridge.

"Before you panic, remember that this is also the best stargazing spot in town."

"You want to stargaze with me?"

He reached for her hand. "Yeah. And anything else you want."

Eve's wanted a lot more than kisses from Jackson, but her mind hadn't yet caught up to her body. Her thoughts were reminding her that, for her, being intimate was a huge step in a relationship.

Jackson pulled the truck past the entrance to Holiday Lake, which was less a lake than a large pond. But when he drove the truck straight out into the field, past the trees, she remembered why she'd loved it here. The clearing gave way to the best view of stars in Stone Ridge. Jackson helped her out of the truck, taking her hand and leading her to the tailgate.

The June night was warm and there seemed to be no sounds at all in the quiet of the night.

They both hopped on and sat, their legs swinging over the edge, holding hands.

"Tell me about the last eight years," Jackson suddenly said. "I know about two of the worst things that ever happened to you, but I have a feeling there may have been some good stuff I missed."

"Eight years? That's a long time."

"A recap."

Touched that he'd want to know what she'd been doing, what he'd missed, she didn't quite know where to begin. She told him about Marisol, her roommate and good friend, about her dorm room, and later the apartment they shared.

"Tell me about this dude you almost married."

"I didn't almost marry Bobby!"

"You said you might have married him someday."

"Wow, that's not at all the same thing."

"What was he like?" Jackson pressed, squeezing her hand.

"Nice. Bobby was good to me, very sweet."

"But not as sweet as me, right?" He grinned.

That made Eve laugh. She couldn't remember laughing as much as she had recently. "I probably wasn't really in love with Bobby."

"Good." He nudged her. "Keep going."

For the next hour, Eve shared the life she'd had so far. She told Jackson about her veterinary program, how hard she worked, and how she'd excelled. Whenever she came near anything to do with the attack, or the setbacks she'd had, she glossed over that. She took him all the way to her graduation, with honors, to coming back to Stone Ridge with no money and a pile of student debt, and later joining Annabeth's practice.

"I should meet her." He'd pulled Eve between his long legs and as she talked, from time to time he'd rest his chin in the crook of her shoulder.

"You will," Eve said, leaving out the part where Annabeth didn't think Eve had any business rekindling something with Jackson. "Annabeth loves country music. She's from Austin."

"Did you ever think of staying in College Station to work as a vet? Or any larger city?"

"No," Eve said. "This is home."

"I'm beginning to realize that."

"Good, because we've missed—I've missed you." Sitting up, she turned in the circle of his arms to face him.

"Yeah?" He grinned and his face took on a positively boyish look.

They were nearly nose to nose, so close they couldn't tuck a breath between them. His mouth came crashing down on hers in a long, deep kiss that had her fisting his shirt, moaning softly. When his hand slipped under the skirt of her dress to glide up and down her leg, she let him. That seemed to heat things up and he groaned when he dipped a finger inside her panties and touched soft flesh. The delicious touch filled her with a sweet ache. She arched her back, wanting, needing so much more.

"God, Eve," he breathed. "Baby."

He covered her with hot, wet kisses. Up the column of her neck, his tongue darting in and out of the shell of her ear. But when he rolled on top of her, his big body pinning her, Eve froze. She hadn't seen that coming, but he was so strong. So much bigger than her. She almost couldn't move and her mind went to a dark place.

"What's wrong?" He took some of his weight off her, pulling back to search her eyes.

"Nothing, I'm..." She fought for composure, worried she'd offend him. "I'm sorry."

God, she was such a mess. After all that therapy, and all this time. Why couldn't she just be normal again?

"Don't be sorry," Jackson said gently, bringing her hand up to his lips. "This is going too fast for you."

"It's not that I don't want you. This. I want you. And I want to be ready." Fingers on the pads of her eyelids, she pushed back the tears.

"But you're not. That's okay." He brushed a kiss across her knuckles, then pulled her close. "Let's just sit here for a few more minutes. If we don't get back soon, Mima might just call the FBI."

# CHAPTER 20

*L*illian didn't think she'd ever get Hank to understand. Then again, he was so dense he didn't realize Lillian knew about him and Brenda. She'd been his first love, he still cared about her deeply, and had likely never stopped.

Hank, who rarely came off that hill at calving time, had been checking in more often, not coincidentally on the same days Brenda would drop in. Brenda, too, had been coming by the ranch and Lillian was certain it wasn't only to see her daughter. They'd dated once, years ago, but then Brenda had married Ricardo, and Hank had his eye turned by the hurricane that had been Maggie Mae. Then she'd gotten pregnant with Lincoln and that was the end of Brenda and Hank.

There wasn't a thing she could do about those two now. But there was still a world of possibilities for the next generation.

This matchmaking business was serious, exhausting work. She was an old woman if anyone cared to notice. A little help here and there would be welcome.

Instead Hank had complained the entire ride home. "He's

just going to be mad we left them, Mother. You can't push those two together. Believe me, I wish you could."

"Just leave it to me. I've already made progress. Those two were *laughing* the other night. Making jokes. They're spending a lot of time together."

"Just because they're friends again doesn't mean much. Look at me and Brenda."

"Hank, I don't have time for you and Brenda right now. You should see the way those two look at each other. Do you realize that if Jackson reconciles with Eve, he might actually stay in Stone Ridge? Don't you want that?"

"Well, of course I want my son back home. But he doesn't much care what I want, does he?"

Lillian sighed. Hank had a way of turning everything back around to himself. Ever since Maggie had left him, he'd been a bitter and angry fool. Having done the right thing by her, his resentment made sense, but he'd let it spill into every aspect of his life.

So many times, she'd tried to give Hank advice on how to talk to his youngest son. She'd done the same with Jackson, giving him advice on how to reach his stoic father. But Jackson was too much like his mother, and neither one could take the high road. Both he and Hank continually baited each other.

"I see he's been spending time with you. Jackson is a cowboy at heart. He'll come back home. We just have to make being home a good option."

"I just don't know if Eve is enough to keep him home. She wasn't before."

That might have been true then, but Jackson now realized what he'd lost. She'd caught Jackson following Eve with his gaze as if he couldn't help himself. Yes, there was still something there. All it needed was a little watering.

And the quilt.

She'd heard about the quilt from Sadie, bless her tender heart. She was on Lillian's side. Eve had *kept* her marriage quilt, given to her by the SORROW ladies. All these many years later, a quilt that should have surely been lost in a move at some point might be somewhere in this house. Unless it could still be somewhere in Brenda's tiny cottage but that was doubtful. Sadie was already searching in her cabin where Eve still had some boxes but had suggested looking in the Carver home's attic. Lillian was hardly in a position to search up there with a broken arm.

She remembered some boxes in a corner of the barn and set out to look there after Hank had dropped her off and headed up the hill. If she found the quilt, she planned to have it cleaned, pressed, and maybe presented to Eve as a sort of "wake-up" call. She still loved Jackson, and they could have a second chance. With no help, because after the rehearsal dinner, Daisy ran off Lord knew where, Lillian didn't know where to start. She went for a box in the corner, one marked "memories" but there was nothing in it but old yearbooks and concert tickets. They all appeared to be Jackson's things.

"What are you doin' now, woman?" Albert asked.

Lillian jumped at least a foot. "Don't sneak up on me like that, old man! You're going to give me a heart attack."

"Alone out in the barn with all the spiders? What should I think? You've finally lost your marbles."

*Spiders.* She cringed. "I'm l-looking for something important."

"Must be, to risk walking into a spider web like you just did."

"What?" She did a little dance, turning in circles, brushing herself off.

Albert laughed and slapped his knee. "You fall for that every time. Never gets old."

"You're wrong about that. It got old a long time ago. Everything gets old and damaged. People. Quilts."

"Barns. Clothes. Books."

"Would you stop? This is important! Years go by. First eight years, and then twenty. Thirty. Pretty soon a lifetime. And I can't let that happen without finding this quilt!"

She continued to the next box. Nothing but clothes. Eve and Jackson would be back soon. She would have to continue this search another time. Tomorrow she'd call Brenda and get her searching, too. Lord knew no one else was going to help her.

"What quilt you talkin' about?" Albert leaned back, having settled himself on a bale of hay. "Ours?"

"No, you fool! Eve and Jackson's quilt. She kept it and I believe it could very well be somewhere in this house. Maybe if I find it, and get her to look at it again, she'll see."

"See *what?*"

"That eight years have already gone by. She can't let another *month* go by."

Lillian would rather eat dirt than admit it, but she still missed her ornery cowboy. He'd always been on her last nerve, and had she known she'd miss him this much, maybe she would have enjoyed the years more. Been kinder to him. At least she'd had the years, which was more than she could say for Eve. The girl had to get on with it! Time was a tickin'.

What had to be an hour later, her results netted her a big fat zero. She'd have to bring Brenda into this. Maybe Eve had left it behind at her mother's house before she moved to college.

Then she noted the time and wondered where on earth those two could be, anyway.

"Oh, Albert, maybe they've been in an accident." She wrung her hands. "I threw them together and maybe Jackson got distracted by her beauty and veered off the road.

The truck rolled and spun and landed in a ditch. Now they're cut and bleeding. Maybe unconscious. What have I done?"

"Woman, sure wish you'd taken up writing true-crime novels. Always did have too big of an active imagination when it comes to blood." Albert shook his head and sat up. "It could be that your plan is working. They're talking. Or maybe doin' *more* than talking."

"You think so?" The thought encouraged her. "I still have to find that quilt. Lord only knows where it could be, and I can't very well ask Eve. Then it won't be a surprise."

"I'll keep an eye out."

"Thank you, Albert." She shook her head, shocked by her thoughts. But they were true.

"Sometimes you're the only thing that keeps me sane."


JACKSON HELD Eve's hand all the way back to the ranch. Seeing her fall apart in his arms, crying because she thought she'd disappointed him somehow…that ripped away at his heart. Just tore whole chunks off. So, she wasn't ready. Not a big deal for him. He was just going to have to stop teasing himself and working himself up. From now on it would have to be her idea.

He opened the front door for Eve, watched her walk in first, then followed her into the kitchen, where Mima sat at the kitchen table, boxes filled with wedding-favor jam jars lined up in neat rows.

She stood up, hand on hip. "Lawd have mercy, where in tarnation you two been? I was about to call the law."

Jackson slid her a smile. "Don't pretend y'all didn't leave us at the restaurant so we would have no choice but to ride back together."

"Didn't mean for you to take half the night." She waved

her hand in the air dismissively. "Hope you two had a grand old time. You just earned me ten more wrinkles."

"I'm sorry, Mima," Eve said in a soft voice.

"No, she's not sorry. It's my fault. Blame it on me. I took her for a drive, and we lost track of time. Not that it matters much since we're both adults."

"I'm going to bed," Eve announced.

"You go right on ahead, sugar. Jackson knows the rest of us are all early risers 'round here."

"Maybe Eve could sleep in tomorrow," Jackson suggested.

It was as if he'd suggested that Texas was the worst state in the country. Mima looked flabbergasted. "What on earth *for?*"

His voice went up a notch. "Because she's been workin' too *hard* around here. She deserves a break."

"Are you sick?" Mima asked her.

Now Eve slid him a surprised look that made him feel she didn't much appreciate his interference. But her getting up so early to feed them plus all the ranch hands breakfast, slaving over a hot stove, didn't sit well with him.

"No. I'm fine."

"Good night to you then," Mima said.

Eve gave him a long look and turned to go. "Night."

"Good night," he grumbled and watched her walk away.

"There, isn't that better? You and Eve, friends again. Good night now."

"Not so fast."

Mima stopped in her tracks and turned. "What is it?"

"You should have told me about Eve."

"Now *that* really wasn't for me to tell."

"I know everything. And while I wanted to kill the man when I first heard, Eve is right. My anger is only going to poison me. Not…him. But I wonder if y'all know how much it kills me that I wasn't there to help."

"It wasn't my place. And I found out two *years* after the whole ordeal had even happened. Too late for any of us to do a thing. My poor sweet Eve, she felt so guilty about what she'd done to our family."

*My poor sweet Eve.*

What about *his* Eve? She wasn't a poor thing and she wasn't always sweet. She was feisty. Ornery. Ready to take on the world. Now she was frightened. Shell shocked. Damaged.

"You be careful not to pity her now," Mima said. "She won't have none of that."

"Hell, no. I know Eve better than anyone else in this family and I know she'd kill me for feeling sorry for her. There's nothing to feel sorry about. She's strong. Beautiful. Kind."

"Son, you knew the old Eve. She's not the same young woman anymore. I suggest you get to know who she is now."

"And I suggest y'all let me remind her of *who* she is. That Eve is still in there somewhere and I intend to find her."

"Just be careful. I see what's happening here, and it's no secret that I'd like you two back together. But you can't start something up with her and leave again. Of course, you're more than welcome to come home to stay. We have the land. You could build a beautiful home not far from the one Lincoln and Sadie will be livin' in. Soon enough, Daisy will find someone, too, and live in her own house on our land. All of us together again."

He snorted. "I guess this is what you wanted all along. But I live in Nashville now. I have a home there. Good friends and connections."

"And Eve is here in Stone Ridge. Along with the rest of your *family*."

"I'll visit often now that Eve and I are talkin' again. We tour through Texas all the time. She'll come visit me."

"We both know this is about more than that. It's about

you taking your rightful place beside your brother. You're a rancher at heart."

"I can be, but I'm also a hell of a musician."

She cocked her head. "Do you like that life? Traveling in a bus and sleeping in hotel rooms on a bed one million people have slept in before you?"

Jackson rolled his eyes. "They change and wash the sheets, Mima. But no, I don't like that part."

Lately he'd been thinking of how he might make Texas home base and hit the road from here. Or he could open up a home recording studio and record here. Unfortunately, access to the best engineers was in Nashville, or Los Angeles. Both not exactly a commute to Stone Ridge. There were lots of details that would have to be worked out before any of it could happen. But more than ever before, he was tempted. It didn't mean he had to give up entirely on music. He could find a different approach to it all.

When Mima retired for the night, Jackson went to his bedroom in search of his guitar. He plugged in the headphone cord and started strumming. Before he'd left Nashville, he'd started work on a song that was to be a gift to Lincoln and Sadie on their wedding day. Since arriving, he'd completed it. Jackson believed it to be the best song he'd written in years, and he planned on recording it. This would be his baby. His song. He was tired of being a hard-working midlist musician and had paid his dues. Maybe he didn't have the big name that would cause a song to jump to number one, but he wrote the songs. If one didn't work, he could write another.

Years on the road still left him feeling at times that he'd gotten nowhere. He'd watched others record his songs while he paid his dues touring and opening for bigger names. It hadn't been the plan to sell his songs, but when he'd needed money and others wanted his songs, he'd sold them. Then just gone back on tour with the band. Someday soon it would be his turn for a runaway hit. For now, there was something calming about being out in the country, away from the bright lights and hustle of the city. He was enjoying the break.

While he hadn't enjoyed the bull-sperm complaining from Hank, he appreciated riding Taco again and doing the hard and sometimes punishing work of a rancher. The past few days he'd helped tag cattle, lifted one out of a muddy ditch, and nearly been kicked by a pissed-off mama when he'd tagged her baby. Fortunately, he was still fast on his feet. By the end of each day he'd been so spent that he'd collapsed in his bed, Winston at his feet. There was no time to sit around feeling sorry for yourself on a ranch. Something needed attention every second, or so it seemed.

And he'd forgotten something else: he kind of loved the life. The physical exertion left his mind free to wander and daydream. It was how he'd written his first song. Sometimes the best songs came when your mind was free and your body was too tired to interfere with random thoughts.

He might not sit a horse like Eve did, but he could hold his own in the saddle.

Just like that his thoughts were back to Eve. He couldn't have possibly expected to feel so connected to her after all this time. But he'd already fallen in love with her all over again. As he had the first time he'd seen her riding bareback at the Truehart ranch, he admired her courage even more than her obvious physical beauty. She'd endured more than any woman should in a lifetime, but she still didn't want anyone's pity. She was still putting herself out there every day working, struggling. He'd known some women to make more of a fuss over a hangnail.

No, Eve was not getting away from him a second time.

"Daisy, I'm going to be needin' your help today," Lillian said from the breakfast table.

"Why? Where's Eve?" Daisy spun around the kitchen searching for her.

"She's taking the day off. Jackson insisted. She's over at Brenda's having breakfast. Jackson went with her."

"Wait. What? Jackson did?" Daisy squeaked. "You mean those two are—"

"Friends again."

"How did I miss this?" Daisy slid her coffee mug on the table and sat. "Have I really been away that much?"

"Keep up, child. Things happen fast when your Mima Carver has a plan. Those two will be headed for the altar again or my name isn't Lillian Pearl Carver."

"I don't know about that. Jackson lives in Nashville now. He really likes it there."

Lillian waved that thought away. "That isn't *home*. He'll move back. All he needs is a little motivation. You'll see."

"I mean, I like Eve and all but..."

"But *what*?"

"She *left* Jackson."

"Well, in a lopsided town like ours, a woman sometimes wonders if she's picked the right man. We hold the record for most runaway brides in history."

Lillian realized this was generous of her. Eve couldn't do any better than a Carver man if she lived a thousand years.

Bless her heart.

"But sometimes you *know*. You don't need to date anyone else no matter how many other choices there are."

Lillian had a bad feeling Daisy referred to that Wade, the no-good rodeo circuit bareback rider. Because of him, for years Lincoln had also risked his life on the circuit. Thank the good Lord he'd come to his senses because of Sadie. "Rodeo Wade" and Daisy would wind up together over Lillian's cold dead body.

"What do you need my help with today? Breakfast? I can get that done and then I'll be out of your hair."

"What I have in mind could take a while unless we get lucky."

Daisy winced. "It's my day off and I'd planned to go up to Daddy's and help more."

"If by 'help' you mean flirt with that no-good Wade, then you can forget your plans."

"But Daddy needs help."

"Come on now. Cattle know what to do seeing as they've been doin' it for millennia without help from any cowboy. They don't need any supervision. It's mother nature."

"Um, well..."

"Admit it, Daisy. You've done run out of excuses to help your poor old grandmother. Now, here's what I need you to do for me. We're on the hunt for a very special quilt."

Lillian's cast was to come off tomorrow, the day before the wedding, and she'd like to shake a leg on this project.

More importantly, Eve would return to work and Lillian was certain she'd make plans to move before long.

If Daisy had no luck today, Lillian would have to help Brenda turn her place upside down. Then she'd help Sadie do the same. After all, Lincoln and Sadie weren't coming back to the cabin after their honeymoon. They were set to move into Lincoln's cabin once the kitchen was complete.

A few minutes later, Lillian had Daisy in the attic while she stood at the bottom of the ladder instructing.

"How do you know it's not at Brenda's?"

"I've got her lookin', too."

"I curse the day you broke your arm!" Daisy said, shoving a box. "There are a lot of boxes up here. Oh, and a tricycle. Is that mine? Good Lord, do we ever throw anything away around here?"

"Hush now. Look for boxes with Eve's handwriting on them. It should be in one of them."

"Great. That's a lot of help!"

"Look against the wall."

Lillian heard shoving and pushing, grumbling, and a curse word or two. "Sadie said it *might* be in one of these boxes. She said Eve kept it."

"Then maybe Sadie should come up here and look."

"I'm sure she would if I asked her, but I'm *askin'* my only granddaughter."

Daisy squealed. "Oh my gawd!"

Lillian hardly dared hope. "You found it?"

"I think I saw a spider! Help!"

"What's up?" Jackson's voice said from behind Lillian.

She jumped. He'd snuck up on her. And as luck would have it, Eve was right behind him. Of course she was.

"Good mornin'. We're just…lookin' for something old for Sadie's weddin'."

Jackson quirked a brow. "I thought you already found something when you broke your arm."

"Oh *my* goodness. You're right, I did. Guess I'm gettin' forgetful." To be convincing, she tapped her temple.

Jackson cocked his head and studied her, his forehead creased in concern. She was apparently too good of an actor.

"Not *that* forgetful!" Lillian swatted him.

Daisy came down the steps and brushed her hands together. "I'm *so* done. I just had a traumatic experience up there with a spider and his entire family."

"Aw, Daisy," Eve said, putting her arm around Daisy's shoulders and leading her toward the kitchen. "Let me make you some blueberry waffles for lunch. Breakfast for lunch used to be your favorite thing."

"I thought you had the day off," Daisy said.

"I do, but I don't mind cookin'."

Eve was in an awfully good mood this morning. Then again, so was her grandson as his smiling gaze followed Eve's movements. And there had been an awful lot of smiling and lingering looks between those two. Progress had been made. Now she simply had to open up Eve's eyes to the facts. Jackson loved her plain and simple, and if she asked him to stay in Stone Ridge, by golly he would. He wouldn't be the first country musician to live in Texas. The fans and all the other musicians could have Nashville. Jackson needed the privacy and relative anonymity of his hometown. He needed his family close. What he needed more than anything was unconditional love and acceptance and to never be abandoned again.

"Want to tell me what's really going on here?" Jackson turned his gaze back to Lillian.

"Spending time with my granddaughter, keeping her away from that no-good Wade. Why? You suspect me of committing a high crime or somethin'? Hiding a body in the attic?"

His eyes crinkled with a smile. "I could see you hiding a lot, but definitely not a body."

Lillian could hear the sounds of pans and the mixer going. Daisy chatting with Eve, recovered from the trauma of a spider. The moment felt normal. But nothing felt business as usual since she'd started her search for that quilt. It was ridiculous to think that a piece of cotton could bring two people together, permanently, but Lillian was convinced if she could locate it, everything else would fall into place. They would both remember that, once, they'd had forever in their sights and could have it again.

"Hey," Eve said, coming down the hall. "Y'all having blueberry waffles with us?"

Jackson strolled past her toward the kitchen and as he passed, Lillian noticed when he reached out for Eve's hand. "Try to stop me."

Eve smiled and the pinch of joy in her eyes gave Lillian a gallon of hope.

# CHAPTER 22

*W*edding day arrived and with it a set of nerves Jackson didn't know he still owned. He no longer had any worries that Sadie would show up. Instead, his fear was entirely focused on performing the love song he'd written as a gift to Sadie and Lincoln. He'd now played in clubs across the US. But today he'd sing an emotional song in a close and intimate setting.

A few months ago, Jackson had started writing this song for Lincoln and Sadie as an homage to true and lasting love. The kind he wished for Sadie and Lincoln. At the time, he'd hoped and dreamed about a love that felt completely out of reach for him. Foreign.

But now the once-hazy picture had solidified to that of a woman who was no longer out of reach. No longer a dream. No longer just his painful past. Eve was warm and loving and everything he'd ever wanted. She clearly carried a great deal of emotional baggage, some of which was not his responsibility. It didn't mean he wouldn't try to fix it, but it did mean this all might take a long time to resolve.

When he considered all she'd been through, and how

hard she was still fighting to get her spirit back, he couldn't ask her to give up her life here and come with him to Nashville. She had a life in Stone Ridge, and a profession she loved that was fulfilling and secure. Show business was the opposite of secure.

That alone had made his decision so much easier.

"Jackson! Telephone," Mima called out from the kitchen, holding the phone in her right hand and wiggling it. "Oh, it's so good to have my hand back! Says his name is Billy."

"Thanks," Jackson said, taking the phone. Billy was an old band member, currently making bank working as a studio musician in Nashville. They'd remained in touch over the years. "How are you, my man?"

"Hey! Your manager gave me this number. Been trying your cell nonstop. Just thought I'd tell you I laid tracks down for Winona last week and she asked about you."

Winona had always meant trouble for him. For one, they'd spent too much time drinking when they'd first met. The memory he had of her was more of a drinking buddy than a wife. But facts were, she *had* been his wife, if even for a few months. She did like to lord that fact over him, as if he owed her something for the honor. He'd eventually walked away from all the hard drinking, but Winona still had a reputation as a hell raiser. She'd close out her stadium shows by announcing to the audience that she'd worked hard and was now going to go have herself a few tequila shots.

"What is she up to?"

"No good, I'm sure," Billy continued. "She said she needs to talk to you and when someone told her you'd gone back to Stone Ridge, she said it was *urgent* that she talk to you."

Jackson spoke between clenched teeth. "Did you give her this number?"

"Hell, no, brother. Just thought you should know."

Jackson hoped his manager would have the foresight not

to give out this number to anyone but his closest friends. He'd check his cell phone when they got into town where reception, though still spotty, at least existed.

"Thanks for the heads up," Jackson said and hung up.

He had a feeling what this might be about. Winona was ridiculously jealous of him when she had no right to be. Occasionally, he'd post a photo on his IG with him and a woman he'd dated or even a fan with a backstage pass, and she'd become irate. She'd text and private message him that he was making a mistake dating that woman because she knew her to be a man-eater. The truth was that Winona, a full ten years older than him, was pushing forty and beginning to feel irrelevant.

"Thanks for looking out for me, Wy," he'd text back because he'd learned the hard way not to get on her bad side.

He took one last moment to fool with his tie, grabbed his guitar case, and met Mima in the family room.

"There you are! Oooh don't you look handsome, cowboy," Mima said, finding her purse. "Now, Eve has gone on ahead because Sadie had some kind of emergency. You know weddings. Something always goes wrong."

He snorted. "You mean like the bride not showin' up?"

"Not usually *that* bad." She clutched her chest. "Lord love a duck, you don't think Sadie will run off?"

Attempting to reassure his grandmother, Jackson placed a hand on each of her shoulders. In recent years his aging grandmother had seemed to get tinier. Thinner. But the firecracker spirit was still there, a strong lady who took crap from no one.

"She'll show."

"Sugar, I want you to know something. Eve leavin' you at the altar had nothing to do with you. She loved you as much as a woman *can* love a man. With her whole heart and soul."

"I know she did, and I loved her. But her leaving me at the

altar had everything to do with me. She'd wanted to be reassured that I was choosing her and not just going through with the wedding because it had been planned before the chance to go to Nashville came up. I should have gone after her. She was scared and nervous. We both were." He took a breath. "And I'm afraid she was right. I would have rather waited. Gone to Nashville with the band and been married to her later. But it was too late to change our plans, so I was going through the motions. Eve had more courage than I did."

"That little girl is a fighter and she won't play second fiddle to anyone."

Boy wasn't that the truth. And in a town like Stone Ridge, women did not play seconds to anyone.

"Thank you for taking her in when you did."

"Well, son, you loved her first."

He nodded. "I did."

"And now? You still love her."

"Yeah, I love her." He grinned, knowing he'd made Mima's day.

"Just tell her how you feel. You'll see. Everything will work out."

He glanced over at his guitar case sitting near the front door and thought of the song he'd perform today. After that, Eve would have no doubt as to where she stood with him.

* * *

SADIE WOKE the morning of her wedding overjoyed, even if she was in bed alone. She reached for Lincoln's pillow beside her and hugged it, taking in the wonderful scent that was all his. They'd decided to spend the night before their wedding apart, an old-fashioned throwback which had pleased both her mother and Mima.

Today, Sadie would marry the man she'd adored since she was sixteen years old.

Her phone buzzed, a text from "My Cowboy":

Love you, my bride. Can't wait to get hitched.

Her heart filled with a wave of love tugging her hard with its intensity. She typed back:

I love you, cowboy. Forever and Ever. xoxo

She added a dozen heart emojis.

This morning, her mother wanted to take Sadie to breakfast at their favorite restaurant in Kerrville. Her last breakfast as a single woman. It was a sweet idea, and Sadie appreciated her mother accepting Lincoln. Last year there had been a doctor visiting who expressed interest in Sadie. Mom had run with that, thinking that a physician in the family would ensure Sadie would always be financially secure. But Mom came to accept that Lincoln, one of her son's best friends, would now be an official member of the Stephens family.

As Mom drove them to Kerrville, Sadie could hardly contain her excitement. "Are you sure we'll be back in time? Eve is going to do my hair and makeup before we leave for the church."

"We have plenty of time, honey. You are getting dressed in the bridal suite? No point in driving anywhere in that beautiful dress. It might wrinkle."

"Of course." Her foot jiggled. She didn't like being this far away from her wedding dress.

Though the idea was ridiculous, she couldn't stop thinking something might go wrong today. Maybe someone would spill juice on her wedding dress. Horrors! Or...today would be the day her waist would have expanded enough to where she couldn't fit in it. The thought made her stomach clench. The dress was gorgeous, taffeta, with a sweetheart collar, and a long train. Instead of a veil, she was wearing a simple tiara. Eve would do her hair in a regal bun.

"There's just a few things I wanted to talk to you about before you're married."

"Yeah? What about? Please don't tell me about the wedding night. I already know everything."

Mom made a face. "Yes, I *know*. This is about the bigger picture. Longevity."

Her mother wanted Sadie's marriage to Lincoln to last, and that warmed her, so she'd listen to every word of advice. No matter how outdated. Once they were seated inside The Pancake and had ordered their favorite coconut macadamia nut pancakes and waffles, Sadie steered the conversation.

"I already had the bride's lecture from the women of SORROW. I heard all about the men of Stone Ridge and how special they are. How I should always let Lincoln believe he won the argument even if he didn't."

"I don't care what any of those biddies had to say." Mom took a sip of her coffee.

Sadie laughed. "Tell me what you really think."

"If I'd listened to their advice, I probably wouldn't still be married for more than thirty years."

Sadie patted her mother's hand. "Please don't worry about me and Lincoln. He's never going to leave me, and I'm never going to leave him."

"And you think that's good enough?"

"What do you mean?"

"Two people can be together for decades and still be miserable."

She had a point, of course. "Well, we won't be."

"You've been so in love with Lincoln for so long that you can't even see a single one of his faults. But he does have them, believe me, and you will notice them at some point in the first year of your marriage."

No. Not *her* cowboy.

Sadie was going to object that she already saw some of his faults, but she didn't think Mom meant stuff like being messy.

"Marriage is work, honey. I know you think it's a dream come true right now but eventually the work will come."

"Okay. That's good to know. I'll have to be ready for it."

"You will be. And with love, you can work anything out. Why, look at your father and me. We had our issues last year, but we got through them. I love him now more than ever."

Oh, all this, and her wedding day, too! Sadie couldn't possibly have a fuller heart. Her eyes began to water. She was glad her mother had told her all this before she'd applied her wedding day makeup.

"Other than that, the only real advice for you is to never lie to your husband. Or keep anything from him, because he'll think of that as a lie. Men are funny that way. I speak from experience."

Sadie froze and her voice formed in a tiny squeak once she got some sounds out. "Um, but what about a surprise?"

"I don't mean a surprise, silly goose. That's fine. Just nothing, you know, important. Life changing."

Nothing *life changing*.

Sadie wasn't sure how she got through the rest of the meal, but somehow before long, she and Mom were headed back to her cabin to meet Eve.

Sadie took a shower, her hand lowering to her belly. She wanted to be happy about her baby, and deep down she was doing cartwheels. She'd always wanted children. Loved children. For goodness sake, she was teacher for a reason. But Lincoln had helped raise Jackson and Daisy and he was in no hurry. She and Lincoln had talked about a family, of course, but not right away.

Sadie slipped into her bra, panties, slimming garments, and

hose. She spritzed perfume twice and walked through the mist. Even though she hadn't yet applied makeup, she tried the dress on again. Just to make sure it still fit since this morning, when she'd last tried it on. Yes, it still zipped up as if it held only Sadie, and not Sadie with a little extra surprise in there. *Surprise Sadie.* That almost made her laugh. When there was a knock on her door that she knew must be Eve, Sadie wiggled out of the dress.

Eve breezed in, carrying her backpack, and a clothing bag with her dress. "Ready for this?"

"Oh, yes. My dress still fits."

"You probably won't start showing until another couple of months."

Sadie still felt guilty about telling Eve about the baby before Lincoln. "Do you think you could, you know, keep it to yourself that I told you first about the baby?"

Eve made a motion as if she'd zipped her lips and thrown away the key.

In the next hour, Daisy and Lucy arrived, and Sadie's cabin was filled with straightening irons, curlers, fake eyelashes, hair extensions (Daisy), and spandex undies. Eve set up on the kitchen counter, leaving the small bathroom to the others. Hours later, Sadie's hair was in a beautiful bun, with ringlets pulled out at strategic places. Her makeup was flawlessly applied. The last item was the tiara, and as Eve eased and pinned it on, Sadie did feel like a princess. She was so ready to be a bride today.

Eve drove them to the church, and Sadie and her bridesmaids strutted into the bridal suite annexed to the church. Outside, the air smelled sweet with fresh-cut grass. She'd been gifted with a mild Texas day. Inside, fresh flowers lined windowsills, bright and cheery. Sadie changed first behind the amber carved wood room divider. Eve, Daisy, and Lucy followed, all looking beautiful and slim.

"See ya out there, sis!" Daisy waved and left.

Lucy gave her a hug, then left, too. Eve, of course, was last. She gripped Sadie's shoulders. There were tears in Eve's eyes.

"Don't. You're going to make me cry."

"That's okay. We have false eyelashes today for a reason." And even though a tear slid down Eve's cheek, nothing smudged.

"Thank you for everything," Sadie said. "For being my friend when I cried because Lincoln didn't know I was alive. For having the patience to listen to me go on and on about him. For years."

"That's what best friends are for. Thank you for supporting me even as I made the biggest mistake of my life." She tugged on Sadie's hands, squeezing. "Have I told you how happy I am for you?"

"Yes," Sadie sniffed, not trusting herself to say more. Emotions clogged her throat.

"Okay, I'll see you out there!"

No sooner had Eve left than after a quick knock, the door opened. It was her father. "You about ready, sweetie?"

She held up her finger. "Just one sec, Daddy."

He shut the door. The quiet enveloped her, with thoughts that were too big for this room. Doubt hovered deep inside her.

Lord! Why hadn't she told Lincoln before today? By now, any disappointment would have settled, and he'd have adjusted to their new reality just as she had. Waiting for the honeymoon was a terrible mistake. He'd hate her for keeping this from him. She couldn't start their marriage off with a lie. With something this life changing. Sadie's stomach roiled and pitched and ten minutes before the wedding, she knew that she couldn't go through with this.

She found her phone under a pile of chiffon and dialed the only woman on earth who would understand.

"Eve, can you please come back?" Sadie could barely hold back the tears. "I need you."

"What happened? Did a seam rip?"

If only it were that simple. "Just…please come get me."

"*Get* you?"

Less than two minutes later, Eve strolled inside. "What's wrong?"

"I can't get married."

Eve laughed. "That's funny. Tell the runaway bride that *you* can't go through with your wedding day?"

"I'm serious. I can't marry him…not like this."

"Oh my God, you're serious! Sadie. You can't *do* this! Jackson is going to kill me. And okay, it's not all about me. What about Lincoln? He'll be devastated." She was quiet for a beat. "Is this because you haven't told him about the baby?"

Sadie nodded, trying to bite on her quivering lips. "Waiting for the honeymoon was a bad idea. It's all a big lie."

"Of course it's not a lie! You're going to tell him."

"I wanted to wait, but now I realize not telling him is like lying to him. It's too big. Too…too life changing." Her mother's words. A wise woman Sadie should have confided in before today.

"What do you want me to do? We can fix this."

"I'm going to have to talk to him. I need to see him right *now*." She wrung her hands together. "Can you go get him?"

"Um, sure. We'll just delay the start. I'll talk to the pastor, tell your father, and…" Eve held up her fingers, counting off "to do" items. "What should I tell Lincoln?"

"Just tell him I need to talk to him. I don't know, tell him I'm nervous, and thinking about running!"

"I wouldn't dare!"

"Do whatever you have to do but get my fiancé here so I can tell him he's going to be a daddy."

* * *

Outside, people were still arriving. Mr. Stephens was pacing nearby and stopped to say hello to Beulah and Lloyd Hayes as they arrived. Others were already seated inside, waiting. Jackson was off to the side, seeming to want to blend into the background. Eve took in the sight of him, and her heart nearly stopped. This was exactly what he'd looked like on their wedding day. He'd worn a black tux. He'd been lankier eight years ago. His hair had been longer, down to his neck and parted in the middle. He now walked with a confident swagger he hadn't possessed at twenty-one. He was a man, whereas she'd almost married a boy.

He stepped right in front of her. "What's happening?"

"Oh, n-nothing," she lied. "I just wanted to talk to Lincoln for a sec. Where is he?"

"He's inside waitin' with everyone else. Weddin's about to begin."

Eve's gut burned like a wildfire. "Can you get him for me?"

"What? Now?" Jackson's eyes narrowed. "Are you *serious*?"

"Sadie just needs to talk to him real quick."

Jackson scowled. His voice rose in volume. "This is ridiculous. You *promised* me this wouldn't happen."

"Don't you yell at me. This is none of our business. I'm *tryin'* to fix this." She hooked her thumb behind her. "Go on."

He met her gaze for several seconds and then hoofed it inside the church. A minute later he came back with Lincoln in tow.

"What's wrong?" Lincoln asked, his brow creased. "Is Sadie alright?"

"Lincoln, she just needs to talk to you about something. She—"

Eve didn't get another word out. Lincoln opened the door so fast he was like a streak of lightning.

"What's going on?" Mr. Stephens asked. "Where's Sadie? What's Lincoln doing in there?"

"They'll be right out, Mr. Stephens," Eve said.

"They better be. We're gettin' a late start." He glanced at his watch, then began pacing again.

Eve and Jackson waited outside the suite like guards. Or statues. Or statues of guards. Lord, she was nervous. How would Lincoln react? She couldn't picture him being unhappy about the baby, but he might be angry that she'd waited until now to tell him. Or at the least, shocked.

"She'd *better* get her act together," Jackson said through a tight jaw. "There are a lot of people in the chapel."

"She will."

"I was afraid of this."

"I know."

A moment of silence later, Jackson rolled his shoulders. "This is awkward."

"And way too familiar."

"Isn't it supposed to be bad luck for him to see the bride before the wedding?"

Eve snorted. "You didn't see me. How was our luck?"

"Good point. What is it, anyway? Do *you* know?"

"I do, but I'm not sure if I should say."

"Just tell me this: is she runnin' out on my brother?" His voice sounded deep and dark.

"No. Never."

Because Sadie was a lot smarter than Eve had been. She was going to work this problem out even this late in the game.

"Then what do they have to talk about right before the

weddin' that can't wait?"

Eve sighed. "She's…pregnant."

Jackson's neck swiveled like he'd been slapped. "Is she afraid she's going to have a wardrobe malfunction?"

Eve didn't think it would be possible to laugh, but Jackson's puzzled expression pulled one out of her. "No. She hasn't told him yet, and doesn't think it's fair to wait until after the wedding."

"Like he's going to back out now? Is she nuts? Why scare him like this?"

"She wants to start the marriage off by being perfectly honest. She was going to tell him on the honeymoon."

"Well, I'm glad they're working it out." Jackson was silent for a long beat. "Eve, that day?"

No need to ask what day. *Their* wedding day. She simply looked up at him, wordless, feeling her legs shake and tremble.

"You should have talked to me before the wedding. Then you would have known that I wanted to get married. I loved you and I would have *never* regretted staying behind. Maybe Nashville would have come later for me. For *us*. Who knows? But when you left me? I was so angry." He reached for her hand, threaded his fingers through hers. "I made a mistake, too. And I need you to forgive me for that."

Eve never thought she'd hear this out of Jackson. An apology. For a moment she froze. "Forgive you?"

"It was a mistake not to come and find you. I should have swallowed my pride and maybe we would be married today."

"Maybe so, or maybe we would be divorced."

"I doubt that. But I'm sorry for my part." He pulled her into his arms. "So sorry."

"I know, Jackson. I know." She pulled out of his arms. "I need to tell the pastor we're startin' late."

"Let's both do it." And Jackson held out his hand.

# CHAPTER 23

*L*incoln's heart pounded in his chest like a horse stampede. He was about to find out why Sadie had been acting so strangely these past two weeks. It couldn't be because she wanted to back out. Sadie was his and his alone. And he was hers. But somehow, he'd failed to reassure her that he wanted this moment. Marriage and commitment. A true partnership and real love. It had taken so long to find her, and when he did, turned out she'd always been there. Right under his nose.

He wouldn't lose her now due to nerves, or whatever else. When he threw open the door to the suite, she was already facing him. Dressed in white, she was a cross between an angel and a princess. In her hands she held a bouquet filled with purple flowers which she carefully set aside. She looked radiant. A little like the sun. He'd never seen anything or anyone more beautiful in this life and for a moment, he couldn't speak.

"What is it, baby? You wanted to talk to me?" He drew her into his arms.

"Oh, Lincoln."

He nearly had a heart attack at the anguish in her voice and pulled back to search her eyes. In them, he saw no change. She loved him. Still. Thank the Lord for that.

"Tell me."

"I have news. I hope you'll be happy. I'm…we're…having a baby. You're going to be a daddy."

Stunned at the news, he was robbed of the simplicity of words. Words like, "what?"

"I wanted to tell you the minute I found out, then I got nervous, because we didn't plan for a baby this soon. So, I thought I'd tell you on the honeymoon, as a surprise. Maybe you'd be relaxed and take it well. But then, my mother took me to breakfast for a talk, and she told me I should never keep *anything* from my husband. And I—"

"She's right," he finally spoke.

If someone would have told him a year ago that he'd be happy about this news, he'd have called them a liar. But everything changed when he fell in love with Sadie. Everything. And, it was still changing. The thing of it all was that he'd always loved a good ride. And Sadie was giving him one. Every day.

"Please forgive me for not telling you before today." Her eyes were wide, watery, and filled with…worry.

She was afraid *he'd* be the one to back out now.

"Baby, how could you ever think I wouldn't be happy about this?" He brought her hands to his lips and brushed a kiss across her knuckles.

"Because…we're not ready."

"And it's happening anyway." He grinned, bringing his palm to rest against her belly.

"You… You're happy." She seemed genuinely surprised.

He tipped her chin up. "From the moment I fell in love

with you, I've been on the wildest ride of my life. I figure this is going to be another interesting turn, just a little sooner than we'd planned. But there's nothing you could ever do or say to make me walk away from you. We're together and nothing, or no one, can come between us."

"I love you so much." She gripped his hands and squeezed. "Let's hurry up and make this official before we lose the pastor."

"Great, because you had me wonderin' there for a minute."

She blinked. "Like I would ever run out on you?"

"Well, our town is known for runaway brides. And… there's Eve. It did occur to me."

"Never. I would never abandon you." She palmed the side of his face. "I love you."

"Then I'll see you at the altar."

"Hurry!" She laughed and shoved him toward the door.

Lincoln rushed out and clapped his hands together. "Okay, let's get this show on the road. Mr. Stephens, she's ready for you."

"Well it's about stinkin' time." Mr. Stephens rushed inside.

"Everything okay?" Jackson asked.

His poor brother. The worry and fear etched in his eyes were a reflection of the day Eve had left him. He wished it could have been as easy as a conversation for Jackson and Eve, but their situation was different. Far more complicated.

"Looks like I'm going to be a daddy." His chest felt so puffed up with pride he might lose a button.

"Congratulations are in order, then." Jackson gave a big grin and slapped Lincoln's back. "You stud. Let's go get you married, brother."

* * *

OTHER THAN A SLIGHTLY DELAYED START, the rest of the Carver wedding went ahead without a hitch. Tilly McGregor the flower girl, dropped rose petals down the aisle without tripping once, and the ring bearer had possession of the ring. Jackson and Eve walked down the aisle and separated at the altar without a single wedding guest snickering. Rings and vows were exchanged. Tears were shed, but not by Jackson. He was in another place.

He'd never seen Eve on their wedding day. Something ridiculous about that being bad luck. But maybe if he'd given in to his desire to see her before the wedding, to be reminded of how much he loved her, he wouldn't have felt like a man being led to the brig. All of the months of preparations and planning had meant they'd spent less time enjoying each other and too much time thinking about one day out of the rest of their lives.

Yes, he'd wanted Nashville, but ultimately, he wanted *her* more. They could have reassured each other, just as Lincoln and Sadie had done, and he'd have married her sure as he was currently in the great state of Texas.

Whether that was a good or a bad thing, he still didn't know.

He couldn't say for certain that their marriage would have worked, but he'd loved her enough to try. He *still* loved her. Which was going to make all this way too complicated. She'd built her defenses up so well that he often couldn't be sure of what she was feeling unless they were kissing. Then, he could feel her. He could taste her.

One thing for certain. *He'd* reverted to behaving like an idiot minutes before the wedding. He'd lost his temper again and behaved illogically when he'd blamed *her* for Sadie's issue. But doubts were powerful. Especially when they got fed on a regular basis.

He should know.

Everyone headed over to the lodge at the ranch for the reception, but the wedding party was held back for photos. Eve looked beautiful in a blue bridesmaid dress, wearing fancy cowgirl boots with inlays that matched the dress. Though they were on either side of the bride and groom, he kept catching Eve's eye. The first two times, she looked away. The third time, she squinted at him. The fourth time, she stuck out her tongue and laughed when he did the same.

"Folks let's save the funny faces until the end," the photographer said.

Finally, they left the bride and groom to even more photos and the wedding party made their way to the lodge. But he and Eve took separate trucks. He'd wanted to ride with her because he had some groveling to do, but she'd wound up getting into a truck with the other bridesmaids before he could intervene. Instead he found himself with fellow groomsmen Beau Stephens and Wade Cruz.

"Can you believe it?" Wade said. "Our Lincoln is a married man."

"Never thought I'd see the day," Beau said. "But if anyone could have gotten him to settle down it was my little sister. She's a charmer."

"Made an honest man out of him," Wade said.

Jackson turned into the lot following a long line of trucks and noted when a single limo pulled up to the curb. Out piled the "rented dates," hired by the ladies of SORROW to attend the wedding reception, another Stone Ridge tradition. "Rented" was actually misleading, as they simply came for the free food, champagne, dancing, and all the eager men. They were instantly recognizable by the fact that no one recognized them.

"Thank the good Lord, someone to dance with," Beau said, looking out the window.

"According to Beulah, some of these ladies might actually

someday move to Stone Ridge if they find the right man," Wade said.

"She only says that to keep us on our best behavior," Beau said.

Wade chuckled. "I'm sure you'll manage."

A man on a mission, Jackson carried his guitar case toward the lodge. He was met by Jolette Marie.

"I thought we had a DJ. You're performing tonight?" Jolette Marie was accompanied by all three of her brothers.

"Nope. Just one song for the bride and groom."

"I'd hoped we could get a whole Jackson Carver concert here tonight," Jolette Marie said, tossing her hair.

"This day is about Lincoln and Sadie. Not my show."

Besides, he was on vacation. If "vacation" included back-breaking labor mending fences and helping pull a heifer out who'd gotten stuck in mud. His trainer had never worked him this hard. He should be in the best shape of his life, but all he needed was a few more days of Eve's cooking and he'd be as solid as Lincoln.

"Y'all seen Eve?" Jackson asked, scanning the crowd.

Jolette Marie's youngest brother nudged his chin in the direction of the lodge. "She's already in there."

What neither Lincoln nor Sadie knew was that the song he'd perform tonight would actually take the place of the best man's toast. Other men had the gift of gab. Like Lincoln, and even Wade, who were funny when they wanted to be. Jackson had never been funny, except to Eve, who had laughed at every one of his lame jokes. When he'd been racking his brain for material for his best man's toast, considering hiring a comedy writer to do it, it was his manager who had suggested he sing instead. And heck, he could do that. These days, it was about the only thing he felt he could do well.

He hightailed it inside, sticking his guitar case in a corner.

The lodge had been transformed. There were white drapes hung from the beams at key places. White fairy lights strung. A wide dance floor and a DJ in the corner.

Jackson was stopped frequently for conversations with some folks he hadn't seen in years. Beulah Hayes and others wanted to chat and welcome him back to Stone Ridge. Asked him to consider putting down roots and staying awhile. He was grateful to see folks in a relaxed and normal situation in which he wasn't the center of attention. To residents like Beulah, he was special, but only because he was one of the men of Stone Ridge.

Jackson took his place beside Lincoln at the head table and clapped his back. "Congratulations."

"Were you totally freaked out?" Lincoln said under his breath.

"Nah," Jackson lied. "I knew Sadie wasn't going to walk out on you."

"Not with Eve there." Lincoln chuckled. "I have to thank her for lettin' me know soon as I get the chance."

"Another runaway bride in this family? Not possible." Jackson cleared his throat. "Hey, I've got a little surprise for my toast."

"Don't worry, figured you hired someone to write your speech. Knew you'd be nervous."

"I would be insulted if you didn't know me so well. But no, I didn't hire anyone. In fact, I wrote it myself."


FOR EVE, nothing on earth could ruin this night. Not only did two of her favorite people in the world get their happily ever after, but Jackson was going to eat his words. Slowly. And painfully. He was always so cute when he was remorseful. She was going to have her fun with him tonight, that's for sure. Because hey, she was right, and he was wrong. Sadie and Lincoln were hitched.

The lodge was busting at the seams with guests, practically everyone in Stone Ridge, plus the women who'd been invited as they were to even out any big event. Ever so kindly organized by Beulah, who loved nothing more than even numbers. Eve hugged her mother, seated at a table with Hank, Mima, and some of the SORROW ladies. She'd just said hello to Sadie's mother, Wanda, and father, Merle, when Jolette Marie walked up to her.

The Trueharts had money and Jolette Marie wore a sequined gown more appropriate for an awards show. Eve was always kind to the family, even if they hadn't always returned the favor. She knew her place. Her mother was the Truehart's maid and cook, and even though Eve now managed a veterinary practice, she didn't expect their immediate respect as a doctor. She'd have to earn it.

"Congratulations, Eve," Jolette said sweetly.

"Thanks, but you should really congratulate Sadie."

"I did," Jolette Marie said. "I'm congratulating you for hanging on to Jackson. He's a catch and you've always had him. You should know, I made a pass at him and he turned me down flat."

"Um, oh. Okay." Eve was momentarily rendered speechless. "Now why would you tell me that?"

"There might be a lot of men in town, Eve, but none quite like Jackson. He's yours if you want him. You're welcome." She patted Eve's shoulder and went to find her table.

Eve kept the smile glued on her lips, but her gut burned with anger. Was Eve supposed to *thank* Jolette Marie for making a pass at Jackson? It wasn't as if she'd done it for Eve. But despite all the words, all the kisses and embraces between them, she reminded herself that she had no claim to Jackson. He might love her, but she was obviously still stuck when it came to intimacy. Unable to move forward, and sooner or later even Jackson would lose patience with her like all the other men had. But she couldn't and wouldn't let that push her into doing something a minute before she was ready. She'd come too far.

Determined not to let Jolette Marie's news ruin this evening, Eve joined the others at the head table where they were beginning to serve dinner. Sadie's father said a few words thanking everyone, and so did Hank. Before long, it was time for the best man's toast. But instead of reaching for the microphone to speak to the large gathering, Jackson moved toward a stool and accepted the guitar that someone from the catering staff handed him.

"Y'all know that I'm a man of few words. Instead of a speech, I started this song for Sadie and Lincoln several months ago when Lincoln asked me to be his best man. I just finished it last week and I'd like to play it now."

A collective swoon came over the lodge as Jackson strummed his guitar before he'd even uttered a sound. It seemed the entire room hung on his every word. Sadie laid her head on Lincoln's shoulder and he draped his arm around her waist as they listened to a love song. The chorus made Eve think the song could be titled "One True Thing."

Jackson sang about a man who had almost missed what was right in front of him. One true love to last a lifetime. One true thing. It was about a woman who'd never given up on the man she loved. Like so many of Jackson's songs, it told a story. This one was about finding your true love, marriage, children, and a lifetime of love. He sang to Lincoln and Sadie, but each time Jackson got to the chorus, he met Eve's eyes.

*There's only one true thing.*
*You and me.*
She froze and wouldn't turn when Sadie elbowed her. Jackson was singing to *her*. But she didn't feel the abundant

joy she should, the heart swell she'd felt on the day Jackson asked her to marry him on bended knee.

Instead she was still stuck in that parking lot at the Piggly Wiggly, with the anguish and fear of knowing she'd lost him for good.

*This is real. Everything that's right in front of you is real. The past isn't real anymore. It's gone. Over. He can't hurt you anymore.*

*Why am I doing this? Why can't I just allow myself to be happy again?*

Maybe the answer was that she was a different woman now than the one who'd first fallen head over heels for Jackson Carver. One who wasn't quite as trusting of the world. But she wanted to be. It would be nice to believe in fairy tales and rainbows again. To believe again in happily ever after. In good outcomes. Might also be good to feel safe in places other than Stone Ridge.

Finally, the song was over, and a swell of applause followed Jackson back to the head table. Mima, Wanda, and Brenda were wiping away tears. So were all of the SORROW women. And every woman at the singles' table, Jolette Marie included, studied Eve. She squirmed in her seat.

"Eve." Sadie elbowed her again. "That song was for you, too."

"I know," she said, her voice shaky. "It was…nice."

"Nice?" Sadie whispered. "It was so *romantic*."

"Baby, it's time for the first dance." Lincoln offered his hand to Sadie.

Eve smiled when the two danced like there was no one else in the room. No one else in the world. The DJ played Thomas Rhett's "Die a Happy Man." With Lincoln, Eve believed it. He could lose the family ranch and still die happy needing nothing more than Sadie by his side. He'd already given up being a regular on the rodeo circuit. Something told Eve he would give up everything, not that Sadie would ever ask him to, and that was the beauty of their relationship. Selfless.

"Dance?"

Eve looked up to see Jackson, his blue eyes shimmering under hooded lids, his hand held out in invitation.

# CHAPTER 24

Eve took Jackson's hand and he led her to the dance floor. She'd been so caught up in her own head that she hadn't noticed others had already joined in on the first dance. Sadie's mother and father had cut in. Hank led Mima onto the dance floor. Wade and Daisy were dancing. Lucy, with a handsome older man Eve didn't recognize. Beau with Jolette Marie.

Eve rested a hand on each of Jackson's broad shoulders putting a good safe two inches between them. If nothing else for the sake of appearance because after the song people were probably assuming too much.

Hands low on her waist, Jackson held her close. "Forgive me for being an idiot."

She felt her lip curl up in a smile. "I confess my life flashed before my eyes."

Funny how she could even joke about this kind of thing now. Maybe it was true that time healed all wounds. If so, she was on her way. A few more years and she'd find her way out of that Piggly Wiggly parking lot.

"Not funny. You know I would never hurt you."

"I know."

Jackson cleared his throat. "What do you think about my song?"

"It was beautiful. Lincoln and Sadie loved it. I think Sadie tried not to do the ugly cry."

He squinted. "The *ugly* cry?"

"Never mind." She shook her head.

"But what did *you* think about it?" He met her eyes.

"What I was thinking…I don't know. Can we just pick up where we left off?"

"Not quite, but we can turn the page."

"Start a new chapter?"

"Excuse me, but may I cut in?"

This was from one of the Truehart brothers. Jimmy? Jamie? Eve couldn't recall. He was young, maybe in his early twenties. Handsome. Puffed up like a peacock with can-do attitude.

"No, you can't," Jackson said, and spun her away.

"Jackson." Eve laughed. "This is a wedding. We can't just dance with each other all night long."

"We'll see about that. I'm not letting you go. Not a second time." With that, he spun them.

"Lincoln and Sadie are off to their honeymoon tomorrow." Eve looked up, meeting his eyes. "We're all going to have to get back to our lives. I'm going to have to go back to work. I've already taken too much time off and Annabeth must hate me about now."

"I'll be helping my dad during the day and writing songs at night."

"I'm sure Hank is happy about that. And Lincoln ought to be relieved."

"Maybe ranching *is* in my blood. Hank is right. Once a cowboy, always a cowboy."

"Don't let Hank's influence do this to you. He might not

respect what you do for a living but that's no reason to change who you are."

Jackson could never again be the same man he'd been when he left Stone Ridge. And that was okay. She wasn't the same, either. It's just that she wasn't who she wanted to be while Jackson at least seemed settled.

He lowered his lips to meet hers and kissed her tenderly. For a moment, Eve's breath hitched. A ripple of self-consciousness pulsed through her. Now *everyone* would know. Jackson and Eve, round two. Would she run again? Place your bets, ladies and gentlemen. It wasn't her imagination when she received a wry look from Beulah Hayes, dancing nearby with her husband.

She was aware some didn't think she deserved Jackson in the first place, much less his forgiveness for leaving him at the altar. She might have believed so at one time, too, but Jackson had her convinced she deserved this moment. This precious time with him.

"You too," he said after he broke the kiss.

"Me too? What do you mean?"

"You also need to remember who you are."

That struck her as funny coming from someone who lived in the bright lights of Nashville. From a man who had completely reinvented himself.

"I *know* who I am."

"Then what happened to the girl I used to know? She was fearless. You dared me to skinny dip in the creek and joined me when I did."

"I was seventeen years old. I'm older now."

"Nope. Not buyin' it. People don't change who they are at their core."

He'd hit a nerve. It wasn't just intimacy with her. There were still times when she found herself afraid to speak up. She'd wanted to scold Mr. Mansfield for not calling her sooner about Holly's colic. And even though she knew better, she'd backed down without even mentioning it to him. She hadn't let Jolette Marie know what she really thought of her making a pass at Jackson.

It happened too much. Still, she didn't like the knowledge that Jackson *was* right. It would be nice to find her fighting spirit back with others and not just with Jackson. Somehow it was easier with him. He'd been, in some ways, her safety net.

"Do you think I'm holding back from you?" She shook her head, realizing all she'd kept from him until someone else had told him. "I mean, anymore?"

"Honestly? Yeah, I do." His voice lowered. "I understand why you might be reluctant to give us another chance. I hurt you."

"No more than I hurt you."

He pressed his forehead to hers. "But I also get why you might not have the kind of courage that you once did."

The courage to fight for her patients when she knew the best course of treatment. It hurt to think that she'd been less than competent due to her own doubts and fears.

"When I'm with you, I remember who I used to be."

"I was kind of countin' on that." He slid her an easy smile. "The woman you used to be was wild, carefree, strong. And mine."

"I'M GOING to miss you so much," Sadie said, wrapping her arms around Eve and squeezing.

Eve squeezed back. "It's only a week."

"Are you going to be alright?" Sadie met Eve's eyes, clutching both of her hands. "Promise me that you'll be okay."

"Of *course* I'm going to be okay."

"I mean, even if Jackson, you know…" She lowered her voice. "Even after he leaves."

Sadie might as well have added "again." Eve knew exactly what she meant. Poor Sadie had endured the brunt of Eve's pain at discovering Jackson had left for Nashville the very next morning. Sad? No, not sad. She'd been *inconsolable*. Jackson had torn up his room? Eve had retired to hers and not left her bed for a week.

"Yes, even then."

She decided not to add he claimed to be staying longer. That might not work out, either. She had to be ready to say goodbye at any moment. Whatever they were to each other now, it was new. No promises or firm commitments. And no intimacy for her to regret.

"Just please don't let him go this time without laying it all out. Throw your pride out the window. *If* you figure out you still love him while I'm gone."

Eve couldn't help but smile at that. "I already figured that out."

Sadie squeezed her again. "Don't forget I'm only a phone call away."

"I'm not calling you on your honeymoon. Some things are sacred."

"You damn right," Lincoln interjected, hauling his bride into his arms. "Say goodbye, Sadie."

"Goodbye, everyone!" Sadie waved. "Wait! I almost forgot. The bouquet. I'm supposed to throw it to some lucky future bride."

"Throw it, baby," Lincoln said, not putting her down. "You have a distinct advantage from up here to go long and deep."

"Line up, ladies!" Sadie shouted and once the crowd of women were lined up, she threw it. "Catch!"

Eve wasn't trying to catch the bouquet, not really, but it sailed past her like a Hail Mary pass and landed right in the eager outstretched hands of one of the women from out of town.

"Woohoo!" She danced around like a receiver in the end zone making a touchdown, nearly tripping over Daisy. "I'm next! Watch out, world."

Lincoln deposited Sadie in his truck and within minutes they drove off, waving goodbye to everyone.

"I literally always stand with my arms at my sides during these things," Lucy said. "Once it landed right at my feet. Two women nearly headbutted each other to get to it."

"I have *never* seen such a display in my life, I declare," Mima said, shaking her head at the woman.

"Arrogance doesn't look good on a southern woman," Beulah added. "It's just plain ugly."

"Oh, I've seen worse," Lucy said.

Eve fought a rising sense of panic. The wedding had taken so much of her spare time, months of it, and it was done. Mima's cast was off and she'd go back to taking care of the ranch hands. Eve would go back to work, and she'd have to find another place to live. More changes. The same stone of anxiety she felt whenever a huge change happened lodged itself in her throat. She could almost feel her palms grow clammy. And Lord, wasn't she sick of herself? She *had* to get over this. Had to move past it, but how, when shame and regret still pierced her? Logic didn't seem to work. Words and positive affirmations lasted a short time. Going through the motions worked, but at night she had nowhere to run as thoughts chased her to bed.

*I may be alone for the rest of my life.*

*I may never have children.*

*How can I love my job, love my friends and family, and hate my life?*

While everyone went back inside the lodge to dance some more, Eve wandered away for a quiet moment. Maybe if she was alone, she could stop these shallow breaths. She could tamp down the anger that had suddenly resurfaced.

*That bastard took my life.*

*I'll never be myself again.*

In the next thought, she realized that if that were the case, she'd let him win. Her life had been saved for no good reason other than possibly the health and well-being of Stone Ridge's large animals. And that wasn't good enough. Her work wasn't *enough*. She wanted to be free again to laugh, scream, and make love without reservation. To be held by Jackson all night long with nothing but flesh between them. To feel loved and precious.

She might still be technically young, but she felt old. Washed out. Nothing left to give. She walked until she took a seat on a bench tucked beneath an oak tree nearby. Her breaths were coming short and shallow. All the effort hadn't worked. She fought a rising tide that would surely pull her under. She wrapped her arms around her waist and bent her head. A panic attack like this one hadn't happened to her in at least a year. She had to think calm, happy thoughts. Her happy place.

Then she looked up and Jackson was standing in front of the bench. If he'd called out to her, she hadn't heard him. His face changed from a curious cocked head, dimples flashing, to a deep crease between his eyebrows.

"What's wrong, baby?"

Rather than answer she bent at the waist, her breaths coming shorter. "I'm…okay."

"You're not," he said sitting beside her, tugging her into his arms. "Tell me what happened. How can I fix this?"

Lord help him, he *still* wanted to fix everything. And that, more than anything, was what finally snapped her in half.

"No! You can't fix this," she wailed. "Don't you get it? It's too late for me."

Every thread of emotion she'd held back since she'd decided that she wouldn't waste any more anger rose to the surface and Eve sobbed and wailed about the unfairness of it all. She cried over how one snap decision could lead to so many painful outcomes. She cried because as long as that man was alive, she might never feel safe. She sobbed for the woman she used to be. For all the time she'd wasted.

"I want to be the woman you fell in love with. I want to be whole again, but I can't. That Eve is gone."

She sobbed, and cried, and Jackson just held her without saying anything at all. His hands glided up and down her spine in a comforting motion and he made soothing sounds. After a while, the panic ebbed, and as always, she felt completely drained. Exhausted.

"I'm s-sorry."

He wiped away her tears with his thumb. "Don't do that. Don't be sorry. You have to know there's nowhere I'd rather be than right here with you."

"B-but I'm guessing you wish I hadn't wet your shirt."

"Big deal." He pressed his forehead against hers. "I'll get another one."

"I haven't had a p-panic attack like this for a year."

"Then you were due." He stood and offered his hand. "Let me get you home now and put you to bed."

She rose and took his hand. "Is the party still going on?"

He took her hand, leading her to his truck. "When I left to find you, Hank had pulled Brenda out on the dance floor. Mima was dancing with Sadie's father. Sadie and Linc may be gone, but the family will close the house down. No point in renting the lodge and the DJ till ten if everyone leaves early."

"The Carvers do know how to throw a party."

Jackson smiled. "This time, let's leave *them* to figure out their way home."

# CHAPTER 25

Jackson pulled out onto the road, then took Eve's hand in his and brushed a kiss across her fingers. He did his best to concentrate on the road before him and ignore the whole-body ache he'd experienced while listening to Eve's hitched breaths and sobs. She'd had a complete meltdown, probably a long time coming. He told himself she'd needed this moment to let go, to let go of all her emotions and fears along with all that anger she'd claimed to have conquered. She'd simply buried it somewhere deep inside.

But anger and pain were funny things. He ought to know. They seemed to reoccur now and again, just when a person thought they'd conquered them and forgiven someone or something. Sometimes, it was a process, but other times, anger and pain became a way of life. For him, it had taken simply seeing Eve again to eventually let his anger and pain go. But Eve might always have to deal with the repercussion of her attack, and his heart splintered over that. She was right that he'd wanted to make this better from the moment he'd heard, and he couldn't. It wasn't that easy.

But she was also wrong. She could be the woman she'd been again, if she was willing to take a risk. In the end it didn't matter to him because he loved this new Eve, too. He loved her, whoever she chose to be, because she had the same heart. The same soul. He'd take her any way he could get her. Whole again, or in pieces. And if he found her in pieces, he'd put her back together again no matter how many times it took.

As expected, there were no trucks, clear evidence that no one was back at the main house yet. Now he could get Eve to bed without any questions from anyone about the streaks down her face and her pink nose.

"Maybe you should change and take a warm bath," he suggested.

"That does sound good."

"I'm going to bring you some hot chocolate," Jackson said, pulling off his jacket and hanging it on a hook in the mudroom.

She didn't protest and a few minutes later he heard the sound of the water rushing as the tub filled. Jackson busied himself locating the cocoa mix and sugar. He pulled out the cold milk from the fridge. There were few things he could make, and this was one of them. Really great hot chocolate. He still remembered how.

Taking care of someone wasn't new to him, it had just been a while. Far from taking care of Eve in the past, she'd been the one to take care of him. But long ago, there was someone Jackson had taken care of as well as he could. For as long as he could.

"Bring me some hot chocolate, Jackie, baby," his mother would say when she'd been laid up in bed, which was often. "Your father doesn't have time for me."

He was probably only seven when he learned what a "rat bastard" and "selfish man" his father was, straight from his mother's lips. He believed her, too, because Hank was mean as the devil some days. Other days, not so much, and Jackson tried to figure out which dad he'd get when he walked in the door every evening. It was anyone's guess.

He heard the door open and close down the hallway and figured Eve had finished soaking. Pouring the hot chocolate into a large mug, he carried it to her bedroom and knocked once before coming inside. She turned to him wearing a white bathrobe tied at the waist, her long hair loose and falling over her shoulders. Face scrubbed clean of any trace of makeup, she looked younger. Her eyes shimmered, and he was hit with a pull of longing so strong it nearly brought him to his knees.

"You made that for me?" She grinned as she accepted the mug.

"It's the best comfort food I know."

"Mm," she said after taking a sip. "It's really good."

"Real chocolate. Real sugar. Real milk. Can't fail."

"It should be a commercial. The simple things. Thank you for taking such good care of me," she said.

"You would do the same."

"I would," she said. "But I'm still sorry you had to see me fall apart like that."

He leaned against her dresser, crossing his arms. "I'm not. I want you to do something for me. From now on, if you ever need anything, you let me know. No pride. Zero bullshit. *Promise* me, Eve."

"Okay. But what if…what if I need *you*?"

"Not a problem. I think I've made it pretty clear how I feel about you." He came to her bed and pulled the covers back for her, an invitation for her to climb in.

She set the mug on the nightstand and obliged, getting in still wearing her bathrobe. He'd have thought she'd remove it, revealing pajamas, but when she didn't, he tortured himself with the knowledge that she might be naked under that robe. She'd probably get dressed when he left the room. Unless she slept naked.

Lord, please let her sleep naked.

He was about flick the lamp off when she reached up and touched his forearm. "Wait. Don't go, please."

Desire spiked through him. He wouldn't make it another few minutes in this room without ravaging her. "I should. I have to."

"Don't leave me."

He squatted beside the bed and tucked a lock of hair behind her ear. "Guess I could sit here until you fall asleep."

"No," she said, still holding his hand, bringing it to her chest. "I'm ready."

He actually heard his heart slam against his rib cage and swallowed hard. "Are you sure?"

She nodded, laying her head on the pillow, her long dark hair fanning out to the side. "I'm falling in love with you."

Her eyes shimmered, and desire had replaced pain. It felt good to know he'd been the cause of that switch. Though he couldn't change her past, he could be a part of her future. And damn if he wasn't determined to do that from this point forward. He didn't know what that future would look like, or how he would get them there, but he wouldn't give up.

She rolled to her side and stood to help him off with the rest of his clothes. "Let me."

He smiled down at her as she unbuttoned and unzipped his slacks. He stroked the curve of her jaw as he watched, wanting the contact. She guided his slacks down past his hips and let them fall to the floor. He was hard as a baseball bat. He kicked off his boots, then pulled off his shirt.

When he covered her body with his and slid a hand under the partition of her robe, he discovered she was indeed naked under there. This lit a blaze in him and did crazy things to his tenuous grip on self-control. He devoured her mouth in long deep kisses that had them both moaning and gasping. He slid down her body, kissing her stomach, and found a little surprise. A tiny sparkly belly button ring. He tugged at it with his tongue and teeth.

His conservative Eve had at some point in her life given in to a flashy belly button ring.

"Hmm. This is new. And I like it."

He stopped, braced above her, and simply studied her for a moment, a smile tugging at his lips.

"What?" she whispered.

"I'm just remembering you. All of you. I'd forgotten."

"What I look like under my clothes?"

"How beautiful you are." He stroked her soft warm thigh. "I thought about you a lot over the years. About this."

"Me too. We've always had this connection. But I thought this would go away somehow. No matter how angry I get with you, this *never* goes away. I think that's love."

"I've never felt like this about anyone else."

"I have to tell you one more thing that I may have misled you about," she said.

Jackson tensed, wondering what else she'd kept from him. He didn't breathe.

"I really don't think I would have ever married Bobby. I loved him but I was never in love with him. At least, not like this. Never like this."


JACKSON STILL HAD the same light smattering of chest hairs but now there was sinewy muscle beneath. His abs were hard planes and a thing of beauty. She no longer doubted for a moment that he'd spent hours with a trainer. Were it any other man but Jackson, she might worry about her fleshy body measuring up. But she read those eyes that she knew so well, and they were filled with heat and desire. For her.

When he pressed kisses to the inside of her thighs, it wasn't just conversation that stopped, but coherent thoughts. He remembered her. Remembered *this*. They'd always been good here. She'd always anticipated his needs and he'd done the same, moving in tandem like a dance. Nearly stupid with lust, she pressed against him, her breasts luxuriating in all that sinewy hard muscle, skin on skin.

He fisted a hand in her hair and pulled her up to meet his hungry mouth. They devoured each other, lips, tongue, and teeth tangling. He tasted salty in the very best way and desire pulsed through her entire body. Then it got crazy as it always had between them. His mouth was on her nipple, sucking each into a hard peak. His fingers slipped deep in her warm wet folds. This was her undoing. Her body tightened like a cord and she clawed at his behind.

"Jackson," she pleaded, gyrating her hips, tugging him closer.

He reached for a condom from his wallet, and when he pulled off his boxer briefs, she helped roll it on, stroking and getting more turned on in the process. She straddled him and gasped when he thrust inside her, the angle and position deeper, filling her completely. Jackson groaned and gripped her hips, trying to control her movements and set their pace.

But she got bold with him. "Let me."

He listened, and she proceeded to gyrate and undulate her hips, slowly riding him, the pulsating waves inside of her staying barely beneath the surface. Holding back, she forced him to slow down and ride the crest even higher with her. When his eyes almost rolled back in his head, she knew she'd succeeded in making her point.

"Eve," he groaned. "Keep riding me just like this."

Not trusting herself to speak, she kept up the agonizingly

slow movements, a trickle of sweat slipping down her back. A moment later she had no control left when her entire body shook and quivered with the most intense climax she'd ever experienced. She worried that her moan sounded like that of a wounded animal and not a woman experiencing the deepest pleasure of her life.

Jackson took over then, flipping her onto her back and thrusting into her again and again. His strokes were faster and deeper. When she began to feel the pressure building up, she realized with some shock that this would happen again. She tried to hold back, but it was almost as if holding back helped push her over the edge and she moaned as she climaxed.

A moment later, Jackson joined her, his own seeming to dovetail from hers, as both of their bodies shook together.

"Jackson," she whispered, clinging to him, completely spent.

"I know." He rolled off her and took her with him, tucking her to his side and bringing the sheet over them. "I know, baby."

Satisfaction rolled through her giving her a warmth and peace in her heart that she hadn't completely forgotten. The knowledge that intimacy like this could be amazing and earth shattering with the right man.

"I'm sorry I made you wait so long for this," she said, her hand resting on his chest.

"Two whole weeks." He kissed her temple.

"I didn't think you'd have the patience."

"You don't make it easy, walking around looking the way you do."

She laughed. "Thank you for waiting for me."

"What changed your mind?"

She thought about that for a moment and had the answer. "Once I realized I'd fallen in love again. Your song, which I love, by the way, ripped something open inside my heart. And I realized I was holding myself back because I felt stuck. But I don't want to lose you. Not again."

"Let's get this straight. You won't lose me. I would have waited another…" He hesitated. "At least another two weeks."

She laughed and swatted him on the butt. "Really? Two weeks? That's *it*?"

"Well, two weeks before I tried to seduce you again." He brought her hand up to his lips to kiss it. "Just kidding. Forever."

"Jackson?" she whispered. "I trust you. With my life."

"You don't know what that means to me, baby."

The next words were harder for her to say out loud and she swallowed back a sob. "I know it seems like I'm broken. Like I'll never be whole, the girl you loved. But—"

"No. You're better. Baby, if you're broken, then I love your pieces. Every one of them." He braced himself above her.

She felt him grow hard against her, smiled, and stroked his cheek. "Eight years older, but some things never change."

He made love to her again, this time slow and sweet.

Afterwards, they lay arms and legs entwined until Jackson suddenly sat up straight and rushed to turn off the light.

"What is it?" she whispered, realizing he'd heard something she hadn't.

"They're back," he said, pulling her with him under the covers. "If we're quiet, they won't look for us."

"This is embarrassing," Eve said. "I feel like I'm sixteen again."

Eve turned her ear toward the door and the voices grew louder as they got closer.

"Sadie's father was hilarious," Daisy said.

"The man can certainly cut a rug," Mima said.

"If that's what horrible dancing means, then I agree."

"Where *is* your brother?" Mima said. "I didn't see him leave but he took the truck."

"Probably somewhere with Eve," Daisy said. "You ought to be happy."

"I would be if I knew where they were."

"Considering they're grown-ups, why don't you let it go?"

"You're right. Daisy, let me tell you a thing or two about rodeo cowboys, while I have you alone for a minute..."

The voices drifted as they moved away, and Eve cringed. "I feel like I should save Daisy from that talk."

"Never mind. She just saved us, and I'll thank her later. You didn't see that self-sacrificing move of hers?" Jackson's hand glided up and down her spine and came to rest on her behind.

"We have all night."

# CHAPTER 26

When Eve pulled up to the Lone Star Veterinary Clinic on Monday morning, she took a few minutes to gather her thoughts. Somehow it seemed like more than two weeks had passed since she'd been gone. The outside of the building still looked the same and she was certain nothing inside had changed either. The little blue building where Eve and Annabeth had hung out their shingle sat right in the middle of downtown near all the major storefronts. She walked to the door and traced the letters of her name:

Eve Iglesias, DVM
Annabeth Dantzer, DVM

Nothing was the same for Eve as the day she'd left for her scheduled vacation, after having had a small anxiety attack at the Maddox ranch. She didn't think she'd ever been this happy in her life.

This morning she'd woken to a cup of coffee on her nightstand that had to have been Jackson's doing. A note beside it said that he'd let her sleep in and would be with Hank most of the day. He'd spent the night in her bedroom, loving her all night long. Speaking tender words along with the sexier raunchier ones about what he was going to do to her and how much she'd enjoy it.

Whew!

She'd decided to skip her regular morning ride and slept in a little longer.

Last night, the sexual intimacy alone would have been enough, but she'd fallen in love with him. Head over heels, can't-stop-thinking-about-him-love. She was happy about that, but she had a feeling Annabeth was going to wake her up to a few truths Eve didn't want to face. She'd enjoyed the little bubble she'd lived in recently, where the past collided with the present and created something new and fresh. Precious. Something she'd never believed would be possible. But she feared Annabeth was about to burst that bubble with a sledgehammer.

She was already there when Eve opened the door and let herself inside the clinic.

"Good mornin'."

"Hey, stranger. I sure hope you enjoyed your time off." She handed Eve a Styrofoam cup. "Sorry. I still can't figure out how to make the coffee."

Hoping for the best, Eve took a sip, and tried not to grimace. "You'll get the hang of it."

"So, how did it go?" Annabeth perched on the edge of the front desk.

"Good." Eve set her cup down. "Better than I could have hoped."

"I heard."

"What did you hear?"

"Just that you and Jackson were pretty cozy on the dance floor." She crossed her arms smugly. "Did I call this or what?"

Okay, so Annabeth had warned her that she could wind up being tossed aside like all the other women Jackson had apparently been through over the years. But Eve regretted nothing. She was living her life again, fearless, and brave. He'd brought that out of her again. And he loved her as much as she loved him, even if he had yet to say it when she was awake. He'd shown her, and that mattered more.

"It's complicated," Eve said and sat at the reception desk's chair to power up the desktop computer.

"No kidding. I would have never dreamed that taking up with the man you left at the altar would be *complicated*." She smirked. "So…tell me. Was it just one kiss or are we talking some heavy make-out sessions?"

Eve might have blushed. Either way, her face hot, she got busy trying to locate this week's schedule.

"Oh, crap. Are you…are you being serious with me right now?" Annabeth went hand on hip and swiveled her head. "That fast? After everything he *did* to you? He abandoned you."

"*After* I abandoned him."

And she should have known better. He'd already been abandoned once. Being abandoned by his fiancée in a church full of people had cut him in places she hadn't even imagined. But she would give herself a pass because she'd been caught up in her own needs. Too young and immature. Too proud.

"We already talked about this. You were just nervous. Marriage is a patriarchal system and it's no wonder you thought twice. It wasn't like you didn't *love* him."

"But it's just not that simple."

"It is exactly that simple. You live here, and he lives there." Annabeth pointed outside as if Nashville was in the parking lot. "It isn't going to work even if I thought you *could* trust him. Unless you're leaving me and our practice."

"No, no, I'm not. You know I'm not." Eve sighed and

found the day's schedule. She was actually amazed Annabeth had managed to put one together.

Routine usually helped but not so much at the moment. The first appointment of the day was Mr. Mansfield. She did not want to deal with him again. Not on her first day back.

She glanced up. "Does Holly have colic again?"

"He left a message on the machine and spent twenty minutes over the phone mansplaining." She pointed to Eve. "He did ask for you, so you're dealing with him. Only you can handle this and not throat punch the man."

"Poor Holly." Eve stood and went to the medicine cabinet to gather some analgesics. "I'll get going right away. I meant to tell him that he shouldn't wait long to call us."

"Don't let him intimidate you," Annabeth said as she helped Eve load her truck.

"I won't. I've got this."

She spent most of the drive to the Maddox ranch thinking about how best to approach the situation. In the past two weeks she'd come to understand that it was better to lay everything out in the open. Like she'd done with Jackson. He made it easier, that was true. But if she could stand up to Jackson, she could stand up to Mr. Mansfield. The courage was in her, she just had to pull it out and put it on.

There *were* good men in the world. Just because she'd happened upon one of the worst of them didn't mean that every big and burly man meant to hurt her. And no man was *ever* going to intimidate her again. She was Eve Iglesias, DVM, and damn proud of it. Once, a man had tried to take her apart, but hadn't succeeded. She'd come out stronger in the end. Having been through the physical and emotional pain taught her that she could survive. Now, she'd learn how to thrive again.

She strode up to the stables, finding Holly in the same

state she'd been in two weeks ago. Pawing at the ground, head down. In agony.

"How long has she been like this?"

"Two days," Mr. Mansfield said.

Her stomach tightened, but she went ahead and gave him the benefit of the doubt. "My partner would have helped. You didn't have to wait this long for me."

"Got around to callin' y'all as soon as I had a free moment."

"If you're too busy to take proper care of the horses, then maybe you need to hire some more hands." She took a deep breath. "Or find another job."

For a moment, the only sound heard in the stable was Holly's horseshoes hitting the ground. No other sound, because a horse always suffered in silence.

And then Mr. Mansfield cleared his throat. "Guess I do need to hire a few hands. You hear of anyone lookin', let me know."

A pleasant surprise flowed through Eve, taking the place of the tension she'd felt up to that moment. "I will."

And then she got busy helping Holly.

The end of the day came quickly, and satisfied at a great first day back, Eve headed back to the Double C. At the turn to the ranch, her curiosity peaked when she caught sight of a black limo turn, too, just ahead of her. A friend of Jackson's coming to visit him from Nashville? It could be someone famous, like maybe Miranda Lambert, or Toby Keith. Eve could get an autograph. Excited, she caught up with the limo. She would try to remember not to be a total fan girl. This would be difficult, as she loved country music.

The limo pulled in front of the house and Eve parked behind the barn and quickly walked toward the house. She made it inside the door just in time to see the beautiful blonde who was Jackson's ex-wife jump into his arms.

Everything in Eve froze, including her stupid heart. In a flash, she was back at the Piggly Wiggly parking lot. Her breath hitched and for the life of her she couldn't seem to draw in another one. She'd been stupid to think that she and Jackson could just go back to the way they were. They'd spent years apart, and other people had been involved.

He had an ex-wife.

And now she was standing in their living room, her hands all over Jackson.

"I missed you, husband!" Winona said.

Jackson gently put her back down on the floor and took a generous step back. "Ex-husband."

He supposed this was what he got for not returning her calls. The woman didn't handle rejection well. She had resources in every state and though he'd stayed off social media, she'd tracked him down. He hadn't seen or talked to Winona in months and now she was standing in his family's living room calling him her husband just as Eve walked in the door. Perfect.

The timing of his troubled and talented friend was impeccable as usual.

A few years ago, his first record label had thought it would be a good marketing angle for their two newest up-and-coming musicians to be seen together. Someone had dropped a rumor that they were engaged, and the tabloids had their fun until the next big story came around. Winona had done a lot for his career, recording one of his first songs, and carrying it into the top ten nationwide.

And one night, drunk off his ass, he'd married her in Las Vegas.

Mima threw her hands up. "What in tarnation is this mess? Jackson is divorced. Didn't expect any marriage that took place in a drive-through would last, but maybe I'm old-fashioned. Y'all got some explain' to do. Go on."

"We're divorced. I have the paperwork." He stared Winona down.

The happiest day in his life was when the lawyer had said a no-contest divorce would take a couple of months, tops. He was actually married to her less time than it took to divorce her.

"No, I'm sorry," Winona said. "It's a...joke between two old friends."

"Well, then, it's not very funny, is it?" Mima said. "Now that we've got that straightened out, I'm Jackson's grand-mother, Lillian Carver. Pleased to meet you. Over there is Eve Iglesias and she lives here. Jackson's ex-fiancée. Nothing funny about it, either. I don't know where you're from, young lady, but here in Stone Ridge we don't make jokes about marriage."

"I'm from Okla—" Winona began.

"I think you had better stop talking," Jackson said.

He led Winona out to the front porch, making sure to keep enough distance between them so as not to even acci-dentally touch her. He'd made such great progress with Eve, and now this. He spotted two suitcases by the front door, not a great sign.

He moved them to the side and sat on the top step of the staircase, bending his head. "Want to tell me what in the hell is going on?"

Winona sat next to him. "I've been calling you and leaving messages ever since I heard. Jackson, you can't do this. Eve destroyed you and I'll *never* forgive her for what she did to you. I saw how she ripped your heart out. I picked up the pieces. I took care of you."

"It isn't any of your business whether Eve and I are back together or not."

She went palms up. "Listen, honey. I was afraid this would happen. I heard about the family wedding from one of your band members. You're thinking of getting back together with Eve, aren't you? After what she did to you? That would be a mistake!"

Jackson shook his head. "Good thing it's not up to you."

"If I'm not too late, and I hope that I'm not, I want you to think carefully about this. I saw what she did to you, how broken you were."

"This is still none of your business."

He and Winona had been better drinking buddies than lovers. But he'd once made the mistake of confiding in her. To get a woman's perspective, he'd told himself. He wasn't looking for sympathy, but simply to understand. When had Eve fallen out of love with him and how had he missed it? Winona had rallied to his defense, telling him Eve obviously didn't love him enough in the first place if she'd let him go. He'd appreciated the support, while telling himself he hadn't really expected to hear the honest truth from a woman he was sleeping with on and off.

Then came the ill-fated short marriage and Jackson's guilt over wanting to immediately divorce her and move on.

"We haven't so much as talked in months. Where is this coming from? We've both moved on and had other relationships since then."

"But I've never been with anyone quite like you."

Jackson wished he could say the same, but the woman inside his family home was the only woman he'd ever loved. Even though he'd disappointed her in ways he wasn't sure he could ever make up to her.

This wasn't helping. "I love Eve. I'm sorry, but I don't love you. I can't help how I feel."

"Can we talk? There's just so many things I want to say to you. In private." She threw a glance over her shoulder at the house. "I have regrets. So many. I'm not getting any younger, you know."

The old song and dance she'd been doing since she turned thirty-five. Winona had been a beautiful woman a few years ago, but all the hard drinking and touring had caught up to her. There were dark circles under her eyes. She was too thin. Even so, she didn't look anywhere near forty.

Jackson raked a hand through his hair. "We'll talk, sure. We're old friends. But not …now."

"I got it. She's here. We need some privacy."

"No. That's not it. I don't keep secrets from Eve." Jackson stood. "I'm going to take you to Kerrville, where they have a full-service hotel you can stay in. Until you can get your travel arrangements in order to leave."

"I thought I might stay here in the family home."

"I'll get some truck keys," Jackson said, without further explanation.

The screen door opened and slammed shut and Eve stomped out. Ignoring both of them, she passed him on the steps headed to the horse stables.

"Oh, wow. She's pissed," Winona said.

Jackson scowled. "And thanks so much for your contribution to that."

"Let me go talk to her." She stood and smoothed the skirt of her dress.

"No. If I were you, I'd stay clear of Eve. Stay *here*."

Jackson went inside, grabbed a set of truck keys, and called out to Mima, "Tell Eve I'll be right back."

He heaved all of Winona's luggage in the bed of the truck, and when she still stood nearby simply observing his efforts, he opened the passenger side door and unceremoniously waved her inside.

With a huff, she climbed in, adjusted her seat belt, and he shut the door.

Rolling down the hill, the truck's wheels kicking up dirt, he had a mind to tell Winona never to look him up again. Lose his number. Forget his face. But in the music business, contacts were important. You couldn't burn bridges. Winona still had a large following in Nashville. She hadn't had a hit for a couple of years, but he figured she'd just taken some time off and was probably in the studio working on something new. She was a regular presenter at the CMA Awards shows and knew a lot of Nashville royalty. But he still wasn't going to bow to her whims. He never had and wasn't about to start now.

"Don't you have a hotel in town?" she asked.

"We used to have one in town, but it closed down. Kerrville's about a forty-minute drive."

"Wow, y'all really are in the boondocks." When he didn't chuckle along with her, she said, "Sorry. I don't like small towns."

"You might like Stone Ridge."

"Yeah, I saw some signs coming into town. Is that some kind of a joke?"

"Nope."

"Why do women eat free at Papi's?"

"Because we don't have many of them."

"Get out of here! What happened to the women?"

He shrugged. "There seems to be a shortage."

"Hmm," Winona said, and he could almost hear her wheels spinning.

They rode in blessed silence for a few minutes. Of course, Winona wouldn't let that last. "Can we talk soon?"

"The wedding's over now so I have a little more time."

"My manager and I've got a lot of stuff in the pipeline. Shows, even working on a possible Netflix special. A movie made from one of my songs! But I mainly wanted to discuss an important venture where I need the best partner I can find. Come by the hotel tomorrow night, and I'll get us room service. We can catch up on old times."

"I'll meet you in the hotel restaurant. Not going up to your room."

"Can't resist me, huh?"

"I can." He said this through gritted teeth.

Even though Mima was not fond of the woman that he'd married and divorced within less than six months, she had raised Jackson better than to drop off any woman at a curb. So, dutifully, he walked her inside and waited until she was able to get a room. Winona immediately got recognized by some of the staff, who fawned over her, asked for her autograph, took selfies, and managed to somehow find her a vacancy on the penthouse floor.

He sat on the lobby's sofa, legs crossed at the ankles, Stetson tipped, until Winona waved him over. "Yeah?"

The hotel clerk grinned. "It is you. Y'all were so cute together. Wish you'd never been divorced. You make such a cute couple!"

"That's what I keep tellin' him," Winona said, handing over her black Amex card. "Maybe I'll get lucky and he'll give me another chance."

"Oh, how sweet," the clerk said, hand on her heart.

That wouldn't happen in a million years, even *if* there was no Eve Iglesias. But there was, and he didn't want or need anyone else. The concierge gathered Winona's luggage and she turned expectantly to Jackson.

"This is where we say goodbye."

"You mean good night," Winona said, giving a little wave. "See you tomorrow, sweetheart!"

Jackson scowled, grunted, and then got the hell out of Dodge.

* * *

*Deep, even breaths.*

Eve had watched as Jackson piled Winona's luggage in the truck's bed and they'd both left in a hurry. Why was he in such a hurry to get rid of her? Did she have news for him, like she was pregnant with their child? Eve drew in a sharp breath. Everything in her life could be upended again, just when she and Jackson had started something. She'd have to step aside, this time for an innocent child.

Eve went for a long ride with Thimble and tried to cool her temper but that didn't work this time. Ever since her meltdown, her anger wasn't staying below the surface. She couldn't tamp it down and ignore it. Her therapist had told her that righteous anger was a good thing. The problem became when a person wasn't angry at a person or situation, but instead was simply an angry person to begin with. That's where she'd been years ago and refused to become that woman again.

However, she told herself, thinking even her therapist would agree, she was angry at *Winona James*. This might be just fine. Who showed up out of the blue the way she had, without an invitation?

Hopping off and holding Thimble's reins, she led her back into the stables and unsaddled her. She bent to pick up the bucket containing the brushes and hoof pick. Right now, she craved routine. Comfort. Watching that beautiful woman jump into Jackson's arms took her back in time to a dark place. After seeing the photo of Winona and Jackson, she'd sat in the parking lot of the Piggy Wiggly and made the biggest knee-jerk mistake of her life. She'd called Matt even though every instinct told her not to.

Her heart and mind knew it wasn't her fault. Nothing Matt had done could be excused by her own behavior. But she should have never called him in the first place as a reaction to seeing that photo of Jackson and Winona in the supermarket tabloid. Another rash decision made in the heat of the moment that had changed the trajectory of her life. But she'd been lonely and in such pain from losing Jackson. She had to be kinder to herself. Forgiving. This was what the therapist had told her.

*That was then, this is now.*

Yes, but *she's* here. Why? Eve wasn't ready to fight for anyone but herself. She'd carved a precious life in Stone Ridge, straight out of smoke and ashes. And she would cling to that reality because it was all she had. Now, she could support herself with the solid and respectable living she made as a veterinarian. Jackson was no longer her entire world.

"Sometimes I'm afraid I'm going to lose myself in him again," she spoke softly to Thimble as she brushed her body with the bristle brush. "That's how it's always been with us. Because when we're together it's addicting. He's larger than life and he takes my breath. Bet you wish you had my problems, right? And maybe I wish someone would brush *my* mane every day."

"Baby, if you want me to brush your hair every day just ask."

Eve jumped at the sexy baritone sound of Jackson's voice in her good ear. She hadn't even heard the truck pull up. Then he did something even sexier. He picked up a brush and started on Thimble's other side.

"I know you have a hundred questions dancing around in your head right now so let me hear it."

"Your ex-wife is very beautiful." She started with the question that had been simmering on a low flame. "Did you invite her here?"

"Why would I? She just showed up. That's what she does."

"No one shows up like that unless they think someone will be happy to see them."

"Did I *look* happy?"

"You looked…shocked."

"Exactly, because Winona has a way of showing up unannounced and making trouble."

"Maybe you shouldn't have married her if you felt that way."

"When I married her, Eve, I was at the lowest point of my life. Still drinkin' too much. Still hurting. Winona is ten years older than me and I was just a country bumpkin to her."

"You said you hadn't talked to her in months."

"I haven't."

"How can she just show up like that, with no encouragement?" Eve brushed Thimble harder. "I'm not sure I believe you."

"I won't ever lie to you. I told Winona we have no secrets between us anymore. Lies are a big deal, especially since we just forgave each other for a lot of crap. If you lie to me, you're going to piss me off."

"I'm not the one who's lyin'!" She shot back.

"Neither am I!"

"Where did you take her? She can stay here, if you'd like."

"Why would *you* want her to stay?"

"I don't, but if you do, that's fine with me."

He snorted. "Yeah. Okay, Eve."

Well, shit, he didn't sound like her believed her!

Since Jackson was helping with the brushing, Eve went for the hoof pick. "We didn't make any promises to each other this time. Maybe that's for the best."

"I'm going to stay home longer," Jackson said, meeting her eyes from across Thimble.

Her heart seemed to literally jump in her chest, which pissed her off to no end because this was *not* good. "H-how much longer?"

"I don't know. Indefinitely. Been writing more songs

here, maybe because I'm more relaxed than I've been in years."

She had noticed the stiffness in his shoulders was gone. "Well, okay. It's fine with me if you do stay longer."

"Eve, cut the crap." He dropped the brush and moved beside her.

"What?" She dropped Thimble's leg. "I'm trying to make this easier for you."

He pulled her to him. "I'm trying to fight for you, for us, but you need to let me."

The tingle that radiated through her body when he said those words was exactly the wrong thing to feel. It shouldn't matter, but her body wasn't listening.

"Why is she here, Jackson? What was so important?"

His brow furrowed. "She seems to think I'm making a mistake falling in love with you all over again."

"Did she *tell* you that? She doesn't even know me!"

"She's heard about you. You're all I talked about for a while. And I'm sorry to say, no one who heard my end of the story took your side. But there are always two sides, aren't there?"

She remembered how hard life had been for her during that time, but she'd had Sadie, and her mother, and a handful of true friends who understood. Then she'd had the benefit of starting over in a new town where no one had to know or hear about her sad love story. The jilted groom. The runaway bride. But the people closest to her had heard all about Jackson. Her roommate, and Bobby.

She threaded her hands around his neck and rose on tiptoes. "Where did you take her? The airport?"

"I took her to Kerrville. She asked to meet with me tomorrow."

"Where?" Her stomach dropped. "In her *hotel* room?"

"I said I'd meet in the hotel restaurant. I'm sure she wants to talk about some kind of musical partnership. I feel like I owe it to her to listen, because I do feel bad for her. She did help my career once, maybe I could help her now somehow. Not sure how, but it's hard to watch someone so talented waste away with boozing. I came too close to that myself."

Eve swallowed hard at the guilt by association. It wasn't her fault he'd chosen to drink but she still felt responsible. "Guess I'm bein' selfish. You're right. If you can help her, you ought to. She did seem kind of desperate."

"Jumping into my arms and calling me her husband when we were married for three months five years ago? Yeah, I'd say so."

"Well, I know what it's like to feel desperate."

He pressed his forehead to hers. "Not like that, you don't. You've always had a lot of self-respect. I can't tell you how rare that is in show business."

Eve took a deep breath and buried her face in Jackson's warm neck. She'd told herself she would trust.

And he hadn't done anything to make her doubt him.

# CHAPTER 27

The next morning while she cooked breakfast for the cowboys, Mima read Eve the riot act. "Have you taken leave of your senses, child? You're letting that she-devil get close to your man."

"Jackson wants to hear her out and maybe he can help her. I remember that not long ago someone very dear helped me." Eve looked at Mima significantly. "Don't you want me to do what the good book says, too? I'm helpin' my neighbor."

"Don't help her to your man! I see what you're sayin' but a woman like that doesn't come around here, call Jackson her husband, if she doesn't deep down inside have designs on him."

"It takes two to play that game. I refuse to be a jealous woman."

The words hit uncomfortably too close to her own personal fears, but Jackson had done everything he could to reassure her. Besides, if he wanted Winona, Eve had given him every chance. Of course, the jury was still out on *what* Winona wanted from Jackson. Eve doubted it was innocent.

She probably did want Jackson back, because she was no fool. Jackson was the best man Eve had ever met, and no doubt he was the best Winona had met.

"Where's Jackson now?" Mima asked, as she cracked an egg with her right hand.

"He heard Hank wanted help mending a fence line, so he's gone up there."

"Good, that boy needs to remember ranching is in his blood."

"He's never going to be a rancher. He's doing what he loves but maybe we can help him to find a way to do it here."

"Now you're talkin'."

"He said he's stayin' indefinitely. I have the feeling that he's tired of show business. All the business part of it anyway. He loves the music, but he can do that anywhere. I plan on making him want to stay home, don't worry."

"You're a gosh dern genius!"

"I like to think so."

"Like my dear old departed Albert used to gnaw on and on about, keep your friends close and your enemies closer."

With that, Eve was off to work where she checked in with Annabeth. Eve's day involved driving two hours in each direction to care for a pig with the swine flu and check in on a pregnant mare who'd been bred with a champion stud. Another cloud had lifted. The progress had encouraged her, and she felt happy. Happier than she had been in a long time about work. Her life.

Later that night after a quick dinner, Eve had just finished showering when she heard heavy footsteps coming down the hall. Jackson must be back from mending fences. Poor man had to be exhausted. Personal trainer or not, a hard day at the ranch was like no other workout. As had become her custom this week, she pulled a bathrobe over her naked body and opened the door to Jackson's room, shutting it quickly. Jackson lay on the bed fully clothed with only his boots off. Face first, it appeared he'd crashed as soon as he hit the mattress.

He groaned. "Got in a fight with a fence."

"Did the fence come at you from behind or was it a frontal attack?"

"Don't know, but every side of me hurts."

"Aww, baby. You're just not used to ranching anymore, that's all." She sat on the edge of his bed, ready to rub the kinks out of his shoulders.

But Jackson suddenly rolled over and pinned her under him in two seconds flat. He gave her a slow smile. "Maybe I should reconsider acting lessons. Got a real gift for it. Had you going."

"You tricked me!" She laughed from underneath him.

"I'm strong enough to take the physical punishment of ranching. Still got to prove it to my dad, but that's what today was about."

Confusion pulsed through her. She'd have thought Jackson left that struggle behind. He'd found his own success.

"You don't have *anything* to prove."

"Yeah. Try telling that to Hank, who thinks that all I do is prance around the stage, sing, and make good money." Braced above her, his thumb traced her bottom lip and then tugged it.

"And there's a lot more to it than that." She didn't know but she hazarded a guess. Nothing in life was as simple as it seemed from the outside.

One hand skillfully loosened the belt of her bathrobe. "Baby, you don't know the half of it."

"I *want* to know." She didn't know anything about that part of his life apart from what had happened with Winona.

"We've never talked about that part of my life."

"Don't you want to share it?"

"Look, I know I've got it good and can't complain. But it just isn't all a fun house twenty-four seven." His thumb now slowly circled her nipple and her entire body tightened in response. "There are takers all around. People who want something, who think I can do something for them, who need me to keep them working. I feel responsible for my backup band. They depend on me to tour, so they have steady work. It's a lot of pressure sometimes."

"I can believe it. You mean takers like Winona?"

"And much worse." He unwrapped her the rest of the way like a present and moaned when he saw that she was completely naked. "But right now, I feel like I'm the one who hit the jackpot."

She smiled. "Ever have any regrets?"

He studied her with a deep, soulful gaze that made her womb squeeze. "My only regret is that music took me away from you."

"Funny. I have the same regret."

"I'm not surprised. It's why so many marriages and relationships fail. The road is tough on couples."

While this wasn't what she wanted to hear, the truth was better than a fancy lie. "That makes me sad for you."

*For us.*

"And you." He kissed her, a long deep kiss that reached all the way to her soul.

When he pulled back, she was breathless again. "Do you think you'll ever marry again?"

"I'd have to find the right woman, that's for sure. Someone who knows me. Someone who has my back. Maybe even someone who doesn't need me to do anything for *their* career. Someone who already has their own career." He winked. "Why, you know of anyone?"

"I might. Anything else?" She grinned, because he made it sound as though he'd put a lot of thought behind this.

"Obviously, I seem to prefer women who challenge me." He nuzzled her neck. "I think that's because Lincoln dropped me on my head as a baby."

She framed his face. "A strong woman is a good thing."

"Uh-huh." He grinned. "A very good thing."

"What else is on your list for the perfect wife?"

"I'm done talkin'," he said, unbuttoning his shirt and pulling it off. "I need a shower, and you're coming with me."

"I already—"

But when Jackson yanked her off the bed in one swoop, Eve decided that two showers in the space of thirty minutes wasn't crazy at all.

As he'd promised, later that evening, Jackson left for Kerrville and met Winona for a late supper in the hotel restaurant, a large and modern place with wide open spaces. Lots of sterile couches in bright primary colors outside the eating area. He would have preferred to sit there, but of course Winona led them to a private table in the rear.

He pulled out her chair and sat across from her, removing his Stetson. "What's this partnership you wanted to talk about?"

"Right to the point, huh? I thought we might chat for a while and catch up." She took the wine menu from the waiter and perused it.

"Should you be drinking?"

"How sweet of you to worry. I've cut back substantially. Only wine now. And if this partnership of ours works out, I swear I'll give it up completely." She held up her palm in the universal swearing-in style.

"What *partnership*? Winona, you should know that I'm

thinking about stayin' here. Not going back to Nashville. I called my manager about putting up the house for sale."

He'd done that this morning, and he still hadn't told Eve or Mima. He wanted to surprise Eve first.

"You're serious?"

"It's been a long time comin'. Our original band broke up a long time ago. Cory is a producer, Rick and Clay studio musicians. They're all married and raising families. I'm still the only one touring and writing songs with a studio backup band."

"Do you want to stop?"

"I want to stop touring and I'll make sure to get the guys other work. I'll keep writing songs, but I don't need to live in Nashville to do that."

"But you can't be a major success without touring! Without putting in the blood, sweat, and tears. I've already explained this to you. Don't you want to be a *star* like me? You're so close. Jackson, you're the full package. Looks, talent, charisma. It's just a matter of time now."

"Maybe I don't want that anymore."

"But you—" She set the menu down and waved her hands dismissively. "Okay, okay. I think you'll change your mind, but this partnership of ours could work either way. I could get a place in Texas and we'd work it out."

"Work *what* out?"

Winona leaned in and whispered. "I want to have your baby."

Everything inside him stilled and he seemed to be walking through thick molasses. He couldn't have heard right.

"*What?*"

"I thought we might do this the old-fashioned way, but now that there's Eve, I don't have a problem collecting your sperm."

She didn't have a problem collecting his sperm! Good to know. He straightened, hands on his thighs, pushing his spine against the back of his seat.

"Are you out of your mind?"

"Far from it. I'm no longer going to wait around for a man to be sure enough of himself to mind occasionally being called 'Mr. James.' I want a baby, and if you do this for me, we'll be square."

He scoffed. "We are square. I don't owe you anything besides my thanks."

"I gave you that divorce pretty fast. You have to admit."

"Because you *cheated* on me."

"News flash, Jackson. I did not cheat on you, just let you think I did because I could already see you wanted out. All you wanted was a reason. I also didn't make you sign a pre-nup, and you could have taken me to the cleaners."

"But I didn't." He sighed and took her hand in his, trying for the reasonable approach. "Honey, we were never in love. We were drinkin' buddies who occasionally fell into bed together. What you're asking is nuts. And I say that in the nicest way."

"I'm sure you're thinking of Eve, but if I could just talk to her, woman to woman."

He let go of her hand. "I would much rather Eve never hear about this insanity."

Jackson considered leaving, but he felt a pinch of sorrow for his friend. He understood what it was like to feel lonely. "Why don't you go to one of those um, banks?"

"I would rather *hand* pick the father of my own child. Someone in the music business with both talent and looks. I know you, and you're one of the best men I've ever known. Even when we divorced, you were kind to me. Out of all of my exes, you're the only one I still call a friend. Plus, you're so handsome you're sure to make me a good-looking kid."

"You should care about a healthy kid."

"That, too."

"You could ask someone else. Another ex."

"I'm starting with you because you're my first choice."

"What can I say? I'm honored, but I'm going to have to give this a hard pass. Sorry."

"Won't you at least think about it? I'll give you whatever you want. I'll pay you."

"Here's something I never thought I'd say, but my sperm isn't for sale."

Winona had worked herself up into a whine. "Not even for one hundred thousand dollars? Think of the new start you would get with that. It's a big chunk toward building a recording studio of your own, if you insist on moving here, or use it for whatever you'd like."

Jackson slowly shook his head, arms crossed. "Your money was never important to me and it still isn't."

"That's one of the things I love most about you, even if it's working against me now. Can you see how perfect you would be for me? Your homestyle, down to earth values would complement my more extravagant ones."

"Values are not in the DNA. They come from the way we're raised."

"Oh, of course, and you could be an involved father if you wanted to be. Is that what you want? Because I'm open to it. I just thought you'd want to make your deposit and be on your way."

"Is there anything else you wanted to discuss, because as far as I'm concerned this subject has been beaten to death."

"Fine." She ordered a glass of wine when the waiter returned, and Jackson declined. "Look, let's have a nice meal together and you just think about what I said."

"There's nothing to think about."

They got through the meal without talking more about

her ridiculous partnership request. He couldn't help thinking of his father's prized bull and the sperm he seemed unable or unwilling to produce. Jackson never thought he'd find himself commiserating with a bull. But hell, a man's sperm was as personal as someone could get. It was his, damn it. He wasn't going to have any child of his raised by a woman he didn't trust. A woman he didn't love. There wasn't enough pity in the world to make him want to help Winona with this.

And if that wasn't enough, there was Eve to consider. He could only imagine how thrilled she'd be to hear of this latest development.

Before he left, Winona couldn't resist one more parting shot. "Promise me you'll watch your back with Eve. I don't trust her, and neither should you."

He drove back and decided not to mention any of this to Eve. He'd said no secrets, but this wasn't a secret. This was a big fat nothing burger which would be just the kind of thing to upset her and feed her insecurities.

He didn't need the drama just when everything had been going so well between them.

On the way home, he stopped in the Shady Grind for a beer and to check in with Priscilla. He hadn't seen enough of his old friend since he'd been back in town, and now that he had made the decision to stay, he thought she should be among the first to know.

The crowd was light on a weekday evening, just a few stragglers sitting on the barstools. He waved to Riggs Henderson, a local rancher, as Riggs left.

Priscilla wiped the bar and gave him a big smile when she caught his eye.

"Hey, cowboy. You alone tonight?"

"Yep. Just wanted to come by for a beer and some company."

"How's your day going?"

He tipped his Stetson. "You wouldn't believe me if I told you."

"Try me." She crossed her arms. "Bartender here. I've heard it all."

He kind of doubted she'd heard this one, and given by her wide eyes, he'd been right. "I trust you can keep this between us."

She made a motion to lock her lips and throw away the key. "I wouldn't know where to start if I *wanted* to talk. No one would believe me. The nerve!"

"She helped me out during a difficult time in my life. Now she thinks I owe her for giving me a fast divorce and not making me sign a pre-nup."

"You didn't sign a *pre-nup*? But you could be—"

"A very rich man right now?" He took a pull of his beer. "Maybe. But that's not me. I always wanted to make my own way. You know that."

"'Course I do. But you could accept help now and then, you know. We have a great community right here."

"I know that. And if there's ever anything you can help me with, I'll ask. But hey, let me know if I can do anything to help you."

"Think you might stick around for good? Lillian would be so happy. She mentions it every Sunday at church. 'Jackson will be coming home. It will just take a spell.'"

Jackson chuckled. "The spell lasted eight years, but I think it's worn off. Tarnished. I'm tired of touring, I'm tired of the lifestyle. The original musicians disbanded a while ago."

"Are you under contract?"

"Between them. I got out of my contract due to creative differences." He set his beer down. "I don't know, maybe I've been trying to control everything when I should have just trusted the label to make me a star."

Priscilla took out a towel and polished a glass. "Maybe being a star isn't all it's cracked up to be when you're pushing forty and have to go around asking your exes to part with some of their sperm and make a baby."

"Life's crazy, isn't it?"

"What are you going to do next? You can't give up music entirely. Will you perform locally?"

"Maybe that, plus keep selling my songs."

"Might think I'm crazy, now, but what about buying me out? The Shady Grind is going up for sale. I'm retirin'."

At that Jackson leaned back, hands splayed on his thighs. Priscilla and the Shady Grind were fixtures in their town. "Why?"

She gave him a small smile. "Why am I retirin'? How about I'm sixty-five and have worked hard enough all my life?"

"I guess that's fair."

"You young 'uns. Think everything in your hometown is always going to remain the same. Sometimes maybe the buildings do, but people don't. We grow old, we move on. We push up daisies because somebody has to, and none of us get to live forever last I checked. I've got family in Arizona. I'll go up there for a while. See my grandkids."

"Damn. Gotta admit, never thought of you quittin' but it makes sense."

He wasn't sure what the Shady Grind would turn into without Priscilla. And who would want to move out to Stone Ridge just to take over an old bar that had seen better days?

Jesus, he was depressed now.

"Can I get another beer?"

Priscilla set it down. "Don't look so glum. Why don't you buy me out?"

That made two ridiculous offers he'd had in one day. "Me? I know nothing about runnin' a bar."

"It's not as tough as it looks." She smirked. "You don't want to be here every night, you hire good help. Lots of good men looking for jobs. It's a business, after all, and you know about the cattle business and show business. How different can it be, right?"

He was going to go out on a limb and think they were as different as apples and salami. But he supposed all businesses had some commonalities. He'd once been a part of the daily operations of the ranch and all that entailed. There was not only the actual manual work behind running the ranch but also taking care of the accounts, clients, equipment, and other details. The entire family had done their part at one time or another.

He took another pull of his beer. "I don't see myself owning a bar. I was thinking something like opening up my own recording studio so that I can make my demos and keep selling songs to other artists."

"Just think about it. It's an option. You could turn it into a real honky-tonk. Right now, it's just a small-town bar and grill with a limited menu. You were the last person to play here. I'd love to see you play here again."

"Sure, I can do that."

Coming right on the heels of being asked to be a sperm donor, the thought of turning the old Shady Grind into a passable honky-tonk was too overwhelming for today.

Still, the idea was worth considering.

# CHAPTER 28

$\mathcal{L}$ate that night, Eve went to Jackson's door.

"Feeling formal tonight?" He slid her a dark and sexy look that made roasted melty marshmallows out of pink places. "Usually you just walk right inside after a quick knock."

"I don't want to interrupt if you're busy."

"Yes, you do." He hauled her in the room and shut the door, then pinned her against it.

The hot kiss he gave her was a promise of a hot night of intense pleasure. He plundered her mouth, deep and wet. And she wanted him. More than anything. When he broke the kiss to nibble on an earlobe, her entire body pulsed with desire.

"If you're writing a song, I can come back later."

"I'll finish later." He pulled her toward the bed and moved his guitar to its stand.

She sat on his bed. "Why don't you play me something?"

Without breaking eye contact with her, he reached for the guitar. Started strumming again. "Workin' on something new. Upbeat. But I can't get more than the chorus."

"It will come to you." She took a deep breath.

She'd reached another realization that had been a long time coming. She could have been more supportive of Jackson's music. There had been nights when he'd played at the Shady Grind and she hadn't come out to see him. He'd always said he understood. Busy with work as the Truehart's groom, school, and keeping her grades up to get into veterinary school, it all hadn't left her a lot of free time. She'd always believed music was something Jackson enjoyed, like a hobby, but that he'd always be a rancher.

But she hadn't recognized just how determined he'd been, or how talented. When the offer had come for the band to go to Nashville, she'd been taken by complete surprise. Suddenly it became obvious that Jackson's music could take him far away. She'd been naïve not to have anticipated that when they'd planned for everything else about their future lives together. They should have prepared for the possibility, and then maybe Eve wouldn't have felt the ground open up under her and take everything she'd hoped for away.

Until Annabeth had revealed her five-year roadmap for success, Eve hadn't even realized how important a plan had been to her. But she'd had them, all her life. Plans to excel academically, get through veterinary school, marry Jackson, and have five children in short order. Own a horse or two and work as a vet. Okay, so maybe she'd been a tad ambitious. At the time she hadn't understood the difference between a goal and a dream.

Because Jackson had been her dream.

"Eve?" Jackson said, because apparently, she hadn't spoken in several minutes. "Baby—I can hear you thinking."

"I'm pretty tired." She stood. "First week back to work and all. I have to get up so early if I want to take Thimble for a ride."

His eyes narrowed. "But we always get up early."

"I know, but tonight I'm tired." She moved toward the door, stretched her arms, and faked a yawn.

Jackson's hand cupped the nape of her neck and he met her gaze. His eyes were soft. Tender. They were killing her. "You okay?"

"Yeah," she lied. "Sure."

"No," he said. "Don't lie to me. Where are you going?"

"To my bedroom."

"No. I mean, where are you going?" he asked again, and this time he gently touched her temple. "Don't go. Don't pull away from me because you're scared."

"I'm not—"

"Don't you think I'm afraid, too?" He took her hand and held it to his lips. "I'm terrified. I lost you once and it nearly killed me."

When he kissed the pulse point on her neck, she had an all-body shiver. "Oh, Jackson." Her fingers grazed along the stubble.

"You're scared. I get it. You're afraid of being hurt. Don't you think I'm right there with you?"

"But I would *never* hurt you again."

"You wouldn't mean to." He pressed his forehead to hers. "But just giving up on us would hurt me. More than you know."

Her own heart ached at that thought. The fact she could do that to him stunned her. It meant she held the same power that he had over her. He kissed her deeply and his warmth wound its way around her heart to give a powerful tug. She was lost in him. Just…lost.

"It's… Okay, yes I'm afraid!" She pulled away, frustrated. "And just…so *mad* at myself."

"Okay, that's more like it. Why? I want to hear this."

"No, you don't. I made so many mistakes when I was younger. Instead of making plans and goals, I had dreams.

Dreams have a way of not coming true because they tend to involve other people. But I couldn't control everyone, or everything." She sighed. "I guess I just wanted to."

He chuckled. "I think that's fair. We really haven't talked about how we're going to do this. How we're going to work it out this time."

"What do you mean?"

"I want to marry you. We can make it work this time." He kissed the palm of her hand.

"Oh, Jackson, I love you so much, but I want to stay here in Stone Ridge. I have a good job, and a great community I know and love."

"Okay," he said. "Then I'll stay here. I won't go back to Nashville."

She blinked. Twice. "You can't do that. What about your music?"

"I'll do it here. Figure something out."

"But will you be happy here if I'm the only reason you're staying?"

"You'd be reason enough for me, but I do love our crazy town. Hank and I have been spending more time together, and small miracle, we're not always yelling at each other. And of course, there's Mima. I don't kid myself into thinkin' she'll live forever."

"But I want you to be happy, too."

"I am happy. The minute I decided I'd stay, it was like a weight lifted. I didn't know how much I dreaded going back. My management isn't going to be thrilled to hear it, but I don't have any loose ends. The last contract fell through when the producer walked off. We hadn't scheduled any tour dates because I was supposed to be in the studio recording."

"What will you do?"

"Well, Priscilla wants me to buy the Shady Grind." He laughed. "Wouldn't that be something? The first place I ever played. I'll think about it, but either way I'll fit my music in. The part I love. Writing songs. And Hank needs me from time to time. Guess I'll be a part-time cowboy."

Eve opened her mouth to speak, but she couldn't. She didn't trust herself not to sob. Instead, she felt a tear slip down her cheek.

Jackson wiped it with his thumb. "Did I upset you, or are these happy tears?"

She nodded. "Happy ones."

Then she jumped him, wrapping her legs around his waist. She kissed him, and made love to him, until he was as happy as she.

# CHAPTER 29

It hadn't taken Lillian long to see that something substantial had shifted between Jackson and Eve after the wedding. The two were no longer making any effort to hide the fact they'd pretty much moved in together. Normally Lillian wouldn't approve, but these two deserved a little leeway. Substantial progress had been made, and all this without the quilt.

She probably no longer *needed* the quilt, though it would be nice to have as a backup just in case those two got themselves a wild hair. Unfortunately, their type of intense passion was at times the problem itself. Love like that could go sideways in an instant with two such headstrong personalities.

Such as when a blond, shiny obstacle showed up on one's doorstep…uninvited.

As always when she was in need of help from up above, Lillian strode outside into the cool, brisk morning and held out her arms to the heavens.

"Dear Lord, what am I supposed to *do* about this mess?"

Albert casually observed from the fence post where he sat

perched, his Sunday Stetson tilted back. "Just can't help your-self, can you?"

"I worry that Winona James could mess up all my wonderful progress."

Albert snorted. "*Your* wonderful progress?"

Lillian waved him away. "Suppose you're goin' to tell me I didn't have anythin' to do with this beautiful reunion happenin' right now under my own roof."

"Was the weddin' brought them together again in the same place. Thank Lincoln and Sadie."

"Ha!" Just like Albert not to give her any credit where credit was due. "Now the hard part starts."

"Hard part?"

"Keepin' him here, you dunce! Don't you get it? Jackson belongs at *home*. And Eve will get him to stay."

"Or she'll go with him."

"Bah!" Lillian wouldn't even consider that possibility. "You're wrong again, old man."

"Who are you talking to, Lillian?"

Lillian whipped around to find Brenda scanning the area. "What? Oh, no one. Just talkin' to myself. You know...praying."

She smiled. "I do that sometimes, too. I talk to the Lord when I'm cleaning. It's being alone so much, I think."

"That, too. Any luck finding that quilt?"

"The quilt?" Brenda looked confused.

"*Eve's* wedding quilt? The one I've been turning up the house to find. You were supposed to help." Lillian crossed her arms. "Well, isn't that why you're here?"

"Yes, yes. Of course." Then she looked at the ground and shook her head. "I can't seem to find it."

"Oh, dear. Well, it has to be *somewhere*."

"Maybe Eve got rid of it?"

It was as if the woman hadn't been listening to Lillian, or was preoccupied. "She *told* Sadie that she kept it."

"Oh, that's right. But she may have lost it and doesn't even know she did. If she hasn't looked at it in a while, that might be the case."

Lillian hadn't thought of that. Had she been wasting all her time on this quest? As if she didn't have enough on her plate!

"You should know, Brenda, we may have a problem. *She* showed up. Jackson's ex-wife. Winona."

"Why is that a problem?"

"The woman has designs on him. Just you wait and see."

"I thought they were married for such a short time."

"Yes. It wasn't a real marriage if you ask me. Maybe that's the problem. She's back to ask to extend the contract."

Brenda gave a little smile. "I guess that will be up to Jackson, then."

"Huh." Lillian didn't know how the woman could remain so calm. Maybe because she hadn't seen the blonde throw herself into Jackson's arms.

"Lillian," Brenda now said, kindly. "Please don't worry yourself about this. When two people want to be together, they will find a way even with some challenges. But it does have to be both, not just one of them."

"I'm sure you're right. I need to relax." Lillian fanned herself. "Eve...she's just been through so much. And people were so...unkind."

She could count herself among those people. The guilt still ate her alive some days. Anger could be such a powerful thing. Wielded like a sword which cut both ways. It had taken her a while to realize the anger she felt for Eve was slowly killing Lillian.

Brenda touched Lillian's shoulder gently. "I hope you're

not blaming yourself any longer. It was natural for you to be angry with Eve. She did a foolish thing."

"She was just a girl. I shouldn't have been so hard on her." Lillian turned then, at the sound of a horse's hooves.

There was Hank, atop a gelding. He stopped a few feet away from them, hopped off, and walked toward them holding the reins.

"Hey, Brenda," he said.

"Hello."

"Son, what are you up to today?" Lillian said.

"The usual," Hank said and narrowed his eyes. "I thought you had physical therapy today."

"I rescheduled."

She'd had the cast removed the day before the wedding, a huge relief. But now the doctor wanted to further torture her. He said mobility was lacking or some such thing, and she ought to have some therapy for it. Lillian offered to do the exercises at home, but they still insisted on an appointment. She figured she'd keep rescheduling until they gave up on her.

"Mother, you can't ignore this," Hank warned. "If the doctor said physical therapy, you need physical *therapy*."

"Thank you for caring. It makes me feel alive." She realized it sounded sarcastic, but she did mean it on some level. "Why are you here, anyway?"

Hank rolled his eyes. "Came to check in on you. Knew you'd probably canceled. I thought Daisy was supposed to take you and she's over at the ranch now helpin' out."

Lillian tossed her hands up. "With *that Wade*? Oh good Lord. Son, you have to keep those two apart."

"Huh? Why?"

"I should get back to work," Brenda said, and waved goodbye to them both.

After Brenda had gone, Lillian turned to Hank. "Honestly,

Hank. It wasn't *Daisy* taking me to the doctor. It was Jackson. I'm surprised you don't remember that."

"Oh, right. Forgot."

Forgetting to be annoyed with him, Lillian felt a fresh tug of affection for her only son. At fifty-six, he was still such a strapping lad. Tall, built, full head of silver hair just like his daddy's. He'd done the best he could after Maggie left him with three young children. It had been natural to be angry when he'd given up so much to make her happy. Including possibly the only woman he'd never loved.

But he'd never given up on his children, or the ranch. He was indeed his father's son.

"Come inside, sugar. I've got a slice of apple pie for you."


EVE AND ANNABETH were having a slow day. No large animal calls for Eve. Their office days usually fit a pattern of feast or famine. But it was a good time to review and do some planning. The business part of being a vet was overwhelming at times for Eve. Annabeth was much better at it. She both understood and enjoyed accounting ledgers and spreadsheets. She'd created a five-year plan at the end of which they should be completely in the black. Then they could afford to hire a full-time receptionist and some admin help.

When it was time for lunch, Annabeth was elbow deep into next year's budget, so Eve offered to walk over to the Shady Grind for burgers and fries to go. She and Annabeth would eat at their desks.

"Hey, Priscilla," Eve said. "Can I get two Shady Burgers and fries to go?"

"Sure, darlin'. I'll go put the order in," Priscilla said, and walked through the double doors to the kitchen.

Eve chatted with a few of the locals about the crazy Texas weather. A few months ago, a tornado had ripped through a small town southeast of here and practically taken every business establishment and most homes with it. There had never been a tornado through Stone Ridge, as they usually passed right over, but they'd had plenty of thunderstorms and ice storms.

Priscilla was back within seconds. "It should just be a jiffy for those burgers. Jackson was just in here couple nights ago. Good catchin' up with that boy. I'm trying to talk him into buyin' the Shady Grind." Priscilla gave the bar a wipe. "He said he didn't think it was right for him. But I think it's worth thinking about. He could do what he wants with the place. Maybe turn it into a good old-fashioned honky-tonk. Put in a good word for me, yeah?"

"Of course, I will," Eve said. "But I think everyone forgets that Jackson does what he wants, not what I ask him to do."

"You have more pull than most," Priscilla said. "Either way, I'm sellin' the place and retiring."

"Oh no. The place won't be the same without you."

As long as Eve could remember, Priscilla had lived here. A tough single mother who'd raised three boys and one daughter, who had all moved out of the area. She'd never married again after her rancher husband died and left her with a ton of bills to pay.

When Eve's orders were up, she paid and started the short walk back to the office. There was a small commotion at the General Store, and Eve looked over to see Winona, surrounded by men, signing autographs and posing for selfies. Eve's gut tightened, because no matter what Jackson had said about Winona getting older and insecure about her looks, the woman was drop-dead gorgeous, whether or not she was nearly forty.

Eve still didn't know what Winona was doing in Stone Ridge, but Jackson had assured her it had nothing to do with him. Last night she'd forgotten to ask him what Winona had wanted to talk to him about but assumed it had to do with music. Eve walked faster to the office, hoping no one would notice her. She was a little bit embarrassed by her temper on the day of Winona's arrival and hated for her to know that she'd rattled Eve.

"There's a bit of a commotion," Eve said, dropping the food on the desk where Annabeth sat, riveted to a profit/loss statement. "Winona James is out there, and she's got every man's attention."

"Winona James?" Annabeth glanced up, her eyes wide. "*The* Winona James?"

"You like her?"

"She's Nashville royalty. I love her music, but I haven't heard anything from her in a while. You know I can't stand country music, but I love the twist she puts in her songs. She's more indie inspired. Used to play a lot in Austin. All her songs are angsty. Nasty. You cheated on me, watch me key your precious truck. I *love* it."

"Um, okay…"

"C'mon, Eve, you really do need to listen to other people's music. Jackson Carver isn't the *only* one who can sing."

Just the best, but Eve wasn't in the mood to argue. She shrugged. "She was married to Jackson for about a minute."

Annabeth cocked her head. "And how do you feel about that?"

"I've known he was married and divorced from her for quite a while. He says they don't even talk anymore."

Just then the door to the clinic opened and in waltzed Winona. For a country music star, she dressed more like a runway model. Eve would bet her clothes were designer and they fit her like they were tailored to her body. She had a little silver purse and matching ankle boots. Eve glanced down at her boots, Wranglers, and flannel shirt over a Henley top.

"Winona James!" Annabeth stood and went around the desk to shake Winona's hand. "Such a pleasure. I'm a big fan of yours. "

"Oh, honey, aren't you sweet? Everyone in town is so lovely and I have to admit, the men! They're so courteous and attentive. Every one of them a looker. I might just have to move here."

Eve swallowed hard.

"Hey, there, Eve," Winona said. "You doing okay? I'm so sorry we didn't get a chance to chat the other day."

"That's okay."

At Annabeth's curious look, Winona said, "I must have forgotten my southern manners. I dropped by unannounced and just about got kicked out on my rear. That will show me to call first."

"Can we help you with anything?" Annabeth asked, falling into professional mode.

"I'd actually like to talk to Eve, if that's okay." She turned to Eve with the fakest smile she'd ever seen.

"Actually, I'm at work so I don't have time to—" Eve began.

"Go ahead, Eve," Annabeth urged. "It's a slow day, after all. If we get a call, I'll be sure to come get you."

"I guess I'll eat my burger later." Eve threw a longing look at her yummy lunch.

"Or I'll treat you to something," Winona said.

"No, but thanks." Eve didn't want to spend too much time with Winona.

Maybe that was unfair, but in addition to the fact that Winona seemed to still care about Jackson, she was a trigger for Eve. Just looking at Winona made Eve's palms sweat, the normal precursor to an anxiety attack. But not this time. She'd keep her cool using the techniques she'd learned long ago. Deep breaths. Counting. Going over routines.

They walked just outside the office and Eve shut the door. With her back to the door, as if ready to take flight back inside, she turned to Winona. "What can I do for you?"

"I want to apologize for shocking you the way I did." She sighed. "But Jackson and I were always so close, I thought he might welcome me."

"I'm sorry if that upset you."

"It didn't upset me. He didn't mean it. I know Jackson and he's kind. I nursed him through a terrible heartache, and we grew so close during that time, as only two people who are both hurting can do. I guess that's how we fell in love. Our marriage was short lived, but I blame that mostly on our horrendous tour schedules. We were apart more than together. I honestly think if not for that, we'd still be married."

Eve felt an uncomfortable, sickening feeling spread to her churning gut. She'd seen this kind of thing before. Women fighting over a man, trying to intimidate each other in passive aggressive moves. Winona didn't know this sort of thing just didn't happen in Stone Ridge.

"I don't know what to say." Eve crossed her arms.

*You're lying.*

*I don't believe you.*

*I believe Jackson.*

*I love Jackson. He loves me.*

"I'm sure you and Jackson don't have any secrets, so he's probably talked to you about me."

"Yes, he has." Eve threw her a significant look. She'd heard the story and it was nothing like the one Winona had just told.

Still, a tiny seed of doubt planted itself. If Jackson had been devastated by his and Winona's breakup, maybe he wouldn't have been honest about it with Eve. To save his ego. And surely, Eve considered, it was fine that he'd loved

Winona at one time. Eve thought she'd loved Bobby. Everybody made mistakes.

"Did he tell you I asked him to father my baby?"

Eve nearly fell, grateful she had her back against the door. "Wh-what?"

"Oh, crap. I'm not going about this very well, am I? I seem to be shocking everyone. This is a small town and a bit of a throwback. Y'all probably are just not up on the times. But here's the thing, Eve. I'm going to be forty this year, and I don't have time to waste with pleasantries. This is my last chance to have a baby and I want this more than anything. I put this off too long, thinking I'd always have a family later. Later is *here*. Jackson and I have a connection, a deep friendship, and I think we'd make good parents."

Lord! Why on earth wouldn't Jackson tell her about any of this? Unless he was quietly considering fathering Winona's baby, Eve didn't see why they couldn't both have a big laugh about it. She burned with heat.

"I can see you're shocked and I'm sorry. Jackson turned me down, if you want to know the truth. I even offered him money. While I hope he'll think about it, I have a feeling he's done with me."

"Well, I hope you don't expect *me* to help change his mind."

Convincing him to consider buying the Shady Grind was one thing. Fathering an ex's child was far more than Eve would ever be able to accept.

"I'm pretty much resigned to the fact. I missed my chance with him." She looked behind her, at the small group of men that were gathered, watching her with eager smiles. She gave them all a little wave. "But I wasn't lyin' about making my home in Stone Ridge. For now. If I can't find a father for my child here, I don't think it's possible."

Eve snorted. "There are banks for this kind of thing."

"Not here. You don't even have a *hairdresser* in town. Anyway, I prefer to pick my own, up close and personal. Maybe even do this the fun way." She did a little jiggle.

"Well, this has been fun," Eve said, "but my burger is getting cold. If you'll excuse me."

Winona held out her palm. "I know y'all think I'm crazy, but taking risks got me out of a trailer park when I was sixteen years old. So, I just keep right on taking them."

Eve nodded, and with that she let herself back in the office and shut the door on the bright, shiny, and very sad person that was Winona James.

Jackson had just finished a rough day helping Hank with tagging new colts when he rode Taco back to the house. Looking forward to seeing Eve, he quickly unsaddled Taco and put him in his stall.

When he walked into the kitchen, Eve sat at the table, her eyes narrowed, lips pursed at him.

"What?" he asked, reading the room.

She stood. "You have got a lot of nerve!"

"Hell, yeah, I do but you like that about me." He tossed his hat.

"Winona came into town today. She told me about her offer."

Oh, crap. Dread spiked through him. "Did she tell you I said no?"

"Actually, she did. But that's not the point!" She slapped the table.

It had been a long time since he'd seen Eve this mad. Damn, it looked good on her.

"Okay, what is the point?"

Eve tossed her hands up. "Ugh!"

She then went out the back door of the kitchen. He knew where she was headed and started after her.

"Hang on, son," Mima said, walking into the kitchen.

"Did you hear all this?"

"All the sperm talk about Winona? Yes, Eve told me. She needed to unload, I guess. Kind of felt like I was talkin' to Hank about his prized bull for a minute. Go figure, my grandson, a stud."

"That's *not* funny."

"Forgive me, then, son, but you've done met some strange people in show business."

He couldn't argue. "I need to go straighten this out with Eve right now."

"First give her a head start. She needs to cool down and a ride alone usually does that for her."

Groaning, Jackson accepted that. He'd give her a head start, then he and Taco would follow, and he'd explain everything. By tonight they would be back in his bedroom again for another mind-blowing night together.

He took a seat and shoved a hand through his hair. "I didn't tell her because I didn't want to upset her. I didn't anticipate Winona would play her head games with Eve. What could she hope to accomplish? Did she think I'd be *more* willing to help her out now? I wasn't angry with her for suggesting the idea, but I am now. She doesn't get to treat Eve like this. I'll have words with Winona."

"Good," Mima said, sitting next to him. "But you should realize something. You were right, and I was wrong."

That's something he didn't get to hear around here too often. "Yeah? About what?"

"I told you that Eve was a different woman now, and you said you'd have to remind her of who she is." She patted his hand. "That flash of anger and temper? Look at our girl go.

Eve's allowing herself to *feel* everything again and I bet that's scary for her."

He hadn't considered that. Eve had come a long way in the past weeks. She wasn't fighting her anger any longer. He'd say the tipping point was the day of the wedding and how she'd come apart with memories.

And then she'd put herself back together again. She amazed him every day.

"I think I've given her enough of a head start."


WHEN JACKSON finally caught sight of Eve standing next to Thimble at the edge of the creek that ran through both the Carver and Truehart properties, he slowed Taco and headed their way. Thimble drank from the creek, and as soon as Jackson unsaddled, Taco joined her. But as he passed Eve, he snorted unhappily. Safe to say Taco still didn't care much for Eve. Loyal to the core, his gelding.

Eve crossed her arms and jutted out a hip. She threw him a stony look.

He moved to stand beside her but didn't even try to touch her. "I know I'm in the doghouse. Go on and let me have it."

"Why didn't you tell me?" She huffed. "Jackson, you've got to stop trying to protect me! You should have told me before *she* did."

"The whole idea was so nuts, I didn't want to bother you with it. You have enough on your mind."

"She sure takes a lot of liberties with you!" She kicked the ground. "I have to wonder why she's still so connected to you after all this time."

"She *isn't* connected to me."

"Why would she even think to ask you such a thing? Have you encouraged her?"

"No! That's just how she is. She got used to having people

do what she wants. She said it's her last chance to have a baby."

"She should go to one of those banks!"

"That's what I suggested." He winced and pinched the bridge of his nose.

"And she told me that you two talk every week. Your divorce didn't stop you from being together afterwards." She held up air quotes.

Now he was livid. He'd been kind to Winona but that would stop. Some people took kindness for weakness and it surprised him to realize that he hadn't known that about Winona until now. Or understood just how desperate she'd become.

He should have.

"She's a damn liar."

"I know."

The boulder that had taken up residence on his chest eased up. Thank the Lord she believed him. He actually let out a breath. "You believe me."

"Of course, I do," Eve said. "I know you, and now I think I know her. This might never happen in Stone Ridge, but I recognized something she tried. It used to happen a lot at the university. I'd see other women do it to each other sometimes, over a man. She was trying to intimidate me, trying to plant a seed of doubt in my mind."

"You didn't let her." But in the next moment, confusion pulsed through him. "Then why are you so mad?"

"Because you *should* have told me! You can't keep trying to protect me from anything that might be uncomfortable. Or…weird."

"You're right."

She covered her face with her hands and his stomach dove south when he noticed the slight tremor in her hand. "I have a bad memory that seeing her brings up."

"Tell me." No longer able to stay back, he tugged her into his arms and held on tight.

"Some years ago, I saw a photo of both of you in a tabloid magazine. You were walking hand-in-hand and they printed that you were recently married. I didn't have any right to feel the way I did, but I was hurt. It was the moment I realized I'd lost you for good. And it was my own damn fault."

"I never loved her, Eve."

"That hardly matters now. The biggest decisions of my life were knee-jerk reactions, and they were all my biggest mistakes. Leavin' you at the altar when the night before I was ready to marry you."

"That was brave even if it was a mistake."

"Maybe I was brave, but that courage caused me to make some snap decisions I still regret."

"Glad to hear you regret leavin' me. Got to admit."

She spoke into his chest now, her soft voice muffled. Her arms tightened around his waist. "Don't ever doubt it for a minute."

Jackson tipped her chin to meet his gaze. "You okay?"

"Yeah." Reaching to squeeze his arms, she slid him a hopeful smile.

"Kiss me and prove it." The corner of his mouth tipped up in the start of a smile as he leaned lower.

The kiss was sweet and tender, reminding her of what they had. What they were never going to lose again.

When they broke the kiss, Eve met his eyes. "She's crazy to ask you, but I can only imagine how desperate she is. I know what it's like to feel desperate, alone, and to wish that someone would help."

The words kicked him in the gut. "Yeah. I guess you do."

She crossed her arms and gave him her back. "She loves you, I hope you know. As more than a friend."

"The feeling's not mutual." Coming up behind her, he pulled her back to his chest. "You forgive me?"

She climbed back on Thimble. "As long as you ride with me, cowboy."

EVE RODE THIMBLE at a gallop slightly ahead of Jackson, but he always had Taco keep a close pace. She figured Jackson was hanging back, because Taco was faster and stronger than Thimble. They all fell into a gradual easy rhythm as they crossed the hills of Ridge Valley. She doubted there was anywhere else on earth more beautiful than Hill Country. When people thought of Texas wildflowers they mostly thought of bluebonnets and paintbrush which bloomed in the spring. But there were some wildflowers that bloomed year-round. At the moment the hillsides were dotted with goldeneye, snow on the prairie, and bright red cardinal flowers.

She'd never want to live anywhere else on earth. This was home. Rugged beauty. Comfort and safety. She'd already left once before and that had been enough. She would never leave again. Now Jackson realized that he belonged here, too.

She stopped Thimble at the crest of the tallest hill on their part of the ridge. The sun began to slip down the horizon, a beautiful splash of red, and orange bursts of vibrant color. Jackson joined her, reaching to take her hand. When he brushed a kiss across her knuckles again, her body shivered, and she briefly closed her eyes to the powerful emotions spilling over her. She recognized happy when she felt it, but it had been a while. Or maybe just a while since she'd allowed herself to feel anything this intense.

"C'mere."

Jackson reached for her and pulled her into Taco's saddle.

He was strong enough that she had no time, or any real inclination to resist.

"Taco doesn't like me," she protested as she snuggled against Jackson in a saddle meant for one.

"He's going to like you again, baby," Jackson whispered close to her good ear. "Remember when the sound of your voice calmed him?"

"That was a long time ago."

"Have you tried talking to him lately?"

"A few things here and there," she said. "Reminding him that he might like me again one day. And he always hears me talking to Thimble."

"And ignoring *him*."

She didn't like the idea. Had she really done that? "It wasn't ignoring, it was just…I-I sort of gave up on him."

*Oh my Lord. She had given up on a horse.*

"Uh-huh." Jackson's arms tightened around her. "Exactly."

"Oh boy." She leaned back into Jackson's chest, realizing he was right.

"Talk to him right now," Jackson whispered as he tickled the shell of her ear. "I think he needs to hear your voice."

"He's content with you riding him. He loves you best."

"Well, he should."

She felt a little bit silly. It had been a while since she'd talked to a horse with anyone else listening. Mostly she'd done that with Hank around, when Taco, who hated doctors, was getting a checkup. Or being treated for colic. Now, she did the same when examining her own patients. And, of course, she talked to Thimble as she would a best friend who couldn't repeat anything.

Jackson's chin on her shoulder, he nudged, and she relented.

"Okay. So, here we are. Yes, Taco, you might have noticed, he's back. Jackson, your favorite. I don't think you've been the same since he left. You might remember, I *tried* to talk to you, and you ignored me. I know you missed him every day that he was gone. Nothing was the same without him. And... the thing is, you didn't do anything wrong. I did. It's all my fault."

"Eve, don't—"

"Shh. I'm talking to Taco." She rubbed his mane, her throat tight. "But you see, I've been forgiven. You have to forgive me, too. That's kinda how it works. We're all going to get along now. You love him. We all love him. *I* love him. So, there it is. Even after all this time."

Suddenly Jackson was tugging her around to face him.

A fistful of her hair in his hand, Jackson moved her to meet his eyes. "Baby, say that to my face."

"Wh-what part?" Her voice shook, knowing exactly what he wanted to hear again.

"You know." His thumb brushed across her chin.

"Okay, okay." She couldn't meet his eyes. "I love you."

An ease and comfort wrapped around her like a cozy blanket. She took in a deep cleansing breath. Some things were inevitable. Mud on her boots. Texas thunderstorms. Falling for the first boy she'd ever kissed. Falling in love and *staying* in love despite everything.

It didn't always happen that way, she'd heard.

"I love you," Jackson said.

He kissed her then as the sun dipped, darkening the ridge, leaving it bathed only in the dim rays of the ambient moonlight.

# CHAPTER 31

Two mornings later, Jackson had just kissed Eve goodbye and put the horses back in the stable after she left for work. They had quite a routine going. Days were mostly spent apart, but nights were spent together. In the mornings their custom was to take Thimble and Taco for a ride before daybreak. Life was comfortable. Calm and routine.

Family life was falling into place again. Hank relied on him in Lincoln's absence and Jackson found that it wasn't the oppressive weight on his chest that he'd expected. He and Hank were talking again without yelling at each other. When Hank needed help, Jackson had found that he was no longer asking someone else. He was coming to Jackson more and more.

"Phone!" Mima called to him from the kitchen back door.

"Be right there," Jackson yelled and hightailed it back to the house.

"It's your manager."

He accepted the phone and spoke into the handheld receiver, walking into the hallway for some privacy. "Hey."

"Hi ho, buddy!" said his manager, Troy Larimer.

"How's everything going? Any luck putting the house up for sale?"

"Well, now, let's slow down just a tad. These things take time."

"Right. Sure. Just let me know if you need anything from me, like a signature. I don't have great cell phone service out here, but I can get faxes."

"A fax machine? How quaint. Yeah, no worries on that. But I have some pretty incredible news."

"Yeah? What's going on?"

"Are you sitting down?"

Jackson rolled his eyes at no one. "No. I don't have to sit down."

"Mick 'da bomb' Mason has agreed to produce you! First, we think we've lost this deal. Now, we have the best in the business bar none."

Jackson was speechless. He wasn't even aware Troy had been looking for a new producer. He'd thought the whole production was dead in the water. Having told Troy that he wasn't coming back for some time, he figured that was the end of that particular deal.

"Are you there?"

"Yeah," Jackson said. "What *happened*? I mean, how did— When did—"

"Turns out, Mick is a fan. When he learned that almost half of the songs on the country charts were written by you, he wanted to know why you don't have your own record out. I explained what we've been through for the past couple of years. He gets it and he's agreed to give you creative control. I don't have to tell you that Mick has created superstars. Taylor Swift, Sam Hunt, Brad Paisley. The list is long. He has the magic touch."

"Yeah, yeah, I know." Everyone in Nashville had heard of

Mick Mason, and everyone had him on their wish list as a producer.

This meant that after eight years of selling his songs, playing in bars and dives, it might actually be Jackson's turn. Just when he'd decided to forget it all and go back to ranching. Timing had never been his strong suit.

"I'm assuming this is what you want?" Troy continued. "Can I start the process? Draw up a contract, schedule some meetings. I figured if anything would get you to come back, this might be it."

Jackson's stomach roiled and pitched. All the twists, turns, and ups and downs of this business were enough to get anyone sick. He'd finally reached a place where he felt good being back home, and now the opportunity of a lifetime had been presented.

But there was so much to consider. He'd worked it out in his mind that music was something he'd always love but he didn't have to be famous to be a success. Stone Ridge was home and he didn't want to leave again. And Eve. After getting through all the crap they had and working it out, he couldn't possibly leave her again.

She'd just have to come with him. End of story.

"Jackson? Hello?"

"Yeah," Jackson said. "I'm here. How soon do you need me back? I need to stay until my brother comes back in a few days."

"That would be fine. I'll start working things on this end." He paused. "And guess I shouldn't sell the house?"

"No." Jackson shut his eyes and pinched the bridge of his nose.

He hung up, a little stunned. A moment later, he did sit down. And shouldn't have been surprised when Mima came in the room, having heard his end of the conversion.

"You're leavin' us." She held a dish towel in her hands.

"You heard."

"Of course, I heard. Jackson, how can you consider going back to that lifestyle? It hasn't made you happy. It isn't what you need."

"Listen. You don't understand."

"I do understand. You want to go back to a rough business that has let you down time and again. You're the only one who still can't see that the only people who love and want the best for you are your own family."

"I wish that were true, Mima, but it's not. My own mother left me, and my father hasn't exactly been my greatest supporter. He always preferred Lincoln to me."

"Hank has his own problems, bless his heart. Don't let him determine your self-worth."

"I'm not doing that," Jackson protested. "But I've been working the music business for eight long years."

Mima twisted the dishtowel between her hands. "What's that going to give you that you don't already have?"

He snorted.

*Money, for one thing. Success.*

"Think of it as a job, like any other. This is my job. Just like Eve's job is a veterinarian, Daisy is an auto mechanic, Sadie is a teacher, and Lincoln is a rancher."

"So are you!"

"That's only part of who I am, Mima. Music fills a part of me that ranching doesn't."

"Son, I understand that. But music is one thing. Wanting to be *famous* is another."

"That's just the thing." Jackson hung his head. "I'd reached the point where I didn't care about any of that. And now…a big-time producer wants to work with me, and I don't know how I can turn that down. I don't know if I want to."

"It sounds like you have a big decision to make and there's no better place to do that than outside."


AN HOUR LATER, Jackson had loaded the old Ford truck's bed with hay. He'd be feeding the cattle in the north pasture this morning. He drove a few hundred feet, climbed up in the bed of the truck, lifted and dumped a bundle of hay, then drove another few hundred feet. Repeat. Sometimes two hands did the task together. One to drive, one to pitch. He and Lincoln used to do the job together when they were teenagers. The sun beat down on him as he worked. He felt in the best shape of his life. The work might be taxing, but because of the mindless repetition of the task that required little to no inspiration, it gave him time to think.

There was a lot that he still didn't miss about his life in Nashville. The lifestyle had many pitfalls. He lived in a cocoon where country music was everything and balance was sadly lacking at times. Because he'd been so ambitious, he'd rarely taken time off to vacation or enjoy the fruits of his labor. He could sometimes still feel the wrenching disappointment of the deals that fell through. It happened several times in an artist's career, sometimes even after great success.

He didn't enjoy what jockeying for position and status did to people like Winona. There were only so many slots for artists and more up-and-coming young and talented artists every day. The most successful artists balanced their personal lives well. Even so, too many relationships bowed to the pressure of a crazy lifestyle. Many of his friends had been through marriage and divorce more than once.

Only when a musician had achieved a higher level of success could touring be cut back and he was far from that situation, even if this album really wound up being recorded.

Which was another thing. That was still not a certainty, because if he'd learned one thing, it was that a deal could be undone faster than he could tune his guitar.

As he drove the truck back, he realized that he had to talk to Eve. He couldn't allow a repeat of what happened eight years ago. She would have to know that beyond all else, she was still the most important choice he'd ever made. The best one.

After checking in with Hank at the end of the day, he took a shower, changed, and decided to drop in at the Shady Grind for a beer. Since the Shady Grind was across the street from the veterinary clinic, he would catch Eve as she returned from her appointments. They'd have dinner, a beer or two, and a long talk. He couldn't put it off. Lincoln and Sadie would be back tomorrow.

Jackson pulled his truck into a parking space in front of the Shady Grind storefront.

He strode toward Priscilla who stood outside the entrance, holding a cigarette between her fingers. "Hey there, cowboy."

"Hey," Jackson said as he watched her light up. "Thought you quit. Those things will kill ya."

"Too late."

She slid him a look that said she meant it and Jackson froze. Words failed to come. He simply stared at this woman who'd been one of his first fans and greatest supporters. The first to give him a chance to hone his skills.

"How? *When?*"

"Now, don't feel sorry for me. I hate that. I'm going to beat this. It's stupid cancer. Not lung cancer, by the way, which I'm tellin' myself means I can still smoke these. For now, anyway. Pretty sure the docs are goin' to kill that fun for me, too."

"Screw cancer," Jackson said and meant.

Priscilla burst out into a smoky laugh. "Yeah. Screw cancer. I'm just glad I got to see you again."

"'Cilla—"

"Don't give me that face. I don't mean before I die. Before I *move*. That's why I'm retirin'. They have a cuttin'-edge cancer treatment center in Arizona where my daughter lives and she's taking me to it. I'm going to beat this damn thing if it's the last thing I do." She cackled. "See what I did there?"

He almost chuckled. Almost. But the thought of cutting-edge treatment filled him with hope. People beat cancer all the time. Priscilla was tough and ornery enough to be a survival story. But hell. First, Mima's broken arm and surgery. Now, Priscilla had cancer and was leaving the state. And the biggest of them, of course, Eve's ordeal. He'd missed all of this by being wrapped up in his career and too self-focused for anyone to think of reaching out to him. It wasn't that his family had purposely kept things from him. They just thought he'd been too busy to care.

And God help him, maybe he had been. That had to change, especially when he went back to Nashville.

"You let me know if I can do anythin' for you. I mean, anything at *all*."

"I don't need anything, especially not after I sell this bar, but I'm not too proud to ask if it comes to that. And you let me know if you change your mind about buying me out."

"I don't think there's much chance of that now. I'm goin' back to Nashville."

"Hey! Good news, right?"

"The best."

He didn't know why he wasn't more excited, though it might be because this wasn't his first promising opportunity. None of them had worked out, not in the long run, and though he tried to be optimistic nothing was guaranteed.

He scanned the area for an Eve sighting. From here he had a good view of the veterinary clinic, but no sign of her truck. She sometimes traveled hours out of her way to see her patients. Even if he could wait to see her tonight at the house, he itched just to see her face right now. He wanted a night out with her, a chance to show her that if she came with him to Nashville, he'd take care of her. He wanted to tell her the news. Wanted her to be happy for him. This time, they would talk. They'd make plans like grown-ups. Work it out. Give and take.

Priscilla stepped aside as a group of men entered the bar, probably fresh off a day on the ranch. And they were still coming, as trucks pulled in, and men piled out.

"Hey, Winona!"

Jackson heard someone shout and he followed the sound, his gaze landing on none other than Winona, who should be on her way out of town.

"Hey, y'all," Winona said as she strode up to him and Priscilla, a small group of men following her.

He introduced Winona to Priscilla, who after pleasantries excused herself back into the bar.

"I decided to stay in Stone Ridge awhile. My manager is scouting a place for me right now. I'm looking for a good-sized property if you hear of anything. Something with room for horses, and a big house, too."

Jackson gaped. "*Why* would you want to stay here?"

"You might have found your woman, but all these men over here"—she waved in the direction of the small crowd of admirers—"are still lookin'."

"Seriously?"

"I'm not kiddin'. I wish I'd known about this place a long time ago. Interesting you never mentioned there are all these young, virile men, all looking for a good woman."

"They're hard-working ranchers. They appreciate country music, but other than that I don't think you have a thing in common with any of them."

"Maybe you'd be surprised." She moved toward the entrance, but before she could get far, a man was already opening the door for her. "Oh, thank you, sweetheart."

When Eve's truck still hadn't shown up, Jackson followed Priscilla and her entourage inside. Because cell reception was much better in town, he texted her:

I'm at the Shady Grind. Come by if you can. I'll buy you dinner.

"Hey, how about a song, Jackson?" someone asked. "It's been a long time since you played for us here."

Priscilla took Jezebel down from the hook on the wall where it hung by its strap and handed it to Jackson. "She's been dying to play with you again."

Laughter from the crowd.

"It's true. She was my first love. This brings back memories."

Jackson pulled the strap over and actually had to loosen it. He'd been a kid when he played this guitar. Someone brought out a stool and Jackson sat and tried to tune the old beast. He did the best he could with what he had to work with and launched into a rendition of his first big hit, "You're the Only One for Me." It was his song, recorded by Brad Paisley.

When he finished the song to applause, Winona was at his side, beaming. "I love that song. Always did."

"Why don't you play one?" Jackson offered her the guitar.

A woman from the audience shouted, "Play the song about the guy who cheated on you!"

Jackson hoped he would not be associated with "You're Not Good Enough to Be My Man," because that hadn't been about him. Winona had written that song about her former husband and manager.

"If you don't mind, I'd like to sing a little something new I wrote recently." Winona accepted the guitar from Jackson. "Home to You."

Eve finished up with the Martinezes' sick pig by prescribing a course of antibiotics and hopped back in her truck to head back to Stone Ridge. She glanced at her phone and smiled at Jackson's text. Dinner and a beer sounded good. But any time she spent with Jackson was a good time. She was so deeply in love with him it had become hard to leave for work in the mornings.

Their routine happened to be the best part of her day. They'd wake up before dawn most mornings, have coffee, and then head out for a ride. And Jackson seemed so content now, so calm. Maybe he finally understood where he belonged.

Eve pulled in near the clinic to check in with Annabeth before she headed home and found it already locked. Unusual, because Annabeth always waited for Eve to check in before closing up shop. She caught sight of Jackson's truck, a sharp pull of joy flooded through her, and she turned to cross the street to the Shady Grind. He'd be there, having a cold beer after a hard day, and catching up with Priscilla.

Eve smiled curiously when she noticed all the action

centered around the Shady Grind and followed several patrons inside. She didn't have to be curious for long. Winona and Jackson were in the very back, each sitting on a stool, giving their audience of mostly men a private concert.

Eve spied Annabeth and walked up to her. "Hey. What am I missing? A special performance?"

Annabeth scowled. "She's gone totally soft on me. The song she played was about wanting a second chance with the one that got away."

"Interesting."

"Oh, crap," Annabeth said and slid Eve a pitying look. "Sorry, Eve. I think she's in love with him."

"That doesn't bother me. He doesn't feel the same way."

"Are you sure?" Annabeth pressed.

The photo of Winona and Jackson in the tabloid flashed through her memory like a slap. But the old sense of utter loss and desperation that had gripped Eve and threatened to pull her down was gone. That was her past. She now had a future because she'd fought off the darkness like a lioness. Driven out of the Piggly Wiggly parking lot where she'd never be back again. She'd clawed her way to the surface, and she wasn't ever drowning again.

She'd once been a victim, but she refused to be one again.

Eve caught Jackson's gaze and they exchanged a knowing smile. "Yes, I'm sure."

Once Winona finished singing, the crowd began to slowly disperse. Some ambled over to the bar and still others to the pool table in the back. Winona sat talking to her mostly male fans, smiling, holding on to Jackson's old guitar, flirting with the men surrounding her. One of the Henderson brothers. Wade, which would kill poor Daisy if she saw. Even Beau seemed to be hanging on her every word. She would have her pick of them were she to go looking for a donor.

Jackson slid Eve his easy smile, dimples flashing, and he

joined her in two long strides. Hand on the nape of her neck, he plastered her against him and planted a kiss on her lips right in front of Annabeth.

"Hey," he said when she came up for air.

Eve regained her footing and breath, cleared her throat and turned to Annabeth. "Jackson, this is Annabeth Dantzer, my partner."

"I guess it's about time we meet." Jackson smiled, and let go of Eve long enough to shake Annabeth's hand.

"Yes, it is," Annabeth said, and seemed to size him up. "You sounded good up there."

"Yeah? Thanks." Jackson tugged Eve closer.

"Well, have fun, you two. Don't worry, I locked up. Guess I'll see ya tomorrow, Eve." With a wave, Annabeth was gone.

"See ya." She turned to Jackson. "Do you want to have a beer?"

"Nah, already had one. But let's eat. I already ordered our food." He led them to a couple of stools empty at the end of the bar.

Priscilla brought their food out minutes later. "Two Shady Burgers and fries. Enjoy, you two."

The burger was greasy, with a fresh-baked bun and Shady's special secret sauce. The fries were warm and crunchy like she liked them. Eve took a bite and sighed in pleasure.

"Is Winona serious about stayin'? When she came to see me at the clinic the other day, she said she was thinkin' about it."

"I'm guessing she sees how many men are available to her, so yeah, if she really wants a baby…"

"I think she's going to find her donor." Eve threw a look in the direction of Winona, sitting at a table with no less than four men. "She should have no trouble."

They finished their burgers in silent companionship until

they were interrupted by Riggs Henderson, the oldest Henderson brother, whom Jackson hadn't had a chance to visit with since he'd returned.

"You must be busy," said Riggs, a cattle rancher and former lawyer who ran Henderson Grange. "Haven't seen hide nor hair of ya lately."

"Yup," Jackson said, shaking Riggs's hand and throwing a sly look at Eve. "Busy."

"Boy, that's the kind of busy I'd like to be," Riggs said with an equally lazy smile.

Riggs was one of the most eligible bachelors in Stone Ridge and a real catch. Unfortunately, a widower for years, he mostly kept to himself. They chatted for a few more minutes and then Riggs excused himself to join his brothers for a beer.

"Poor sucker," Jackson said, watching him go. "Any place else and you'd have to peel the women off him. Baby, thanks for sticking with me."

"Aw." She patted his cheek and kissed him square on the lips, eliciting a dimpled smile. "You are so *welcome*."

Jackson pulled out his wallet from his back pocket, paid at the bar, then tugged Eve off the stool. "C'mere."

"Where are we goin'?"

He pulled her out the door, and down the steps to the alley between the Shady Grind and the General Store. "There's somethin' I have to see."

He pinned her to the side of the building, holding her arms tightly to her side.

"What is it you want to see?" she said.

His callused hands slid down her bare arms and came to rest on her waist and then...lower.

"Everything." A single dimple flashed, and she might have climaxed. "If that's okay with you."

"I think you know that you have an all-access pass."

# CHAPTER 33

*L*illian wrung her hands together. "Oh, Albert! What have I done? He's leavin' us again and I'm about to lose them both."

Albert lay on the couch, arms crossed behind his neck, boots propped on the couch pillow as he watched his favorite John Wayne movie. Lillian had put it on for him and sure enough, two seconds later, he'd shown up. Her old man loved his westerns. Maybe he wasn't really "here" among the living but interesting how old habits never died.

"Serves you right interferin' the way you done. Now Eve's probably leavin'. What a fine mess you've made."

Just the thought of that precious child she'd come to love like one of her own leaving Stone Ridge was enough to make Lillian's poor old heart want to plum give out.

She paced the living room, clutching her chest. "I might be comin' to be with you sooner than we both thought."

Albert pushed back his Stetson and rolled his eyes. "Woman, stop. You're not joinin' me just yet."

"How do you know?" Lillian clutched her heart. "I swear it hurts so much right here somethin' must be givin' out."

"That's a good kind of hurt. Reminds you that you're still alive."

"Well, I'd rather be dead. Worked so hard to get those two back together, and now they're both leavin' me."

"You don't know that."

Lillian could tell that Eve wanted to be with Jackson but was afraid. And all of Stone Ridge could take the blame for that. Because Brenda, Hank, Lillian, Sadie, Lincoln, and the entire town had become her safe place after the attack. They'd coddled her. She'd only felt safe here where she knew almost everyone, including the good and protective men of Stone Ridge that she'd known most of her life. In Nashville, life would be different.

She'd be in a larger city again, maybe even some triggers would rise up, and she might be miserable. And even with all that, Lillian saw clearly in Eve's eyes that she wanted to be with Jackson, no matter what. She just needed a little push to get past that last wall of fear, but surely Lillian shouldn't be expected to be the one to do this. That was asking too much. Leave that one to Brenda, or Sadie. They probably had stronger hearts, anyway.

All Lillian had ever wanted was to have her entire family surrounding her. They had enough land not to be crowding each other. Room for every Carver grandchild to build a house and fill it with her great-grandchildren. Why were kids always growing up, everything always changing, and people always leaving? She yearned for the security of knowing exactly where her little chickens were every night. Back in the old days, when all three were underfoot making messes everywhere they went, she'd taken it all for granted.

A Texas storm had kicked up suddenly in the early after-noon and the wind now battered against the willow trees. A sudden flash of lighting with the resulting crack seconds later had Lillian jumping out of her skin. Lord have mercy.

Speaking of her heart! Albert was gone after the flash, like he'd been a figment of her imagination all along. In that terrifying moment, she feared he wouldn't be back.

Not even in her dreams.

And she was alone now, *really* alone.

There was a knock on the door, and when she opened it, there stood Jolette Marie looking like a drowned cat. Lillian had never been happier to see her.

"Brenda said you were lookin' for this." She held a cardboard box.

She waved the poor wet woman inside. "Come in."

"Thanks," she said, shutting the door. "I got caught in the shower. One minute, it's dry, the next a monsoon."

Lillian quirked a brow. "Now, honey, how long have you lived in Texas?"

"All my life." She handed Lillian the box with a scowl. "I'm sorry that I kept this longer than I should have. Brenda didn't know I had it. I don't know what good this is going to do you, but it wound up in storage in the main house's outside shed. I think my mother was storing a few things for Eve. You know how she adores her. Anyway, I guess I kept it because I thought I might have a chance with Jackson. Now I know it's just a pipe dream."

"Sugar, that boy had eyes and a heart for one girl half of his life. Don't let it get you down. There are plenty of bachelors in Stone Ridge and you're lovely when you're not trying to take another woman's man."

Last year, it had been Lincoln she'd been after. She had a thing for the Carver men, that much was certain. Then again, seemed like Jolette Marie wasn't terribly particular at times. She liked men. Period.

She winced. "You're so nice but I don't deserve it."

"Not everyone *deserves* forgiveness. The good book tells us to give it anyway."

"But I guess perfect Eve deserves everything."

Lillian almost laughed at that. She thought of how much energy and time she'd spent hating Eve after she'd broken Jackson's heart. Lillian's forgiveness had been a long time coming.

"Eve isn't perfect. Far from it." Lillian set the box down and went to the linen cabinet to gather some fresh towels. "Here, get in front of the fire and see if you can get warm and dry again."

Lillian sat and opened the box. She found old sweaters, cowgirl boots, and some old and worn western romance paperbacks. Near the bottom of the box, but perfectly protected between all the other clothing was the wedding quilt.

"Well, butter my biscuit."

The quilt was in fair to middling condition. It looked a little ratty and faded but nothing a good wash and pressing wouldn't take care of. And even though Lillian hardly needed this quilt anymore to remind Eve of how much she'd once loved Jackson, maybe it could serve another purpose. She was still deep in thought considering that purpose, the quilt spread out on the couch, when Jolette Marie came next to her.

Jolette Marie traced the embroidery lettering with the date and the names of Eve and Jackson. "I'd want to hide this, too."

The poor girl had been to the altar three times and run off. No wonder no man was interested in anything other than a temporary dalliance with her.

"What did you do with all your quilts?" Lillian asked.

"I got rid of them."

"Of course you did. That's the logical thing to do."

"What a tough memory. They never got married on this date and yet here it is embroidered into the quilt so…permanently."

"Yes, well, we were all so certain it would happen. And yet she still kept the quilt. All these years."

Lillian's own marriage quilt was in her closet exactly where she would always be able to find it. Worn and yellowed with age now.

She'd probably clung to Albert longer than she should have.

Another flash in the gray skies and crashing thunder following closely on its heels had Jolette Marie jumping, too.

"Hank will probably be over to check on me in a bit." Lillian patted Jolette Marie's hand. "We're safe here."

"Do you mind if I fix us some tea?" Jolette Marie asked.

"Go ahead."

Two hours later, Jolette Marie was curled up on the couch reading one of those paperback novels, Hank still hadn't shown up, and the late afternoon sky had darkened as if it were midnight and not five o'clock. Eve was usually back by now, same as Jackson. Daisy should be home as well unless she was spending time with *that Wade*. A striking fear pulsed through her at the thought any of them were in trouble in this storm. Lillian picked up the phone to dial Hank and found that the lines were down. Wonderful.

She found her cell phone but as usual reception out on the hill was nonexistent. When all the lights went out a few minutes later, Jolette Marie screamed.

"Get a hold of yourself, child. We have a generator." And in the next two seconds, the lights flickered back on.

"Whew. I was just at the good part." Jolette Marie went back to her novel.

"Wish I could lose myself in a fantasy," Lillian muttered.

Although, some would consider that her frequent talks with an imaginary Albert had been a bigger flight of fancy than any book. Her vivid imagination had always gotten the better of her. Like now, when she pictured Jackson and Eve lying in a ditch on the side of the road injured. And Daisy. She might have run off to Las Vegas to get married to that Wade. In this weather! And what about her Hank? Albert had always known where to find their son. Lillian felt so out of touch.

"Where are you when I need you, old man?"

She tried the phone again and wished she could remember where she'd put the satellite phone Hank had given her for emergencies just like this one. She was about to ask Jolette Marie to stop fantasizing and help her find it when Hank burst through the front door.

"Oh, Hank! Thank the good Lord."

But Hank's face was ashen. "There's been an accident."

# CHAPTER 34

The long-predicted rainfall arrived and ruined Eve and Jackson's secret marathon make-out session.

"Damn rain," Jackson muttered against Eve's lips, his hand under her shirt.

Lighting flashed, and thunder crackled. Everyone that had been outside quickly dispersed indoors. But rather than rejoin everyone at the Shady Grind, Eve tugged Jackson toward the veterinary clinic. Just crossing the street and down a few storefronts drenched them both. Eve unlocked the door and hurried inside, Jackson right behind her.

"Nothin' quite like a Texas rainstorm," Jackson said, smiling as his gaze did a slow slide down her body. "Um, yeah. Definitely nothin' like it."

Normally Eve dressed casually for work and never in her best. She had on an old pair of Wranglers which, though clean, were faded and had seen better days. She wore another pair of older boots that hadn't been shit on by Holly, and her blue Lone Star Veterinary Clinic tee. But now her too-tight Wranglers were soaked and clinging to her legs and her tee was showing off the fact that she'd worn a red push-up bra today. She was practically see-through.

She groaned. "I'm glad we ran in here and not into the Shady Grind. I had only planned on you seeing this bra, not the entire crowd."

He slid her a dark sexy look and stepped right into her space. Achingly close.

She took a step back with a smile. "I want to give you the grand tour."

Taking his hand, she led him through the office. First, she pointed out the receptionist desk, next the coffee and snack room, the medicine supply cabinet, the surgery room, and the kennels where they kept recuperating pets. Finally, her office. The door had a placard with her name: Eve Iglesias, DVM.

"And this is my office."

There was no small amount of pride in showing Jackson the fruits of all her hard work. Only the residents of Stone Ridge knew that little Eve Iglesias, Brenda's daughter, had gone away to school and come back home a doctor. Jackson quietly studied the letters on the door. So quietly, she wondered what he was thinking. But in the next moment she knew because he turned and made her face him.

"Baby, I'm so proud of you."

Every word was laced with such emotion that it reached all the way into her heart and twisted. She closed her eyes. A sudden wetness on her lashes threatened to ruin the light mood they'd been enjoying, so she fought back the tears and opened the door.

She waved him inside. "And this is my desk."

"Then this must be your chair." Jackson strode past her and stood behind the chair, spinning it once.

"Actually, I don't spend much time at my desk."

Now he sat and reclined in the chair, making himself at

home. "This is a comfortable chair. I could do a lot in this chair."

"I took a nap once."

"Boring." He beckoned her to him, gazing at her from underneath his eyelashes. "We can do better. Lock the door."

She did and joined him. "What did you have in mind?"

"Everything." He reached for her wrists and pulled her into his lap.

"I'm all wet," she said, barely protesting being this close to him again.

"I have to tell you something important." His hand glided up and down her spine, creating a friction that warmed her.

She settled in to him, resting her head on his shoulder. "Is it good news?"

"I hope so, for both of us. Got a call from my manager this morning. One of the best producers in Nashville is interested in working with me. It's the opportunity of a lifetime. I don't think I can pass this up."

"Oh," she said, her throat tight. "No, you can't."

This moment was far too familiar.

*"Our band got an offer to play in Nashville," Jackson said.*

*"When?"*

*"In a couple of weeks. Don't worry, I turned them down. We're gettin' married."*

*"But—"*

*"I'm happy, baby. Maybe we'll both go out to visit them someday."*

*"We could wait to get married—" she offered, even as she fully realized that all the deposits had been made and this late in the game, no refund was possible.*

*"No," he said, brushing a kiss across her fingers. "We're doin' this. It's too late now."*

"Eve," Jackson said now, tipping her chin to meet his eyes. "I want you to come with me. Please think about it. The next few months to a year are going to mean hours of hard work in the studio, hashing it out. But the upside is huge. This producer is a hit-maker. I would say that I'll come back to visit but I wouldn't be able to realistically do that for close to a year. That's too long for us to be apart."

"I agree." She breathed in his scent. Woodsy with a hint of leather. "And after that?"

"Probably a US tour to support the album. Some local appearances. Travel."

"If I go with you, what will I do?"

"Whatever you want. And be with me, every morning and night. Just like we've been doing here. I'm addicted to you. Obsessed." He glanced around her office. "I know what I'm askin' you to give up and I wouldn't do it if I didn't think it's our best bet long-term. For our future. Our children."

"Our children?"

"You've got to marry me and have my babies. You know that, right?" A single dimple flashed.

She squinted. "Is that a proposal?"

"Call it a pre-proposal. The actual one will be big and flashy, or soft and quiet if that's what you want."

"Soft and quiet," she whispered.

His hands slid down to her wrists and cuffed them. "All I'm asking from you is two years. Then we'll both come back to Stone Ridge for good, build a house here, and you'll go back to your practice."

Two years. Two years without practicing medicine, unless she could figure out a way to do it in Nashville. She'd have the horses and dogs that Jackson had on his small ranch on the outskirts of Nashville, but likely that would be the extent of it. And yet she'd already lost him once before to pride and the worry of holding him back. Everything had changed because as a grown woman she realized neither one of them could be everything to each other. She understood that sometimes sacrifices would have to be made, on both sides.

"Eve?" he whispered, since she'd been silent for several minutes.

"I could save you on your vet bills by taking care of the animals myself."

"Is that a yes, you're coming with me?" He grinned.

Eve swallowed the ball in her throat. "Yes," she said, threading her fingers through his hair. "You better believe I'm coming with you."

"You've just made me the happiest man in Stone Ridge." He tugged off her tee. "You need out of these wet clothes."

"Right. I could catch my death in here."

He traced the edge of her silky red push-up bra and then followed that action with his tongue. When he lowered the cup and sucked in her nipple, Eve's body trembled and it had nothing to do with the cold.

She tugged on his button-down shirt and it came off his shoulders in one swift movement. Then they were skin on damp skin. Jackson unhooked her bra and tossed it to the side. He kissed her, a warm, hot demanding kiss that had her hot and bothered in two seconds. Then they both moved quickly as boots were kicked off, Wranglers removed, and underwear tossed.

Naked, she straddled him in the chair, and her hands roamed free over the hard planes of his chest and abs. Her fingers dove into his hair, pulling him closer, as if she couldn't get enough. And she'd never *had* her fill of Jackson. Never got tired of him. Nothing had changed in that regard and never would. Every microscopic cell of her loved this man. She needed him, and she needed this connection that she'd never felt with anyone else. It always felt fresh and new and took her by surprise each time.

In one swift move, Jackson gripped her hips and sat her on the edge of the desk facing him.

*Surprise!*

"What are you—"

But when he spread her legs and lowered his head between her thighs, she knew exactly what he was doing. He was undoing her, bit by bit. His magic tongue teased and tortured her until a big wave of pleasure crested and she moaned his name.

Wanting him inside her, she wrenched herself from his grasp and straddled him. His neck snapped back and he groaned. "Condom?"

"Don't have one here," she said, breathing like a locomotive. "It's okay. I'm on the pill."

In that moment she handed him a trust she didn't take lightly. But she'd already risked her heart, now she'd give him every last piece of her. The trust she'd once given him so instinctively as a younger woman was tougher to give now but worth everything it cost.

She rose over him and he thrust into her, making her gasp. But she set the rhythm again, moving on him slowly. He met her with warm and lingering deep kisses. But when he gripped her hips tightly, every muscle hard as granite, she realized they were fighting a losing battle. They were both frenzied by the sound of the thunder, the rain pelting the roof, and their own crazy passion. Slow wasn't going to work this time and he took control.

Taking her with him, he rose and moved them to the closest wall. "Wrap your legs around me."

He thrust into her again and again, the sweet pressure building until she couldn't hold back the onslaught of extreme pleasure. Her orgasm had her trembling and she gripped his shoulders tightly like she would never let him go. He swallowed her moan with a kiss, and she felt him grow rigid the moment before he followed her over. Both spent, he carried her back to the chair and deposited her on his lap.

"That was the best use of my chair…ever," Eve whispered. "And the wall, too."

He smiled against her mouth. "Told you we could do better than a nap."

"You weren't lyin'."

Eve rose bare-ass naked and walked to the blanket she kept to comfort scared small animals. Annabeth didn't believe any such comfort to be necessary and usually got down to business but if Eve had anything to say about it, her soft and colorful acrylic always did the trick.

She threw it over herself and then joined Jackson, covering them both. "We should probably go soon."

Their damp clothes lay on the floor and while she didn't relish getting back into them, sooner or later the torrential downpour would stop. Lock on her office door or not, this was unprofessional behavior. Probably.

Jackson groaned. "You move that way over me again and we won't be goin' anywhere for a while."

She snorted. "Sorry."

Her phone buzzed. It could be important. Maybe a colicky horse emergency. Mr. Mansfield had her on speed dial now and he'd been sworn to call her immediately about Holly.

"I've got to get this." She reached for her phone from the back pocket of her Wranglers laying on the floor. A text message sent from Hank read:

Your mother has been in an accident. Come to ranch. Now.

The text had been sent an hour ago but maybe due to sketchy Wi-Fi at the ranch it was only now getting to her. "Oh no."

Jackson was behind her in an instant, reading over her

shoulder. "Leave it to my father to leave important details out. What *kind* of an accident?"

"A car accident!" Eve's hand shook. "It has to be. In this weather she must have lost control of her Jeep."

"Then why does he want us coming home, and not, say, to the hospital?" He turned her to face him, cupping her chin.

"Because…because maybe it's too late." Eve threw the blanket down and started shoving clothes on. Panties. Damp jeans over them. Tee shirt. Socks. Boots. "I've got to get to the ranch. The ranch. Can you…can you lock up? H-here's the keys."

She didn't seem to know what she was saying or even thinking. Her only mission was getting to the ranch. Why was her mother at the *ranch*? Maybe looking for Eve, who'd spent far too much time there lately and not enough with her own mother. She would text Hank, the text minimalist, and ask him for details, but better to save time and get herself on the road. In this rain it could take a good thirty minutes or more to get to the ranch.

She wasn't sure how, but Jackson was dressed and waiting at the door for her. He locked the door to the clinic with the keys she'd given him.

"You can't think for a second I'm lettin' you leave here without me." He dangled the keys to his truck. "And I'm drivin'."

Eve didn't answer, just followed him, somehow feeling outside of her own body. The movements were hers, but they didn't feel natural. As the rain continued to come down, Jackson pulled out onto the street. In rain like this, windshield wipers on the fastest mode hardly did the work of giving a driver much visibility. It was like driving by braille. Or hope. Eve couldn't see outside to the landmarks of town that were comfort. Routine. She needed a slice of normal. Usually she'd be driving, part of her routine. She'd adjust the mirror, turn on the radio to the country station and hold her hands at two and ten on the steering wheel in this kind of rain. But she had an alpha man taking control of the situation.

*Oatmeal.*

*A lemon scone that Mrs. Hopkins had brought into the clinic as thanks for taking such good care of Pookie, her little Cavalier King Charles spaniel.*

*Lunch?*

Eve hadn't had lunch! No wonder she'd inhaled that Shady Burger and fries.

"Eve." Jackson's strong hand was on her knee, pulling her out of her daze.

*Jackson.* He was right next to her.

"Did you hear anything I said? While you were getting dressed, I called Mima's satellite phone and got through. She said your mother's okay but banged up a little. Fell off a horse, apparently. Hank doesn't want to drive her anywhere in this rain, so he wanted you to come and take a look."

He'd called while she was dressing. How long had she taken to get dressed? And she thought she'd been quick.

"She fell off a horse," Eve repeated.

It happened sometimes, even with experienced riders. Her mother *wasn't* an experienced rider. And what on earth had she been doing on a horse? Earlier, she'd told Eve that she was going into town to buy groceries for the week.

"Yeah, baby. She's okay." Jackson squeezed her knee, never taking his eyes off the road. "He may have overreacted."

Eve let out a deep breath, rested her hand on his, and stared at his profile. Jackson always had a way of reassuring her, of calming her fears, when no one else could.

"Drive faster, if you can."

# CHAPTER 35

Jackson had questions. Quite a few. The first had to do with Eve's mother, who had apparently been riding a horse. With Hank, or around Hank. Somehow, *he'd* found her. How? And where?

His main concern right now, correction, his *only* concern was Eve. She'd been in a daze, barely tracking, thinking she was moving but often just staring at a piece of clothing before she slowly put it on. For a moment he'd been worried about *her* more than Brenda. He'd put his hand on her knee to get her attention away from whatever scenario was playing in her head. Then he'd held on to her hand all the way back.

The wind whipped one-hundred-year-old willow trees like they were made out of straw. The sky was gunmetal gray and thunder cracked every ten minutes. Eve didn't jump quite like she used to when they were younger, and then his chest tightened when he remembered that she only had half of her hearing.

A fifteen-minute drive took forty minutes and Jackson

pulled in beside the barn to get closer to the house. He shut the truck off and turned to Eve before she could get out.

"Look at me, baby." One hand on the nape of her neck, he pulled her close enough to take every other distraction, even the ones in her head, away. "You're okay."

"I need you." Her eyes shimmered with wetness.

"You've got me."

"She…she was there for me after the attack. When I woke up, she was there. She didn't leave my side *once*."

Raw, fresh pain hit him as he thought of Eve on that hospital bed so badly injured. Without him.

"Thank God for her."

"Nothing can happen to her, Jackson. *Nothing*."

Then she pulled away from him and nearly jumped out the passenger door. He sprinted, getting ahead of her to open the door and let her fly inside.

"Well, it's about time." Mima had come to the front door and after one look at Eve, she understood. "Sugar, she's okay. Got her lying on my bed. Why don't you go check on her?"

Eve disappeared down the hallway before the last sentence. Wanting to go with her, but also wanting to give Brenda her privacy, Jackson hung back. Hank stood by the fireplace staring into the flickering flames. Jolette Marie and Daisy were huddled together on the couch.

Mima followed his gaze. "Jolette Marie came over and got caught in the downpour so I asked her to stay."

"What happened to Brenda?"

"Maybe I should let Hank explain."

"Someone better. I didn't even know she *liked* to ride horses."

"She doesn't know how." Mima pursed her lips. "Apparently Hank was teaching her, and they got caught in the rainstorm. Her horse went right when she went left, and well, that doesn't work."

"Yeah, no kidding."

Jackson strode over to Hank. His father's face was as ashen as the stormy sky. "Want to tell me what's goin' on here?"

"What's goin' on is, I'm an idiot." Hank scowled, using the poker to stoke the fire.

"You're goin' to have to give me a little more detail than that."

"Want detail, do ya? I was stupid enough to think that at my age I might also get a second chance. Lot of that seems to be goin' around here." He gazed significantly at Jackson. "Brenda has always said she wanted to learn how to ride a horse, and so last week when I saw her at the feed store, I said she could come by anytime. She picked *today* of all days. I dropped everythin' I was doin' when she came over unannounced but sure didn't expect the thunderstorm to start this early. It wasn't supposed to rain until tonight. If then."

"Doesn't sound like your fault."

"Maybe not but she got hurt on my watch."

"How bad?"

"I'd say maybe a mild concussion, some cracked ribs. I don't know, I'm not a doctor!"

"Calm down," Jackson said. "Eve will know what needs to be done."

"Glad you finally wised up, son." He glanced at Jackson again. "That girl is the best thing to ever happen to you and don't you forget it. Don't care if you win yourself a hundred Grammys."

"I know. I got my second chance. I'm lucky."

"I shouldn't have made a dang fool of myself going for it at my age."

"Dad, you're not *that* old."

"Ha! I have to take blood pressure pills now."

Jackson was surprised Hank hadn't been taking those for

decades. He'd been angry for as long as Jackson could remember. Naturally he'd assumed it was his cowboy nature, ornery like his father had been, tired all the time, working the land. With a bad back for the last ten years Hank had popped anti-inflammatories like they were candy. Jackson's mother leaving was no small amount to blame for his hostile nature, but since that had been about twenty years ago, he'd have thought his old man would have moved on. So, either he still loved Maggie, or he loved someone else.

*Someone he thought he couldn't have.*

"Hey, if you feel something for Brenda, you might want to tell her."

"That's not my way." Hank bristled. "A woman has to know how I feel by my actions."

"And your action was…to teach her how to ride a horse?"

"My *action* was to give her what she wanted, to drop everything I was doin' because she showed up."

"Sometimes a woman…" Jackson was about to school his dad but there was really no point. The man wouldn't listen anyway. "Nah, never mind."

But words were his business. Words mattered. A woman wanted those words, too. Those "I love you" and "I've got your back" declarations. Jackson had given those to Eve and then some.

"What? Go on and tell me, you're such the expert!"

"I'm no expert," Jackson said. "But I think the words matter. Or at least, they do to women. Brenda might want to hear you tell her how you feel, not just assume you didn't have a full schedule you dropped because she showed up. How's she supposed to know that?"

"She *knows* I'm a busy man."

"We're all busy. I'm just sayin', words matter."

* * *

"MIJA, PLEASE." Brenda waved Eve away. "I'm fine. *Really.*"

Eve had known that her mother was going to live the moment she walked into the bedroom and saw her half reclined, half sitting up on the bed, looking like she'd get up and run out of the room at any minute. Her mother would hate all this attention.

"But you fell off a horse. That's not a small thing."

Eve had already checked for signs of a concussion and found none. She continued to examine her mother, poking gently at her ribs.

She winced some, but other than some bruising, minor scratches and abrasions she didn't even seem to have a cracked rib.

She covered her face with her hands. "I'm so humiliated. I should have asked you to teach me how to ride a horse. Not Hank."

"You know I would have taught you. Anytime."

"But you've been so busy lately, and I didn't want to bother you."

Eve felt a deep throb of guilt. "I'm *never* too busy for you."

"Oh, I didn't mean that," Brenda protested. "Don't feel guilty, please. That's only half the story."

"What's the other half?"

Her mother wouldn't look at Eve. "I wanted Hank to teach me."

"I guess he *does* have more experience with horses than I do. But I could have—"

"No." Brenda said significantly and met Eve's eyes. "I wanted *Hank* to teach me."

"Oh." Eve let that sink in.

Her mother and Hank.

Hank and her mother.

Eve's brain hiccupped. The idea was...weird.

"I'm sorry I never talked about this, but when we were in

high school, Hank wanted to marry me. My parents wanted me to marry Ricardo. I always did what my parents told me to do."

"Oh," Eve said. Again. Maybe she could come up with another syllable. Perhaps "ah."

"And then Maggie came along, got pregnant with Lincoln, and that was the end of it."

"Mami—"

"That's why I never stopped you from leaving Jackson at the altar when I knew what you *should* have done. I let you make up your own mind about everything without much counsel from me. For that, I'm truly sorry. I went a little too far. Maybe I could have saved you some grief."

"No, that…" Eve shook her head and stood. "Wait, are you trying to change the subject? You and *Hank*?"

"Are you upset?"

"I'm just…shocked." She could barely formulate thoughts, much less words. "Um, I guess I always thought of Hank as a father-figure. He almost became my father-in-law. I love him like a father. But I never saw you two together. I just never…I never thought…"

"I know." Brenda studied the floor.

"Does Jackson know about this?"

"No. There's nothing *to* know."

"But if you two want to…um, date? You should be able to do that. Regardless of what's going on between me and Jackson."

"What *is* going on?" Brenda patted the bed next to her. "Tell me all about it."

"He wants me to go with him to Nashville. And…I said I would go."

"That's wonderful!" Brenda stroked Eve's cheek.

"It's complicated."

"What *complicated*? I hate that phrase. Complicated is for

calculus. Love is simple. Tell me, querida. If you don't love him, that's okay. It's not your fault. You can't choose who you love."

Up until this moment, Eve had been prepared to go with Jackson. But now, a sharp pang of fear hit her. She didn't want to be away from her mother, from Sadie, Mima, Hank, and everyone she knew and loved. What if something happened while she was gone?

They were her safety and comfort as much as Jackson was.

"I love him. Maybe too much. I forget myself. Forget what *I* want just to give him what *he* wants. That's not normal or healthy."

"Maybe not." Brenda laughed. "It's true love, especially if he won't *let* you give everything up."

Eve considered this. Jackson wanted her with him in Nashville, which would effectively mean giving everything up. Her practice here, her family, the town she loved so deeply. But tonight, there'd been such a deep pride for her in his words that he seemed to understand what she'd accomplished *meant* something. He understood what she'd be giving up and there was an expiration date.

She'd seen the kind of money that a successful career could provide. Certainly, more for their future children than she ever could. The problem was that money had never been all that important to her. Lord, she was so confused.

LATER THAT NIGHT, even after the storm had stopped raging, everyone but Jolette Marie and Hank stayed in the Carver main house. Mima in Jackson's room, Brenda and Eve in Mima's bedroom.

When Eve came out a couple of hours later to get a drink of water after everyone had gone to bed, she found Jackson on the couch. He lay arms crossed behind his neck, staring up at the ceiling. When he heard her come in, he turned and gave her a slow smile. Despite the fact that she still wanted to sleep with her mother and make sure she'd be okay through the night, Eve felt a strong pull of longing wash over her. Seeing him so lonely on that uncomfortable couch wasn't helping the situation.

"Hi," she said, squeezing next to him. "I hope you don't mind me staying with my mom tonight."

His arm curled around her waist. "Is she okay?"

"I think so."

He quirked a brow.

"Physically she's okay. Emotionally? I'm not sure."

"Hank told me something tonight," Jackson said. "Apparently he wants a second chance with her."

"He *told* you that?"

"In so many words."

"Wow," Eve whispered. "Just…wow."

"I know."

"I haven't been able to think in anything other than one-syllable words since she told me about them. 'Oh' and 'Wow.' Our *parents*."

"Yeah." He pulled her from her sitting position until she was sprawled over him. "It has nothing to do with us."

"I know." She kissed him. Tender and chaste, her lips barely brushing against his. "Tomorrow Sadie and Lincoln are back."

"It feels like much longer than a week since they've been gone."

"When do you have to leave?"

"Don't you mean we?" Big warm hands curled around her wrists. "Soon."

In Nashville, Eve wouldn't know anyone but Jackson. He'd be busy and couldn't babysit her all day. And what if they didn't work out? If Jackson loved her, if this was *true* love, he was going to have to show her in some way. He would have to give up something, too. From where she was sitting, he wasn't giving up anything at all.

"I'm sorry. Jackson, I can't leave." She traced the firm ridge of his jawline and the rough bristles there. "I want to, but I have obligations here, too."

"After tonight, somehow I knew you were going to say that." His arms tightened around her.

"Are you mad?"

"No, I can't be. You're being honest. Disappointed, yeah. I'm not hearing what I want to but I'd rather have the truth." He brought her hand to his lips and brushed a soft kiss across her knuckles.

"Me too." Her voice was thick with emotion. "But nothing changes the fact that I love you."

"I love you, baby."

She wished with all her heart their story could be different and more like Lincoln and Sadie's. But the truth, important though it was, could be downright heartbreaking. She pressed her face to his neck and felt the salty wet tears come.

# CHAPTER 36

When Eve woke early the next morning, she didn't remember how she'd made it back to Mima's bed. The last thing she remembered was feeling Jackson's slow labored breathing beneath her and somehow falling into the blessed oblivion of sleep. She'd dreamt of her wedding day. Eight years ago, in her alternate reality, she'd walked down the aisle to join the younger and boyishly handsome Jackson Carver. And there were no complications. Just love.

Until this morning, Eve didn't know it was possible to cry in one's sleep. But because she woke up with tears in her eyes, a raw ache in her throat, and pain like a weight on her chest, she would have to say that it was.

Her mother was no longer in bed next to her. Eve had slept in her clothes and so she used Mima's attached bathroom to clean up and smooth her hair down. Her eyes were red-rimmed from crying but she couldn't do much about that.

She heard familiar voices as she walked into the kitchen.

Then both her mother and Mima turned from where they stood at the stove.

"I made flour tortillas." Brenda waved her to the table. "Have a seat. They're almost ready."

When Brenda Iglesias made tortillas, they were homemade, not store-bought and warmed. She must have been up at the crack of dawn to get started.

"I asked him not to, but Hank called me in sick to the Trueharts. I unexpectedly have the day off." She smiled. "Isn't that lovely?"

Her brain sluggish from lack of caffeine, Eve tried to take it all in. Soon enough she realized that all the men were gone. Even Jackson. Jackson, who had held her so tightly in his arms last night, as she quietly cried herself to sleep.

"Here, sleepyhead." Mima handed her a cup of life, otherwise known as coffee. "Hank and Jackson got an early start. They've gone to the feed store, will run some errands, and then later they'll pick up Lincoln and Sadie at the airport."

"Oh, right. That's today."

Lord, it was going to be good to see her best friend. Eve would cry, and Sadie would bake chocolate chip cookies and force her to marathon rom-coms all day. Sadie would help remind her that life would go on, with or without Jackson Carver.

And it would. It just wouldn't be nearly as sweet.

Eve sat to eat a quick breakfast with everyone, but she had no appetite. She picked at her eggs, chorizo, and tortilla and half listened to Daisy talk about the rodeo coming into town.

"No more spendin' time with that Wade!" Mima interjected with no small amount of judgement. Her lips were twisted into a scowl that would be comical had Eve felt any kind of lightness about today.

Daisy switched to talk about suspensions and brakes and

other things that Eve could hardly pronounce much less understand after only one cup of coffee.

"I have to work today," Eve said to no one in particular.

Both her mother and Mima glanced at her and Eve noticed when they shared a look between them.

There was an awkward pause in conversation and then Daisy spoke up. "Me too."

Eve would check up on Holly, then drive out an hour to the Wilson cattle ranch for a recheck on the breeched calf she'd brought into the world a few months ago. She'd offer to help Annabeth with any small-animal checkups or emergencies. Offer to be on call seven days a week. She really needed to throw herself into her job. All this would keep her busy. Work was what she needed. More and more work. Maybe more animals would get sick. Wait, no. Oh Lord! What was *wrong* with her? She may have winced.

"Eve, honey, are you okay?" her mother asked. "You didn't eat much."

"I'm not hungry," she said and rose. "And I have to get ready for work. After I take Thimble for a ride."

But even Thimble couldn't help her this morning. Oh, she was patient and kind and she listened as usual. She didn't even mind when Eve wet her mane with tears.

"I love him so much, but I won't lose myself to him again. And that's what he wants. Face it, he could have any woman he wants, and any one of them will likely give up everything for him. And I could, too, I know I could. But with what I've been through, and how hard I worked for this life, he should understand why I *can't.*"

Later, Holly passed her checkup with flying colors and Mr. Mansfield smiled and thanked her for caring enough to make him see the error of his ways. Work went swiftly and efficiently. It was something she could count on every day of her life. Routine. The expected. Animals needed vaccines, they needed checkups, and required medication at times. Some horses were prone to colic. Some pigs got the swine flu. Smaller breeds had their own issues with allergies, ear infections, and overbites.

In the afternoon, after her rounds, Eve helped Annabeth with a large golden retriever named Shadow that had been hit by a car in a hit and run. Eve's thoughts went to Winston and the way Jackson always let him in the house when it was too cold.

"Who would do this?" Eve asked Annabeth as she helped review the X-rays. "No one in Stone Ridge could *possibly* do this to an animal."

"I think you overestimate the residents here." Annabeth squinted at the X-ray.

"Maybe it was someone passing through town."

"Uh-huh. Well, he's lucky. Nothing broken. He's so thick."

They both turned to look at Shadow, who still had a smile on his face. Just emerging from his mild sedative, he happily wagged his tail.

"Who's a good boy?" they both said at once.

After they let Shadow go home with his grateful owner, Eve turned to Annabeth. "I've been thinking that I should be on call seven days a week. We don't need to split coverage anymore."

Annabeth's jaw dropped. "Are you out of your mind?"

"Why would you *say* that?"

"First, I can't get you to take a vacation for years. You finally did because of the wedding. But Eve, this is a partnership. You give some, and I give some. It would make me feel awful to have you cover all the time."

Right. Wonder what she would have said if she'd instead told her that she was leaving their practice for two years. Eve let out a nervous laugh to cover the fact that she now wanted to burst into tears. In a true partnership, every person gave up a little something to make it work.

"You're right. I don't know what I was thinking. Thank you for being a great partner."

"But I *am* going to go on vacation next month. There's an Indie music festival in Austin and I'm going for the entire week. You're welcome to cover for me then."

"Awesome. Consider it done."

At the end of the day Eve drove home to the ranch to make a welcome home supper for Sadie and Lincoln.

When Eve walked in the front door, Daisy was already decorating the entryway with flashy banners that read, "Welcome Home."

"Your mom left," Daisy said. "Said to call her later."

"Thanks." Eve got busy immediately. She peppered and salted the pot roast and put it in the pan. She washed and chopped vegetables. Boiled potatoes. Started the cake.

"Eve," Mima said from behind.

Eve jumped. "Lawd, don't scare me like that."

"Sorry. You seemed very involved with mixing those egg whites. I've been standing here two whole minutes."

"You have? I just want this to be a perfect supper."

Contrary to the banana cream pie that was Jackson's favorite dessert, tonight she was baking Lincoln's favorite. Angel food cake.

"I know you do, sugar. I have something to say and it's very difficult for me, so you have to listen to me carefully."

Eve stopped the mixer and turned to give Mima her full attention.

*Please.*

*No more bad news.*

She took a breath and steeled herself. "What is it?"

Mima took a deep breath. "I want you to go to Nashville with my Jackson."

Eve snorted. "What?"

"You *have* to go with him, sugar. Show him what you're willing to give up for him, and he won't ask you to do it."

"Have you been talkin' to my mother? I'm stayin' right here. My mother needs me even if you don't anymore. And Annabeth needs me. Next month she's going to an Indie music festival and I'm coverin' for her like she just did for me. Relationships are about compromise. And I live here, not in Nashville. I *don't* want to live there."

"But you love him!" Mima said. "Maybe y'all could live half the year here, half the year in Nashville."

"That wouldn't work, either." She turned the mixer back on.

Mima tossed her hands up and yelled over the raucous noise. "Young people! I broke my arm and been breaking my back to get you two back together and fix the foolish mistakes of youth. But you need to work with me here!"

Just then a truck pulled up outside and Eve wiped her hands on a dishtowel. Finally, she'd have someone to truly confide in. Someone who would understand. But not tonight. She'd save all her tears and angst for tomorrow. Tonight would be a coming home celebration.

Eve, Mima, and Daisy fought to get to be the first to hug the returning Carver newlyweds.

# CHAPTER 37

"San Francisco is so beautiful," Sadie continued, taking another bite of angel food cake. "We went to Alcatraz Island and took the audio tour, ate the best seafood I've ever had in my life, and we even went on a ghost tour in an old Victorian neighborhood."

The farmhouse table was crowded tonight with the entire family. Jackson sat next to Eve, occasionally reaching for her hand under the table. Hank and Brenda had joined them, and they were seated next to each other.

"Eve, this feast is delicious," Mima said. "You've absolutely outdone yourself tonight."

"You have," Brenda said. "Bravo."

Hank quietly smiled and nodded his agreement while everyone else added their approval to the mix.

"Best damn meal I've probably ever had." Jackson pushed back his chair and stood. "Eve? Need to talk to you. Outside."

"Not this again," Daisy said.

"Hush now." Mima patted Daisy's arm.

Choosing not to look at anyone, Eve rose, dabbed at her mouth with a napkin, and followed Jackson outside. She wasn't frightened like she'd been almost a month ago. And to her, Jackson had never been someone to fear. She'd been afraid of his intense anger for her and for good reason. For a long time, she'd associated intense anger with physical pain.

But now, her heart ached. Just like it had on her wedding day when she'd had to let him go.

Jackson braced his arms on the wooden fence of the deck and looked out at the sun cresting the hill, a splash of orange and red. There was nothing more beautiful than a sunset in Hill Country.

"I bet they don't have sunsets like this in Nashville."

"No." He turned to face her. "Eve, I'm leavin' tonight."

"Tonight?"

"They're sendin' a car and a private plane for me. Don't see why I should stay another day. This is too hard."

*Hard? I'm dying.*

"It's hard for me, too."

"You made a choice, baby."

"So did you," she bit back.

"Yeah." He closed his eyes and pinched the bridge of his nose. "Let's not do this. We tried, didn't we?"

"I didn't want to hurt you, just like you didn't mean to hurt me."

"Remember I told you the only thing that would hurt me is you givin' up on us. But I was wrong." He turned to the sunset view again. "It isn't hurtin' me. It's killin' me."

With a smooth stone lodged firmly over her throat, Eve wasn't sure she could speak. "In a partnership, both people have to compromise. Give somethin' up. You aren't willin' to give anythin' up. You just want me to."

"I told you we'd take turns. All I wanted was two years." He crossed his arms and faced her again. "But I'm not askin' you to come with me anymore."

"Y-you're not?"

Her heart skipped a beat in anticipation, hoping there was good news coming. Yes, yes. Maybe he would *stay*. He'd come to his senses. Because she loved him, and he loved her. They'd have to find a way to make it work here.

"I know that's not fair to you. That's why I've got to leave tonight. I don't see the point anymore. I'm sorry, baby." With that, he turned and walked back into the house.

Eve stayed outside until the sun had disappeared and the darkness of the night encompassed her. She stayed until Sadie found her and simply walked up next to her and took her hand. They remained like that for what felt like hours but was probably only minutes.

"Are you okay?" Sadie asked quietly.

"No," Eve hiccupped.

"You will be. You're stronger than I am." Sadie sighed and put her arm around Eve. "I would have given everything up for Lincoln. That doesn't make me someone to admire, I know. Not like you."

"Don't be silly. I'm no one to admire."

"You're strong, Eve. You put yourself first when you stood Jackson up. He wasn't ready to be the kind of husband you *deserved*. You fought your way back after that monster hurt you and could have taken your fighting spirit away forever. Now you're a doctor, and an important member of our community. Remember what you told me the night of my wedding? You were going to be okay, either way."

"I lied. I'm not *going* to be okay." Her voice broke.

"Eve? Jackson is leavin'," Mima called out. "Y'all come say goodbye."

"Oh God."

"You don't have to," Sadie said, squeezing Eve's shoulders tightly. "Stay right here with me."

"No. I want to say goodbye."

Jackson said his goodbyes to Hank, Lincoln, Mima, Daisy,

and the rest, giving them all a quick hug. Eve was last. As everyone watched, Jackson pulled Eve into his arms and rested his chin on the top of her head. Closing her eyes against the pain, Eve whispered goodbye.

She and Sadie stood watching the limo as it drove away, kicking up gravel.

Brenda gave Eve a quick hug, then turned away, but Eve caught the tears in her eyes before she did.

"Ice cream?" Sadie said.

Eve simply nodded, unable to trust herself to speak and not burst into tears. Everyone else had dispersed.

"Eve Iglesias!" Mima's voice called to her loudly and urgently the moment Eve crossed the threshold.

Eve ran toward the sound, which came out of the bedroom she'd been staying in. Mima stood in the center of the room, and laid over Eve's bed was her marriage quilt.

"Where did you—?" Eve stepped closer. Her and Jackson's names were still embroidered on it, but the date had been carefully unstitched. Removed. It was a blank space. "Why did you—?"

Bringing this quilt out was really hitting below the belt. Her hands trembled, and her throat clogged with a sob.

"Because," Mima said. "You needed to remember."

"That I loved him enough to marry him? I haven't exactly forgotten that."

"It's to remind you that everything that's been broken between two people who love each other *can* be fixed. You only have to care enough not to give up or give in. The old date is blank now, and *that's* your future. It's wide open. Sometimes with love you have to give just a little bit more and meet in the middle. Love is a fine balancing act. Sometimes you give more, sometimes he does. But if you don't take a risk right now, you may never have a chance again."

"It's too late."

Mima handed her the truck keys. "No, it's not. You go and catch him at the airport."

*And then what?*

Eve didn't know but suddenly she didn't *care*. One of her biggest faults was being the martyr. She'd let him go once before without a fight but not this time. Now she was strong enough to realize that she could love him without losing herself. Maybe she could show him by being the bigger person, swallowing her pride, and letting him know she'd come with him to Nashville. A year was too long to be away from each other.

"This is crazy. Stupid." Eve took a deep breath. "And I'm doin' it."

"Yay for crazy stupid love," Sadie cried from just outside the bedroom door.

"That's my favorite kind," Lincoln said as Eve flew past him.

She jumped in her truck and started it up. Rolling down the long driveway she kicked up gravel and followed the tracks of the limo.


*THEY'RE SENDING A CAR. And a private plane.*

Jackson couldn't have said "we live in two different worlds" any better than if he had actually *said* those very words. He might be clueless in some ways, but he'd meant what he said. No point in staying a day longer when she'd already made up her mind. When he thought about what she'd seen of his world so far, he couldn't blame her for not wanting any part of it. She'd seen nothing but takers like Winona. Nothing she could relate to or understand. But that wasn't Nashville for him. The city was filled with people just like him and Eve, who'd come to find better lives and a chance at their dream.

He'd done everything he could to tell her how he felt. Wrote a song for her. Told her he loved her which was gut-wrenching considering his fears of abandonment. His words had told her all she needed to know about his commitment to her.

*I showed her how I feel. I dropped everything I was doing because she showed up.*

Shit, could his old man be on to something here? The knowledge went through his skull like a sledgehammer. He'd done everything *but show* her how he felt. The only real way he'd shown her was through their making love but that could be construed many different ways.

Jackson had told Eve how he felt, but what had he really given up for her? She was right, he'd been asking her to give up everything while he gave up nothing. And being a man of Stone Ridge, he'd been taught better than that. He'd been taught "ladies first." Ladies foremost. It was old-fashioned, yes, but that was his town. His people. They were always there for each other, helping those in need. He wanted more of that, and less of coveting all of the things that he thought meant success.

He'd really made a colossal mess.

"Turn around."

"But what about the plane?" the driver asked.

"I'll take care of that." Jackson pulled his phone out. A minute later when the driver still hadn't turned back, Jackson yelled, "Turn around!"

"Yes, sir." The driver executed a flawless U-turn and they headed back to Stone Ridge.

Now Jackson had to think of a grand gesture. Something he could show her that she'd understand meant he'd do anything for her. Give up this opportunity and live in Stone Ridge. There had to be a way for him to find a balance. He could buy Priscilla's bar and carve out of niche for himself right here in Stone Ridge. Or maybe he could work out a way to take this opportunity on his own terms.

A truck sped by them going in the opposite direction and damn if that didn't look just like— "Turn around!"

"I did," the driver protested.

"No, I mean turn around again."

"What?" Through the mirror the driver quirked a brow. "Wait. Am I being punked?"

"No! Look, we're wastin' time here. Turn around, back to the airport."

"No problem, sir. I live to serve!"

This time the turn had a little spice in it as the brakes squealed and tires burned. Jackson wondered if he'd pissed his driver off.

"Look, I swear I'm not some entitled celebrity asking you to follow my every whim."

"Not at all, sir. Turn around! Turn around again! Nothing crazy about that."

"Call me Jackson. I'm not a sir. This is about a girl. My girl. I mean, I swear that's her truck, just ahead of us. Can you catch up to it?"

"Ah, romance! Why didn't you say something? I've been married forty years myself."

Jackson could almost feel the accelerator press down. "Then you understand. This girl was supposed to be my wife eight years ago."

"Kind of a slow burn there, yeah?"

"Long story," Jackson said. "See if you can get her to pull over."

The driver followed closely enough that Jackson read the license plates of Eve's truck. In the darkness he couldn't get a close view of inside the cab, but it was definitely her truck. Where the *hell* was she driving like her pants were on fire?

He'd have a talk with her about the difference between racing a horse and racing a truck like a speed demon.

While the driver honked and even pulled his hand out the window in the universal sign for "stop" Eve kept right on driving.

"She seems clueless, sir."

"Shit fire! She isn't. She's just ignoring you. Just follow her, wherever she goes."

"You sure this is the girl, sir?"

"I'm sure."

"Dale Earnhardt Jr., that one."

"Not usually."

Another few miles and one thing became quite clear. Eve was headed to the regional airport and she wasn't going to pull over. Had he forgotten something important, and she was rushing to catch his plane?

"Guess you will make that flight after all," the driver said as he smoothly turned into the regional airport minutes later.

"Pull over," Jackson said and hopped out of the limo. He sprinted and caught up to Eve, just as she nearly fell out of the truck.

"Jackson?" She narrowed her eyes at him, and then at the limo. "That was you behind me?"

"You didn't think about pullin' over?" he yelled. "Did that not sound like a good idea to you?"

"Don't you raise your voice at me! I was in a huge hurry and I thought it must be a crazy person back there thinking I wasn't goin' fast enough. So, I went faster. Why were you *behind* me? You should have been way ahead of me."

"We turned around." His heart kicked up and his chest constricted. "I was comin' back."

"You were comin' back?" Her eyes were wide, her wild

brown hair flying all around her. "Did you...forget somethin'?"

He took a step closer, hope spreading over every fiber of him.

"Yeah. I don't care if we live in Nashville or Stone Ridge, I want to wake up next to you every morning for the rest of my life."

"Oh, Jackson." She smiled, and that tiny piece of hope sprouted. "I already made a mistake lettin' you go and all I know is I don't want to lose you again because I'm too proud. Everybody thinks I'm so strong but I'm not when it comes to you. I came here to ask if you'd still like me to come with you. I know you said you couldn't ask that of me, but I love you, so that means I have to be with you. Wherever we are. I have to trust there's a way we can work this out. Please tell me you still want me to come with you."

"C'mere." Jackson pulled her into his arms, her head fitting so neatly below his chin. He bent to press a kiss at her temple. "You have a backstage, all-access pass to Jackson Carver and I believe you know that."

When he'd been coming back to her, she'd been heading back to him. And if that didn't say compromise, well, he didn't know what did.

"Funny thing is, I just decided that I don't want to go back to Nashville and the lifestyle that made me crazy. When I came back home, I was wound tight as a cord. I like the slower pace here. Not sure what I'm going to do, Eve, but we'll work it out. You and me. When it comes right down to it, I'm way more cowboy than I am Nashville."

"I love you, cowboy," she said.

"And I love you."

Maybe sometimes it really was that simple.

*Six months later*

Eve sat in the bridal suite of Trinity Chapel, getting last-minute hair primping. This time, her long hair was down and around her shoulders curling in their soft natural waves.

Eve would be married today, come hell, or another Texas thunderstorm.

"How do you feel?" Sadie asked, concern furrowing her brow. "Scared? It's normal, remember."

Eve reached for Sadie's hand and squeezed it. "I'm not even a *little* bit scared."

"Because it would be *totally* normal."

"I know."

To say that everyone attending their ceremony was a tad nervous about Eve was an understatement of epic proportions.

"You're not gettin' out of *this* weddin'," Beulah Hayes had half warned, half joked with Eve, right after the SORROW ladies had handed her yet another marriage quilt with a different date on it.

Same people, different date. Take two. But Eve would always treasure and keep the first quilt, the one where Mima had removed the date to signify that she still had a future with Jackson. Until then, she hadn't realized that date had reminded her time and again that she'd had her chance, and her happiness was in the past.

To Eve, it was almost laughable for anyone to think she'd back out of her wedding, but she understood their concerns. She knew what it was like to be excited, nervous, and worried. Today, excitement ruled the day. She was going into this wedding day eyes wide open, and so was Jackson. Almost nine years and much heartbreak later, they both understood what they would give up to be together.

And just in case there had been any doubts, Pastor June insisted Jackson and Eve attend marriage counseling before their second wedding day attempt. Eve thought the whole thing to be a huge waste of time, but in the end, those sessions were where they'd made the biggest concessions and compromises about their future.

No one in Nashville understood why Jackson had turned down working with the mega-producer, and instead decided to keep his music local. But everyone in Stone Ridge understood. A hometown boy, Jackson was a true man of Stone Ridge, one who wanted to remain in the tight-knit and loving community he'd grown up in. With Eve's approval, Jackson sold the song he'd written for her, Sadie, and Lincoln. Best of all, it went to a new artist who planned on releasing it as her single. And the producer? No one else but Mick Mason, who wanted Jackson to keep him on speed dial for any future songs.

Full circle.

Between the money from the sale of his ranch and the

song, Jackson had more than enough to buy the Shady Grind. These days he was learning the business and between impromptu performances, he was a part-time bartender. And part-time cowboy. For Eve, the best part was him being just across the street from her veterinary clinic and she'd walk over several times a day just to see him.

They'd decided to break ground on a new home right on the Carver ranch, ten acres away from Lincoln and Sadie's home. After their honeymoon, they'd move into that large split-level home that was far grander than any place Eve had ever lived. Most importantly to Eve, there were stables where they'd keep Thimble, Taco, and Silver, the quarter horse Jackson had given to Eve as an engagement gift. He was forever spoiling her with both big and small gifts, but her favorite was the one-carat solitaire ring.

"Is everybody ready?" Eve asked, when she noticed Sadie peeking out the window.

She joined Sadie and saw Jackson's "posse," the former band members who had become like a second family to him over the years. They appeared to be standing guard, much like Jackson and Eve had all those months ago on Sadie and Lincoln's wedding day.

"The important thing is, are you ready?" Hank held out his arm. Today, he'd be walking her down the aisle.

Eve took his arm as Sadie handed her the breathtaking bluebonnet bouquet. "I've never been readier."

As the door to the suite opened, the band members met her.

"We're here to make sure you don't run away again," Mac, the drummer, said with a wink.

"Insurance," Kyle, the bass player, said. "Can never be too careful."

"Well, get out of my way because I'm gettin' hitched."

They chuckled and as the music played, one of them

opened the door to the sanctuary. The bridesmaids and groomsmen filed in two by two. The same people who'd been at Lincoln and Sadie's wedding. Sadie and Lincoln brought up the rear and then it was Eve's turn.

She went a little faster than she should have, losing step with the music, and Hank slowed her down.

"He's not goin' anywhere, darlin'."

"I've just waited so long for this. If I could, I would run to him."

But she slowed down, keeping time with the wedding march as they made their way down the aisle. Everyone stood. Mima and Brenda were already clutching tissues to their quivering lips. Annabeth gave Eve a thumbs up. Priscilla, who'd come back for the wedding with her daughter, gave Eve a wink.

Eve glanced at them all and smiled, trying to appreciate this moment and all the love and support coming at her big as a Gulf Coast wave during a hurricane. But as was usually the case, within seconds her gaze gravitated to the man waiting for her. Her whole heart. The man with the dimpled smile. The love of her life. Her handsome groom, older now but still the boy she'd fallen for before she understood love. She saw him, and everything fell into place and locked tight in her heart.

Jackson took a step toward them, as if he, too, couldn't wait.

And Eve walked confidently toward her future.

# ABOUT THE AUTHOR


Born in Tuscaloosa, Alabama Heatherly lost her accent by the time she was two. Her grandmother, Mima, kept both the accent and spirit of the southern woman alive for decades.

After leaving Alabama, Heatherly lived with her family in Puerto Rico and Maryland before being transplanted kicking and screaming to the California Bay Area. She now loves it here, she swears. Except the traffic.

www.ingramcontent.com/pod-product-compliance
Lightning Source LLC
Chambersburg PA
CBHW031616100726
47898CB00006B/1820